# DARK HAUNTINGS

## PARANORMAL TIMES, BOOK ONE

C. C. SOLOMON

*CatDog Publications*

*Dark Hauntings* is a work of fiction. Names, characters, places, and incidents are either the product of the author's imagination or are used fictitiously, and any resemblance to actual persons, living or dead, business establishments, events, or locales is entirely coincidental.

## COPYRIGHT © 2021 BY C.C. SOLOMON

ISBN: 978-1-7361329-1-3

# ACKNOWLEDGMENTS

Thank you to all my friends and family who supported my dreams. Thank you to my betareader, Ophelia. Thank you to my editors at Real Indie Author, you push me to be a better writer even if it's no fun sometimes. Thank you to my proofreader Madeleine from Mad Skillz for your expert eye and formatters at Yours Truly Book Services for your awesome services at every level. And thanks to my readers for keeping me going. Your enthusiasm and feedback has made a huge difference.

# A NOTE FROM C.C.

To find information on prior books by C.C. Solomon go to
www.ccsolomon.com

# PROLOGUE

## TWO MONTHS AGO

*I* looked on at the madness facing us on the wide snow-covered street. This was it. This was the battle we'd all been preparing for the last several months. I just had to play my part and help kill off a hundred or so demons. No biggie.

Yeah, right.

Felix Gonzalez placed a large hand on the small of my back. "Ready wifey?" he asked, looking down at my with a soft smile.

I rolled my shoulders back, pumping myself up for the fight. "Please don't call me that." I took my sword out of the sheath strapped to my back. The sun's reflection gave a bright glint off the sword as I swung it forward toward the encroaching chaos. Although my trusty sword was golden and should have been heavy, it was comfortable to hold, a combination of magic and my own supernatural strength.

Felix's smile turned to a wide grin as he removed his magic infused machete from his waist sheath. "You know you like it. Now, let's go kick some ass."

"You dick," I muttered as I teleported into the madness.

When I reappeared, I had no time for assessing the situation further. A large naked beast with long, black hair stormed towards me. She had short, thick legs and arms propelled her through the fighting bodies at a speed that did not match her sizable frame.

I stood my ground and met the creature's beady, black eyes set in a flat face.

"You killed King Alister," the creature roared through a mouth full of sharp, yellowed teeth.

"Heeere we go," I muttered, my teeth gritted as I raised my sword to cut into the creature. Of course, all the demons would hate me for having previously killed one of the Kings of the underworld. Especially when said King had been my ex-fiancé. I'd known I'd have a target on my back in this fight. I'd been prepared for the extra hate I'd receive on the battlefield.

My sword chopped into the side of the demon, but it only succeeded in making a dent in the beast's red scales. I figured it wasn't going to do much damage, but I had to try. I could keep chopping into the demon and hope to inflict damage eventually, but I'd probably get squashed before I could.

"You betrayed us all," shouted the demon before slamming into me and knocking me into the cold, hard ground.

I ground my teeth as I felt the painful crunch of my right arm upon contact with the demon. Well, I guessed my arm was out of commission as it healed. It looked like I had no choice but to use my faerie magic. I was a warrior faerie, after all. Fighting was my thing.

With my left hand, I reached into my pocket and pulled out my magic infused *shuriken*, flinging two of the throwing stars at the demon in hopes they'd penetrate. To my relief, they sliced into the demon's thick skin, leaving deep gashes before boomeranging back towards me. I caught them and threw them again, aiming for the eyes and throat. The demon moved to the right, but its large body was too massive to miss getting stabbed in the eye by the *shuriken*. It screamed in pain and struggled to remove the star, but I pushed my magic outward, forcing the star deeper into the demon's eye, through the bone and out the other side of the creature's head.

I ignored the shrieks of pain from the creature as I ran forward and leapt in the air. Angling my sword downward, I stabbed my weapon into the remaining eye of the demon, pushing it through the head before I touched the ground. I made a come-hither motion with my hand, and the sword reversed course and flew back into my grasp. I tilted my head expectantly as I gazed at the creature.

"Come on, now," I whispered, waiting for it to dive.

The demon stumbled to the side before falling backwards with a loud thud, dead.

I gave an approving nod, which brought a grimace of discomfort as the bones and muscles in my right arm continued to heal. It might not be brand spanking new in minutes, but it wouldn't be too far off. As long as I had my left hand and my faerie magic, I would be fine.

I spun around and searched for my next fight. I caught sight of Felix bulldozing through several demons with his giant frame. He didn't look like he needed my help. These demons were just bodies to tire us out and intimidate those who didn't know any better. They weren't great fighters. Most rank-and-file demons weren't that tough. At least not to other magical beings.

Something resembling a slug the size of a large dog slithered towards me. I ran up to it and sliced the creature in half, jumping back as acidic slime squirted into the air.

"Ugh. Okay, now they're just putting on a show with this one," I muttered, shaking off my sword. "Where are the real fighters?"

Several other nightmarish demons, clearly thinking they were up for the job, rushed at me, and I cut them down, my sword and magic making it almost too easy.

"You seem bored," came a deep voice from behind me.

I turned sideways, scowling, disturbed that someone had caught me off guard. A man appearing to be in his fifties, with cropped wavy, black hair and coal-black eyes against mahogany skin stood behind me. He was dressed in black full-body armor. On top of his head rested a red crown. It was high, with dangerously pointed ends and did not move when he walked despite not being clamped onto his head.

I took a step back, a feeling of gloom falling over me like a heavy blanket. The last time I'd felt that dread was when I'd first met Alister, my now dead ex-fiancé and one of the Kings of hell. After that first meeting, the feeling had disappeared, which I was sure was through Alister's magic. I'd almost forgotten what it felt like to be in the presence of a demonic ruler.

The fighting was further off and no new foes moved or even looked our way. For now, it was just me and this stranger.

The man tilted his head slightly, the crown still not moving from his head. "Francesca, it's nice to meet you. Do you know who I am?"

I shook my head slowly. Although I had an idea, I'd rather he told me.

The man straightened and clasped his hands behind his back. "I am King Herrod. Have you heard of me?"

Had I heard of him? Of course, I had. He was one of the strongest leaders in the underworld. He made Alister and his regular flayings seem tame. I was thankful I had never met him before. I'd known the risks of this battle. The original soulmates were an ancient and powerful force that had to be eradicated. Yet, I had hoped to last longer than this. There was still so much more I wanted to do and learn.

Herrod threw a hand up in front of him, an easy smile on his lips. "Relax. I have no plans to hurt you. You look so much like her."

"Like who?"

Herrod didn't respond for a long moment as he stared intently at me.

I grew uncomfortable under his gaze and shifted in my stance. "If you don't want to fight me, then what do you want?"

The demon king blinked several times and then let out a throaty chuckle. "Fight? Do you think there would be much of one between me and you?"

I'd heard he could snap his fingers and make someone explode. So, no, I didn't actually think it would be much of a fight with him. "Then, what is it that you want?"

He threw his hands out to his sides. "To see you in action."

Why was he being so cryptic? Why did he care anything at all about me? "Why?"

He looked around.

It was interesting that no one had dared approached us in all this time. It was as if they didn't even see us. I was smart enough to know that the demon king had made that happen. He didn't want to be disturbed. But why?

"You children are in over your heads," he replied with a sneer.

I rolled my eyes, trying to maintain my appearance of calm. No point in letting him know how terrified I was. "Yeah, I've heard that before. The first soulmates are big and bad. We should just roll over and let them win. Well, I'm not a coward. That's not how I work." I let my sword down, no longer even considering fighting him. "I'm surprised you're even fighting on their side. You're a King of the underworld. They have no power over you. Especially if you go back to where you came from."

He raised a brow in disdain. "Do you believe I am here because I fear them?"

I shrugged. "Well, then why?"

He sighed, seemingly bored with the conversation. "The

first soulmates eat souls. But they can also collect and transfer them to others who might have use of them."

I snorted, even though what he'd said was anything but funny. "So, this is a business deal? You want the souls they collect? That makes sense, I guess. I mean, it's a bad deal since we're going to win this fight, but, you know, do what makes you happy, even if it'll just end up wasting time and resources."

The hair on the back of my neck stood to attention.

I spun around, my sword out and already swinging.

A gremlin was mid-leap in the air when its head exploded, coating me in a shower of green blood and gore.

Yuck.

"You're welcome," Herrod said.

I wiped the gremlin blood out of my eyes and turned around, wishing I could stab him without getting my own head blown off.

Herrod raised his brows. "What? No thank you? Come now. Surely your mother raised you better than that?"

"Thank you," I said through gritted teeth. "Although, I could have handled it on my own."

"I'm sure you could have, my dear."

Why was this guy helping me? "Look, I don't know you and don't want to. And I definitely don't want to owe you a favor."

He gave me a slight smile and his eyes flashed a disquieting gold light.

Was he happy or had I pissed him off? I was good at pushing buttons.

"You owe me no favors, child." He looked around the battlefield again. Trouble had still kept its distance from us. "I think you are right about me wasting my time here. Perhaps this fight is not worth my troubles. I'll be taking my horde and leaving." He gave me a curt nod. "I'll be seeing you again."

I shook my head, confused. I hadn't thought I'd made much of any argument to him and now he was just running home with his tail between his legs? "Why?" I called, but he was already disappearing before my eyes into a mass of smoke.

I definitely did not want to see him again, but something told me this was far from the end. Just great. What was it with demons?

# CHAPTER 1

PRESENT

*I* collapsed on the gym mat panting like a dog as exhaustion hit me. "I'm not on my A game today."

My friend, Nadia Andrews, sat beside my outstretched body and made a tsk-tsk noise. "Everyone has their bad days, Fran."

I grumbled as I sat up and attempted to touch my toes. I managed to do it, but my screaming hamstrings were not happy. I was a paranormal being. I had many, many more years ahead of me compared to an average human. Plus, I'd just fought in a battle against supernatural evil a couple months ago and our side had won. How had my body betrayed me in such a short time? "I used to be able to kick your butt in a practice fight with ease."

Nadia scrunched her dark brown eyes and frowned. "Looks like you lost more than your memories. You lost your mind, too."

I huffed in pretend anger. "Rude." I mean, she wasn't far off. I *did* have my memories stolen by angels who thought I would be a big baddie just because I was half Unseelie fae and half demon. While I wasn't exactly a saint, I'd never harmed an innocent person, and never intended to, despite my lineage. Angels could be real jerks.

And of course, 'something had gone wrong' and now the angels couldn't return my memories. So, I was left all alone to piece together my past. I still wasn't sure I should believe the angels. They had never been truthful to me yet.

"Look, woman," Nadia began as she brushed loose strands of her brown hair off of her face towards her long ponytail. "You're still in great fighting shape. You just have to keep at it. Never let your skills rest. But, you know, being the fiancée to a demon king kind of slowed you down. But it didn't slow you down on the battlefield which is the important thing."

I struggled to my feet and bent backwards as far as I could, stretching my back. I used to be a warrior, until I was whisked away to play housewife to Alister. I had to admit, I missed the fight. "I really think Misandre sent me there to get rid of me."

Nadia nodded slowly. "Probably. Good thing she's dead, huh?"

I did a little shoulder shimmy. Yes, celebrating the death of the queen of my court seemed a little treasonous, but I really hated Misandre. Having an Unseelie queen dead, especially a sadistic, self-absorbed, destructive fae like her, was a good thing for me. It made me one step closer to my ultimate goal, being the queen of a fae court. "On that note, I got an invite to a banquet in her old court in about a week. It's for anyone vying for her throne. I'm going," I declared. "I've got to go make a play for it."

Nadia squinted her dark brown eyes and tilted her head from side to side in consideration. "Do you really want all that hassle? Just stay here with me!" She jumped to her feet. "Rule by my side. You were already going to be queen here anyway."

"Uh-huh, and then I killed the king. Not so sure I'd be welcomed to run anything here after that." I waved my hand around the gym, although ruling consisted of much more than our current location.

Alister had run the older part of Las Vegas that also crossed over into the underworld. I know, it was cliché that Vegas would be a gateway to Hell, but in all fairness, there were several gateways, some of which were in highly religious areas. This location was just a funny coincidence. You could still gamble and party in Vegas, but you had to be prepared to do it alongside demons, succubae, and vampires.

As for Alister, the demon lord and unofficial mayor of Las Vegas, I had kind of sort of killed him with the help of another man whom I may or may not have been seeing romantically before my memories were taken by the angels.

The fact that I wasn't being rotated over a fire at that moment was all because of Nadia. Honestly, being any kind of ruler of the underworld was a kill or be killed type of lifestyle. No one gave complete loyalty, and many rulers came into their positions by killing the prior ruler.

However, my leadership goals remained only with the fae. Demons gave me heartburn. Most were untrustworthy, and even more were just plain dumb. No, the fae were a wise bunch and if I was going to be a queen, I would rule over intelligent, loyal individuals. Therefore, I stepped back from my role as soon-to-be queen of a part of the underworld and gave the title to Nadia who gladly accepted.

She patted my shoulder, focusing my attention. "Think of it. Two Queens in one court. We don't have to be romantically linked to rule together. Kind of like a President and Vice President.'

I sighed and dropped my shoulders.

Nadia waved a hand in front of me. "No, no. Give it some time before you answer. I don't see why you think you're better off with the fae. Do you think you'll be any more accepted by them?"

Okay, she had a point there, although I hadn't actually

killed Misandre. I hadn't even been present when she'd been attacked. But I was still friends with the people who had killed her. I really needed to pick my allies better, but Misandre's killer was a good friend to Felix, and I couldn't exactly turn my back on him. Beyond my own confusing feelings about the man, he'd also fought by our side when demon supporters of Alister had attacked Nadia's home. I hadn't even asked for his help. He'd just come to our aid like he'd owed us something.

I released my reddish brown hair from the ponytail and ran a hand through the strands in annoyance. I was not much of a demon—which I was fine with-- if I cared about things like loyalty. There was nothing binding me to Felix. I could easily distance myself from him and his friends so I'd have a better leg to stand on when I came for Misandre's throne.

Yet, the thought didn't feel good in the pit of my stomach. Guess that was the Unseelie side of me.

"I have a payment to collect," Nadia began, heading to the door. "Come with me and check out my work. Maybe this is something that could interest you now that we know you're part demon. You could work the crossroads like me."

I'd never seen Nadia at work. I think, in part, it was because I didn't want to see my bestie as the demon she really was. I'd made mental exclusions in my head about who were okay demons and who weren't. Having been around enough demons, I'd encountered a handful that really weren't evil. They were simply a product of their nature. Not all of us chose who we'd become. Nadia's fierce loyalty to me and support as a friend definitely made me question the nature of demons. Well, some.

~

*W*hen Nadia said she would collect a payment, I hadn't quite been sure what she'd meant. But I had been certain it wasn't going to be the two of us walking into an orgy in a South Beach mansion.

To clarify, we teleported inside the mansion that belonged to Zach Coles, the popular movie star. The fact that he was still popular even in a post-apocalyptic world was a credit to his talents. In the past couple of years, movies were being made again, and humanity started to see symbols of what we used to know ten years ago.

Zach was not only a star of action and romance movies, but was also a sex symbol. His face and body were all over the internet.

In that moment, though, I saw all of that body, including his pale behind while he pumped in and out of some random woman on his California king bed. On either side of him, naked women purred for his attention. In other parts of his gigantic bedroom, couples or trios were getting it on in all manners of sexual positions. If I had pearls, I would have clutched them.

Sexy pop music flowed through the scene from some hidden speaker. The room, bigger than an average one-bedroom apartment, was filled with the sounds of moaning and grunts, and the smell of sex was thick in the air. I wanted to crack a window. Instead, I waved my hand in front of my face, but that did absolutely nothing.

I leaned into Nadia as we stood in the middle of the room, looking very out of place. "Did we have to pick right now to show up?"

Nadia pulled a bit of lint off of her fire engine red fitted suit, looking nonchalant. She actually looked like a badass in her suit, which popped against her deep bronzed skin, and six-inch patent leather black heels. Her eyes were done up in a smokey style and her deep brown hair was slicked back in a high, braided ponytail. I felt like her bodyguard in my dark jeans, combat boots, and black leather jacket. I wasn't used to seeing Nadia look so polished, but she had definitely stepped up her style game since becoming a Queen of the underworld.

Nadia side-eyed me with a smirk. "Now's as good a time as any."

I looked across the room at a woman receiving oral sex from a man between her legs and looked back to Nadia with a raised brow. I was sure that woman would disagree.

Nadia clapped her hands and the music stopped. Actually, everything stopped.

Zach paused his thrusts to look around at his frozen companions. "What the hell is going on?" he yelled, removing himself from the woman in front of him. He turned to face us, and his blue eyes widened in horror. He ran a nervous hand through his strawberry blond hair, which was damp with sweat. "Nadia, what are you doing here?" he asked with a nervous twinge to his voice.

She lifted her shoulders with a smile. "Just came to collect my payment."

He moved to the edge of the bed. "Has it been ten years already?"

"Oh, I think you know it has. Now, we had a deal. I kept you comfortable in this scary new world since you're a human with no magic, and in ten years, you either give me a soul or I take yours."

Zach crossed his legs, thankfully covering his junk, and swung his hands out to the side, trying to regain his composure. "Well, as you can see, there are plenty of souls for you to grab here."

That dick. He was going to try to sell out his friends to cover a crappy deal he'd made. While I usually didn't concern myself with the treachery of humans, especially since I'd stopped being one of them, that didn't mean I didn't judge.

Most humans with no magic had proven to either be impressively resilient in these times or disappointingly disloyal. They could be as bad as demons. And yes, I realized I was half-demon.

Nadia chuckled and stuffed her hands in her pockets. "Now, Zach, you know that the soul you give me has to be a willing one. Who here is the willing soul?" She made a grand show of looking around the room, twirling.

She was loving this, I could tell. Seeing her like this was entertaining.

I could hear Zach gulp as he scratched his head. "I still need to confirm some things. Just give me a little more time."

"And you know I don't give extensions." She clasped her hands together. "Look, no one lives forever, even us humans-turned-paranormal will eventually die. Even if our life span *is* considerably longer."

Nadia took a step forward.

Zach froze.

"You had a good time, didn't you? You didn't age. You stayed in great health, lived comfortably while those around you either died from paranormal sicknesses or some other unfortunate circumstances. You never went hungry or cold. You had ten years to find me a willing soul."

I leaned into her again. "Excuse me, but what idiot is going to give up their soul to help someone else out willingly?"

Nadia tilted back to me. "Well, there's more to it. I would make another deal with that person and Zach would get ten more years. Then he and the new soul *both* come to me. No extensions that time. So, you see, only a few get that option." She tsked at Zach. "You should feel honored I gave you such a deal, and yet you still failed to secure me an additional soul. What a waste." Her usually brown eyes flashed bright gold.

Zach fell to his knees, unconcerned about his nudity. He clasped his hands in front of his chest. "Please, Nadia. I'll do anything. Just give me a little more time. I almost have a soul for you. Time got away from me. I didn't even realize it was so close."

That was part of the trickery of a crossroads demon. Humans would make a deal and then forget about it until it was too late. They'd worked so hard to draw the right demonic symbols and to bring the perfect offering to conjure the demon, had signed the contract in their own blood, and then found themselves all wrapped up in whatever wish they'd demanded in exchange for their soul.

It sounded like an awful deal for anyone with full awareness of the afterlife. Even if a person lived all those years righteously, their soul wasn't getting into heaven or whatever utopia they believed in. Instead, they were going to the underworld, or Hell, as it was known in many religions. That was for all eternity. Ten years didn't seem worth it for whatever torture they'd be subjected to forever. Yet, desperate people made desperate deals. Honestly, I didn't think most people believed there *was* a Hell and thought the whole matter was a joke.

What an awful way to learn the truth.

Nadia made a sympathetic mewling noise and walked over to Zach, crouching down in front of him. "I'm sorry, honey. I can't help you. A deal's a deal."

Zach started to cry. Like really cry. Tears and snot, the whole works. It was sad. "What's going to happen to me?"

Nadia took a handkerchief out of her pocket and dabbed at his face. Aww, how nice of her. Playing all motherly before she snatched his soul from his chest like the scary demon she was. "Nothing good for you, I'm afraid. Well, let me take that back. Different souls carry different weight. Different prices. I can either keep your soul and have you work for me, maybe even one day you can become a lower-level demon and work your way up in the ranks. It's not so bad then."

He gave her a hopeful look and his sobbing died down. "Really?"

She nodded. "Or I can sell your soul to the highest bidder and then who knows? You could go to someone who just wants to torture and shred your soul over and over again. Or your days could be filled with endless pain at the pleasure of your owner."

Zach paled and fresh tears met his eyes. I didn't blame him. For being a half-demon, I was far from fine with the horror show that could come with the territory. After all, I had lived most of my life as a human. The dark terrors of the demon world still gave me the shivers.

"Or you could be entered in endless fighting games in a nonstop gladiator style battle that will maim you over and over again. Really there are many possibilities. Too many to name. I'd tell you to pray, but if that was your thing, you wouldn't have made this deal in the first place." She patted his cheek and stood up.

Damn, she was cold.

She snapped her fingers and we looked at her expectantly.

Nothing happened.

She cleared her throat and clapped her hands.

Still nothing.

She rolled her eyes and swore. "Death and Destruction!" she yelled for her demon dogs.

And...nothing.

She stomped her foot. "Damn it, they are useless." She glanced over at me. "Can you try?"

I scratched my neck and twisted my lips, unsure. Usually all Alister had to do was give a shout for the hellhounds. I thought they'd gotten used to Nadia by now but perhaps I was wrong if they ignored her call. They'd always come when I called but perhaps that was only because I was with

Alister. However, I'd give it a shot. "Sure. Death and Destruction!" I shouted at the top of my lungs.

A second later, loud terrifying barks of her hellhounds heralded their arrival, and soon their forms materialized in front of us. The hellhounds had black fur, were twice the size of Dobermans, had red eyes, and a mouth full of razor-sharp teeth.

"About time you two showed up. Didn't you hear me?" Nadia asked with a scowl.

The dogs ignored her and came up to me, butting their heads against my thighs, licking my fingers.

I chuckled and scratched their heads.

Nadia cleared her throat again. "You guys are here for a reason. You have work to do." She glanced over at Zach who had already peed himself upon seeing the terrifying dogs. Lucky for us he'd placed a pillow over himself prior. No need to piss Nadia off further by, well, pissing on her boots. "I do apologize for the delay. I know it just makes it worse."

I tried to look through his eyes at the dogs but they just looked like the lovable dogs I'd known since they were puppies. They were really mine as much as they were Alister's.

Nadia clapped her hands again. "Okay, boys, get to work."

The hounds looked up at me.

I frowned and looked back at poor Zach. I wasn't sure if he was really a bad guy. I did feel a little bad for him. However, I didn't expect my interference to make a difference. Even if I refused to give the dogs my approval, Nadia could still take him on her own. I was just delaying the inevitable. I gave a curt nod.

In unison, the dogs turned to Zach and growled a deep, low sound that raised the hairs on the back of my neck. Then, before I could blink, they leaped in the air and pounced on him. They tore into his body with teeth and claws as Zach's screams filled the air.

Thankfully, we were standing far enough away that we missed getting hit by the spray of blood and more. The whole thing was disgustingly gory. Having been the fiancé of a demon King and the soldier of an Unseelie fae who both had a taste for torture, I'd grown a strong stomach in the past five years, so I was unbothered by the violence.

When the hounds slowed down and relaxed, all that was left of poor Zach were various body parts and entrails. The hounds feasted on his bones and intestines, seemingly content.

A glowing flash of white light zipped in the air as Nadia opened her hand, palm up. The zap of light fell into her palm and she wrapped her fingers around it, reopening them over a tiny glass jar in her other hand. Placing a lid over the jar, she looked up at me with a smile. "That was quick and painless. I really think this will go for a pretty penny." She shook the jar in the air. "Don't feel bad, Franny. Even before the world changed, this guy was a complete shit. He had sex with underage girls, and I'm talking really young ones. He was a complete pervert. An evil soul like his will bid high."

I scowled, shaking my boot free of some bloody flesh that had landed on top of it. Her explanation did make me feel slightly better. I wasn't really a horrible, uncaring person. "I can't believe you even did a deal with him. You gave him more time to harm little girls."

"I made sure he didn't hurt anyone. I keep my eyes on those I do deals with." She huffed. "I might be a demon, but I'm not a monster. There are levels to the underworld. I still have some decency."

She was right. As demons went, Nadia was the least evil I'd encountered. It was actually through her, and to a degree, Alister, that I had learned that demons were more than purely evil flunkies. Granted many were. However, some were insanely intelligent, yet irredeemably bad. Others were unfortunate souls who had a conscience, so they only went after evil beings.

"Well, that's good to know. I guess I still care a little."

She chuckled. "You care more than a little. Especially since getting reacquainted with your angel babe."

I glowered at her. "Please don't call him that. We're just friends."

She snorted. "You know that's a lie. You would jump him as soon as he gave the okay."

I hated that she was right, but I didn't want to discuss that here. "Anyway, can we unfreeze these people and get out of here?" I had no idea how they were going to explain the shredded Zach to the local authorities and I didn't want to stick around to find out either.

She shrugged and snapped her fingers. The hounds and I teleported into her house in Las Vegas. She lived in a five-bedroom mini-mansion, full of floor to ceiling windows, decorated in a modernist style, and so clean I could eat off the floor. The magical line to the underworld lay just beyond her backyard where she had a pool and fire pit. I stayed as a guest with her and it was quite comfortable.

Nadia sat on her couch and kicked her shoes off before placing the soul on her glass coffee table.

Death and Destruction lay in front of her fireplace, still gnawing on Zach's bones.

"I'm giving you the dogs," she said. "They don't listen to me anyway, and they love you. I need my own hell hounds."

I sat down beside her and threw my head back on the couch. "I can't take them. I'm on a journey of self-discovery."

She pfftd. "Okay, *Eat, Pray, Love*, what are you talking about?"

I furrowed my brows and shook my head. Like she didn't know. "Okay, my memory only goes back like five years. I have no idea who I had been when the world went all supernatural. And now I find out I'm half-demon.

Which parent was a demon? Who the hell even *are* my parents?"

I needed to get myself in order. She had to know that. This world was crazy enough as it was. Ten years ago, the Event had happened. At least that's what the media called it. One minute, folks were at home eating dinner and, the next, they were fending off giant trolls, man-eating plants, vampires, and a crap-ton of other paranormal things. And if that wasn't enough, then came some supernatural illness that goes and kills half the world, mostly humans who weren't changed into the paranormal, making them the minority now.

So, in my imagination, I had been some poor teen or twenty-something out clubbing. I wasn't sure of my age. My kind ages slowly, so who knew how old I could be. I might be forty for all I knew. So, there I was, probably dancing on a bar counter or something. Then—bam–I'd sprouted wings and flown away. Well, honestly, I didn't know if that really was the case. I'd become a faerie, but I didn't have wings. I'd seen several who had them, but I'd gotten shafted. Probably because I was half-demon.

I sighed. "I won't be around to care for dogs. Plus, I'm unemployed so I can't even afford to feed them. My old boss is dead, so I have no job working as a fighter in Misandre's court. And Alister's dead, so I don't have him to fall back on to do any hits. I'm officially on my own."

Nadia reached over and smacked me on the forehead. "You can work for me, sis. Being a crossroads demon is pretty easy."

I raised my upper lip in disagreement. "I really want to get my memories back and the angels said they would help me fix their screw up. I don't think they're going to keep that promise if I start working as a crossroads demon." Although the angels hadn't had any success in returning my memories since the world had changed, they'd promised they'd keep trying. I wasn't exactly the number one fan of the angels. Some weren't any better than the demons. Plus, as much as I loved Nadia, I knew that doing anything demonic would harm my chances of becoming a faerie Queen. I'd keep my friendship but I couldn't engage in the deceptive work of being a demon.

"So where are you going to go?" Nadia asked, cutting into my thoughts.

I twisted on the couch and blew out a breath feeling completely lost. I had a goal but my plan to get there was a bit fuzzy. "Well, Misandre knew about my past, but she would never tell me much. I'm sure there are others in her court who might be more forthcoming since all the fighting has died down a bit."

A loud chime rang through the house.

Nadia turned toward a small device on her side table that looked like a picture frame. She tapped it and the black screen became an image of a large man standing at her front gates.

She looked over to me with a sly smile. "Angel babe is here to take you away."

# CHAPTER 2

*F*elix Gonzalez sat on my queen-sized bed, inspecting my room as if he hadn't been there before. This was not really the case. Since we'd first met several months ago, he'd come to Vegas from his town in Silver Spring, Maryland, many times. He'd kept coming by to convince me to move to his town.

I flopped down on the other end of my bed and gave him a doe-eyed blink, intending to have a little fun with him.

Felix shivered and looked away. "Don't look at me like that. You know what those honey eyes do to me."

I gave a wicked smile. "Whatever do you mean?" I knew exactly what he meant. I had a unique mix of bright topaz-colored eyes against warm brown skin that seemed to turn him on. I was certain my eye color came from the fae half of me.

Felix could have also been into my curves and the fact that I was tall. Who knew? I just knew that from the day I'd first met him—well, the day I first remembered meeting him, he'd professed his love and it didn't end. Apparently, he'd had dreams of me before he'd got *his own* memory back and, when he did remember me, he said we used to be close friends who had been about to become more before our memories had been taken from us.

Why could the angels recover his memories but not mine?

Felix was hot as hell and hard to be bitter about. He was tall. I mean super tall. Like six foot five or taller. This girl liked a guy she could climb. He was built like a wrestler, but an in-shape one. He wasn't just mass. He had definition as well. He had smooth, buttery, tanned skin, and long golden-brown hair that he often kept in a low ponytail or bun.

And he was always smiling. Like, for no damned reason. He was just in a jolly mood all the time, like some hot St. Nick. But it was cute.

Felix turned himself around on my bed so that he was fully facing me. He gave me a wide grin then placed his hands on my waist and pulled me towards him until I found myself sitting on his lap with my legs on either side of him.

Okay. I didn't *find* myself this way. I did take part in situating my body in just this position. I was supposed to be keeping my romantic distance from him but it was hard. I actually did like him. I just wasn't sure if I was right for him. I thought well enough of myself but I had to admit, an unemployed person, with bad relationship choices and no memory wasn't the most datable. I didn't want to ruin him. And yet, I couldn't keep away from him. I really was an indecisive mess. I cocked a brow. "Why are we sitting like this? Do you want to kiss me?"

He looked down at my lips, biting his own. "Always."

I moved in closer, but he leaned back. I pulled away and let out a breath of frustration. "Really?"

His gaze penetrated mine. "Do you remember me?"

Always this question. It was so frustrating. Sometimes, I didn't want a reminder of how incomplete I was just so I could feel like crap and not get what I wanted. "You know I don't. You're being a tease."

Felix knew that I didn't remember him beyond a few months ago. It was because I still had magical amnesia that Felix refused to get intimate with me, claiming he wanted the full me when we had sex.

He grabbed my hand and kissed my palm. "I know. I just want you back."

I smiled slightly at his gentle nature. It made me feel way too warm and fuzzy inside, which scared me. I stroked his hair, which was hanging loose today. "Do you really think that if I got my memories back, you wouldn't be the first person I told?"

He looked down at our hands, still locked together, and I saw a look of uncertainty on his face before he looked away. "I'm not sure."

Well, now I really did feel like garbage. Felix was the kindest person in my life. I hated to be the source of any pain for him. I tried not to live my life by being a jerk. "I don't hate you, Felix. You're my friend."

He chuckled before losing the smile and tightening his grip around me until my chest smashed into his. His eyes seemed to almost glow with a desire that gave me flutters. "Just friends?"

I nodded. "Yep, buddy. That's the way you wanted it." I patted him on the head for extra emphasis. I didn't want to hurt him but I didn't mind throwing a couple of jabs at him.

He released me with a groan. "I'm a glutton for punishment. I just can't let you go."

I snorted. "You're going to have to try." Although I wasn't sure I wanted to unwrap myself from around him. Really, he was just like a giant teddy bear.

"I guess I should tell you why I came here. I want you to come back to Silver Spring with me."

Again. The man never gave up. I secretly thought it was an attractive quality but I wouldn't tell him that. It was probably best if he actually did move on.

"But, as a leader. You want to lead something, start being a part of our town council."

I scrunched up my face in surprise. "Why would they want an outsider as their leader?"

"You give a perspective that isn't in our council."

"They have you and Lisa if they want a fae and demon point of view."

He shook his head. "Nah, I'm not into the whole leadership thing. I prefer to just teach. And Lisa's in and out dealing with her own stuff. And she has her store. Not that she'd want to lead anyway. This can give you good practice."

This really made no sense. I wiggled away from him in the least sexy way possible, much to my chagrin. "You're just offering me this job so I stay away from the demons. You don't really think I'd make a good leader. Did Carlos put you up to this?"

Felix leaned back on my bed, balancing on his elbows, and gave me a sleepy look. "Actually, I think you would be a fearless co-leader, which is what we need. What else you got going on? Ever since we defeated the first soulmates you've been kind of aimless."

I rolled my eyes. Yes, I looked hopeless but I wasn't a charity case. I didn't want that path for myself. I wasn't going to rush to the person who offered me the best job if I didn't deserve it. I couldn't be queen based on favors people gave me. I wanted to earn my path in life.

"Why do you even need more leaders?" I asked.

Felix gave a heavy breath and shook his head. "That battle took a lot of people. And Amina and Phillip are still in their sleeping coma."

Amina and Philip were the *new* soulmates, and we all just had to hope they didn't go down the rabbit hole of evil the first ones had. Amina seemed all right, but Philip? I wasn't certain I wanted him waking from his coma.

"So you think your people are going to let a half-demon, half-fae tell them what to do?"

Felix lifted a shoulder. "We welcome people who are powerful and have a desire to help and not hurt."

I pointed to my chest. "You think that's me?" I could have laughed. Nothing about me said humanitarian or helper. I only aided them in battle because I wanted to kill Misandre, and because I owed Felix for getting rid of Alister.

Felix looked at me for a beat as if assessing me and then sat up. "I think that you need some good publicity, so to speak. Work with us. We have allies with the fae and the elves. You know, being friends with Joo-won might get you some points towards getting the throne you so desperately want."

I poked my lips out in thought. He had a point. Joo-won was a neutral elven king who had a past alliance with Misandre. Although he'd turned on her in the end, it hadn't seemed to harm him. This was mostly because no one in Misandre's court had been jumping up and down to work for the original soulmates when she'd aligned with them. That she'd fed some of their souls to the soulmates was something she'd tried to keep quiet.

Maybe it wouldn't be as hard as I thought to win them over if I showed that I had some type of heart and loyalty to protect my people. I shrugged. "I'll think about it."

He bumped my knee lightly with his. "Come back with me and hang for a while. See if you like it. Spend some real time there. It could be fun."

I rubbed my hands over my face. I didn't have a real plan to take over a fae court. Not really. And I didn't know where to start in getting my memories back. I suppose if I had to start some sort of plan it would be the path that got me closer to running a court and that wasn't here.

As if sensing my changing attitude, Felix pressed on with a twinkle in his eye. "Your apartment is still there."

"I'd hardly call it mine. I didn't stay there that long."

Felix massaged the back of his neck, looking slightly tired. "Be that as it may, I made sure no one moved in there. The town's grown a lot, so it wasn't an easy task. I don't think I can hold it much longer."

"You should give it up then."

He side-eyed me.

I smirked. "Fine. I'll come for a visit. But I'm not staying. I want to lead fae, not vampires and witches." Though, did it *really* matter?

"Why are you stuck on that goal?"

I flopped backwards, lying on the bed. "Because I am." Yeah, I knew that wasn't an answer. Some days I questioned myself as well. I'd just seen Misandre and Alister do it so wrong over the past five years that all I could focus on was doing better for others who looked to me to protect them. A passion was lit in me and I couldn't shake it.

Paranormals could live hundreds of years. So, I had all this life I was going to live, and I needed something to live for. Even if I got my memories back, it didn't mean I'd be satisfied. I still had a life to live and if I never got my past back, I didn't want to die fixated on it. I also didn't want to keep living as a low-level hitman or flunky in a fae court. I couldn't explain it, but I felt like I was *meant* for more.

Maybe I couldn't run a fae court yet, but I'd get there at some point and that would only happen if I kept moving upwards. I wasn't sure serving as a council member would get me to my goal, but it could certainly be a step up.

Felix chuckled and patted my thigh seemingly unbothered by my lack of a real answer. "All right, future wife, pack your stuff. I'm taking you home."

I lightly punched him on the back. "I told you not to call me that."

CHAPTER 3

*I* packed pretty lightly. Just a large suitcase and a bookbag. I really didn't have much anyway. I said goodbye to Nadia who seemed a little amused by my decision. She had been a fan of Felix even before our memories were snatched, or so she said.

We then teleported to the town's entrance. Felix's community was surrounded by a giant, steel wall that encompassed six square miles that made up the downtown area of Silver Spring. Although they were covered by magical wards, the wall also helped to keep out strangers. They were the by-invitation-only sort.

The town had everything you could possibly need or want; schools, a hospital, shopping, dining, entertainment, plenty of housing, a farm, and its own brewery. It really was impressive. Not every town had it all together like this, outside of government-run communities.

Those towns controlled by the reemerging government served more as a federation with individual governors that worked together to rule their towns. An opening in the steel wall appeared and a guard stepped out. He had a petri dish in hand and a small knife. He first went to Felix who held out his arm as if this was an everyday occurrence. Felix's blood trickled into the dish. The guard then waved his hand over the wound, quickly sealing it with whatever healing magic he possessed. He then produced a small vial filled with dark liquid and added a drop. Satisfied with whatever he was looking for, he gave Felix a nod then walked over to me.

I leaned back with raised hands. "What is all of this?"

"Checking to see if you have the paranormal illness," the guard replied in a gruff tone as he cleared the petri dish with a swipe of his hand. Now it was sparkling clean.

Felix *had* mentioned that his town had found a test—though no cure yet—to the new paranormal illness floating around.

I pushed up my puffy jacket and held out my arm, bare against the cold winter breeze. This world just never had an end to its surprises. An illness to kill regular humans wasn't enough. Now we paranormals were at risk. Even if we paranormals could live long lives, it didn't seem like Earth was going to let us get there.

Once the guard gave me the all-clear, he let us go with another nod, and I followed Felix into the city.

Many paranormals were trying to live here after they learned the town defeated the greatest evil we'd ever seen so far. It made sense. The Six, a special group of paranormals brought together by some mysterious being, were famous and they lived here. They had succeeded in killing a powerful fae Queen, a demon King, an alpha weretiger, and the original soulmates in less than a year. So, if there was a safer city to live in, I couldn't think of it.

And it seemed that people were beginning to feel safe again after the battle. Everything appeared as normal. The apartments looked well-kept, the street was clean enough to eat off, and the restaurants and storefronts were maintained. A large snow-covered park on my right piled with kids running after each other, throwing snowballs before the last winter snow left.

Felix grabbed my suitcase. "I can teleport us to the apartment."

I looked around as we stood at the entrance to the town. I could hear the presence of life everywhere around me. Kids laughing, dogs barking, neighbors greeting each other and cars honking. The feel of the end of our six-month supernatural winter welcomed me with a warm breeze. Nadia's town was nice, but it wasn't always pleasant. This place felt good. "Let's walk. How far is it?"

"Two miles."

I nodded. "We can stop and have an early dinner on the way."

Felix grinned. "I like that plan." He snapped his fingers and my luggage disappeared. "Sent it to my place. I can bring it down to your place after."

Felix had conveniently moved me into his building when I'd first arrived. Not that I minded.

We strolled through town, and I tried to contain the stupid feeling of happiness growing inside me as I saw kids riding bikes and cars zooming past. People walked in and out of shops. Highrise buildings stood clean and well maintained. The sidewalks and roads were also smooth.

Most highways outside of the towns still weren't repaired from the damage. The abandoned cars were starting to get cleared, but when giant monsters had erupted from the ground or had stomped down highways, destroying the pavement, it had been hard to put in the energy or costs to keep up with repairs.

The people of Silver Spring kept everything in order. There wasn't even trash on the ground. The air smelled like honey dew. Birds chirped from branches, practically singing like we were in some fairytale cartoon. It was like the world had been untouched here.

Really, the town was in a great position to thrive. Having magic just made things better.

I looked over to Felix who walked with his hands stuffed in his pockets, his sunglasses over his eyes to guard against the bright sun. He seemed so content.

"You like it here." But would I? "You're just teaching?"

He nodded. "Yep, I like it. Seeing a kid's face light up because they got a complex math problem right makes my day."

I chuckled softly. This man was pure light. "You're just a big old softie, aren't you?"

He glanced down at me, although I couldn't see his eyes. "You know it. But I don't mind being a king by your side."

I wasn't so sure we lived in the same world. He seemed so sweet and normal. Yes, he had this amazing magic, but it seemed he was fine living his life like he was a regular human. I didn't see how we matched at all. How could he? I began to wonder if he was so sure of us because he was stuck on the memory of who we both used to be, and not who we were now.

He tilted his head towards an Italian restaurant on our right, just off the main road. It was one of several restaurants, bars, and lounges on that block, not far off the entertainment and shopping blocks.

We stepped inside the small, darkly lit space. It was moderately busy as people sat around the bar and high tables over drinks and light food. I could see a wider space towards the back with larger tables and more of a dining setting.

The host smiled at us with menus. "Table for two? We have happy hour still going if you stay in the front area."

"That work for you?" Felix asked, removing his sunglasses.

"Always," I replied, glancing over at the fully stocked bar.

Several flat screen TVs were showcasing a basketball game. The government had decided that the real return to normal would be to bring back certain televised sports. So, we now had basketball teams again that came from government towns, although non-government citizens could be recruited to teams. Basketball players didn't make nearly as much money as they used to. No one did, but they lived an entirely comfortable life and were still treated like rock stars.

We sat down at a high table near the front window. Our waitress quickly appeared, and we ordered martinis.

Felix glanced down at his phone.

"Being summoned somewhere?" I asked, looking over the menu.

"No. Well, Faith wanted to know what I was up to. I texted her that I was here with you. Mind if she joins us?" He gave me a sheepish look, assuming my answer.

Faith was not only part of the Six, but she was also Felix's best friend. They were almost like brother and sister.

I wasn't jealous of them. If they were going to be a couple, they'd had years to have gotten to that stage. My issue with Faith was that she hated me. She was like some over-protective mother who didn't like any woman sniffing around her Felix. She treated him like he was some idiot kid, not the intelligent, powerful man he was.

I didn't skip a beat. "Invite her." I was going to be the bigger person. That's what good leaders did, right? Only, being good gave me heartburn.

I hadn't even finished my first martini when Faith appeared, another person in tow; Azrael.

Azrael was the androgynous angel assigned to Felix to watch over him after our memories had been snatched. They had no trouble voicing their disapproval of me. Apparently, I was just this big baddie thug that had this magical power over the gentle giant.

I sucked my teeth and chugged down the rest of my

martini before looking for the waitress. Whatever I asked for next needed to have double the liquor.

Faith sat in the empty chair beside Felix. She gave me a slight smile that looked like it hurt her face. "Hey, Fran. Surprised you decided to come back here." She squinted her violet eyes at me over her fake smile.

I made eye contact with the waitress and waved at her to come back for more drinks. "Well, I live to surprise."

Faith tilted her head. Her dirty blond hair was a little longer than last time, having reached her ears, and she had to swipe bangs out of her eyes. A new tattoo was on her hand, fully connecting to the tattoo sleeve she already had on her right arm. The woman was practically covered in them, most of which were magic-based and gave her an impressive boost of power beyond her already strong succubus magic. She looked like the bad-ass I liked to believe I was. I'm not saying I was intimidated by her, but I wasn't so cocky I thought I could easily take her in a fight. I mean, I could still win.

I was already thinking about fighting her, and we hadn't said more than a few words to each other. Luckily our waitress returned, and we ordered more drinks and food.

Azrael, who had sat next to me, turned fully to face me. I could feel the angel's turquoise eyes on me.

I twisted my lips. "Can I help you?"

"So, you decided to join the council? I didn't think you would. Actually, I thought it was an awful idea."

I turned to look at them. The angel smirked at me as if glad they'd annoyed me. Azrael was almost modelesque, tall and lean with full lips, short, wavy dark blond hair, high cheekbones and olive toned skin. The fact that they were so beautiful just pissed me off more.

Was this fool trying to bait me? It wouldn't work. "Thanks for your vote of confidence." I gave them a tight smile.

Azrael winked at me. The stupid angel oozed a sex appeal

34

that made them attractive to practically everyone. And Azrael used it to their advantage. However, I had never been fooled. They weren't much of a role model. My limited encounters with the angel consisted of them cursing, drinking, drugging, and more. There were demons who were more reserved than them.

Our waitress returned with our drinks.

Azrael picked up their beer and raised it in the air. "Shall we do a toast?"

Felix lifted his drink, also a beer this time. "To what?"

I felt mildly betrayed by his change in drinks.

"To old friends. May they not betray us."

The three clinked glasses while I took a sip of my own, rolling my eyes. I was pretty confident that was a dig at me, and I was disappointed that Felix didn't catch on.

He glanced over at me and smiled. "I'd also like to toast the return of my future wife. Your return expands my heart." He clinked my glass, although I hadn't bothered to move it. He did the same to Azrael and Faith's glasses as they gave him disapproving looks.

I put my drink down and glared at both of them. "Really, guys. You're acting like he's becoming BFF with Satan. I did help fight the bad guys with you, you know. I'm not evil incarnate." I raised a finger in the air. "I even turned down a job to be a crossroads demon."

Faith bared her teeth at me in an attempt at a smile. "Well, gold star for you."

Azrael gave me a slow clap.

I was so mad I could spit. I really hated them. However, I wouldn't fall for the bait. I would be the bigger person as was required of a good leader. Being mature sucked. I looked around for our waitress. "Can I get my food to go?" I could be mature, but I didn't have to sit there and get treated like hot garbage. There was an inner part of me that was really hurt that they didn't like me. It further strengthened my fears that maybe I would drag Felix down. I thought I was awesome, but some days I didn't feel so secure, especially with no long history of memories to aid me.

Felix slammed his beer down, bringing my attention back to the table. "You guys don't have to be dicks. This is my future wife. Show her some respect."

I opened my mouth to protest and let him know I could handle my own. It wasn't worth him fighting, and I wasn't sure they would ever respect me, so it was a wasteful cause. However, something told me to close my mouth and let this play out. His usually jolly brown eyes looked darker, and his brows were furrowed together in a scowl. I felt like this was not the time to interrupt him.

"She isn't the only one who's half-demon. Cut her some slack. Because of her, we got Nadia's people to fight on our side when we went to battle, which is why, in part, we won in the first place." He looked around at us, face still set in anger. "You all have to work this shit out. Sooner rather than later."

I raised a brow, slightly impressed. I'd never had anyone stick up for me like this. It touched me. Also, seeing this side of Felix was kind of hot.

Faith grumbled and folded her arms. "We're just looking out for you, man."

"I'm not a kid."

Azrael put down their beer and leaned back in the chair. "Just because the soulmates are gone doesn't mean the world's at peace. You still have to be on your toes. Especially now that you're famous. People will want to exploit any weakness you all have."

Well, I was back to feeling like garbage again. I didn't have to have my memories to know that I was better than what Azrael and Faith were implying. I'd had the opportunity to exploit Felix's giving nature, and I never had. Never would. Our food arrived. On plates. With silverware. I looked up at the waitress. "Can you fix this to go, please? I won't be eating here. Sorry."

Felix shook his head. "Ignore her. Can you get us another round of drinks?"

The waitress nodded and disappeared before I could argue.

I glared at Felix. Okay, him getting all bold and aggressive was cute. He still saw me as good, despite his friends and for that I had to acknowledge it made me like him more. However, I still didn't want to sit through this punishment with his friends. "I'm not going to leave town just yet, but I don't have to sit and eat with them either." I pushed my seat back to get out.

Felix got up and made his way towards me as I walked past Azrael. "Stay."

I poked him in the chest. It was like he was made out of brick. Still, my nether regions did a wiggle as my mind wandered to picturing what he would look like under that shirt. What was I standing for? Oh yes, I was trying to leave. I was failing at winning over his friends. I wasn't sure how I could win a whole court this way. I needed to be alone and think. "Move."

He folded his arms, a twinkle in his eyes. "I'm not afraid to pick you up and put you back in your seat."

I placed my hands on his hips. "That would be fun to try." I gave him a wicked smile, daring him.

"Don't tempt me, woman. I want you here."

Ok, that desire in his eyes practically emanated from him. I kind of wanted to climb him, but this was a public place and I was still mad. "Your friends don't want me here. We could teleport away together." I added a wink for good measure.

He stepped closer to me, my hands still on his hips, as if he were daring me. "Forget what they said. It's not about them. Stay here. Please."

I glared up at him while he smiled down at me. We stood that way for several seconds not really wanting to leave his side because I was kind of getting turned on by his assuredness and also wanting to preserve my ego by not continuing to take the hits from the angel and succubus.

Azrael let out an exaggerated sigh and gave me an apologetic smile. "Fran, sit back down. We apologize. Perhaps we've been too quick to judge."

I glanced over to Faith, who had started eating, ignoring the show. She eventually looked up, her cheeks swollen with food. She then gave me wide innocent eyes before responding. "Yeah, what Azzy said," she said through a mouth full of food.

I didn't think they'd changed their opinion of me and that hurt, but knowing that Felix accepted me dulled the throb enough to allow my wounded pride to power my legs back to my seat. "Well, *Azzy*, it looks like you lucked out today." I raised my glass for a toast. "Here's to another chance."

"Okay, demon faerie," Azrael muttered, clinking their glass with mine.

I decided to ignore the angel for now and take a bite out of my food. Felix walked back to his chair and took another swig of his beer, still visibly upset. I fought the urge to reach over and pat his hand soothingly like some kind of wife. We were *not* a couple, and I wasn't the sweet type.

But I *was* developing emotions for him.

Faith put her fork down to grab the gin and tonic she had been nursing. "I thought you were going to be some big fae boss."

Why did Felix have to tell her my business? "I will be."

Azrael lifted a brow. "Out of curiosity, how will you become a queen?"

I adjusted in my seat. Why did this angel have to catch me without a plan? Ok, I could come up with something. "I am only here on a visit. I haven't decided to be a part of your council leadership. In fact, I'm going to a banquet next week for those vying for Misandre's old throne."

Faith frowned, taking a sip of her drink. "How does that work? Some type of battle royale?"

"As cool as that would be, no." I wasn't going to pretend they were even remotely interested, but I'd give them a chance. "We get voted in. It's actually very civilized. Well, the voting part is. It's everything before that stage that gets cutthroat. Cutting deals, making threats, sometimes killing. It's actually a very nasty game." And I really needed to be there earlier to make all of that happen.

Faith snorted, seemingly intrigued. "Sounds like fun."

I agreed. Maybe she wasn't a total ass.

Felix deepened his frown. "Sounds dangerous."

I stabbed my fork back into my pasta. "Everything is dangerous nowadays. But I *am* going to assess my competition. I'm no fool."

Felix softened his eyes. "Need me to go with you?"

Need him? What kind of woman did he think I was? I was no damsel. I could handle my own. He had to have known that by now. "They won't let non-fae attend." That was the truth.

"Seems dangerous to go alone. Especially if people are upset about Misandre's death."

I waved a hand as if swatting a fly. "Nothing I can't handle." That was a lie, but I didn't need to give them something else to harp on me about.

Felix rubbed his chin in thought. "Good, then bring Lisa with you as support. Just for my peace of mind. If something goes down, she can let me know telepathically."

I sighed. Lisa was Seelie fae so I wasn't quite sure she'd be welcome, but it couldn't hurt to try. As part of the special Six, she was able to speak to anyone in that group telepathically.

I agreed that walking in alone without support would be foolish. All the other contenders would have their entourage.

I had never been one to have a bunch of friends, at least not in the five years I could remember. I could bring Lisa and Bella, the only other faerie I trusted, to come with me.

Maybe going after the queen position now was a little hasty.

I wagged my fork in Felix's direction. "You know, you're a pretty smart guy."

He puffed his chest out. "I'm reaching the next level of genius since I got my memory back."

I laughed. That felt kind of good. To feel happiness. To have someone truly care about me. I wasn't going to get all sentimental, but I knew how to cherish a moment when needed.

Next week at the fae banquet, I was most likely not going to have such pleasant moments.

# CHAPTER 4

*I* didn't like dressing up. Heels, tight dresses, pounds of makeup and keeping my hair smooth and sculpted felt like extra work that I didn't need. However, here I was in a deep red, off the shoulder, floor-length gown, with open toed heels. My hair was piled up in some intricate series of knots and curls, and make-up that made me look glamourous.

All this for a banquet.

I hadn't made it early enough to make deals or do much more than scope out my competition, so I was feeling a little nervous. However, I still had one or two eyes and ears in the old court to know the players and know what had been going on since Misandre's death, so I wasn't going in totally blind.

Lisa Xu's emerald green eyes practically beamed when she stood beside me at the gates of the gloomy-looking castle that had once belonged to Misandre. "You look crazy hot. I can't believe you didn't let me show you off to Felix before we left."

I didn't feel hot, unless she meant temperature wise. I was

currently sweating underneath the girdle she made me wear to smooth out my form.

Lisa looked like she was totally at home. She wore a hot pink asymmetrical gown, and her jet-black hair hung sleek and straight down her back.

Bella huffed on my other side. "Are we sure we need to be here?" She spun around slowly, scanning the growing crowd.

Several other groups of fae began to walk towards us to enter the party from the black stoned walkway. Bella moved us to the side of the steel gates as they opened inward to let us all in.

I was sure she was nervous being here. The Seelie community looked like a unicorn threw up everywhere. The Unseelie realm was darker and was lit from within like New York or Tokyo. It was all tall buildings, and bright lights. However, a thick forest surrounded the cities with trees as tall as the buildings, and thick vines ran everywhere.

Tonight, a thick bluish gray fog hung in the air, blocking any light from the pink moon and stars. Fortunately, the castle, located on the outskirts of the town up a tall hill, was lit like a light house. The walkway was lit on both sides with floating orbs as fae of all shapes and sizes, humanoid and nonhuman shaped, teleported onto the grounds.

I gave a tight smile as some familiar faces passed us with greetings. Some fae looked over to Bella with looks of distain. She had her own baggage, something I should have considered before inviting her.

"If you really want to be a leader, come to Arwa's court." Bella glanced over at me with pleading blue eyes against honey-toned skin. Her big curls framed her face like a lion's main and complemented her long green v-cut gown.

Lisa scrunched her face. "Can an Unseelie fae become Seelie?"

Bella shook her head, rolling her eyes at a fae who scowled at us. "No. It's a blood thing. Our DNA. The best we can do is go neutral. That doesn't mean she can't join our court. I'm sure Queen Arwa would welcome you."

I didn't understand this need, this *drive* to become Queen, but I *knew* I'd be unhappy pursuing anything less. "Yeah, and then I'll have to start from the ground up. Here, people at least know me. So, let's put on a fake smile and get this show over with."

I linked my arms with theirs and yanked them forward before they could have any more second thoughts about being there.

Lisa gripped my arm with her other hand. "The last time I was here, a ghoul tried to eat me alive. You know that would make the third time someone tried to eat me."

I snorted as we continued to walk to the grand doors of the castle. They were maybe ten feet high, and inside we stood in an equally grand foyer with a wide marble staircase facing us. "Welcome to being a fae. I almost had my arm torn off when some loupe gorilla attacked me. It was hanging by a cord of muscle like—"

Lisa made a barfing noise and pulled away. "Please, I think I get the picture."

We followed the crowd past the foyer and further through the castle, past elegantly decorated rooms that looked like they had come right out of a French palace from hundreds of years ago. We then entered a grand ballroom decorated in crystals, golds, and dark velvets. It was opulence bordering on gaudy.

Someone had decided to maintain Misandre's taste.

"Who's that guy?" Lisa asked, gesturing to a long table near what was the front of the room.

A golden cloth covered the table, which stood in front of floor-to-ceiling gold paned windows. Ten people sat there. In the middle, in what I could only call a throne, sat a man with an upturned nose and beady, purple eyes.

I sucked my teeth in annoyance. "That's Sylvester, Misandre's second. He's been power tripping ever since she died. I know he's throwing his hat in for her spot."

"Why wouldn't he get it automatically?" Lisa asked.

I looked around at the many round tables scattered throughout the room. Our names hung in magic gold lettering in the air above our assigned tables. I spotted my name on a table all the way in the back, practically next to the door.

Well, that wasn't unexpected. I wasn't royalty but I was higher up in Misandre's court as a top warrior. I deserved better seating, or so I thought. "He wouldn't get it because no one likes him. Does that guy look like someone you'd want leading you?"

While his small frame didn't mean that he couldn't be a good leader—it was about our magic after all—he had the face of a rat and was petty beyond belief. He also lacked big ideas and was a snitch.

I moved us to our crappy seating past more extravagant tables with people I needed to be networking with to get support from. I could only imagine what rejects would be at our table.

A deep baritone laugh caught my attention, and I glanced to my left to see a man with his head tossed back. He was surrounded by a group who all focused on him with awe. He was handsome and tall, with very short, black hair and ice blue eyes against skin the color of desert sand. He looked vaguely familiar, but I couldn't place a name.

He stopped laughing and glanced over in my direction. For a moment, he looked surprised, then he recovered and winked at me before turning away.

I leaned my head back. Uh, cocky much? I deducted a point from his attractiveness for that.

Lisa leaned in toward me. "You know that hottie?"

"Not a clue who he is. Let's go to our table." I didn't have time to be distracted by pretty faces. I had a throne to secure, and building supporters was the best way to do it.

I made chit chat with the other fae at our table in an attempt to network and make new friends. While smoozing wasn't my thing, I think I put in a good effort throughout our four-course meal.

Lisa put her hand over her mouth and whispered. "We are back here with all the senior citizens and booger eaters. What did you do to get us back here?"

Bella leaned past me and glared at Lisa. "One, keep your voice down. Some of these older fae have a lot of wisdom they can share with us."

I glanced at her. "When will that start happening?" The elders were pretty old with white hair and wise eyes. I couldn't imagine how old a fae had to be to actually well, look old.

Bella ignored me, rightfully so. "Two, I'm pretty sure you offing a fae queen didn't endear Fran to anyone."

I practically choked on my fae liquor, a mildly sweet blue concoction that would make any weakling drunk before finishing the first drink. Luckily, I was no weakling.

One of the older fae at our table chuckled, the corners of her blue eyes crinkling even more with her laughter. "It was a fond farewell when she was killed. You'll get no enemies at this table from her death."

The other fae nodded in agreement. "We should thank you," said another male fae with long white hair.

I gave them a grateful smile. Maybe I could boast this angle instead of hiding it. I glanced sideways at Lisa. "This city practically broke out in dance like she just killed Evaline from *The Wiz.*"

Lisa scrunched her face. "What's *The Wiz*?"

I rolled my eyes. "I'll try not to be upset by that question. It's the 1970's more soulful version of *The Wizard of Oz*. Evaline is the wicked witch and when she gets killed, her peons get out of their ugly suits and high kick it to an amazing song sung by the great Diana Ross, aka Dorothy."

Lisa gave me a deadpan face. "You remember some ancient movie but can't remember where you were when the world went to crap ten years ago?"

I raised my glass and sighed. "I know, right? I can remember tons of pointless things but not my own mother's name or face for that matter." I gulped down the rest of my drink, trying to wash down the rising anger. I'd always been frustrated by my memory loss, but the rage came whenever I sat too long with my thoughts about how it had happened. To be controlled by the angels in such a way made me feel powerless and weak.

I looked down at my empty glass and swung it around. "I'm going to the bar to get another drink. Be right back." I rose and walked with purpose to the bar near the right of the room.

When I got to the bar, there was already a line, and I reined in my annoyance. I looked at the other bar not too far down and it was equally busy.

I felt a presence behind me and turned slightly to see the laughing man from earlier. He wiggled a bottle of fae sparkling liquor at me. "Need to be topped off?"

I pushed my glass towards him. "Thank you. Do I know you?"

He concentrated on pouring my drink, but a smile played on his lips. "You seem familiar." When he was done, he looked up at me with those shocking icy eyes. "I'm Marcus Livingston from King Fredrick's court of the Northwestern Region. You're Francesca Ross, right?"

I noticed he had what sounded like an English accent to my limited ears. The fae realm wasn't as large as the earthly realm. On a map, it would probably cover Europe and Africa, which still made it a considerable size. If he was of the Northwestern region he could be attached to the European

Fae. There was a slightly snobbish tone to his accent, as if he were royalty.

Perhaps he was. On closer inspection, Marcus seemed like he came from privilege. He was dressed in human clothes in a maroon, fitted three-piece suit tailored by the gods to cover every muscle of his body in the most flattering of ways. He wore a simple, crisp, white shirt underneath and a silver tie that seemed iridescent. The swirling pastel colors actually appeared to move before my eyes.

Wait. He knew my name? I tilted my head. "How'd you know my name?"

His grin widened and I noticed his incisors were sharper and longer than other fae or humans. I looked down at his hands holding his bottle and cursed myself for only now noticing that he had claws. I wondered if he was using his fae magic to hide his true appearance, well sans claws and teeth. The fae were a very diverse race. Some were as small as your hand, fluttering about like birds. Others were as tall as trees or as wide as a truck. Still others resembled animals but not quite weres, with many tails, horns, and furry ears. Marcus' incisors and claws let me know he might have another look he was hiding. He probably kept those to intimidate folks.

"You're associated with the Six, and everyone knows them. And you killed a demon King. That's not an easy thing to do. I should get your autograph on a napkin." His voice had a lazy drawl to it that felt like liquid down my spine when coupled with his accent. His voice was indeed a weapon.

I took a sip of my drink. This was not the same as what I'd been drinking earlier but I wasn't going to complain. "I'm sure my autograph isn't worth anything."

He tilted his head, assessing me politely. "Well, a picture together would be even better, but that might be more for personal reasons."

I kept my eyes neutral. Was this guy flirting with me?

47

Hmm, no, I couldn't trust anyone here. If he was flirting, it was because he wanted something beyond my body. What was he after? "I feel like I've seen you before. Maybe when I was with Alister?"

He squinted his eyes. "Long ago, before this world changed, I knew a girl named Francesca. I called her Franny. We were like twelve when I last saw her. She looked a lot like you. Eyes and everything." He narrowed his. "That's a rare combination."

Was he a clue to my past? "Not for a fae it isn't."

"True, but fae weren't out back then. We were still in secret. Do you still like to race? You were always a runner." He raised his chin in challenge. "You beat me every time."

I frowned as a pang of recognition rocked me. An image of two small kids sitting in a stuffy living room surrounded by faceless adults. The female's face was blurry as well, but the male looked vaguely like Marcus, eyes and all. Then the scene left my mind as soon as it appeared.

Did I know this guy from before? If I didn't seem like I did, it might give way to the already growing rumors about my memory loss, making me less fit for the throne.

I tapped my chin, pretending to recollect. "Aww, yes, I remember visiting with your family when we were little." At least I hope that was what I had seen.

His eyes didn't seem to betray that he knew I was lying. "Yes," he replied before taking a sip of his drink.

That was it? Damn it. I was hoping he could give me a little more information. Maybe he could help jog my memories back since it seemed we did know each other.

"How's Ms. Dalia?" he asked.

Who? Of course, I didn't remember any Dalia. Should I have? Crap, what if she was my mother? What if he knew where my mother was and I didn't answer right? I had to say something. I gave a tight smile. "Oh, she's just fine." Please let that be the right answer.

He cocked a brow. Did I say something wrong? Was this woman really dead and I just failed his test? "I'm surprised she's not here with you. Actually, I'm shocked you're even bothering with this throne."

Crap, crap, crap, crap, crap. How was I going to play this off now? I had no idea what he was talking about. Why wouldn't I want *this* throne? What the hell had my life been like before? Why'd I decided to be a stupid hitman for a demon if I was a fae? The only thing the angels had told me was that I hadn't known I was a demon.

I gave Marcus a crooked grin as my mind raced with some type of fitting lie to come up with. "Well, you know me. I always have to do the opposite of whatever anyone expects of me." Here's to hoping the old me was similar to the me of now.

Marcus gave me a hard stare before he snorted in a chuckle. "Well, that's true. My Franny always had to do things the hard way."

His Franny. First of all, I hated that nickname. Second of all, what was he talking about *his*? Had we been close? If we were twelve the last time we'd seen each other, I doubted we'd been dating. Hell, maybe we had been. I decided to let that part go for the time being. It was the least of my concerns in figuring out my past. Why was getting Misandre's throne the hard way? If there was another kingdom I needed to focus on that would prove easier to rule, I needed to know about it. However, finding out that information without giving away my memory issue would be tricky.

Marcus emptied the rest of his bottle in both our glasses before putting it on the edge of the bar and moving us further away. "You know, Franny, I actually don't blame you for wanting this throne. You're like me, a second born." He took a sip of his drink, assessing me with his eyes.

I tried to keep my face neutral. Was he setting me up? Was

it true? I had a sibling? And if I did, why did it matter that I was a younger sibling? What significance would that play?

"What have you been doing with yourself all these years?" He continued. "You just disappeared on us. My family was very disappointed."

My mind continued to race with questions I could not ask.

"I heard you were engaged to a demon. That seemed so beneath you. I'm glad you came to your senses." He smiled again and flicked his tongue over one of his incisors as he looked down at me with flirtation in his arctic eyes.

Was that supposed to be sexy? I mean, it kind of was but that wasn't the point. I needed to get him to tell me more about my past. "Why do you think being with a demon was beneath me, out of curiosity?"

"You're royalty, of course. Fae's shouldn't mix with demons if they plan to get ahead. It brings our value down."

Royalty? I joked about not being royal before, but clearly I was wrong. I had to know more. Was I descended from a court?

"Well, well, well. If it isn't the betrayer," came a nasal voice behind me.

I twisted my lips in annoyance and turned to face the source of the noise—I mean voice. Sylvester.

He glared up at me with those tiny mouse eyes, and I fought the urge to knock him on the head. He was barely five foot three inches and had a bald head and pointed ears slightly longer and sharper at the tip than an elf's. He wore a gold suit with a silk collared shirt underneath, exposing dark chest hairs.

"Call me what you want, Erik the Gnome. Sticks and stones and all that," I replied.

He jutted out his chin. "I'm surprised you dared show your face here. There are people here who would have your head for befriending those who killed Misandre."

I leaned my head toward him. "Here, go ahead and try to get it." I widened my eyes in my best crazy lady glare.

Marcus chuckled.

Glad I could amuse him.

Sylvester reared back and grimaced. "This is hardly the time or place. This is a classy affair, but I'd hardly expect you to know what that is."

I looked him up and down. "You're dressed up like a golden leprechaun, and you talk to me about class?"

He opened an elegant fan in front of his face in one snap. "I'm going to announce those running for the throne. I'm going to make sure no one votes for you."

Marcus tilted his glass slightly from side to side in front of him, studying the swishing liquid contents. "Oh, Sylvester, why be so cruel? Let's all be honest with ourselves here. No one loved Misandre. Not even you."

Sylvester made a noise of protest, but when Marcus met his eyes, the smaller faerie pursed his lips and fanned furiously.

What was that all about? Marcus could be intimidating, but the only other person I'd ever seen this gnome back down to was Misandre.

"No one really liked those first soulmates she aligned herself with either. They were more trouble than they were worth. And we all know why she really followed them. She was planning to run the other courts with whatever backing they promised." Marcus took a sip of his drink, and we all stared at him for his next words. "Honestly," he began in his slow drawl, "anyone associated with her should feel uncomfortable. So, you see, you can't be angry with our Francesca here."

Our?

"She's actually quite smart. You might take heed and separate yourself from Misandre's destructive ways."

Sylvester sneered, but I could see a slight look of concern in his eyes before he huffed and walked away.

Marcus leaned down toward me.

My body buzzed to attention. Why was I like this around him? Was he using magic on me?

"That was fun."

I furrowed my brows together. "I can handle his insignificant insults."

He shifted upright, a lazy smile on his lips. "Oh, I know you can. How about we make an alliance for now. See, I have it on good authority that there are about eight to ten fae vying for the throne, including you, me, and Sylvester. You and I can join forces and slowly take out our competition, metaphorically speaking."

I cocked a brow. That plan sounded intriguing. Working with him would also give me the chance I needed to see if he could unlock any more of my memories. "And then when it's down to just the two of us?"

"Well, then we duke it out like any other just with fewer people to bother with, giving us a fifty-fifty shot. And I'll make you my second in command when I get the throne."

I snorted. "Cute. I suppose I can do the same for you when I get it." I pushed out my glass to his. "Clink on it, ally?"

His grin widened before he touched his glass to mine. "I hope to see a lot more of you, Francesca. We have a lot of catching up to do."

Yes, we did. Maybe having him as an ally would be better than I thought. I could become a fae Queen and learn who I really was. However, I had to be careful. I knew there was more to Marcus and if we hadn't seen each other in years, I wanted to know why. What kind of danger was he?

# CHAPTER 5

*S*omeone pounded on the door to my apartment in Silver Spring the next evening.

I cracked open my eyes in irritation and looked at the clock. It was after six in the evening. I cursed and sat up in my bed. While I realized that getting up on a Tuesday evening might make me seem a bit loser-like, I had just returned from the fae realm at the crack of dawn. Time worked differently between the human and fae realm. While it seemed like I was just out for a few hours in fae time, I had been gone for nearly a day in human time.

I rubbed my eyes and threw on some jeans before shuffling to the door. I looked through the peephole and found Felix waving at me. I opened the door and waved him in but he remained at the entrance.

I raised a brow. "You can come in."

He scratched his beard with a frown on his face. "I'd love to, but there's a certain angel waiting in my apartment who wants to also speak to you."

"Who? Azrael? They can wait."

He slowly shook his head, eyes wide.

I already knew by his look who it was. Monica. "Damn it."

I ran a hand through my hair and sighed. "Okay, give me five minutes." I paused before turning away. I needed to ask this question before I got too sidetracked. "Did you ever hear me mention a Marcus?"

Felix narrowed his eyes. "No. Why?"

I shrugged. "I met him at the banquet and he said he knew me. Of course, I didn't know from where."

"Well, don't give away too much about your situation. You don't want people taking advantage of it."

"On it." I walked back to my bathroom, a little pleased at his concern.

He nodded and turned away. I quickly washed my face, brushed my teeth, and put on a bra and t-shirt to go better with my jeans, then trudged downstairs to Felix's. I knocked on the door before turning the knob and walking in.

A tall, stern-looking woman with a braided bun on the top of her head, a white wrap blouse and gray, wide-legged pants over shinny black heels paced in Felix's open living area.

Zaphkiel—or Monica—as we knew her. She turned her silver eyes to me and gave a small smile. "So glad you could join us, Francesca. It's very good seeing you again. How was your trip to the fae realm?"

I rolled my eyes. Damn angels and their all-knowingness. "It was a ball." I didn't need this small talk. Monica was my least favorite of the angels I'd met. It was her fault that I didn't have my memories. I still wasn't convinced that she couldn't give them back or that she didn't know who I used to be.

I flopped down on the couch and laid back. "Why are you here?"

Seeing that small talk was over, Monica walked over to the glass dining table and pulled out a chair before sitting. She crossed one long leg over the other before speaking. "I need the both of you to go on a mission for me."

That was unlikely to happen. Feeling renewed with my agreement with Marcus, I planned to spend more time in the fae realm making my rounds. Being on the council here was no longer high on my list, and helping the angels was even lower.

"In exchange, I will help you find out more about who you are, Francesca. Felix, I'll help you find your family."

Felix sat down beside me, shifting his large body towards Monica who sat adjacent to us. "I thought you couldn't do any more. It's been months."

I knew she'd been lying. "Let me guess. You'll try a little harder if we work for you. Really, we shouldn't have to do anything since it was you who wronged us in the first place."

Monica nodded slowly, her silver eyes giving away no emotion. "Interesting. Was it us who caused you not to get your memories back? We did try. There is a greater force at work. We kept an eye on you, but we shared only what we knew. You had a whole life before the return of magic that we did not track. Your history is very secretive. Why don't you ask Felix here about yourself since you were both so close and he has his memories back?" She looked almost amused when she made the suggestion.

I was sure it was because she already knew the answer.

I'd asked Felix many times before about his memories of me. He said I'd been raised by a mother and step-father who had adopted me. I'd had no siblings and I was in college when the world had changed. I hadn't been able to locate my parents after that and had no clue if they were living or dead. Felix didn't know their names. The rest of what he knew was more personality-based but was nothing of significance.

Monica didn't wait for me to ask before she began talking. "Honestly, Francesca, we didn't pay much attention to you outside of your connection to Felix. You aren't an angel, so we'd have no reason to care about you. However, if you help us, we might be persuaded to help you more."

So much for Monica being altruistic.

Felix cleared his throat and sat forward at the end of his seat. "I thought angels were supposed to be helpful."

Monica tilted her head toward him. "We are, but we like assurances. And—you'll have to excuse me—being part demon does give us pause in how much of your past we want to uncover."

Felix looked over at me with uncharacteristically irritated eyes.

I shrugged. I needed my memories. I didn't know how to approach Marcus or if he could even be trusted, but I also needed to be campaigning for votes.

I was, however, curious about what kind of mission she wanted us to do. "Okay, what's the job?"

Monica pursed her lips, assessing me with squinted eyes. "I need you to visit a town and check things out there."

I sighed. "Care to elaborate? What's so interesting about this town?"

"It's grown at a rate not common, and more importantly, there are a couple of lower-level angels and their human associates who have entered and refuse to leave. I could, of course, retrieve them by force but I am curious as to what kind of town is more appealing than heaven."

I wouldn't be surprised if they liked it better than working under her, but I kept that comment to myself. "So, you want us to see what's so special about this town?" With the possibility that *we* might not want to leave. "Sounds easy enough." Which likely meant it wasn't. "Did they have some sort of spell that trapped their citizens inside? Do you know what the deal is? Do you have a guess?"

Monica uncrossed her legs and leaned forward, leaning her forearms on her thighs. "I've lost people to this place. I'm not inclined to lose anymore. I've forbidden any of my people to step foot into that town. I haven't gone in and only met with the town leadership at a neutral location. They claim to be on the up and up, but their auras are cloudy. That doesn't necessarily mean anything sinister, but it could mean there is more and they are covering their evil with magic."

Felix scratched his beard in thought. "Have you spoken to your people who refuse to return?"

Monica shook her head. "It's all very mysterious."

I snorted and shock my head. "So, you want us to risk our lives to go inside this town and, should we be able to leave, give you the deal on what's going on?"

Monica gave a curt nod.

Felix frowned, clearly disturbed. "You think we're dispensable, don't you?"

Monica leaned back. "I think you both are half-demon and that—" She paused and turned up her upper lip in distaste. "—part of you might make you resistant to evil magic. Low-level angels are not immune but even a higher-level angel could have trouble, depending on the strength of the evil doer."

Was this mission worth it? Having my memories back would give me a better play at a crown. I could work on Marcus while having the angel's continue to work on my memories as well, thus increasing my chances. If I only had to go in the town and report back, then this wouldn't be a significant distraction. Time moved slower in the fae realm so I wouldn't miss much. "Where is this town? And when do you want us to head out?"

"St. Michaels, Maryland and this weekend. Spend some time there to really see what's going on. It'll be almost like a vacation."

In the middle of a campaign for Queen.

"So, will you do it?"

I crossed my arms. But I really *did* need answers and my memories. The few hints I'd gotten from Marcus led me to believe that maybe there was more to my past than I realized. Could I really trust Monica to return my memories? I guess I could go for a few days, and if she couldn't deliver, I would go to the fae realm. "Will you cover all expenses?"

"Of course."

I lifted a shoulder. "Why not. Could be fun."

Monica stood up. "Wonderful. I think you both will be quite useful to our cause after all." She turned to leave, then paused. "And when you return, Francesca, I do have something to share about your family. I think you'll be quite pleased."

Before I could press her further, she disappeared into a cloud of smoke.

I twisted my lips and flipped the empty space she'd just occupied with my middle finger. Of course she would hold out on telling me anything until I returned. If it wasn't big, I was leaving. "I have a feeling she is going to be a thorn in my side for quite a while."

Felix nodded, a soft smile on his lips.

I leaned away from him. "What's with the face?"

He raised a shoulder. "You and I going away for a romantic getaway."

I got up, shaking my head. "Ok crazy man. This is a job, not a vacation. You and I aren't a couple. In fact, it might be smart to invite Faith and Azrael with us. More power in numbers."

He stood up as well, glancing down at me with the same amused face, his full lips stretched in a lopsided smile that gave him an annoyingly sexy appearance. Something shifted in his gaze, and it was like he was seeing me for who I was, touching my soul in places I couldn't even reach.

Why were men insisting on making me get butterflies? I had no time for such things. I was a big girl.

"Are you afraid to be alone with me?"

I laughed dryly. "Uh, no." Okay, maybe I was. He was a very sexy distraction after all. And the way he looked at me made me want to throw myself at him.

As if seeing some desire in my eyes, he reached over and stuck two fingers into the pocket of my jeans, yanking me forward. I braced my hands against his hard chest, momentarily distracted by the definition of his body. He really was massive. It was hard not to cuddle up next to him. Normally I wouldn't be a fan of such alpha behavior but Felix had always proven respectful, bordering on boy scout. But then he had his moments, like this, where his presence showed me that he was no kid. The look under his partially lowered lids exposed that he was very much not in an innocent mood, and it did something to my nether regions.

"You are not focused," I began. "We need to look into this place. We could be getting sent to our doom. Besides, this back-and-forth flirtation thing is just going to make us frustrated. We should just keep it platonic." But only if I truly wanted the throne. Did I want it more than him?

He groaned like I just suggested he eat wilted asparagus. "We can take things slow but platonic? You're killing me, woman." He bit his lower lip and tilted his head. "This is part of the fun."

My knees were starting to feel like jelly, and I could not have that. I wiggled away from him and pointed. "I will not be tempted by you into another high school make-out session."

He lost the heat in his eyes and replaced them with a sort of happy sadness that made him so endearing to me. "I am focused, Fran. It's just that you've practically been running from me for two months and now I have you here. I'm happy, and I just want to be near you for the time that we have together. I know that when you get that throne, because you will, I won't see you again."

My heart stabbed a little. I hadn't thought about that. If I were a Queen of a court, my comings and goings would be a big deal. I couldn't just go off for visit on my own without an entourage. Then there was the deal I'd made with Marcus. I still wasn't convinced it was a real thing, but if it was, I was sure there would be strong disapproval of me spending so much time with non-fae. Marcus seemed like the type to take advantage of that and steal my crown right from under me.

Besides, where could things go with Felix and me? He wasn't any part fae so he could never rule beside me. We couldn't get married.

I frowned and looked over to Felix. He was still staring at me with sad eyes. "Just realizing it, huh?" he said in a low voice.

I nodded slowly. "Then why do you even want to be around me? It'll just hurt more later."

"Guess the pain is worth it to me."

I wanted to run up to him and kiss him for that. It was the saddest, sweetest thing I'd ever heard. But I also didn't want to hurt him. Maybe he could take the pain but I couldn't take causing it. No, it was better that Felix and I stay friends.

I cleared my throat. "Well, we should get the others over and talk strategy."

He gave a nod and turned from me, closing his eyes. I assumed he was calling Azrael and Faith. Since the angel was his guardian, they had a magical connection. As for Faith, as a member of the special six with Felix, they could keep in contact through their minds as well. It was better than a cell phone.

I sat down on the couch and Felix's golden retriever bounced over to me from a back room. "Dexter! Where have you been hiding?" I asked, scratching the dog's head.

"She doesn't like Monica," Felix replied.

"Smart dog."

"She likes me though," Azrael stated.

I jumped slightly and saw the angel sitting in a leather armchair to my left. "Don't you knock?"

Azrael gave me an unbothered wave of the hand. "Felix is family, I don't need to knock."

As if on queue, we heard a knock at the door. Felix jumped up to get it and seconds later he reappeared with Faith. I gave Azrael a pointed look and the angel wiggled their eyebrows at me in defiance. Angels were unnecessarily annoying.

The others joined us in the living room and we gave them a recap.

Azrael scooted further in the chair, their cocky look being replaced with concern. "Should have known Zaphkiel would be on top of this. Losing angels and humans under her rankings doesn't look good on her ability to lead. So she's sending you two to fix it."

"How dangerous is this town?" I asked.

Azrael shrugged. "That's the thing. We don't know. There's a whole ward around the town and you can only get in by invitation. They aren't stingy with the invites so it shouldn't be hard to get in. It's the getting out that's a bit more challenging."

Faith swore and twisted in her seat on the couch beside Felix. "Well, this doesn't sound smart. We don't need to go. Azrael and Fran's angel, Carlos, can keep helping us get your memories back."

I opened my mouth to mention Marcus. He clearly knew about my past as well. Maybe I couldn't get the spell to be broken but I could still learn who I was. Assuming I trusted him. Which I didn't. I glanced back over to Azrael. "Do you really think Monica will help us or prevent others from helping us if we don't do this?"

Azrael tilted their head from side to side in thought. "I think she has an agenda and she's using you as a means to get there. If she can keep feeding you nuggets, you'll keep doing as she says. Even the unsavory things other angels won't or can't do."

Felix hunched forward beside me. "Can angels say no to her?"

"Yes, if it's to do something against our policies, for a lack of a better word. But you guys don't have those kind of restrictions."

"Would you go if it were you?"

Azrael sighed and crossed their arms behind their head in thought. "I'm an angel whose goal is to eradicate evil. I would feel it my duty to investigate. Neither of you have such responsibilities. However, Felix, you're part of the six and you are a hero. This is what you would be expected to do. Both of you are part demon. There's nothing good in that." I held my tongue to argue. "Doing good work like this, possibly helping people, will lessen the stains on your souls. The more you do such things, the better it will be for you in the afterlife."

Felix nodded, appearing settled in the matter. "Well, I like the sound of that."

Faith huffed. "Felix, this isn't smart. Fran can go with some of her demon friends. That's the smarter thing to do."

Of course she would throw me out there on my own. Monica made a deal with both of us and I was going to get the power of the Six to help make this situation a success because I had no real idea of what I was dealing with in that town. I leaned forward and looked past Felix to Faith. "Excuse me? Why is it okay for me to go but not him?"

She rolled her eyes. "He doesn't need Monica and her troubles. This is all about you. It's not safe. Felix just needs to stay here and teach. We've had enough trouble this past year. Amina's still in a coma and Lisa's running around trying to help an elf King. The six are already a mess as it is."

I pressed my lips together and squinted, thinking of the right words. Nothing came to me. "So, you do realize that Felix is an adult person? He can take care of himself."

She twisted her lips and glared at me. "I know that. It's just dumb for him to risk getting hurt for nothing."

"Wow, okay. Well for someone named Faith, you surely

have none for your friend here. I've seen him fight enough to know that we don't have to build a wall around him like he needs to be protected."

"I know he can fight. More than you know. I just think he should stop chasing after you like some love sick kid because we all know you're playing him."

Azrael snickered. "Cat fight. Where's my popcorn?"

Felix scooted forward to block us from each other. "We're going to go on this mission. Faith, I know you're looking out for me but this is what I want. It's not just about Fran. If Monica can help me find my family, then I have to do this."

I grabbed Felix's arm and pushed him back so that I could see Faith again. "And I'm not playing him. I'm just trying to figure out my life. It's not like you got it all figured out Ms. I'm-going-to-date-an-original-soulmate-that-tried-to-kill-us-all!"

"Damn it, woman," Felix sighed.

Faith jumped up. "I didn't know she was evil. No one knew. Like you can talk since you were getting *married* to a demon lord who worked for her!"

I lowered my head. Touché. "Shut up." I mumbled.

"Great come back."

Felix cleared his throat again, looking pained. "It seems to me that we all have made relationship mistakes in the past. Maybe this will bond you guys." He looked back and forth to us both but we didn't respond. "We'll give it a little more time. Until then, Faith, will you go with us?"

She looked over to Felix with still engaged eyes. "Fine, we will go on this stupid mission with you because I'm your best friend and I have to have your back."

I opened my mouth to retort that I too would have his back but Felix raised a hand in my direction to keep me silent. I leaned back, looking at the hand. There he went, being alpha again.

"Fine, then it's settled. Friday, we leave for a vacation. It's going to be fun!" He said in a forced shout as if him yelling it would make it the truth.

Azrael snorted, a confused look on their face. "It probably won't be but I'm packing popcorn and whiskey anyway."

What was I getting myself into?

# CHAPTER 6

*S*t. Michaels, Maryland, was a tiny town off the Chesapeake Bay. According to Azrael, it used to be a reasonably popular weekend getaway on the east coast until a supernatural tsunami-like flood had destroyed the area. Population decimation and fear of another devastating flood had left the town abandoned for years until recently.

Instead of teleporting, we drove to the town's warded entrance off the main road near an abandoned restaurant. A giant welcome sign warned us about the ward a quarter of a mile ahead.

I couldn't recall the last time I'd bothered with a car. It was such a sluggish way to go nowadays. Add in that riding in a car with two people that hated me made the trip even more painful. I leaned out of the front passenger side window. "So, what do we do now?"

Azrael opened the door, got out and stretched. The angel tilted their head back as they took in the warm spring sun, although it felt like the middle of summer. "We wait. Somebody's watching."

Not that much later, two people in mopeds rode toward us dressed in black suits and sunglasses like secret service agents. We remained in place until they stopped their vehicles and got off simultaneously. They then approached us at the same time, same pace. Right foot, left foot.

I moved my head back in the car. "Do they seem kind of …weird?"

Felix opened his driver side door. "I don't know. Seem kind of cool to me."

Faith scoffed. "You would think that."

We all got out to join Azrael, who was giving our approaching duo an amused grin.

"How may we help you?" They said in unison.

Were they twins? They didn't look like it. Both were men but that was where the similarities stopped. One was tall, over six foot, the other was short, no more than five foot five inches. The tall one looked black with short, brown hair. The short one was white with cropped, blond hair.

Azrael stepped forward. "We have reservations at the Sweetwater Harbor Inn. We were approved for access."

The pair nodded and went about the standard method for testing us to ensure we weren't carrying any supernatural illness. Once they approved of our health, they gave us a simultaneous smile and asked us to follow them to the inn.

Had Azrael's angel magic made entry so easy, or was there something else going on here? "That was so weird," I mumbled after we got back in the car and followed them down the street.

The ward tingled over my skin as we slipped through them. Monica and Azrael's words about not being able to leave jumped into my mind. "Stop!"

Felix pressed on the break. "What?"

"Reverse and see if we can get back out past the ward. I just want to see if we get locked in."

Felix reversed and the tingle passed over us once more but with no issue. He glanced over at me.

I gave a curt nod for him to continue.

"Guess we can rule out the missing angels being trapped in."

I expected the place to still look devastated since, according to Azrael, the town had only resurfaced a little over a year ago. However, it looked totally void of any damaged buildings or land. In fact, it looked exactly like the old pictures of the town before the great flood. There were small shops and restaurants, grocery stores, beautiful two-story houses with well-kept lawns and other buildings all surrounded by a harbor with crystal clear water and clean boats of various sizes.

I wasn't surprised. Magic could make anything possible, and it was the common tool among paranormals to bring life back to an area.

Other than our two escorts, nothing seemed out of place. People walked about. Dogs barked. There were no kids but that wasn't odd in and of itself. It was early on a Friday and it was possible they were in school or that the town just did not cater to families. Old photos on the internet gave the appearance that this was more of an older person destination.

Our escorts paused in front of a large three-story inn overlooking the water, then waved at us in unison before riding off.

An older woman greeted us at check-in with a plastic smile and wide eyes like she was both shocked and happy. It was both odd and unsettling.

I was slightly annoyed to find we weren't given our own rooms. Instead, we had a total of two rooms. Before Felix could say what he wanted, I nudged Faith to stay with me. She looked perturbed but followed me to the elevator anyway.

Faith glanced over at me as we waited at the elevator. "I know you're avoiding being with Felix. Don't want to get his hopes up. But why'd you pick me instead of Azrael?"

The elevator doors opened, and we stepped in with our

luggage. It was tiny, fitting no more than two people, which seemed fitting of the old-fashioned waterside inn. It looked like the place was in need of an upgrade. I found it odd that they'd chosen to make the inn the same when they had done the reconstruction.

I sighed. "Except for Carlos, I'm not a big fan of angels. Don't worry. I won't ask you to stay up all night, eat pizza, and talk about boys."

The elevator opened to the third floor. "Well, that's no fun," Faith said with a smirk before stepping out.

Once we got settled, we met Azrael and Felix in the lobby. It was still early out, only around noon, and, with it being May, we'd have plenty of daylight on our hands to walk around and investigate.

Everywhere we went, the townspeople stopped what they were doing to smile and wave at us. Joggers waved. Diners stopped eating and waved. Even people on bikes and in cars. It was like Mr. Roger's neighborhood here.

About an hour into checking out the town, Felix suggested we grab an early dinner at a café. With such a small town, I didn't expect it to take long at all to cover the area, so we'd already seen everything, although I wasn't quite sure what we were looking for.

There was, however, one thing I did notice already. I wasn't certain at first, but as we began to stroll around, now I knew. That icky gloom. Like a film of sweat on the skin that made you want to jump in the shower and wash it off.

I paused the group before stepping into the café and turned to Azrael with a pointed look. "I sense demonic energy in this town. Don't you?"

The angel tilted their head, unbothered. "Since we went through the ward."

I threw out my hands. "You didn't want to say anything?"

"I assumed you knew. If we thought this place was fine, we wouldn't be here."

I rubbed my temples. Damn, these angels. "Okay, there are a lot of evil things in this world. It's not just demons who cause problems."

Azrael shrugged and walked past me to enter the café. "Well now that you confirmed what I suspected, we have a better understanding of what we are dealing with."

Felix rolled his shoulders back, looking around. "I could tell there was magic in the town, but I couldn't tell what type. Is it all demonic?"

I shook my head. "That I don't know. I can only tell fae and demon magic and I can't tell strength. I don't know if there are a lot of demons here or even just one. I just feel a trace of it. That doesn't mean it's the whole town. Honestly, you'd be surprised how often I feel demonic presence in the world. They're everywhere."

Faith walked forward, following Azrael. "Why am I not surprised?"

A hostess greeted us at the entrance with another bright smile. She was young but she was dressed as if she'd stepped out of the 1950s, including flipped hair and a poodle skirt. I looked around the café. All the patrons were young but dressed in attire from decades long passed. Fashion was only recently reemerging but wearing clothes from so long ago was odd. *Everyone* wearing vintage clothes was even more strange. We saw people in 1950s poodle skirts, bell-bottom jeans, 80s track suits, fringe vests, slip dresses and oversized plaid shirts. What in-the-time-warp was going on?

The sound of a 1950s doo-wop song played from some unseen speaker. Was this a theme café? It certainly wasn't designed as such. It appeared to be a modern design from the time right before the world had changed.

The hostess sat us down at a circular table near the window and gave us four menus.

"Excuse me, is this a theme party?" I asked, accepting a menu.

The woman gave me a quizzical look. "Why, no. It's just a regular old café, sweetheart." She giggled and turned away.

"I feel like I'm in *Back to the Future*," I began. "What's going on?"

Faith leaned back and looked at the menu with a slight shake of her head. "I'm nobodies fashion expert but this town looks like they fell in a time warp they couldn't get out of. Did you see the guy jogging in that neon windbreaker suit?"

"I tried to ignore it. So where would we find these missing angels? What are their names?"

Azrael tossed the menu on the table, having made their selection. "They'd be going by Dean and Nancy here."

"Should we ask around?"

"That might draw suspicion. I was hoping to just run into them."

Felix made a slight excited noise. "Did you see the description of this roast beef sandwich? I know what I'm eating."

I snatched the menu from him. "Hey, pay attention. This isn't a vacation." They were going to throw me on my own to my doom because it was possibly too dangerous. Now, they were chatting about meal options like they were on a cruise to the Bahamas.

He squinted his eyes at me with a smile. "But isn't it though?"

I gave the menu back at him. "I feel like you're not going to be any help." I looked back over to Azrael. "What do your angels look like?"

Azrael nodded. "That pastrami sandwich sounded good. Ooh, and I was thinking about the mozzarella sticks. Who wants to split that with me?"

Were they ignoring me to be a jerk, or were they being affected by whatever was going on here?

Felix raised his hand.

I looked up at the ceiling. "I'm going to flip this table if you don't answer me."

Azrael let out a much put-upon sigh. "Dean is a tall, skinny white guy with spiked blond hair. Nancy is a full-figured Hispanic woman with blue hair. They will stand out here."

A hostess appeared and gave us four glasses of water. I looked up at her. She was dressed in 70s style bell bottom jeans and a fitted turtleneck with a fringe vest. Her red hair was feathered back to perfection. She smiled at us with pale pink lips.

However, her style was not the concern.

Although she appeared no older than thirty, her face sagged. Not in the way skin did due to age. It was almost like she was melting. Bags hung low under her eyes. Her jawline hung loose. Her neck was lumpy, and even her ears seemed to droop.

I looked around at the others. Felix seemed unperturbed as he gave his order. Azrael, ever the poker face, gave their order with no look of concern. Faith avoided looking at the woman and gave her order with no pause.

I was the only one gawking at her like she was an animal at the zoo. Admittedly, this was not polite. I gave my order quickly and waited for her to leave before saying anything.

"Is there such a thing as looking young and old at the same time?"

"Not like that," Faith snorted. "Maybe she's got a condition or something. I didn't want to be an asshole and stare." She picked up her water and gave me a pointed look.

I mean, she wasn't wrong, however, we didn't come to this town to just relax. If things were weird we should be questioning them. "I get it, I was being rude. It just felt off and aren't we here to find 'off' things?"

She gave me a wary look. "And her skin condition is the cause for the missing angels?"

Clearly, these people were no detectives. Why did Monica think we could uncover anything?

Felix rubbed his beard in thought. "You know, maybe the angels just decided to stay here. People seem nice. They feel free to be themselves. Might be better than working for creepy Monica."

Azrael nodded, shifting to face Felix better. "The thought did cross my mind, but I'd rather hear that from them directly."

I sniffed my water. I wasn't sure I trusted anything here. "Have angels run off before?"

Azrael raised a brow and gave me an amused look. "Of course. Felix's dad did. Angels sometimes fall in love with those they shouldn't and then they go run off to live their best lives, I guess. Being human is like freedom to us. You may not know this, but angels can be uptight."

I sat straight and put a hand to my chest. "No," I gasped in fake shock.

The angel chuckled. "Yeah. I mean, no offense against heaven. It's a beautiful realm and everyone is nice and good. But you don't get whiskey or weed or deep-fried Oreos. And forget about sex."

Faith gave a pained expression. "Yikes."

"Your body doesn't exactly want it anymore. We're supposed to be above that shit. But, fuck it, you remember." The angel slouched in their chair and tossed their head back.

I could see the wistfulness in their eyes. I had to admit, I felt a little bad for the angel. Just a little.

"Is that why you ran around like a maniac when you came to earth?" Felix asked. He glanced over to me. "They stayed up late, went to the strip club, drank and ate everything. I felt like the parent of a bad teenager."

"I regret nothing."

I crossed my arms and sucked my teeth. "Well Heaven

sounds boring. What do you do all day? Hop on clouds and play the harpsichord?"

Azrael glared over at me. "It's not that bad. There's stuff to do. You hang with your loved ones. You cross realms. You see and learn all the secrets of the world and the universe."

"Do aliens exist?"

Azrael wiggled their brows. "Everything exists. It only sucks for angels like me really, because we actually have to work. It's the trade you make for getting a chance to return to the world and get higher in ranks. Higher ranks mean more privileges and power. Of course, it also means dealing with more politics and personalities. Sometimes I'm not sure if a chance to eat a cheeseburger is worth all this."

As if she heard us, our waitress returned with our food. As she placed our orders on the table, I snuck a glance up at her and noticed in surprise that she no longer had any sagging skin. Everything was as tight and youthful as one would expect for someone in their twenties.

What the…

She flashed us another smile before leaving us to our food.

I looked around at the others at the table. "Anyone care to explain her quickie facelift?"

Felix grabbed a mozzarella stick and popped it his mouth in one go. What was he, Scooby-Doo? Did he even chew?

"If you spit that up in my face, I'm going to throw you into traffic," Faith threatened, obviously on the same wavelength as me.

His eyes widened and he began to chew. Clearly Faith's threat was all bark because one, there was no traffic here and two, he was way too large for her to even break her back trying to pick up.

Faith dipped one of her fries into a small container of ketchup. "Maybe she got a magic surgery just now."

"Why is a twenty-something's face even sagging like that

in the first place?" I looked down at my Philly cheese steak before leaning in to sniff it. Would I be able to tell if the food was magically poisoned? "What if it's in the food? People eat it and then become smiley, wavy, pod people."

Felix paused biting into his sandwich. He gave me the saddest pout ever. "I'm so hungry."

They really weren't taking this mission seriously. Did they think Monica wouldn't send us to our doom? I didn't have that kind of faith in her. I wanted to find these angels and get the hell out. If Monica suspected something was going on here then every place and everything was a suspect, including the food. I shrugged. "Fine. Then eat and we'll find out what happens from there."

He glared at me and I looked back at him with a sugary sweet smile.

The sudden sound of chomping to my right stole my attention and I turned to see Azrael chomping away at their sandwich. "Really?"

"The food is fine. Angels can detect evil, including poison or tampering, in food. We're like those drug dogs in airports who could sniff out cocaine in suitcases. We can't tell you what's in it, but we can tell if something is wrong." The angel closed their eyes and shook their head. "This sandwich is heavenly. Not literally because there's no food up there but you get the deal."

I began to nibble at my cheesesteak, still not certain about the food or even what we were doing here. It seemed everyone was taking it way too easy.

After eating, we settled the tab using government dollars. Most towns not affiliated with government towns still accepted government dollars because there were so many places they could go to buy items. Government towns covered at least half of the country so even if you ended up somewhere else, the town would still take your dollars because there was bound to be a government town less than an hour away for them to shop.

The waitress, still looking youthful, took our money from Faith, slightly grazing her fingers as she took the cash. "You have such smooth skin. What do you do to take care of it?" She ran her fingers up Faith's hand and began to stroke her.

Faith flashed her a smile, seemingly unaffected. "Thanks, hon. I use this all-natural cocoa butter a friend of mine told me about. Game changer for me."

The waitress nodded and backed away slowly. "Thanks, doll."

Felix got up and smirked down at Faith. "I think she was flirting with you."

Faith got up with a smug grin. "It happens."

"Everywhere we go it's like this."

"Life of a succubus."

As we headed out of the café, I took a look back and noticed the hostess and waitress whispering to each other as they looked at us with excited eyes. It was kind of the way a fan would look at some pop idol. Was it all just Faith's succubus pheromones? I was pretty certain it was more than that and I was going to find out.

# CHAPTER 7

*W*e decided to rest up back at the hotel and then head out that evening for drinks to see what night looked like in the town. I suspected it would be quiet and boring. I was annoyed that we were here, unable to determine what was going on. This was a waste of time. I needed to be vying for votes, not trying to find angels I didn't even care about. The information Monica was going to share with me had better be worth this.

Faith took a nap in the bedroom while I occupied my time scouring the internet on things to help me win a fae throne. I knew the internet wouldn't have significant information for me, but I could learn leadership skills and build followers. After all, getting the throne didn't involve a fight or some type of magical challenge like the weres and witches went through. All of the people approved for consideration had proven their power. I had been one of the top fighters in Misandre's court and a former hitman for Alister. All my competitors, including that punk Sylvester, had strong magic.

No, to get the throne, I had to get support which would

be impossible while I was here. It was like running for election. However, I didn't have a ton of money, and my popularity was mixed. So now, I had to find a way to win over the undecided.

Research was not my thing, and so, having almost gone cross-eyed from looking at the screen, I closed my laptop and paced around the living area. We were supposed to head out by nine, so I'd have to wake Faith up soon.

I looked out of the sliding glass doors of our suite, intending to spy on the neighbors. The sooner I figured out what was wrong here, the sooner I could get back to what I *needed* to be doing. The inn was off the main road, and the view from our room looked across the street to a large, dark house. Dusk had given way to night. I let out a deep sigh. If we didn't find anything, how long were we supposed to stay in this sleepy town?

The lights from the top window in the house across from us, perhaps the attic, came on. Who was walking through a dark house only to hang out in the attic?

A tall thin figure, perhaps a man, appeared in the window. I couldn't make out any details from so far away. He just looked like a shadowy figure surrounded by light. The man raised an arm and slowly began to move his arm from side to side almost robotically.

Who was he waving at? I frowned and looked down the street. There was no one there. I looked back and took a step back. The man was still moving his hand, except the lights were no longer on in the attic. There was enough light from the street lamps for me to see that he was still standing there waving. What was his deal? Could he see in my room? I had my lights on, and suddenly I felt very exposed. I went to my living room lamp, shutting it off before walking back to the balcony.

The man was still waving. What in the hell?

I closed the curtains and took a step back, staring at the beige curtains with a rising unsettling feeling. *You're being silly, Fran. You've seen more creepy things than this.*

What if it wasn't even a person? It could be a stupid waving Santa statue they put in the window to scare people. Either that or he was just some guy trying to flirt. I could see Felix doing something like that.

I walked back to the curtains and opened them a crack. The man was still there. Still waving. Except this time, he was smiling. How did I know? Well, I could see his almost glowing white teeth all the way from my suite. I could also see that they were sharp. Then there were his eyes. They shown bright red like floating orbs in the darkness.

I pulled the curtains closed.

Demon. Had to be. And an inhuman one at that. I shivered, standing in the darkness in the living area. Demons still creeped me out.

If a demon was around, that could only mean foul play was in the air. It could gravitate here because it found the souls corruptible. Easy prey. If the townspeople were as kind as they presented themselves to be, gaining their souls would be worth quite a lot. All the more reason for angels to also come here in order to protect the people. However, with two missing angels and some odd behavior, I wasn't sure the angels were winning.

"Why are you standing out here in the dark?" Faith's voice boomed through the silence.

I jumped, in spite of myself, and spun around. "I was mediating."

She flipped the light switch on and gave me disbelieving eyes. "Come on. Let's go meet the guys."

I nodded and then peeked back through the curtains out of curiosity. The waving demon was gone.

∾

"There are no kids here. Or older people. Have you noticed?" Felix leaned into the rectangular picnic table.

We sat on the deck, overlooking the water in a busy restaurant and bar. Tiki torches and the low base of rock music surrounded us.

"For the older people, at first, I just thought, well, maybe they are all just paranormal people since we age slower. But older people got magic ten years ago too. Even if they stopped aging, they didn't get younger."

Faith looked down at her beer, her brows gathered in a frown. "Think they have an age cut off here? Maybe no one who looks over a certain age and no one under eighteen? Just a town full of adults in their best shape?"

That didn't quite make sense either.

Felix shook his head. "But why?"

"Could be that this is like their playground. No responsibilities and immaturity of kids and teens. No having to care for the elderly. It's just you, living just for you, forever." Faith's eyes seem to lose focus as she continued to stare at her drink. "Actually, it doesn't seem like such a bad thing."

"The children are our future, and the elderly are our teachers."

That was sentimental.

Faith tipped her head to the side in thought. "Except what does that mean when you can live for hundreds of years as a paranormal?"

We sat quietly with that thought as we drank and looked around. The plausibility of Faith's suggestion made more sense when I coupled it with the demonic presence in the town. It was possible that deals had been made to preserve the town as it had been.

Azrael jumped up and stormed toward the outside bar in

the crowded deck, beyond where I could see. We got up as well and chased after the angel, spotting them spinning a tall, lanky man around. "Where the heavens have you been?" Azrael cried.

I assumed this was Dean.

He raised his brows in surprise and then turned to a woman with blue hair.

That had to be Nancy.

Dean looked confused back at Azrael. "We've been here the whole time."

"You haven't responded to emails."

Dean and Nancy exchanged glances, but they seemed content, pleasant smiles setting on their faces. "We like it here," Dean stated.

Nancy touched Azrael's arm and ushered us away from the bar to a part of the fence surrounding the deck. "We don't want to go back. This place just feels so good." Nancy relaxed her shoulders, and her smile faltered. "And being under Monica was so tiring."

I had to kind of agree.

Dean shrugged. "This is the perfect place to escape her. She won't come here. Guessing that's why she sent you two. Did she tell you how she threatened the town mayor?"

I wouldn't put it past her, but in order for me to get what I needed, I had to bring answers back to Monica. "Why are people so weird here?"

Nancy glanced over at me, her smile returning. "How so?"

I shrugged. "I don't know. How they dress? The smiling faces all the time."

"We don't judge here. That's the best part."

"Huh. And what about the demons?"

A muscle in Nancy's face twitched. "What demons?"

Azrael sighed. "The energy is here. You have to feel it."

Dean clasped his hands in front of him. "Perhaps you're

getting it confused with the two demons who accompanied you here." He gave Felix and I pointed looks.

I cleared my throat and took a step forward. He thought we were idiots. "First of all, we're half-demon. Two, we can tell the difference between our own scent and another scent. This isn't a fart. We aren't just smelling our upper lips."

Felix released a mix of a snort and a laugh.

Dean tilted his head, his smile growing. "I didn't mean to offend. I only meant to share with you another possibility. The people here have been nothing but good to us. I don't see how any evil could be present."

I crossed my arms. "We didn't say evil. We said demonic."

"Same thing, no?"

There was the judgmental angel I knew and disliked.

Before I could say another word, Faith cut in. "Looks like they're fine. Can we go?" she said with bored eyes.

"Going so soon? But you just got here," exclaimed a woman's voice behind us.

Dean and Nancy's eyes lit up, and their smiles widened like a kid at Disney World.

I turned to see a woman standing there with two other women behind her, wearing black suits like the men who had let us in the town.

"Yasmine!" the angels exclaimed.

Several people around us looked on with gleeful whispers.

Was she a local celebrity or something? She certainly was beautiful with rich toffee colored skin and wavy, deep red hair. Her eyes were almost black but seemed to have a navy tint to them. Perhaps they were really blue. She was slightly shorter than me and fuller with an envious hourglass figure that she had draped in a red wrap dress paired with over-the-knee black boots. "I'm happy you're visiting our small town. I hope that you will enjoy yourselves." She looked over to Felix and extended a hand. "I'm Yasmine Covington, the town mayor. And you are?" She lowered her lids slightly, a pout on her lips.

What was she? A politician or a super model?

Felix grasped her hand with an enamored smile.

Irritation flared within me.

"I'm Felix, and this is Francesca, Faith and Az-"

"Ashton," Azrael cut in, slapping Felix on the back.

So we were giving fake names now? Even Dean and Nancy didn't know the angel's heaven name. However, I was sure Dean and Nancy weren't their real names either.

Yasmine gave a nod to the rest of us, but she didn't shake our hands like she did Felix, whose hand she was just now letting go. "Couples get away?"

Faith gave a dry laugh. "No. Just friends getting away from the horrors of the world."

I glared at her. Maybe I did want Yasmine to think Felix was taken. And yes, I recognized how selfish that seemed.

Yasmine still had eyes only for Felix. "Well, you will see that this is the place to be for an escape. There are no cares, no worries. Only relaxation. We have wonderful spas, great paths for jogging and biking, boating is quite fun here. There is a festival coming up later this month, so I encourage you to come back."

Felix nodded eagerly.

What was going on here? What kind of power did Yasmine have?

She clapped her hands together. "Have you tried the town beer? Oh, you must." She touched Felix's bicep and led him to the bar.

The small crowd parted as we followed.

Once we got additional drinks, Felix invited Yasmine back to our table. I pushed my annoyance aside in favor of the mission. I'd already decided that being with Felix was a bad idea. Why? Because he couldn't be with me when I became Queen. That's why. I needed this mission to finish smoothly and quickly so I could get back to regaining my memories and a throne. If Yasmine was taken with him, then maybe that was a good thing? Maybe we could learn more about what was going on here? But damn if it didn't hurt to see her cozying it up to him.

"So, did you start this town?" Azrael asked.

I tried to ignore the curious glances from those around us. I hated being on display and we would never blend in with the mayor's two women in black standing behind her like a living wall.

Yasmine nodded. "Yes, a few years ago. Before all of this, I was working insane hours as a CEO of a company that's long gone by now. I lost everything. My husband, my life's work. I didn't know what to do. I roamed for years at a loss of what to do with my life. I'm a witch, so I had magic, but I didn't know what to do with it. Then, I remembered my dream. I used to want to run a bed and breakfast by the water. I thought of this place. I'd come here on vacation before. This seemed like the perfect place to rebuild and make my own." She leaned back with a satisfied grin. She then looked around and raised her hands. "And that dream became this. Now instead of running a company that was sucking the life out of me, I'm running a town that has brought me nothing but joy. And I hope it brings the same to you."

I twisted my lips. She sure knew how to give a talk. There were cult leaders with the same kind of backstory.

"And you have great beer," Felix exclaimed, raising his glass.

Yasmine laughed and clinked her glass with his. "That we do."

I looked around at the crowd. Everyone did look happy. Was this town just the unknowing target of a demon who wanted a slice of their good thing? Did Dean and Nancy really want to be here as an escape from Monica?

Movement near the steps leading to the parking lot caught my eye. A shorter figure stood in the shadows. It looked like a child. I squinted and tried to see better. My fae eyesight finally kicked in and I saw that it really was a child. A boy of no more than ten. So, there *were* kids here. He looked around the area appearing lost. Did he need help finding his parents?

The child finally rested his eyes on me. He let out a sob I could not hear and wiped at his face with his sleeve. Could no one hear him? The steps were right near the outdoor bar and there were tons of people just a few feet away, much closer than me. Yet, no one even moved to turn toward him.

"I think there's a lost kid there," I said, cutting into the conversation.

Yasmine frowned and looked around. "A child? Where? We don't have children here."

I started to point to the dark parking lot behind her, but the child was now gone.

Faith leaned in. "Could it have been just a little person?"

I rolled my eyes. "I know the difference between a child and a short person."

Yasmine relaxed her face and gave me a gentle smile. "Sometimes drinking can dull our senses."

Oh wow, they thought I was an idiot. "And if I were drunk, I'd agree." I stood up. I was going to find this kid and prove them wrong. "Excuse me. I'll be back."

I expected Felix to get up and follow me, but he was already back to talking to Yasmine, not even noticing me. Men were so fickle.

Instead, Azrael rose and walked after me. "Disappointed it's me instead of him?"

I huffed and rolled my eyes. "No. He can talk to whatever

84

woman he wants to talk to. I have no claim on him. We're just friends."

They stuffed their hands in their pocket, looking as nonchalant as ever. "Riiight."

Azrael didn't have to believe me. I wasn't sure I fully did either but it didn't matter. Felix and I weren't a thing. I decided to change the subject before my mind went too deep into that statement. "So, why are you following me? Keeping an eye on me?" I questioned as we walked.

"Yes, and I didn't need to hear any more of that founder's tale the mayor was spinning."

I looked at them from the corner of my eye. "You don't believe her?"

"I just wonder about some things. I think whatever we're going to learn about this place, she isn't going to say. So, if we see some odd things, we have to find the answers on our own."

I looked at the small, darkened parking lot. "I couldn't agree more."

"Help!" screamed a child's voice deeper in the lot.

"You heard that, right?"

"Child's voice? Yep."

Azrael and I both took off in the maze of cars. We split up and searched the area, but there was no child.

Azrael jogged over to me. "I would fly, but I'm afraid someone might see me."

I leaped up to the hood of a car and scanned the area from that height. Movement on the ground near the edge of the parking lot, peeking out from behind a pickup truck caught my eye. It looked almost human in shape, but it was lying in a heap. Not good.

I jumped down and took off in the direction of what I hoped was not a body with Azrael on my heels.

We arrived at the area, but it was dark. I snapped my fingers, and floating pinpoints of light hovered above my fingertips. I pointed my hand in the direction of the heap, and my mouth fell open, unprepared for what I was seeing.

It was human alight. Except it wasn't a body. It was what I could only describe as a skin suit and a pool of bloody gore underneath it.

Shit. Looks like we were going to be here a little longer than I thought.

CHAPTER 8

$\mathcal{T}$he only small conciliation of our gruesome discovery was that the skin suit did not belong to a child. It was far too big for that.

A white man with brown hair and eyes walked over to me. He appeared to be in his early thirties, and he was dressed in jeans and a plaid shirt. He looked fit but not overly so. He had "off duty" cop written all over him, and when he flashed what looked like a badge, I mentally chuckled at my right guess.

He gave me his best stern eyes. "I'm Sheriff Milton Dante. People here just call me Dante. I need to ask you both a few questions." He looked between Azrael and I, taking his phone out of his pocket and pushing the record button. "State your names."

We introduced ourselves and recapped what we saw.

"What were you doing out here?"

I hadn't forgotten about the kid who'd drawn me out there in the first place, so I kept my eyes open for him, hoping he'd show himself. "Like I said, I saw a kid from the deck and went to check things out since he was young and all alone."

"And you say you never found the kid." He stated it like he didn't believe me. Like he thought we were making up the child's existence.

I held in my annoyance and tried to remain as cooperative as I could. "No."

He worked his jaw, assessing the both of us. His eyes rested on Azrael a little too long. "Where y'all from?"

Really, what did his questions have to do with anything? "We're from Silver Spring. The town that saved the world," I replied in a tight voice.

He gave a sour expression, mouth pinched. "Yeah, I heard about that. You two part of the Six?"

"No, but we are with two members. Before you ask, we're here on vacation, but can we get back to the dead body or skin?"

Dante lifted his upper lip at me in a slight scowl.

Clearly, I knew just how to make friends.

"Did you know the deceased?"

There we go. Back to the relevant questions. "No. Do we even know who he was?" I looked over to the body not too far from us as a team of paramedics put the remains in a body bag. The skin really was in perfect condition. It was as if someone had simply unzipped themselves out of a costume. Except I couldn't see a zipper or seam. Not so much as a cut. How the person could be removed from their skin without cutting it was a mystery.

I'd had the unlucky fortune to see Alister flay his tortured souls. It was not a quick process. Skin—well human skin— was not super tough. If pulled on, it would eventually rip. One would have to pull skin away from the muscle to get it off. It would be sort of like trying to open a letter without tearing the envelope seal. Harder actually.

Of course, magic was the answer for almost everything nowadays. I supposed there could be a magic that teleported a person out of their body but why go that route? And where was the body? And if someone was going to delicately remove someone from their skin to keep it in tact, then wouldn't they want that skin? Why dump it halfway under a truck in a parking lot? And if the body was more important, then why bother removing the skin so carefully?

My mind rang with questions I just didn't know the answers to. I wasn't a detective. That wasn't my specialty. Outside of fighting I wasn't sure what was, but I didn't think my journey would lead me to being a mystery solver.

"Did you know his identity?" Azrael asked, interrupting my wondering thoughts.

Dante looked over to Azrael again with those curious eyes. "Not yet. Why do you want to know?"

Azrael remained unaffected by Dante's response. "I find a dead body, and I kind of want to know who it is. If nothing else than to say a little prayer."

That could have been the truth.

Dante seemed satisfied with that response. "Yeah, both of you, don't leave town just yet."

Hold up, that was not part of the deal. "Well, we're only here on vacation, so if we have to stay past our reservations, I guess you'll be paying?"

Dante snorted before turning away from us.

I leaned towards Azrael. "I don't think I like him."

They gently patted my back in a shocking show of affection. "Me either. Let's keep an eye on him, shall we?"

I nodded in agreement as we turned and headed to a very horrified looking Yasmine, who was currently leaning into Felix's chest, with a hand to her mouth. I fought hard not to roll my eyes. This woman was the leader of the town. She needed to show strength.

I cleared my throat. "Excuse me, Mayor Covington," I started, trying to pull her back to business. "Do you have any idea who that could be?"

She looked over to me with sad eyes, slightly pulling from

Felix for the moment. "No. But I have my people looking into his identity. It shouldn't take long with our magic. That poor man. How horrific."

Felix rubbed her back. "Has anything like this ever happened before?"

Yasmine shook her head quickly. "Of course not. This is a peaceful sanctuary. We don't have crime of any sort."

I cocked a disbelieving brow. "Then why do you have all the men and women in black here?"

"Better to be safe than sorry. I'm no fool." She pulled away from Felix and smoothed down her dress, standing straighter. I guess my questioning had gotten her mind back to mayor mode. "Did you find the child you were looking for?"

What if whoever had skinned that guy had grabbed the little boy and planned to do the same? I didn't consider myself a softie but the thought of a kid getting harmed bothered me. I had a conscience even if I was half-demon.

I looked around the area as if the kid would just show up. Of course, he didn't. "We lost him."

Yasmine tapped her chin in thought. "I thought it was odd that you saw a child."

I needed to know why. "Why are there no children here?"

Yasmine's lips tightened, her eyes seemingly going dark. "Children bring pain. They are a distraction from allowing us to be our truest selves. Once you become a parent, it becomes your identity."

"You don't like kids?" I wasn't judging. I was on the fence about wanting them myself.

"I don't have a problem if one chooses to have kids. They just can't live here with them. So, you see, if there is a child here, someone must have snuck them in. That would be against our rules. However, I have more pressing matters at the moment." She looked past me. "Excuse me, I have to go." She began to walk away, her security detail shadowing her.

She suddenly paused and looked back at us. "You will tell me if you find this child." She said it more as a directive and less as a question.

I wasn't making her that promise.

However, Boy Scout Felix said that we would, and Yasmine flashed him a grin before turning away again.

"I don't believe that they don't have any crime here. It can't be a coincidence that the day we show up, they have the one crime that happens to be a gruesome one."

Felix shrugged. "It can happen. I listen to this true-crime podcast. It's got supernatural and regular crimes. The most interesting ones are in unassuming places. Actually, when you think about it, nowadays every place is dangerous."

Faith walked up to us with wide eyes as if she had something huge to tell us.

Azrael, by her side, looked less excited.

"Where were y'all?" I asked.

"Eavesdropping on the police," she replied. "And we found out some things."

I waved my hand to encourage her to speak. "Like?"

"Dead suit was apparently a local grocer. The witches tried to do a locating spell to find where his actual body is, and it pointed them to the mess on the street back there."

I tilted my head. I felt like her calling the poor soul a dead suit was really disrespectful, but I would let that slide for now. "You said what, now?" What she said did make sense. Sort of.

She put her hands to the side of her head, still looking too excited for this macabre news. "I'm saying, dude didn't get flayed. He liquified. Except for the skin, of course."

I rubbed between my eyes with my index finger. "So, everything melted. Muscle and bone?"

Felix made a grumbling noise of disgust. "Kind of like deflated."

Azrael squinted their eyes at me. "Ever seen anything like that?"

I leaned back. "Why are you asking *me*?"

"Because you lived in the underworld with a demon King. It's not that hard a leap."

Fair point. "No. I've seen people liquify, but everything goes with it, skin and all. And I have seen someone wear their victim's face like a mask but not the whole body. At least not without there being tears and stitches like some kind of Frankenstein."

Faith gagged. "Damn, your life sucked."

I shrugged. I hadn't known any better at the time. "Anyway, I think it might be safe to say that a demon is here. I can't think of any other being doing that. Not vampire, were, fae, ghoul…" I clapped my hands. "And it's not our problem. We can let Monica know what's going on and go back to our lives."

Azrael crossed their arms over their chest with a shake of the head. "Not so fast. We have to confirm that it's a demon. We want to make sure whatever we tell Monica is accurate so she can plan her next moves accordingly. We need to give her good intel."

I let out a tired breath and looked around at the parking lot. The town was capable of solving their own issues. Why did the angels feel the need to get involved in every—

My breath paused as I saw a dark shadow on the outskirts of the parking lot, away from other people. It was tall and had the same red eyes and sharp white teeth I'd seen from earlier. And it was still waving. At me.

"Shit!"

"What is it?" Felix asked before following my gaze.

But he was too late, the demon waver dispersed into the darkness.

"I think I found our demon. And it looks like he wants to be my friend."

$\mathcal{T}$he rest of the night was pretty uneventful. There were no more visits from the demon, but I had a worthless sleep. I got up early the next morning and went out for a coffee. Finding a bench near the water, I sat down to think about my next move.

I didn't need any more demons close to me outside of the ones I already knew. And this one was teasing me. But why? Was he the same demon who had melted the grocer?

What was I even doing here? This was such a distraction. Every day not focused on getting votes for the throne was a day wasted. Did I care that much if Monica helped me find out who I was? She probably wasn't going to really help, and I had just attracted another demon for nothing.

Why hadn't I followed up more closely with Marcus? He could help me regain some of my memories. But I didn't trust him enough to let him know I was memory deficient.

How badly did I really want the throne anyway? Was I just going after it because I "felt" I needed to? Or because I was trying to find my place in the world?

Footsteps neared me, and I looked up to see Felix staring down at me, eating a donut.

How this grown man looked both intimidating and child-like at times was beyond me.

"Been looking for you. I thought you'd be near the water. Felt like that was your thing." He passed a flat white box over to me. "Donuts. They're pretty damn good."

"Thanks," I replied before opening the box and taking out what looked like a devil's food cake donut.

Felix tapped the uneaten side of his donut with mine and said, cheers.

I chuckled. "You are a silly man."

He leaned back on the bench. "I know." He looked over

the water. There were already a few people out canoeing and paddle boating. "Did you see the demon again?"

"Nope." I took a bite. He wasn't lying. It was good.

"Maybe it's better I stay with you tonight. If this thing knows you're taken, maybe he won't bother you."

I had to admit to myself I was a little happy he hadn't forgotten about me while cozying up to Yasmine. Maybe I was just misinterpreting his friendliness with her. *Maybe, Fran, you shouldn't care because you aren't in a relationship with him.* I nudged him with my elbow. "Nice try. You know, maybe I attract demons because I'm part demon?"

"But I don't."

"Maybe you do, but you're surrounded by your friends. Or maybe your angel father made sure you were protected growing up."

Felix smiled and nodded. "I wouldn't be surprised. My dad was a good man. But if he's really gone, he's not able to look out for me now." His smile fell, and a pained looked overtook his face. I could only imagine what he must be feeling.

It's one thing to lose a parent. It's another thing to know they are gone into nothingness. Not the spirit world or heaven. Just gone. When angels died, they became nothing. I never considered myself religious, but the thought was still unsettling. When the world changed, I'd always taken some comfort in the fact that there were different realms, that people could live on. I felt true comfort when I learned that paranormals could live extraordinarily long lives. However, to learn an angel could still be killed and be gone from any plane of existence was sobering.

I grabbed Felix's hand because I didn't know what else to do. I was the farthest thing from comforting. However, Felix was my friend, and I couldn't just ignore his sadness. I wasn't that heartless...most of the time. "I'm sorry about your dad.

And we're going to find your mother. And you'll find out all about who he really was and who she really is. But I do know one thing about them both."

He gave me a slight smile.

"They must have been good people because they raised a good man." I gave a quick shake of my head. "That felt corny coming out. Was it corny?"

He lifted my hand to his lips. "You can be sweet when you want to be."

I slipped my hand away from his. "Well, don't get used to it. Anyway, back to the demons. Maybe if I knew what this thing was, I'd be able to handle it."

"You've never seen that kind before?"

I shook my head. That had plagued me most of the night as well. "I called Nadia and described it. She hadn't heard of a demon that looked like that before, either. I've seen a ton of demons. I did some research, and I'm wondering if it was a shadow demon."

Felix finished his donut and brushed his hands clean. "I've seen one. Back when we were working for Alister as his enforcers."

"Was I there?"

"No. But what you describe doesn't sound like a shadow demon. What I saw was super tall and skinny with very long, bony limps. And it was faceless."

I nodded slowly, feeling more confused. "Fuck. So I'm being tailed by an unknown demon. Sweet."

He scooted closer to me. "But you have an angel and a Nephilim by your side. We'll protect you."

"I don't need protection." I finished my donut and jumped up. If I stayed seated beside Felix too long, I'd get comfortable. He was like a security blanket, all comfort and warmth. I almost felt like he would protect me. The problem was, I couldn't depend on him if I was to be a leader.

"If we're going to confirm there are demons here, we have to make sure Azrael sees it so he can report back."

"How do you lure out a demon?"

"Let's start with my new demon friend tonight. If it wants to say hi, I'm going to let it."

# CHAPTER 9

*I*n my mind, the demon might go from waving to visiting if I looked more approachable. It also seemed to disappear when others showed up, so Faith begrudgingly agreed to sleep on the sofa bed in the living room. I stayed in the bedroom with the doors closed and blinds open in case whatever was trailing me wanted to look in to ensure I was asleep. I wasn't sure this demon was related to whatever had skinned a person, but I wasn't going to ignore the coincidence either. I needed to speak to it or kick its ass. Whatever the case, I wasn't going to ignore it.

While waiting up for the demon, I closed my eyes, otherwise known as falling asleep. I'm not sure how long my eyes were closed, but something woke me up. I wasn't sure how late it was after I drifted off. There was no clock in the room.

What had woken me up?

A noise. Like a scratching of wood. It was coming from the foot of my bed. I slowly turned my head in that direction.

A blur of darkness moved off the bed to the floor.

I shot up and quickly crawled to the end of my bed.

Nothing.

Damn, it was fast. Something had been sitting on the bed

with me while I was asleep for who knows how long. That was scary.

Child-like snickering broke the silence of the night, and I looked around the room. Squinting my eyes into the darkness, I didn't see anything out of the ordinary.

Something was definitely in here with me, though.

"Okay, I don't know what you're laughing at, but if you're trying to scare me, it's not working. So, come out." I sat up on my bed, my legs folded beneath me with crossed arms.

More laughter.

It sounded like it was coming from under the bed. Oh, this thing really wanted to go for gold in scaring me. Didn't it know I didn't frighten easy? I mean, it was still some nerve-wracking shit though.

I bent over the side of the bed slowly and then quickly lifted the comforter, looking under the bed. No red eyes. No sharp white teeth.

I moved back up and let out a yelp as the waving demon crouched on the end of my bed. It snickered, its glowing razor teeth parted as the laugh emanated from it. I had to admit, it did make for an eerie sight.

I raised my hands in mock surrender. "Okay, you got me. Haha. Now, what do you want?"

It jumped off the bed and stood up. It was tall, his head almost grazed the ceiling.

So, maybe it was a shadow demon.

I slid off the bed, readying myself for a battle. However, the demon just turned and walked to the door, disappearing through the wall. I grabbed my sneakers beside the bed and opened the door to follow it.

The demon stood near the front door as if to wait for me. I looked over to Faith who was sleeping on the couch, her face in a frown and one leg hanging over the edge.

"Wake up Faith, we have to roll," I shouted, stuffing my feet in my shoes.

Faith shot up, but her eyes were still closed. "Show time?" she mumbled.

"Yep, demon is taking us to our supposed doom."

She opened her eyes and slipped on her shoes. "That doesn't sound right. We sure we want to go?"

I turned back to the demon, but he was now gone. I swung open the door and looked down the hall. The demon stood, waiting in the center of the hallway. I walked towards it, keeping my eyes focused on it in case it tried to disappear again.

Faith came up behind me. "I called Felix and told them we're en route. This feels crazy unsafe."

So, far as creepy as this thing was, why wasn't I more scared? Oh, right, because I dated a demon King and was surrounded by far scarier things all the time with him. "Who you telling?" But we were here to investigate, and so we would.

The demon went through a door with a glowing exit sign above it, and we opened the door after it, moving in a jog.

No demon in the stairwell. We went down the steps and exited to the outside of the inn. I looked around and found the demon crouching on a car.

"Would you wait up? We can't walk through walls like you can," I shouted.

It laughed again. The sound pricked my spine. Even though it was child-like, it was far from cute.

Faith leaned toward me. "Like, I'm pretty sure you aren't crazy, but who are you talking to?"

I kept my eyes on the creature who now jumped off the car and began to walk down the street. "You don't see a giant-ass black shadow man right in front of us?" I asked, pointing in the demon's direction.

Faith squinted her eyes, trying to see ahead. "No."

Maybe she didn't have as good of night vision as I did.

However, no one could miss those glowing teeth and eyes or that laugh.

"You didn't hear it either?"

Faith gave me a wide-eyed shake of her head. I looked back in the direction of the demon and cursed myself for taking my eyes off of it. The creature was gone. I ran forward to where it had been standing only a second ago. Then spun around, searching for it.

"Come on, man! Didn't you want me to follow you? Where are you?"

Faith made a noise, her face a mix of confusion and sleepiness as she pointed to her left. "Where did he come from?"

I looked in the direction of her hand and found a little boy standing under a street lamp. He was the same one from the other night.

Okay. This was beyond weird. So the shadow demon and the kid were connected. "Hey, kid. What are you doing out here alone?" I walked forward and then paused.

The child smiled, and I saw the familiar glowing razor teeth in his mouth. His dark eyes suddenly shown a ruby red. Crap, this kid *was* the waving demon. What kind of game was being played here?

"Can you see the kid?" I asked, my eyes remaining on the now little human-like demon.

"Yes. What do we do?"

"Do you want us to still follow you?" I called to the demon.

He nodded and then turned to walk again in the same direction as before.

I shrugged. "Guess we keep following."

We continued to walk in silence for several blocks.

After a while, Faith let out an impatient sigh. "This feels like a set-up."

"That's because it probably is."

The demon stopped in front of a two-story house with a well-manicured front lawn and then began to walk onto the property. It headed to the back of the house and then paused in front of steps that appeared to lead to a basement. It turned to us and pointed to the steps before backing away into the nothingness of nightfall.

I looked at the steps leading down to the darkness of the basement. The entire house was unlit. If this was a movie, I'd be yelling at the screen to go back home. "Yeah, I'm not going down there."

Faith looked around the lawn behind us. "I'm going to have to agree with you on that one."

I stepped back. "Glad we could agree on something."

"Except…"

I sighed. I already knew what she was going to say. "We came here to find out what was going on and bring some sort of proof of it back to Monica. Let's go in.

Faith nodded. "I let Felix know where we are. They can go in if we aren't out in five minutes."

I had almost forgotten she was part of the goody-two-shoed Six and had a telepathic connection to Felix. I scrunched my face in concern, still looking at the steps. I so did not want to go into a fight if I didn't have to. And believe me, if anything attacked, we would be fighting.

"Don't tell me you're scared?" Faith leaned in wiggling her fingers at me.

I scoffed. "Look, you aren't going to peer pressure me like some teen from an old slasher flick. I'm just being justifiably cautious."

Faith gave me a very doubtful look. "Uh-huh. I thought dark fae weren't afraid of anything."

"Not sure who told you that lie. However, I am not scared. That thing could be leading us to our deaths. Just because it was shaped like a child doesn't mean it was good. You didn't see its earlier shape." However, she had a point about us getting to the bottom of this. I needed the information Monica had on my family. I was getting my answers and gaining my throne.

I opened my hand, and my sword appeared. Up until now, I'd had it cloaked in invisibility magic. Most warrior fae kept their swords near them or in a location they could easily conjure them. There was no way I was coming here without my girl with me. I wasn't sure we were going to need to get down and dirty tonight but I sure as hell wasn't walking into that basement with my hands in my pocket looking like a Final Girl in a horror film.

Faith tapped her fists together, and her tattoos became etched in a golden glow. She could do more than just kiss or sex people out of their energy. Succubi had strength, and Faith's tattoos somehow gave her even more.

We descended the steps on tip toes, crouching at the door at the bottom, which had a window above the doorknob. I slowly moved up and peeked inside.

It was dark, but there was definitely something going on. This part of the basement was cluttered and unfinished and I could see a wall on the opposite end with another open door leading to what I assumed was a finished part of the bottom level.

However, the décor wasn't my focus. In the middle of the concrete floor was a man hunched over on the ground digging into a smaller body and...eating. My stomach churned as I watched the man greedily gobble down the insides of a person's torn up stomach. I looked at the victim on the floor and fought a building rage. The victim, a female, couldn't have been more than thirteen years old. She looked up at the ceiling with vacant eyes and an open mouth with a slack jaw. She was surely dead.

I pulled out my phone and briefly filmed the gruesome scene as my proof for Monica.

Faith yanked on my shirt and I ducked down to her crouching level. "A man is eating a child," I whispered.

Her eyes blazed with anger, swirling with orange, red, and yellow. She shot up and before I could stop her, she kicked the door open, breaking the lock.

Faith charged in like a raging bull, me on her tail, cursing. We didn't even get to fully assess the situation. There could have been others in the house and we'd be outnumbered and eaten.

She raced at lightning speed and grabbed the man by the back of the neck, raising him in the air. I flipped a switch near the door, dimly lighting the room. There didn't seem to be anybody else there, just boxes, old furniture and other knick-knacks.

The man, who Faith now had by the throat, looked human except for the bloody mouth and clothes. He was of average height and build, no more than forty years old, a full head of blond hair and angry blue eyes.

He drew his legs up and kicked Faith in the chest, releasing himself from her grip and knocking her to the ground. He by-passed Faith and sped towards me at an inhuman speed. Guess he thought I was the weaker of us two. He would soon find out otherwise.

He whipped around me, and I spun, already prepared for his trickery. My sword swiped out, and I sliced him in the arm hitting bone. He zoomed backwards to avoid another hit, yelling out in pain as he grabbed his arm. When he opened his mouth to scream, I could see that his mouth was full of pointed, bloodied teeth that practically split his face open.

He pressed his back against the concrete wall, looked from Faith, who was now standing by my side, then to me, as if to decide which one of us was the lesser of two evils. His eyes moved behind us, and I glanced over my shoulder seeing a darkened staircase that probably led to the higher floors.

"You aren't getting out of here in one piece," I said before running towards him, sword pointed outward with both my hands gripping the hilt.

He zoomed to the side and then past me, a blur of movement that I wasn't fast enough to catch. Damn, this guy was quick. Seriously, what the hell was he?

Fortunately, he didn't get to the stairs because Faith was able to punch him in the throat, sending him sliding back on the floor. I had to admit, I was pretty impressed with her succubus strength and movement. At least she could match his speed, which was very much not my thing.

Faith wasted no time and grabbed the man by the throat again before slamming his head against the hard floor.

I moved forward, glancing over at the dead teenager. Renewed rage built in me as I returned my attention to the man. I pointed my sword at his head as he squirmed to get out of Faith's release, gurgling for breath. If he broke free, he'd be met with a nice stabby-stab to the forehead. But first, I needed to at least ask him some questions before we sent him to the worms.

"How could you?" Faith shouted, squeezing his neck.

If she squeezed any harder, she'd decapitate him with her hands. That wouldn't get me my answers or my missing memories. "What are you?" I asked through gritted teeth.

He glared at me with hate-filled eyes like I was the one who was crushing his windpipe.

Faith dug her knee into his stomach forcing him to cry out. "Answer her!"

He didn't, just continued to glare.

I kicked him in his injured arm, and he winced. "Talk."

He was still playing it quiet, guess I would have to apply some mild torture. I stuck him in the thigh with my sword and he let out a guttural noise that was cut off by Faith's grip.

"There's no good cop, bad cop here," Faith growled. "We're both assholes, so it's in your best interest to talk."

His cry sounded very human, and his blood came out red. Faith had to use her muscle to keep him down, so it was possible he was supernaturally strong along with being incredibly fast. However, he didn't use any magic against us so he wasn't a witch. Could he have been a were? His eyes still looked very human, and the eyes were the first giveaway of a were. He could have been a ghoul. They did eat human flesh, and he also had sharp teeth, although his mouth was wider than most ghouls. Plus, he didn't have fully black eyes. Also, he was eating more than flesh. In fact, he was eating everything. Organs, skin, muscle. Trolls and gremlins did that along with some demons and some really nasty fae.

Hell, he really could be anything. We were still learning about all the types of supernatural creatures in the world. Ten years in, and there were some paranormals things that were still coming out of the proverbial woodwork. Honestly, it didn't matter to me. That would be Monica's problem overall. Right now, we just needed to document what was going on in this town because her angels were too busy having so much fun to do that themselves.

I took out my phone with my free hand. "Say cheese," I said before taking his picture. I glanced over to Faith. "I'll show his picture to someone who might know what his kind is. You can kill him now."

Faith didn't even hesitate. She squeezed his neck until it caved in. She then ripped his head off and tossed it across the room, where it bounced before coming to a stop next to a few old paint cans. "We should burn this whole place to the ground."

I nodded, feeling a similar anger but trying not to let it get the best of me. Hmm, I was growing up. "Normally I'd agree with you but we need to let this town's leadership know this is going on. They are no longer a crime free town."

I looked back down at the body. The demon's headless body began to quickly deflate before our eyes like a balloon.

The insides of his body seemed to have liquified and were now leaking, along with his blood, out of every orifice of his body including the open wound in his neck. I jumped back in disgust and surprise, quickly taking a picture before it all went away.

Faith jumped up and jogged back as well, avoiding the growing bloody puddle. "The fuck?"

We looked in silence as the body continued to deflate until it was as flat as, well, a pancake, leaving only empty skin behind.

Faith looked up at me with raised brows. "What just happened?"

I put my sword back in the sheath on my back, and it went invisible again. "He melted like the Wicked Witch of the West."

"Is this what happened to the skin suit we saw yesterday?"

I honestly wasn't sure. "It seems like whatever these creatures are, when they die this is what happens. Seems so unnecessary. They could turn to dust like vampires. Who wants the leftover skin?"

Faith brought her hand to her face, presumably to rub her eyes because she looked exhausted, but she quickly caught sight of her bloody hand used to kill the guy and dropped it. No need to give herself a monster blood facial. "I need to get the hell out of here. This fuckin world, man."

I rolled my shoulders back. She took the words right out of my mouth.

Faith looked over my shoulder at the dead teenager. "I thought there were no kids in this town."

I refused to look behind me. I'd seen enough. "He could have kidnapped her. Let's call the authorities and get out of here."

Faith headed to the door and I followed. "What are we going to tell them? That we followed a demon child here?"

"Yep. I don't have the creativity to come up with a lie.

They need to know they have a kid killer here and demon spirit things are haunting the town. Or maybe it's just me?"

"So, if it led you to a body yesterday and to a crime today, is it really a demon? That would seem to be the opposite of what something evil would do."

We walked outside back to the backyard, and I bit back my reminder that not all demons were bad. "Why it came to me, I don't know. Why you can't see it, I don't know."

"Seems we have more questions than answers now. We need to find out where that kid comes from. They probably have a family that needs to know."

I didn't say the other alternative. That this kid had no family. There were a lot of orphans. "I'm sure the police will work on that. The biggest thing is to figure out what the hell he was and make sure there aren't anymore."

I wanted the hell out of this town and back to my life. I had information now. It was time to get out.

# CHAPTER 10

When the police arrived, Sheriff Dante was front and center. He looked at the crime scene then walked over to us with a look of full-on suspicion. He made a show of giving a big sigh and adjusted his belt before finally speaking. "Glad I told you not to leave. Seems you might be set on making trouble after all."

I narrowed my eyes at him, wondering if he was really serious. "Making trouble? Seems we are highlighting an issue —a pretty big issue—that you need to investigate. You should be thanking us."

He chuckled.

I didn't see what was so funny. A kid was dead.

"Everything was fine here until you came. You've been here two nights, and already we have two crimes. I don't believe in coincidences." He gave me a long stare down that I guess was supposed to intimidate me, but I'd been glared at by much worse, so I wasn't afraid.

"Are you accusing us of something? Because if you are, then arrest us. Although, I'm trying to figure out what kind of evidence you have. In both situations, we brought something to your attention. If we were the perpetrators then we could have easily kept quiet."

Dante looked back at the body bags being carried out of the basement as he scratched his patchy beard. "I don't know. Maybe you lost all that attention after winning that big fight we've all heard about and wanted to find something new to get into to get back in the lime light. You come here and make up some trouble, then act like you can fight it off and become stars again."

I really wanted to pimp slap the dumb off of him because that was truly the stupidest thing I'd ever heard. Before I could say anything, Azrael spoke up as they joined us. "Do you feel good about that particular theory? Is that the path you want to go down? If so, I'd really question your effectiveness as any type of leader." The angel crossed their arms and gazed down at Dante like he was a mere peon. For all Azrael's laid back nature, they could also be extremely pompous and they were going hard now. For once, I didn't mind it.

Well, that seemed to rile Dante right up. "You—you don't tell me how to do my job. I have to explore all theories."

"Yes, I see. Well, by all means, keep pursuing that theory that makes the least sense instead of the obvious one that points to a possible demon problem."

Dante looked Azrael up and down with a face of disdain. "You all think you're such hot shit just because you got in a little fight and won. A lot of us have been fighting for the past several years, and before that we fought in other ways. I'm a former marine and been in two wars back in the Pre-World. Y'all ain't better than anyone here."

Sounds like someone had a chip on their shoulder that really had nothing to do with us. He was probably jealous of the six's fame long before Faith and Felix showed up here. We were dead in the water from the start with this guy.

Felix raised his brows and threw out his hands in surrender. "Whoa, whoa, whoa. Look, man, we aren't here to cause trouble or argue. We don't think we're better than anyone. We just want to help with any problems this town has going on. We're on the same side here."

He was such a damn peacemaker. I noticed a colorful bit of movement approaching us and turned to see Yasmine dressed impeccably in a brightly colored shift dress. Most people threw on jeans and a T-shirt when called in the middle of the night, not dresses and heels.

"I'm so very sorry you had to experience this. Like I told you before, this kind of thing never happens, and now it's occurred twice since you've been here."

Felix shifted uncomfortably in his stance and leaned forward. "In case you're thinking it, it wasn't us. We're good people."

Dante muttered something unintelligible, but we ignored him.

Yasmine patted Felix on the arm and gave a slight smile. "I know you're good. And it seems you helped us fix a problem we didn't know we had. I'd hate for you to leave because of all this. We typically don't have such horrible events like this. For all your troubles, allow us to extend your stay a few days. No charge."

There was no way I was staying in this weird town another day. I had to get on the campaign trail. Azrael could stay, and Felix was off for the summer, so he could too.

"We'd love to stay," Azrael spoke up with a wide grin.

I wanted to punch them in their perfect teeth.

I lifted a hand. "Actually, I–"

Faith grabbed my hand and yanked it down. "We are going to have to make some arrangements at work, but we would love that."

Someone called for the mayor, and Yasmine pointed to one of her people and told him to call the inn and extend our stay.

"Are we done here, Sheriff?" Faith asked with a toothy smile.

He looked over to Yasmine who was already on her way to address an issue then looked back to us with irritated eyes. "For now."

I looked at the others, my lips tight with anger, then turned around and walked away. Those fools could stay, but I was getting the hell out of this creepy place. I felt them coming up close behind me and I teleported away to my room to get some distance.

I grabbed my suitcase and began to pack what few belongings I had brought with me. A minute later, I heard the crew in the living area but ignored them.

"Can we at least talk about it?" Felix asked, taking up the doorway to the bedroom. I could see bits of Faith and Azrael behind him.

I paused, putting my hands on my hips. "Why are we staying?"

Azrael hunched forward and wiggled past the bit of space between Felix and the doorway. "There's a mystery to solve here."

"We killed the bad guy. We're done."

Azrael looked up at the ceiling and shook their head as if I said something totally ridiculous. "You're here to get information for Monica."

"And I've done that.

They shook their head. "We do not yet know the full extent of this situation. The skins belong to the bad guys. We found two. Might it be possible then that there are more? And who killed the first one? And why do you have a demon that seems to want to help take down these creatures? One that can only be seen by others when it's in human form. Let us not forget, no one saw him at the restaurant."

I shrugged and flopped down on my bed. I'd forgotten that the demon was more than likely the crying child I'd seen the other night. It would make sense since we were led to the first crime that way. "Maybe he's someone who knew me from the underworld? I was quite popular."

Azrael sat down on Faith's bed and leaned back on their hands. "That's fine. Call it back then."

"Uh, I don't control it."

The angel gave me a condescending smile. "Try."

I glared at Azrael for a beat. I had no idea how to summon a demon, believe it or not. That typically involved spell magic unless you were a demon lord. I had no experience in spells, at least not ones powerful enough to raise a demon. I was a warrior faerie. My powers were all about fighting and inflicting damage and death. However, I would humor the angel because I often liked to make them look stupid.

"Hey, demon boy. Come out and show yourself," I called to the air.

As expected, nothing happened.

Suddenly Azrael's eyes opened wide, and they sat up straight.

Felix took a step forward. "It's behind you."

I frowned. "What?" And suddenly I felt it. Goosebumps pricked the back of my neck. I'd thought it was simply the air conditioning. I jumped up and spun around.

There the demon sat on my bed in its familiar crouch, looking smaller than before. It was still a human-shaped shadow even though the lights were on. It grinned up at me, silent. I was beginning to wonder if it could do anything other than grin.

"Okay, you're here." Was all I could say. How had I summoned a demon without even trying? Maybe I hadn't. Maybe, it'd just been in the shadows, waiting.

Faith entered the room now that Felix had moved. "What are you all looking at?"

Felix pointed at the demon with wide eyes. "You can't see that thing on the bed?"

Faith frowned and shook her head. "What's going on? Why am I left out?"

Azrael sighed and leaned forward, resting their forearms on their thighs. "It's because you aren't angel or demon. In addition to humans, very few paranormals can see spirits not in any earthly form. That would explain why you can only see it when it's in the child form."

Faith leaned forward and narrowed her eyes looking at the bed but not at the exact spot where the demon perched. "Why did it take on the appearance of a child?"

"To be deceptive. Make you believe it's good."

I tilted my head from side to side. Angels could be so singled-minded. "Or it's taking the form of the victims. That would explain why no one knew about the murders. The victims are kids, and kids aren't supposed to be here."

Azrael raised their upper lip with a look of disbelief. That was one demon-hating angel. "Speak, demon. Why are you here?"

It just kept scary smiling at me.

"Speak!" Azrael shouted.

The demon looked at the angel and then crabbed walk to the edge of the bed before dropping to the floor, and lowering down until all we could see were its glowing red eyes.

"I think you scared it," Felix said in a low voice.

I agreed. I bent forward across the bed.

The demon looked up at me. Its smile was now turned down in a frown, teeth still bared. Even with limited features, it really did look scared. "It's not going to speak to you." I wasn't even sure it could even talk. I walked around the bed, towards the creature, and crouched at its level. "Can you speak?"

It nodded.

"What are you?"

"The loooossst." It said in a creaking whisper.

I'd heard of the lost before. I got on my knees, feeling slightly more at ease. This creature was not really a demon. They were a lost soul trapped in darkness. There were all types of spirits. And spirits took all forms. This one also fell into the category of ghost, and it had been taken from this world in a very horrific way.

"Were you murdered by the creatures you led me to?"

It shook its head.

"How old are you?"

It put up both hands. I could tell although this demon could speak, it would be limited speech at least for now. This was not uncommon for *spirits*. There were many who couldn't speak at all. Usually this was because no one could hear them, so they stopped trying to speak and just lost the ability for a while.

"Ten?"

It nodded again.

"Are there more of those killers here?" Azrael asked in an agitated tone.

The demon child flinched.

I glared back at the angel. "Shut up."

The angel opened their mouth, their eyebrows furrowed together in anger.

I looked back at the demon spirit. "Are there more of those killers here?"

It nodded.

Felix made a noise. "See, this is why we need to stay here. To help them!"

I put a finger up to stop him from saying more. "I'll get to that next." I turned back to the spirit. "Why did you come to me and not anyone else?"

The demon reached out for me and touched my arm with both of its hands. "Speeeeciiiall."

The feel of its skin, if you could call it that, felt like icicles. I fought the urge to recoil. Sometimes I cared about not being a jerk. "Why do you think I'm special?"

It lowered its head to my hand, scooting closer.

It was easy to forget that this creature was actually a trapped child.

"Just aaarree."

It thought I was special but didn't know why. What did it see in me then that it trusted? I lifted a hesitant hand and patted it on its icy head. This gesture seemed to make it happy as it moved its head like a dog wanting to be petted more.

"Azrael, can we do something to set his spirit free?"

Azrael humphed. "Oh, now you want me to speak? Well, I can't help you."

I rolled my eyes. "Don't be petty."

"I actually don't have the ability to make a demon not a demon. Once it's in that form, it's out of my jurisdiction."

"It's more like a ghost."

"Not the way we categorize it."

Of course not. Why not just say their powers are limited?

Faith threw her hands out to the side, her face a mask of fury. "I'm seeing and hearing nothing and it's fucking pissing me off." She then took a deep breath as if to calm herself. "But from what you all are saying it sounds like a bad situation. We can't leave a ten-year-old kid trapped in a demon form. We have to do something."

Azrael sighed. "I wish I knew what to do. We can ask Monica. Who we're going to see tomorrow morning. As you know, she won't step foot in here even though I told her there isn't a ward up preventing us from getting out."

"Fine. So, what do we do about the demon-ghost?"

I looked down at the creature. I had no idea but it couldn't stay by my side. It tightened its grip on my arm to the point of pain. I tried to yank my arm away, but that only made it worse. "Okay, you need to go back to where you came from. Rest for a while or something. If you need me, I'm here." I patted it on its chilly back awkwardly. "Come back before something bad happens or when I call you. It'd be nice if we could stop these things from happening instead of coming after the fact." That reminded me of something. "How'd the first guy die yesterday? Did someone kill him?"

Felix walked forward carefully, eyes glued to the demon's grip on my arm. I knew him well enough to know he would try to pull the demon away if he didn't disappear soon. "Why would someone kill it and not report it?"

"Maybe they were just focused on getting the hell out of town." Like I was.

"Staaaaarvvving," said the demon.

That wasn't good. I had no idea what demon spirits ate. "You're hungry?"

The demon swiftly shook its head.

Then what was he talking—oh. "The guy from yesterday starved to death."

The demon nodded quickly.

Azrael scratched their chin in thought. "And therefore, he melted. How fascinating."

I scrunched my face. "Or gross, but we'll go with fascinating." I looked back down at the demon, feeling Felix's shadow practically over us. I could handle this. "All right, buddy, by the way, what's your name?"

"Tiiiiim."

Tim the demon. That was deceptively harmless. "Ok, Tim. I'm Fran. We're going to find a way to set your spirit free, so you can go off to heaven or wherever." I couldn't imagine at ten that he had done anything bad enough in his life to go to hell, so helping him get to the right place seemed like the thing to do. Couldn't hurt to get some cool points on the conscience scale. "So, let us rest some and get to thinking of a plan. Okay."

Tim nodded before releasing me and disappearing into a cloud of black smoke.

Felix reached for my arm and rubbed warmth back into my limb. How he even knew I needed that, I wasn't sure. I instantly felt at ease with him. It wasn't going to be easy parting ways when I went to the fae realm. Maybe I should rethink things and see if there was a way to get him into my world? I had no idea but my feelings for him weren't light. I could talk a good game, but I really liked him.

I thanked him and then stood up. "Okay, let's all get some rest so we can meet boss lady in the morning."

"Are you going to stay here with us for the week? I don't want you disappearing while we're asleep," Felix said with raised brows.

I shrugged. "We'll see how she responds, and then I'll decide."

With the way things had been going, I was pretty sure Monica wasn't going to respond to my satisfaction.

~

We met Monica at an upscale diner in an unaffiliated town several miles away from St. Michaels late the next morning. We relayed the events from the past two days. Azrael kept out the part about finding the angels while we worked up a story that didn't involve them betraying Monica. I didn't care to protect them as much. They had a job to do, and she was their boss, like it or not. Misandre was hardly the pleasant leader I wanted but I endured it. She was killed eventually so I was sure it would work out for them in time. More importantly, this prolonged Monica helping me with my memories, which was the only reason I was there. Azrael believed if we gave her a bit of information she would at least share the news she'd been

117

holding from the last time we saw her. That better be the case, or I was going to snitch.

Our waitress set our plates of food down and I cut into my sausage, waiting for the angel's response to our news.

Monica sipped her coffee, her eyes narrowed in thought. "I have no doubt that there are more of these creatures, and we still need to find Dean and Nancy, so it's important you stay longer."

Azrael nodded in agreement. "That's the plan."

I frowned and shook my head. "Or, you can bring your angel flunkies to handle it. We've given you the intel. You know the place is troubled. You also know we can come and go as we please. We played our role, now give me the information you promised."

Monica pursed her lips. "You still haven't found my angels."

I made a 'pfft' noise with my mouth. Those angels weren't my friends. I didn't need to keep their secret. "Your angels are there. We saw them."

Felix groaned, and Faith muttered some expletive. Maybe Azrael wanted to keep them a secret, but I didn't give a damn. I ignored Azrael's blazing eyes on me. I wanted what I came here to get. Information about my past.

I put down my knife and fork and leaned into the table towards Monica. "Look, your angels don't like you. I'm guessing nobody does. I'm sure you're aware of that. You are a ruthless, deceptive being." I really wanted to say bitch. *Gold star, Fran, for being so classy.* "That Sunnybrook farm town seems like a utopia to those poor put upon angels. I'm assuming. Honestly, the place feels like a cult but that's another story. If you don't want people to desert you, maybe you should act like a leader people want to follow. Someone people want to emulate and go to the front of battle for." I sat back in my chair feeling self-satisfied. "Read that in a leadership book. I can let you borrow it if you play nice."

Monica's silvery eyes glowed and I feared for a moment she was going to zap me. "Are you saying my angels ran away?" she asked through gritted teeth.

Faith cut in with a look of resignation. "Yeah, man. And don't go taking it out on them, okay? They didn't mean any harm."

I wanted to add that I'd do the same if I were them, but I felt I'd said enough for the moment.

Azrael ran a weary hand over their face before speaking. "I was trying to sort that all out, Monica. That's why I didn't tell you. I'm sure we can come to an understanding. Perhaps through mediation. Dean and Nancy are young. We just have to train them better."

Faith nodded. "But you also are a trash-ass leader so, there's that."

I gave a quick clap and pointed at her in approval. Maybe I didn't hate her after all.

Azrael turned to Felix, their eyes wide with anger. "If she speaks again, I am going to electrocute her. She will survive, but it will shut her up for a while."

Faith kicked the angel in the leg. "Try it."

I was confused. I thought they were a thing, but maybe their romance was a little on the violent and aggressive side. Everyone had their kinks.

Monica slammed her coffee cup down, brown liquid spilling on the table. "Enough!"

We quieted down and stared at her. One could never forget that Monica was the most powerful person at this table. She was a high-level angel, and the power she wielded could not be taken for granted. Sometimes it was fun to poke the bear, but I didn't want to be mauled by it.

Monica clasped her hands, resting them on the table. "Being a leader everyone admires is not an easy task. None of you sitting at this table have lived as long as I or seen as much as me." She looked around at us, her face neutral. "I was a Queen when I was human. Beloved. However, none of that love kept my people safe from the cruelty of the world. They were still ripped from their homeland and enslaved." She rested her eyes on me. "Leading is not a popularity contest despite what some of your books are telling you. It is about sacrifice and the ability to see the bigger picture. Now I realize you dislike me for having your memories erased but it was a necessary evil. One I'd have done again. You are all charged with the greater good. That means putting the needs of what is right before your own."

I twisted my lips, not certain I was buying that she'd put her needs to the side but I let her continue.

Probably sensing my doubt, Monica cocked a brow. "It is unfortunate that your memories did not return, but you overestimate how much of your mind you had before we intervened. Both you and Felix are different from your friends. You were paranormal before the world changed. You came from parents who knew what they were. But, Francesca, there are secrets hidden within you that even we did not know before. Secrets we still don't know." She sat back in her chair, relaxing her face. "Now, since you have provided me some information, albeit unpleasant, I suppose it is only fair that I can tell you what we have discovered."

"Finally," I muttered. Her speech was nice but since I wasn't sure she was really practicing those words herself, I wouldn't hold onto them for long.

Ignoring my snide comment, Monica continued. "You know that your mother was Unseelie fae. Her name was Dalia Cruz. She was Queen of a Southwestern Regional Court."

So, that's what Marcus had meant by wondering why I was focused on this court. I really was a freaking princess!

Fae courts, like many paranormal groups, were located all over the world. The Fae realm was its own world, but it represented and influenced cultures in the human world all over the globe. Which was why the fae did not have only one appearance. Misandre was a northwestern faerie and would then terrorize humans in Europe while taking on the appearance of a caucasian woman with a Scottish accent. Marcus was also a northwestern faerie, but he had the appearance of a biracial male with an English accent. Queen Arwa was an eastern faerie and protected humans in the Asia region while taking on the appearance of a middle eastern woman. If my mother was a southwestern faerie then she interacted with South American countries.

"What did she look like?" I asked in a whisper. This was the second time I'd heard that name. Marcus had known my mother and I was even more certain now that partnering with him was a good decision because he had information about my past that I would get him to share, even if I had to trick him into doing it.

Monica tilted her head. "I don't have any pictures of her yet. But she was described by our sources much like you. She was also described as being afro-cuban in the human world. At some point in your life, you stopped residing in the fae realm and lived as human. I don't know much about your time living as a fae, just that you were royalty. I don't know why you and your mother left."

"Is she alive?"

"I do not know."

I lowered my eyes, a feeling of frustration growing. "What about my father? All I know is that his last name is Ross."

"Your father was a demon, this you know. They did not let him into the fae realm. However, there is no information yet about him. I don't know if your parents lived together in the human realm."

"Anything else?"

"That's all I can tell you."

I wasn't certain if she meant this is all she knew or if this was all she was going to tell me.

Monica stretched her lips into a tight smile. "We will continue to look into more information about you and discover how to break whatever magic is continuing to mask your memories. In the meantime, you will rid this town of this evil, and I will recover my angels at the conclusion."

I had my information, and now I could leave instead of sticking around hoping for another morsel of truth from Monica. Yet, now I felt invested. I was getting a bleeding heart hanging out with these guys. I wanted to actually stop these demons. Maybe it would look good on my leadership resume. Fae's were no friends to demons, so being a demon vanquishing princess sounded like something good to write on a campaign ticket.

Felix cleared his throat. "I know I have my memories, but is there anything regarding my mother's whereabouts? I know the neighborhood we used to live in was destroyed by an orc attack. I tried to reach her by phone, but she never answered. I tried to email her, she never replied or showed up at any of the locations I gave her. Is she dead like my father?"

Monica straightened up in her chair and gave her best sympathetic face. "Your mother, the demon," she said that with distaste, "is still in the human realm. Her last location was Boston, and then we lost her. We are still working on it."

Felix frowned, shaking his head. "Why would she keep moving?"

"That is the mystery. Who is to say she's been in the human world these past ten years? She could come and go. Who knows the motives of demons? They are much harder to track, like Francesca's father. For all we know, this could be part of her punishment for falling in love with an angel."

"Except she didn't get killed," Felix stated gruffly.

Nice. Way to push back.

Monica blew out a breath. "They may not know of what

she did. I honestly doubt any angel reported their findings to a demon."

Felix turned his upper lip up slightly in an uncharacteristic look of anger. "Well, lucky me, she got to stick around so I didn't become an orphan."

I pressed my lips together and tilted my head as I looked at Monica for her reaction. I liked seeing Felix be a smart ass. When he acted that way, I better understood why we were supposedly besties before our minds were wiped.

"Kind of makes angels seem like dicks in comparison to demons," he went on, crossing his arms.

Faith put a fist over her mouth. "Damn," she cried in an instigating, heavy voice.

"Not helping," Azrael muttered out of the corner of their mouth.

No, seriously, why did Faith hate me again because I was really starting to like her more and more. She really had that giver of no damns bit down perfectly.

Anger flashed across Monica's face before she rose. "You're entitled to your feelings. However, it won't win you any awards. You are still half-demon, and you are asking the angels to find your demon mother. We've actually completed all that we owe you. Your memories are back in full. Any additional work we do for you is only in relation to the services you provide us. Such as protecting the town of St. Michaels." She looked over to me. "Sometimes, I wonder if letting you two remain together was a good idea." She then turned away. "I'll be checking in on your progress."

Wait, she was blaming me for Felix's clap back? Did she not see his best friend with the dynamite temper and foul language?

"I thought she was paying the bill." I stared after her as she left the restaurant, watching as she passed by the floor-to-ceiling windows and out of sight. I really didn't like—

My mind froze as I lay eyes on a person across the street

looking in my direction. Except this wasn't just any person. She was a woman with a caramel complexion, long brown hair and topaz eyes. She looked exactly like me. Not even the slightest difference. Did I have a twin?

I shot up and ran out of the restaurant to find out.

# CHAPTER 11

*I* almost got hit by a car as I charged across the street.

The woman stepped back and began to walk, turning left down a dark alley.

Of course, she would go to the most suspicious area ever. Without hesitation I turned down the alley and stopped as the woman stood there in the shadows looking at me. Even in the darkness I could see clearly that she was the spitting image of me.

"Who are you?" I shouted.

The woman, who looked like me, pointed at me.

I turned around but saw nothing. Turning back in my look-a-likes direction, I pointed to myself as well. "Me? You're me?"

The woman nodded.

I put my hands on both sides of my head utterly confused. "No," I said more to myself than anyone else.

The woman nodded again.

"Do you mean you're my twin sister?" Could I really have a long-lost twin like some type of *Parent Trap*?

She shook her head, those same eyes almost mischievous.

Monica had said I looked like Dalia. Perhaps, I was actually the spitting image of her.

"Are you my mother?"

Again, she shook her head.

I was getting frustrated with this bogus question and answering period. Clearly this was some sort of shapeshifter. Or it was a spirit, but why would it be my spirit?

"Fine, don't tell me. What do you want?"

The shapeshifter—that's what I decided it had to be because it made the most sense—ran at me with lightning speed quickness.

I caught her by the neck and was shocked to feel how icy she was. Shapeshifters weren't known to be uniquely cold.

Before I could register what had happened, I felt a stabbing pain in my gut. I looked down and saw the hilt of a sword sticking out of my stomach. I looked back at the woman but she was no longer there. However, I could barely register her sudden disappearance because the pain from my wound began to overtake me. I grabbed the sword and dropped to my knees, feeling woozy. Falling sideways, a chilling dizziness washed over me as blood poured over my hands.

In the distance, or perhaps it was closer, I heard familiar voices calling out to me.

Felix's large body soon appeared.

He knelt on the ground beside me. "How'd this happen?" he yelled, his face full of worry and fear.

I scrunched my face in pain. "I'll tell you all about it, but first, can you heal me?"

He was already pulling the sword out before I could finish my sentence.

I let out a pained scream as the sword resliced its way out of me, deepening any wounds to my insides. It felt like fire was scraping my organs.

He tossed the sword to the side and immediately began to

heal me, hovering his hands over my injuries. I gritted my teeth as the warmth of his magic knitted my muscles and skin back together.

From the corner of my eyes, I saw Azrael pick up the sword. Instantly it disintegrated in their hands. "Huh," the angel said, rubbing their chin in curiosity. "I'm more concerned about why someone would use a conjuring weapon. Not many beings have that kind of power."

It felt cold like a spirit demon, but those weren't the only beings with a cold touch. "Maybe it was a shapeshifter?" I coughed into the pain. Fast healing was a great thing, but it hurt like hell.

"Even more curious. Shapeshifters don't possess that type of power."

Faith looked up and down the alley. "The bigger question is why it tried to kill you."

"Did I mention that it looked like me?" I added. "So basically, I tried to kill myself."

Faith paused her alley inspection and looked at me with a frown. "Is that why you took off like a madwoman without saying anything?"

"In retrospect it was not the smartest thing to do, but in my defense, I thought it could have been my mother."

Felix lowered his hands, the healing done, and helped me to sit up. "Do you have any enemies who would want to take you out?"

I snorted. "Probably a lot. Maybe people from my past I can't remember. Now that Misandre and Alister are gone, they might think it's a good time to finally get rid of me. Could be another Unseelie faerie vying for the throne who wants to off the competition. Or who knows what kind of enemies my mother had as a Queen. Maybe that's how I ended up in the human world. We had to go in hiding, and now I've been found. Who knows, really?"

Felix ran a hand through his hair before picking me up in

his arms like I wasn't able to walk, his face full of worry. "Well, until we find out who's behind this, we can't leave you alone. I can't have my future wife getting gutted in the streets again."

I wiggled and kicked my legs out. "Is there a reason why you are carrying me? I'm all healed up."

He gave me a lopsided smile that looked a tad bit sly. "You don't get healed up that quickly. Let's get you back to the hotel so you can properly rest up. And Faith and I are switching rooms. I personally want to keep my eye on you."

I twisted my lips again and rolled my eyes. "How'd I know you would see this as an opportunity to get on in."

He shrugged, tightening his grasp on me. "Eh, you secretly love it."

Azrael cleared their throat as they dusted their hands from the residue of the conjured weapon. "Pause the flirting for a moment. How did a random shapeshifter find you here? Did it say anything?"

I shook my head. "No, it wouldn't talk. I asked if it was me, and it nodded yes, then stabbed me with a sword. It acted like it couldn't talk. Oh, and it was cold to the touch."

Azrael narrowed their eyes. "Like the child demon."

"Yeah!"

"Are you sure it's a shapeshifter?"

I laid my head on Felix's shoulder. Maybe I was still weak. I certainly felt like I needed a rest. Healing was always an energy sucking activity. "I mean, what else could it be?"

"Many things, Francesca. Many things. I think it might be time to give Carlos a call."

My eyelids felt like weights now, and I struggled to keep them open. "Why him?"

"Because he's an older angel, and he knows things."

Made sense to me. I had to admit, I was kind of excited to see my guardian angel again. It had been a while since we talked. I was still a little peeved at him for deceiving me about his role in my memory wipe all this time but other than Nadia and now Felix, he was the only friend I had. And since the world was clearly trying to kill me. It was important to keep what little allies I had around.

~

*C*arlos was away on a mission so he couldn't come right when Azrael rang the angel hotline, or what they used to communicate, but he agreed to come later that night. I decided to take that time to take a healing nap. The sword hadn't killed me, but it sure hadn't been a love tap.

When I woke up that evening, Felix was already settled and had moved into my room. I still thought his reasonings for switching rooms was a joke. For a guy who claimed to want to take things slow until I regained my memories, he sure liked to put himself in situations that didn't help that cause. Perhaps he really didn't believe I'd be a fae Queen or maybe he was hoping I wouldn't go that route and stay with him. I would only end up hurting him if he really thought that way.

He walked out of the bathroom with only a towel wrapped around his waist.

Oh, come on.

He looked momentarily surprised to see me awake and sitting up before he walked over to his suitcase on the bed to rummage through his things.

I couldn't take my eyes off of him. He really was a nice specimen of a man. His hair hung damp around his broad shoulders, and his well-defined chest still glistened with water. He had a strong physique, which I noticed as his arm muscles flexed as they moved through his bag. I stole a peek lower at the deep V of his pelvis. I was very open to the idea of his towel dropping. Maybe if I could make a strong wind happen...

"Did you sleep well?" He asked, interrupting my thoughts.

I forced myself to glance up at his face and he looked at me with a slight knowing smile again. Oh, he knew what he was doing coming in here like that.

"Yeah, I had a great nap. If you are going to insist on walking around half naked, we cannot be roommates."

I got up off of the bed and stretched. I probably needed a shower as well.

"Oh, come on, you're a big girl. You can handle it."

I put my hands on my hips. That didn't feel like a Felix way of talking. Well, I'd show him. I walked over to him and gripped the top of his towel, the back of my fingers resting against his smooth skin. Damn, he smelled good. And his skin looked so buttery, I wanted to lick it. *Girl, get a hold of yourself.*

"Seems to me you have a lot of talk." I looked down at the towel. "Keep playing and this towel will be on the floor." Of course, I was kidding. That was our thing, that was our banter.

So, when he gave me a confident smirk, grabbed my hand on the towel and then pulled it up, I nearly grasped at the imaginary pearls around my neck. However, since he was showing, I was definitely going to take a gander.

And he had on smiley face boxers.

I glared up at his chuckling face and punched him in the arm. He was solid. Seriously, his biceps were like rocks. "You tricked me."

He touched his stomach still having a hearty laugh at my expense. "You're a perv, my love. I just put a towel on because I thought it would be disrespectful to walk around in just my boxers. But perhaps you like that?" He wiggled his brows.

I shrugged, trying to regain some footing. "If they were tighter, perhaps."

"I like to leave a little to the imagination."

I waved a dismissive hand and turned to walk away. "Eh,

imagination is overrated. As I guessed from the start, you're just in here to tease me."

Felix grabbed my wrist and brought me back to him. The playfulness in his eyes died and he gave me an all too serious look. "I'm staying here with you because I love you. You know that."

Oh, God. He'd dropped the L-word. And he did it so casually. "Don't keep saying that."

"It's the truth. All the flirting aside, you know that. If you don't get your memories back, that won't mean anything different to me. Maybe I was being silly by waiting for that to happen." He grabbed my hand again. "You could have died today. And I have you, right here, in my reach, and we're just bidding time. Waiting for this right moment."

I was getting tired. Not physically but emotionally. I wanted this man. That was never the question. Felix was practically perfect. However, I couldn't see how we could fit in each other's lives. The more we ignored that part, the harder it would later be when we had to face it. We could focus on the now and have fun and it would feel great, but there would come a moment when the music would end and it would destroy me. Just thinking about it now tightened my heart. However, the idea of losing him now hurt just as much. He brought me into his arms, and I rested my cheek on his chest. I tried to prevent myself from rubbing my face on his smooth skin like a purring cat. "Stop running from me, Fran. You deserve to be happy. Despite our differences, I think we can make this work. We can break barriers in the fae world."

I moved my head so that I could stare up at him and he dropped his arms to my waist. A sincere glint hit his eyes. He was looking at me as if I was the most precious thing to him. My stomach fluttered and I tried not to reach out and touch him. He passed a hand gently over my hair before leaning forward and kissing me. As always, it was breathtaking, and the slight taste of mint from his toothpaste brought a welcomed sweetness. I placed my hand on his naked chest as we deepened our kiss, his tongue playfully touched mine and sent zaps of excitement to my core.

He moved his mouth to my neck, and I was sure I'd fall over as his hot kisses sizzled on my skin. "I don't think the fae are that understanding," I said in a barely audible voice as he continued to kiss me. "Especially Unseelie. We can be jerks sometimes. I can admit thaaaaat." He twirled his tongue on my neck and my knees really did get weak at that moment.

"If they won't accept me," Felix began between kisses. "Then I will fall back." Another kiss. "I don't want to be in the way." And another. "Of your goals."

Damn it, why was he so understanding? And so good at kissing?

He continued. "I just want you, Francesca." He gave more kisses, and the way he was whispering on my neck, I was sure I'd have to wring out my undergarments. "I just want..." kiss. "...you to..." more kisses. "...let me..." more. "...love you."

I believe my eyes must have fluttered. I wasn't seeing so well now. I wanted to climb this man and let him have his way with me.

But if I did, it would mean something. However, I did not know what to do with the connection he was offering. Ever since our first meeting in the woods, well, the meeting I could remember, he had confessed how he felt about me. There were never any games with him. Even when he didn't have his memories, he knew he loved me. His feelings for me were that strong that he knew we were meant for each other without any real reason. It wasn't easy to find a mind like that. He would offer me security of the heart. I wouldn't have to worry about his loyalty.

I, on the other hand, wasn't certain at first. Although I

found him attractive, I thought he was crazy when we first met. And Felix didn't know if I felt romantic feelings towards him when we worked together in the past as hitmen for Alister. Nadia believed I had loved him back then but that I just would not admit it. All I knew now was that I cared deeply for this man, but those feelings were terrifying because I didn't know how to fit them into my world. I didn't want to ruin his kind heart, and I didn't want to lose myself in another man.

But as his large hands pulled me tighter to him, so close that I could feel him come alive, losing myself for just a little bit didn't feel so bad.

And because fate hated me, we heard a knock at the door at that moment.

"Ignore it," I whispered.

But it was like the knock brought Felix to his senses because he groaned and pulled away from me. "That's probably the others since we have to meet up with Carlos." He gave me a peck on the lips. "Can you answer it while I get dressed?"

I sucked my teeth and reluctantly left to answer the door. Azrael stood there and looked me up and down. "You aren't ready," said the angel in their always annoyed tone with me.

No, I'd been stabbed to almost death and needed to rest to heal fully, so I did not have time to get ready. "Come on in. Let me jump in the shower, and I can meet you all at wherever we are meeting Carlos."

"He's in our suite now with Faith."

I nodded. "Okay, well I'll meet you there in ten."

Felix appeared beside me, fully dressed, his hair pulled back in a low ponytail. "We aren't leaving you alone. I'll stay."

Azrael raised their hand and the front door opened. "Would you mind going ahead, Felix? I need to talk to Francesca in private, please."

Felix squinted his eyes in suspicion but headed out without question. "Don't be long."

Azrael waited until the door clicked and then swiped their hand in the direction of the door.

"What'd you do?" I asked.

"Soundproof us."

I raised my brows. Did the angel think Felix was going to hang around and eavesdrop? Or maybe someone else? This must have been serious. I moved over to the loveseat and sat down. "What's up, angel?"

Azrael walked over to me with a somber look. "Have you noticed a change in Felix?"

I poked my lower lip out, confused. "Uh, no? Should I?" I thought about it then remembered something. Lately, his physique had been top notch. It was impressive actually. "Oh, yes."

Azrael sat on the couch with a wide-eyed look. "You have?"

I nodded quickly. "He has been going hard at the gym. His body is ridiculous."

Azrael rolled their eyes and swore. "So, I take it as a no? He doesn't seem darker to you?"

"Assuming you aren't talking about his tan, then no. I mean, sure he got a little ballsy with Monica, but I think we all know she deserved it. For all I know, he's just coming into his true self. The type of guy he was before you guys swiped our minds."

"I'm being serious, Francesca. Perhaps you haven't noticed because you haven't been around him as much, but the others do. Some days, he's that old lovable guy that seems just a little out of whack. Then the next moment, he's this smart mouth, arrogant, rude and sometimes cruel person."

I let out a breath, racking my brain of my moments with Felix. The closest thing to arrogance I'd noticed was him being more assertive in his attraction to me. But I liked that.

134

"He seems more confident. That would make sense. He was a hitman. He's just getting his swag back."

Azrael massaged the bridge of their nose. "Yeah, and hopefully not killing anymore. Do you know he's not teaching anymore?"

"No, I thought he was on summer break. He told me he liked it. He lied?"

Azrael gave me a pointed look. "See, he's not himself. He finished the school year, but announced he wasn't coming back. He joined the police force instead. Said he was tired of teaching brats."

That didn't sound right. It was just the other day that he told me he loved teaching. I made a face of disdain. "While he's right, kids are brats, but that doesn't sound like him. When was this?"

"Yesterday. It's like Dr. Jekyll and Mr. Hyde."

"Maybe it's this place then. Maybe it's affecting him."

"Possibly. Or maybe it's because he's half-demon? And now that it has been allowed to be let loose, it's gaining ground."

"He was always part demon. The only thing that changed is him being in this town."

Azrael growled in frustration. "Before the mind wipe, he was like this to a degree, but there was something that held him back from going too far over."

Intrigued, I scooted to the edge of my seat. "What?"

The angel's eyes softened. "His love for you."

I lowered my shoulders, at a loss for words and unsure how I felt. At first, I was the bad influence. Now they were saying I actually was good for him?

"Then, when we took his mind, Faith and the others helped him fall on the side of angel versus the demon side. But when we returned his memories, things slowly began to change. Especially since he was held in the hell dimension when Alister captured him. That could have triggered his dark side. He mentioned to me that he'd never gone to the hell realm before. He'd always meet with Alister in the human world."

"Shit," I whispered. I hadn't even thought about that. "So, you think he's going evil. Maybe this town is another catalyst to make that happen? We need to get him out of here. But, wait, it's not affecting me. I feel like I'm becoming nicer."

Azrael raised their brows and looked away as if they were struggling with that realization. "Maybe this place makes people the opposite of who they are." Jerk.

"Well, rest assured he won't go to the dark side. He'll just be a jerk from time to time. The angel side will keep him good."

"Or get swallowed up by the demon side."

That was new. "Can that even happen?"

"Not to you. But he's part angel. It's a tricky balance. After all, Satan used to be an angel."

Now that thought terrified me. Felix as a demon was not what I wanted. Sure, there were a precious few full-on demons who weren't totally nasty like Nadia, but that didn't mean that would be the case for Felix. And while I was still coming to terms with being part demon myself, it didn't mean I wasn't worried. Demons were considered the lowest of the low. I didn't even want the fae to know I was so tainted. Most of them had hated that Misandre had worked with Alister. Yet another reason why her death was not mourned. As much as I hated angels, I hated for Felix to be a full demon even more.

"What do we need to do?"

Azrael tossed their hands out to the side. "Keep an eye on him and get him out of here sooner rather than later just in case there is a connection."

"I think we *all* need to get out of here."

Azrael paused. "Just make him keep loving you. Don't break his heart."

I wanted to laugh, feeling suddenly exhausted because I wasn't certain this was going to work. I wanted to be Queen of a fae realm, and I was beginning to suspect that my draw to that decision was the fact that somewhere in my mind, I still remembered that I was a fae princess with a kingdom of my own. How much did I want my past? And did that outweigh my attraction to Felix? "I can't commit to a relationship right now. I have goals."

The angel stood up with a look of disappointment. "Well, if you can't, then we might eventually lose the Felix we know and love. All because he had to go to hell to save you. Think about that when you run after your goals."

# CHAPTER 12

*C*arlos jumped up when he saw me. He looked the same with kind eyes, gray hair, and a trimmed goatee. He appeared to be in his late fifties, but he was fit and stylish, which gave him a youthful vibe.

He opened his arms and gave me a tight hug, smelling of cigars. One of his few earthly vices. "Good to see you again, my dear," he said in a jolly voice. He let me go and ushered for me to sit beside him. "I'd love to catch up, but I know we must get the serious talk over with first. They told me you were attacked by a shapeshifter."

I nodded swiftly. "Well, I thought it was a shapeshifter, but it was cold so maybe it was a demon."

"Yeah, it wasn't a shapeshifter." He looked over to Felix then back to me with concerned gray eyes. "You're both half-demon, and as such, you attract dark things. I suspect what you encountered was a doppelganger."

I blinked rapidly. I knew nothing about doppelgangers except that they were like unrelated twins, but something told me this just wasn't a stranger who looked like me. "Where did it come from?"

Carlos shrugged. "Who knows? But she is not human.

More of a spirit, and typically they are harbingers of bad things to come."

I snorted. "Yeah, like a stabbing."

"If I were a betting man, I would say that killing Alister is slowly bringing out all the freaks who gravitate to the energy of a half-demon. As a hybrid, for lack of a better word, you're special. Some would want to consume your energy."

"Fun. So, you're saying Alister was protecting me all this time?"

Felix shifted in his seat with a grimace at each mention of Alister's name.

Carlos glanced over at him with understanding eyes, then back to me. "In a way, yes."

"Will it come back?"

"Absolutely. It will try to kill you again. It wants to *be* you. Once you die, it would become you."

"Screw that."

"Indeed. Even if it doesn't kill you, its very existence is problematic because it still means other trouble is meant for you."

I rubbed my face in frustration. "So, how do we get rid of it?"

Carlos waved a hand to the side. "Kill it like you do anything else. If you see it again, just go for the kill. No questions. Of course, killing it won't be easy since it's actually a spirit, just in solid form."

Azrael took a seat at the dining table next to the kitchenette. "Do we just exorcise it?"

"In a manner. The key is to use magic in your killing of it. If you use a sword make sure it's laced in magic." He glanced back over to me, his eyes now seemingly darker. That couldn't be good. "Now, let's talk about the bigger reason I'm here."

I raised my brows and touched my collarbone, pretending

to be insulted. "I'm sorry, me being attacked by a doppelganger wasn't a big issue?"

"Of course, it is and I've explained what to do. It's probably wise to keep people around you at all times. Before you got here, Faith and Felix told me about the child demon attached to you. You will see more such things. Some mean to do you harm, others not."

Great, I would need a chaperone for who knows how long. How was I going to explain that to the fae? What excuse could I use for the amount of demons coming my way?

As if reading my thoughts, or perhaps my face, Carlos spoke again. "I know you are worried about your chances for the fae throne. I've learned a few things about you recently, which I came to share as well."

Well, that was exciting news. "Do tell."

"Apparently, you are a princess, my dear. You were raised under a Queen of an Unseelie court. So, I suppose, it's in your blood to want to run a court yourself."

I lowered my shoulders. If this was all the news he had, he was too late. "Monica told me that."

He swung his fist across his body in mild irritation. "Of course, she would steal my thunder. Did she tell you why you aren't a princess now?"

I shook my head. "Guess she's decided to dole out info piece by piece to keep me at her beck and call."

Carlos rubbed his chin. "Wouldn't be surprised. Well, let me say this. You have an older half-brother. I don't know his name. I can't narrow down the exact court you came from yet, either. What I do know is that you lived in northern Florida with your mother and father. Your brother must have remained behind with his biological father, who was a fae King. Now, I'm just guessing, but your mother probably raised you as the King's biological daughter, and then, when you were twelve, he found out the truth and sent you and your mother away to the human realm."

That made sense, and now I had a whole other thought in regards to Marcus. Was he my half-brother? Who exactly was he to me?

"Your mother married a man later on named Emmett Ross. I don't know if he was your biological father, the demon, or an adoptive human father. I can't find anything about him doing anything extraordinary or criminal. He seemed to be a regular, law abiding citizen. He volunteered in the community and seemed to have been a good man. I'm sorry to say he died of cancer thirteen years ago. This is why I was doubtful he was your biological father. A demon wouldn't die of such a thing. I am searching for your parents now. Finding your brother is more challenging. Fae, especially Unseelie, do not like outsiders."

I took in a breath, feeling finally hopeful that I was getting closer and closer to my identity.

Carlos patted my knee in a comforting manner. "I will keep looking as long as it takes to find who you are and how to get your memory back. Monica, I'm sure, shared that your memory of who you once were was probably wiped before we came along. It's how you ended up with Misandre. If you were going to join a fae court again, it would make the most sense to find a Western connected court. But you went to whoever solicited the best offer. Misandre seized that opportunity, and I would not be surprised if she knew exactly who you were. You are a warrior faerie, and that came ingrained in you from your lineage. More importantly, what you are makes it hard for you to be a ruler in the fae world."

I nodded. I figured that much seeing as faes hated demons who they thought were tainted, uncivilized and untrustworthy. Which was mostly true. "Yeah, with me being half-demon. It's not a good look."

He looked down at the hardwood floor, shoulders slumping. "Not just that. You can't keep your dynasty going."

I scrunched my face in confusion. "What do you mean?"

When he looked back at me, his eyes were pained and he clasped my hand in both of his. "You can't have children."

What?

"Neither can Felix."

That stung. While kids had never been on my mind, I hadn't ruled them out. Especially, if I was coming for a throne. Who would want a queen who couldn't keep a dynasty going? It was the reason that Misandre's leaving had caused this competition. She never had any more children after humans killed them long ago.

Felix let out a heavy sigh after a period of silence. "Well, I guess it's for the best. Kids can be annoying."

Now that was not a Felix thing to say. Aside from his flirting more than normal, I hadn't noticed much of a change before in Felix. Was I so self-absorbed with my own issues that I missed what was happening with him? I looked over to him, sitting on my other side, but his face only gave off a mild sadness as if he just learned he'd have to wait another ten minutes for the train to come, not some life devastating news. That was not what I expected him to say. He was a freaking teacher, after all. He was also patient and kind. He'd make a great father. I shook my head of the thought. I was going into fairy tale thinking again. I glanced over to Azrael, who gave me a pointed look. Clearly, Felix's uncharacteristic response was a solid example of this growing darkness that the angel mentioned.

Carlos squinted his eyes at him. I wouldn't be surprised if Azrael had already spoken to him about Felix's change, if that's what you would call it.

I rolled my shoulders back trying to comprehend what Carlos was telling us. "Why can't we have kids?"

Carlos looked back at me, eyes shifting to sympathy

again. He was a much kinder angel than the others. It's why I always looked at him like family. He was just easier to like than the cold Monica or that smart-ass Azrael. It was also probably why I took him for granted and easily ran away. "It's natures attempt to prevent ongoing angel and demon bloodlines."

"So, we're freaks of nature? And this is nature's way of stamping us out?"

"I'm sorry, my dear, but it seems so. Angels and demons aren't supposed to have kids. In most cases such children don't come to term. The few that make it are anomalies."

"Any chance the big guy or gal upstairs could make an exception for some do-gooders like us?"

Azrael choked back a laugh, and I cut my eyes at them.

"Problem? Felix is a member of the Six and I helped fight the evil soulmates and took out a demon King. You'd think that would earn us some brownie points." It wasn't my fault I was born like this. I felt shafted. Maybe I had wanted kids, regardless if I was to carry on a fae dynasty. I could live my life simply and still have wanted that possibility. A part of me felt sad at that.

The angel waved a dismissive hand at me. "It doesn't work like that. Felix was made a Six to serve a purpose. He has no choice but to do good. And you doing good is no more than anyone else who risked their lives in battle." I huffed and crossed my arms. "Rude much? Can't a girl have some hope?"

Felix nodded, giving me a gentle smile that brought me back to the Felix I knew. "Of course, you can. We both can. I'll find a way to give you kids if that's what you want." He gave me a quick wink and I cocked an eyebrow in return. I wasn't sure how he planned to pull off a miracle, but I was intrigued to find out.

"Well, thanks for sharing all your news. Keep up the good work of finding out who I am while we try to go rid a town of weird skin melting demons and fight off a doppelganger, and I find a way to set a child demon free and win a fae throne." I swung my arm around the room, pointing at everyone. "And let it be known, that none of these things I have to do are paying gigs. If we can't stop what's going on in that town by the end of this week, I'm out. I have campaigning to do."

Carlos chuckled, leaning back comfortably in his seat. "Over-dramatic as always, my dear. I have absolute faith things will work in your favor. This demon child, have you thought of asking him about the melting demons? He knows when they are out, so perhaps he knows more information about them to help you catch them?"

I dropped my mouth open and scratched my head in disbelief. "You know, I normally think I'm a smart woman but then you say the obvious thing that I never think about and I feel like an idiot."

"Me too," Azrael grumbled, rolling their eyes. "Assuming we can trust a demon, that would be a great start."

Well, time to go have another chat with a demon.

◆

*I* tried to call Tim like I had last time but he was a no show. I guess he felt he'd come when he wanted. So, since he was being a little jerk, I'd have to force him to show up by conjuring him.

Like I said, conjuring a demon was never my specialty and working for Alister, I never had to. Carlos gave me a conjuring spell to use but said it would require some form of blood sacrifice, specifically the killing of an animal. The more powerful the demon, the higher in the food chain the sacrifice had to be. Since the demon was just a child, I was hoping a mouse or rat would do.

Carlos left us for the night and the four of us gathered in

a wooded area still in town. Felix procured a small field mouse he trapped in a box.

Faith let out a breath and rubbed her arms as if chilly from the comfortably warm night air. "Anyone else feel bad about killing Mickey over there just to make the equivalent of a phone call?"

Felix shrugged. "It's for the greater good."

"Of course, you'd see it that way, Mr. Give-up-a-toe."

I snorted. Did I mention that when Alister put a non-removable tracking ring on me, Felix gave up his pinky toe to make a spell to remove it? It worked but I felt guilty about his sacrifice.

"Let's begin." I took out my phone to open the spell that Carlos emailed me. Felt kind of weird reading a dark ancient spell from my smartphone. In the movies people always read it from some thick, dusty book. Modern times, I guess. "Okay, we say the spell, inserting Tim's name, then Felix kills the mouse. In that order."

The group nodded in understanding. I called out the spell in my most commanding voice and Felix killed the mouse in a manner I won't get into. I will say, he looked a little too excited about doing it. Seriously, his face lit in an evil smile like some Disney villain. It was unsettling.

"Okay, all done."

We looked around us, waiting for Tim to appear out of the darkness.

Nothing.

Azrael raised their hand, their face fixed in its normal neutral look. "Can I ask the obvious question here?"

I balled my fist up and gritted my teeth, readying myself for his next annoying comment. "Damn it, I know what you're going to say."

"Is his name really Tim?" We both said at the same time.

We quieted and waited another beat.

Faith chuckled out into the darkness. "I'm going to take a guess and say it's not."

I kicked my foot into the grass. "He lied."

"A demon lied? How could that be?" Faith questioned in a mocking tone.

I cut my eyes at her, but I wasn't sure she could see me in the darkness.

Azrael let out a heavy sigh. "We all know that there is power in a name. Even for minor demons."

"But would he be that sneaky? I thought he was trapped. Oh, wait a minute, he probably lied about that too." I wanted to slap my forehead. I was slipping. I really wasn't this gullible, I swear.

Felix put the box with the now dead mouse on the ground in front of him, tossing the knife he used in the box. I flinched slightly. Okay, it did feel a little disrespectful to just toss the murder weapon in the mouses now makeshift coffin. Murder weapon? *Okay, Fran, you're being ridiculous.*

Felix grumbled. "Why would he lie? Why even tell us about these skin demons then? What's his motive?"

I huffed. "Well, that's the first question I'm going to ask when I see him again. Damn, demons. And yes, I know the irony." I stormed off. If we didn't find this demon, I wasn't sure we'd be able to get rid of the town's skin demon problem any time soon.

# CHAPTER 13

*T*he next morning, I decided to treat myself to room service on Monica's dime.

As I waited for breakfast to arrive, I fumed over the lack of success from the previous night. Unsurprisingly, Tim had never shown up and I really expected him to since he liked to appear in the most disturbing of ways. What was his deal? This is why I shouldn't be nice. Everyone was a jerk, including demon kids.

I heard a knock at the door and got off the couch to answer it. Felix was currently in the shower. I'm not saying I wanted him to come out half-naked again, but I would not be upset if he did. I did a slow walk past the hallway to see if the bathroom door would open, when it didn't, I shrugged and went to the door.

"Who is it?"

"Room service," said a muffled voice behind the door.

I looked through the peephole and saw a man standing there with a cart of what I hoped was covered food.

I opened the door wide, and the man pushed the cart in. "Here you go ma'am, your breakfast. I'll put it on your table if that works for you."

I nodded absentmindedly then paused as I peered at him. Something was off. His face was sagging. Just like the waitresses.

I opened my mouth to say something. Did he know?

Of course he had to. No one just walks around with a droopy face unknowingly. And anyway, wouldn't it be rude to say something? What would me saying anything do but make him more self-conscious? Still two unique skin disorders in a small town where we also encountered skin melting demons? Nope, I didn't believe in coincidences. This was suspect as hell.

The man looked up, saw me staring and instantly touched his face. He quickly turned away when he felt the loose skin hanging from his jawline. He lowered his head, one hand to his chin as he maneuvered the now empty cart toward the door. "Sorry about that. I have a condition."

"No need to apologize," I replied with a wave of the hand, then I paused, mid-wave. Wait a minute. Sagging skin was very close to melting skin. Well, sort of. It honestly didn't matter, we didn't have much to go on and I couldn't ignore the oddities in this place. "I hope you can get some rest soon. That usually helps with my ailments," I said lamely. No, it did not but I wanted to keep an eye on this guy, and I needed to know if he was leaving anytime soon. I peered at this name tag. Kyle.

He shook his head as he exited. "Sadly, I just started my shift so I have a ways to go. Enjoy your breakfast."

I closed the door behind him. "Okay, Fran, think, think. Tim said the demons melt into a bag of skin if they don't feed. Dude's face was melting but does that mean he's dying inside? Wouldn't that be painful if all your organs and bones were melting? I would not be going to work, I know that."

"Who are you talking to?" Felix said behind me.

I jumped slightly and turned to him. Sadly, he was fully dressed in a fitted blue T-shirt and dark jeans. His hair was pulled back in a low bun showcasing the masculine angles of his face. Darn it, he was distracting to look at.

"I was talking to myself. The guy who brought the food up had the same skin condition as the waitress from the other day."

Felix walked over to the food and uncovered the dishes. I had ordered fluffy chocolate chip pancakes, bacon, and cheesy scrambled eggs with a coffee and a mimosa. Felix got steak and eggs, a cinnamon roll, and a Bloody Mary. "Strange," he mumbled before sitting down and cutting into his food. He was not focused on the task at hand.

"Uh, yeah. I'm wondering if it's connected to the skin melting demons. Maybe sagging skin is the first stage. Only I can't figure out how anyone can go about their daily business if their insides are melting."

Felix chewed thoughtfully. "Unless they're on a hell of a pain killer."

Nature called and I shook my head, still confused as I headed to the bathroom. I decided to do some quick thinking in solitude and kill two birds with one stone. Maybe the sagging faced people really didn't feel what was happening to them. However, one would think that if they knew this could happen, they would stay on top of eating people. Kyle could have simply tried to attack me if he was really hungry. Why hadn't anyone come for us? Did they know we were powerful? Maybe they were afraid of us.

"Hi," came a creaky voice.

I hunched forward on the toilet, covering my private area and looked up to see Tim perched on the ledge of the tub across from me. "Are you serious! Get out of here, you little pervert!" I screamed.

Tim chuckled and disappeared.

I cleaned myself up and washed my hands. We'd spent all that time trying to get his attention and now he decides to pop up while I was in the bathroom. He really was an asshole.

I swung open the bathroom door and found the shadow demon, leaning against the wall across from the bathroom, whistling.

Felix stalked toward us with a frown. "What's going on?"

I pointed to Tim. "He popped up while I was on the toilet!"

Felix looked at the demon and before I could blink, he'd grabbed it by the throat and raised him off the ground.

The demon clawed at his hand around his throat and kicked his legs in the air.

"Were you fucking spying on my wife? You must want to die." His hand tightened around the demon's throat.

Whoa, angry Felix was very scary and hot. I wanted to correct him on the wife part but thought better of it. I put my hand on his shoulder. "We kind of need him alive to ask him some questions."

Felix gave an uncharacteristic growl and dropped the demon to the floor. He then crouched down and leaned forward, whispering something to the demon I couldn't hear. It must have been disturbing because Tim crab walked away from Felix, who was now standing with a satisfied smile.

I pointed to the living room area. "In the living room, both of you."

They followed quietly, Felix sat at the table and picked up his fork to eat, eyes still angrily on Tim who was crouched on the farthest side of the couch. I sat on the opposite end closest to Felix.

"And here I was feeling sorry for you," Felix shouted, "but come to find out, you're a little perve. Are you even ten?"

Tim raised his shoulders. "Thirteen but who's counting?"

I leaned forward and thumped him on the forehead. "I am, you jerk. You're taking advantage of what little kindness I have."

"Is a teen in danger no less sympathetic?"

What teen talked like that? "Not when he spies on women in the bathroom. Is your name really Tim because you didn't show up when I tried to conjure you. Who are you really?"

Tim looked down at his feet and twisted his bony black fingers together.

Felix put his fork down with a clang. "Answer her or I'll exorcise you back to Hell."

Could he even do that? He was part angel so I wouldn't be surprised.

Tim jumped slightly at Felix's bark. "I'm Yusan and I'm technically seven hundred years old but when I was human, I was 13 when I died."

I nodded. This sounded more like the truth. "How'd you become a demon?" Really what could a teen have done that would have sent him to the underworld?

"What I said earlier was true. I was wrongly changed into a demon by a warlock. He was actually sent by my older sister so that she could take the throne in our kingdom. We were just humans, but magic was still potent in some areas. I'm not exactly a demon to be honest. I'm more like a spirit. I've been roaming the earth all this time. When I first became a spirit, I still looked like me. But slowly I began to change until I became what you see now. It sucks."

"I can imagine. Well, Yusan, if what you say is true, I'm sorry. Why'd you come to me?"

"Like I said, I'm drawn to you. You have a power that is very appealing. The spirit world is drawn to angelic and demonic power and the stronger it is, the more drawn we are."

I tilted my head toward Felix. "Drawn to him, too?"

Yusan squinted his eyes. "Not as much as you."

Huh. Why was that? I couldn't be more powerful than Felix. He was part of the Six. That made him super-powered.

Not to mention that his being half-angel trumped my half-faerie.

"I'm hoping maybe you could help me."

I scratched my head in thought. I had no clue if I could but I wasn't going to tell him that. I needed his assistance. "I can try after you tell me what you want. But first you have to help me. We need to stop these attacks in this town and you seem to know what's going on. Think you can help us? Seeing as you can talk better now. Was that whispering all an act too?"

Yusan lowered his head. "I might have over exaggerated a little for drama. But to be honest, I don't talk much so it wasn't too far off. But as to helping you, sure. Anything for you. You'll still help me too, right?"

I nodded. "Of course. Even though you are a lying jerk. So, how many of these things are here in this town?"

"A lot from what I've seen."

"So, we're outnumbered?"

He slid down on the couch from his crouch and sat properly, kicking his legs out. "For certain."

Well, that was helpful. It meant we had to watch our backs. I'm sure we weren't making any friends by calling attention to the problem.

Felix twisted in his chair to face us. "Can you let us know who in this town is one of these monsters and what are they called?"

"I don't know what they're called, and I can point you to some of them. They work all over town. There's a lot in this hotel because they usually feed on the tourists."

I sucked my teeth. "How kind of them. Should we be worried?"

Yusan tilted his head from side to side. "Not sure. You all are popular so maybe they are too scared to bother you. Of course, it probably makes you tastier."

Felix leaped to his feet, and Yusan shot up, scuttling to the farthest wall.

I bit my lower lip, there he went being all alpha again. I wondered if this was a change in him that I just took for granted as being who he was. My knowledge of Felix was short compared to Azrael so it would make sense that I didn't catch all his changes.

Felix paused, and lifted a brow as he stared at the small demon. "I'm not gonna hurt you, little perv. I just think we should grab that waiter dude from earlier before he wanders off."

I threw on some shoes and took off after Felix who was already out the door.

Of course, when we got to the restaurant, the guy was nowhere to be found. We waited for him to reappear but thirty minutes in, and he had not returned from wherever he had disappeared to. Even his coworkers claimed not to know where he was.

We went back to our room where Yusan reappeared, this time sitting at the dining table eating the rest of Felix's cinnamon bun. My food remained untouched. Yusan really had a lot of audacity.

Felix clapped his hands together and they glowed a brilliant white. "You ate my food."

Maybe I should be more concerned because this was an overreaction. "Really, Felix. You're going to try to exorcise him for eating your food. Hardly seems proportionate. You can have some of my food if you're still hungry."

Yusan dropped the fork and teleported behind me in his usual crouch.

Felix depowered his hands and scowled at Yusan. "It's the principle of the matter."

I turned to the demon. "Do you think the waiter left because he was melting? Maybe he went to kill someone to rejuvenate or something?"

Yusan threw his hands out to the side. "It is a proper guess."

"So where did he go?" Felix asked.

"Why don't you both know this? You are part demon. Can't you sense other demons and spirits?"

I rubbed my face, feeling mildly annoyed. "Clearly not as well as you. Find us a bad guy."

Yusan shrugged, obviously pleased with himself. "Well, there are so many but I can take you to one who is about to feed. I have a good sense of when the blood of an innocent is about to be spilled."

Felix slapped his forehead. "Seriously? You didn't want to lead with that? Teleport us."

Yusan looked up at me.

I shook my head, my lips twisted in annoyance. "Do it now before he kills you for real."

Felix stormed over, grabbed my hand, and I took Yusan's. We soon disappeared in a cloud of smoke.

I waved a hand in front of my face and coughed. "Is the smoke really necessary?" I asked before we reappeared outside of a small one-story house.

Yusan gave a sharp toothed grin. "It comes with the territory."

Felix wasted no time and walked forward, kicking the door open.

I leaned back in surprise. "You didn't want to have a plan or anything? You're just as bad as Faith," I mumbled, following him in.

We looked around the dark living room, which was decorated with dreary beige and brown furniture and worn carpet.

"Where are they?" Felix whispered, looking back at us.

"Oh, now you ask."

Yusan pointed to the back of the house.

Since we were standing in the living room area, I assumed he was directing us to the kitchen.

Felix took off in that direction.

I pushed out my right hand and summoned my golden sword before following behind him. Once I got to the kitchen, I quickly jumped sideways, narrowly missing being hit by a person tossed in the air and landing right outside the entrance. Felix wrestled with another man on the ground and a small, terrified child huddled in the corner near the stove. Yusan stood in front of the small girl, arms out protectively, although I didn't think she could see him. She was looking through him at the fighting.

I looked down beside me at the recently tossed person to find a woman squirming on the ground and looking very dazed.

I pointed my sword at her. "Stay down."

Her eyes darkened to full black and she hissed at me. She backflipped too quickly for my eyes to register. I charged at her with my sword, but she leaped up at the last minute and kicked me in the face with her boot.

I fell on my butt, still gripping my sword. Blood trickled down my lips from my nose and I cursed myself for being so careless before jumping back up. The woman paced slowly in front of me, sneering. Oh, she got one point on me but she wasn't about to get another. She kicked off her boots and I could now see her toenails were long, sharp, black talons. How'd she fit that in her shoes? Did they retract?

I waved her over to me. "Come on, bitch. You like to eat kids? Well, I'll make it so you can't eat a damn thing ever again."

She sniffed the air, leaning slightly in my direction and her smile grew. And by grew, I mean it was so wide, it practically split her face in half and all I could focus on were her massive teeth just like the man in the basement. She could bite a kid's whole head off with one try if she was so inclined. What in the hell kind of creature was she?

I had no time to think because she was racing towards me in a blur of light. Damn it, she was as fast as a vampire. I swung my sword out, missing her shoulder by an inch. She encircled me and I felt excruciating pain as her bear trap mouth landed in my shoulder. She ripped away flesh and muscle and then began to chew.

I was torn between agonizing pain and nausea as she proceeded to literally eat me alive. With my sword arm still good, I jumped high in the air and came down behind her, slicing into her side on the way down. That was not what I was aiming for, but it was better than nothing. She moved so fast it was hard to get a good aim.

The woman tsked. "Too slow. I'm going to enjoy eating you alive. You taste very strong."

Oh, if this bitch thought she would get another bite out of me, she was dead wrong. Time to use some fae magic.

Not wanting to drop my sword, I fought against my painful left arm and punched my fist out into the air. A swirling force of magic lifted the woman off her feet and into the nearest wall, plaster crumbling around her human-sized dent. She looked at me with wild crazed eyes and kicked her feet, struggling to move.

I stumbled forward, vaguely aware that Felix was still in battle, but I had to get rid of her first. My maimed arm hung loosely at my side. I could no longer feel it. It was numb but it wasn't the only thing going numb. My whole left side began to sag until I found myself limping toward the woman.

"What the hell is going on?"

"Paralyzing agent. Our first bite causes you to go numb. It's actually humane. That way you don't feel us eating you whole. But in your case, I wouldn't mind you feeling pain the whole time." The creature woman laughed.

I shook my head as if pushing away drowsiness and

limped on in spite of my injury. I was beginning to feel weak. Not just physically but magically. I didn't have to ask to know that this bite probably numbed powers as well, so paranormal victims couldn't use their magic to free themselves if their body stopped working. Clever design. This only meant I didn't have much time to finish her off before I became her main course.

As if sensing her own demise, the woman broke free of my weakening magic and slid backwards up to the popcorned ceiling with her taloned fingers and toes. She turned her head sideways to hiss again at me.

How did I take her down without killing her? I needed to keep her alive to get answers. This was going to be tough.

# CHAPTER 14

The sounds of a struggle behind me, threatened to take my attention. I knew if I turned away, the demon woman would pounce. I could kill her and hope Felix didn't kill his guy or I could maim her in some way.

She decided she didn't feel like waiting around for me and began to crawl across the ceiling toward Yusan and the child. Bits of plaster fell to the ground as she clamped her steel-like talons into the ceiling.

I crouched low before taking a flying leap up, my sword swinging across me before I sliced into the back of the woman's legs. They detached and fell to the floor in one clean swipe. Of course, the cut didn't come without a nice spray of blood over my face and hair. I landed on the ground and wiped the blood off my face, which I know only smeared it. A shower would definitely be needed.

The woman screamed in agony as she hung by her taloned fingers to the ceiling. A pool of blood spread under her from her dripping knees. She couldn't possibly keep hanging on with all that blood loss. She'd have to pass out soon.

Of course, I wasn't fairing much better. I crumbled to the

floor as my remaining working right leg betrayed me and went numb. "Felix!" I shouted.

I could no longer play warrior woman. I turned my head, thankful that my neck wasn't yet paralyzed and saw Felix stand up over the now dead body of the skin demon. The man, or rather the deflated body of the man, lay sagging on the ground. Felix's hands glowed white and when he looked over to me his eyes shown so brilliant, they were like tiny flashlights coming out of his head. His angel power was still so mysterious to me but I also knew it to be frightening. Angels were pretty powerful beings already, another reason I didn't like them much. For only being half-angel, Felix still had the ability to kill with just one touch. He couldn't do it much so I was surprised he would waste his gift on such low-level demons. Of course, I called them low level, but there I was, paralyzed.

Felix headed over then stopped before reaching me and looked up at the hanging woman. He grabbed her by her torn legs and tore her from the ceiling against the background of her agonizing screams. A few of her talons were left in the ceiling as she broke away and was slammed to the ground.

Geez, he was ruthless. Not that I was complaining. It was always interesting trying to reconcile the big oaf that he usually appeared to be with how hardcore he was in battle. It made sense seeing as we used to be hitmen.

He pointed to the woman, who rolled back and forth in pain. "Stay."

He hunched down in front of me, assessing my predicament.

"I can't move," I exclaimed through closed teeth. "They have some type of paralytic in their saliva."

He looked over to my shredded shoulder and hovered his hand over me. At first, I felt nothing, but soon the feeling of his cool healing magic began to spread down my shoulder and through my body.

My shoulder was fully healed but I was still working up to the movement part. However, that wouldn't stop me from getting answers. I looked over to the woman who had now stopped moving and was panting heavily on her back, her eyes unfocused. "We need to question her before she dies."

Felix glanced at her and then turned back to me. He picked me up and sat me in a chair at the kitchen table. He then went and crouched in front of the woman. "Tell us everything we want to know."

She shook her head.

Felix took out his machete hanging from his jeans pockets and stabbed it in her arm. I'd seen Felix in action before but this seemed more hardcore than I was used to. Not that I thought he was wrong but torture didn't seem like his thing. I realized that I didn't want it to be his thing. If I could move I'd take over to spare him this. "Tell us everything we want to know, or I will slice you up in small pieces and make sure you feel every bit of it."

"Damn," Yusan whispered, and the child behind him whimpered.

I suppose Felix would be frightening to a kid if in a bad mood. Which he definitely was at the moment. I felt bad for the little girl. Sigh, I really was becoming more of a bleeding heart but she was a child after all. I could only imagine her state of mind right now.

The woman stared at him with horrified eyes and then slowly nodded.

He took the knife out of her arm. "Smart lady. What are you?"

Her mouth was more human-like as she pressed her lips tightly together. She looked over to Felix's machete and then closed her eyes. "We're wraiths."

I raised an eyebrow. Huh, that was new. I didn't pretend to know about all the paranormal creatures but I'd seen a lot. Of course, I had no idea what I knew five years ago. For all I knew maybe I had come across a wraith before. I looked to Felix to see if that rang a bell to him but his brows furrowed in thought.

"What's a wraith?" He growled, seemingly annoyed that he had no idea what she was.

"We are physical spirits who use human bodies."

"Like demons," I guessed.

"Close, except we just need the human skin and wear it like our living armor," she replied in an annoyed voice.

I suppose no one was jumping up and down to be compared to a demon.

"So, we don't need to exorcise you," Felix stated, still crouched in front of her. "If we strip you of this skin, we'd see the real you?"

The woman scrunched her face in either continued pain or fear of being skinned. "Yes."

Although I was curious to see her true form, it wasn't necessary for now. "What's with eating people?"

"Once we find a body to wear, we need to feed on humans from time to time to survive and maintain our form."

I adjusted in my seat, fully mobile now. "Is that why your skin sags? When you haven't fed in a while, your body starts to deteriorate?"

She nodded.

I looked over to the small child, still cowering but less visibly frightened now that we had the situation contained. We'd need to find her family after the questioning, assuming they were still alive. "Why eat kids?"

The woman wiggled in discomfort. "They are the most powerful. Other paranormals are strong too. Once you eat them, you don't need to feed for a long time, and you gain strength."

I wondered if the mayor knew that she had such a wraith problem and that children were their main food source. If she couldn't get rid of them, it made sense that she would ban children from coming here to protect them. Of course, it didn't excuse her for letting other tourists like us come and get snacked upon. "How many are you? Do you live in town?"

"We are many and some do," the woman croaked out, closing her eyes. She was sweating and looking very pale.

She wasn't going to last much longer. "Does the mayor know?"

The woman coughed and a spray of blood left her mouth. "She knows of issues but not of the wraiths."

I snorted in annoyance. "So, she at least suspected maybe there was a serial killer on the loose and said nothing."

Felix grumbled something unintelligible and then stood up. Guess he wasn't so happy that his new girlfriend wasn't so innocent. Ok, I sounded really jealous there. It's probably because I was. "I imagine her talking about skin-stealing monsters invading her town would be bad for business. Maybe she thinks we can help."

I huffed, twisting my lips. "Then she should have said something. Don't make excuses for her. She has to know some of her own people are wraiths. This problem isn't new."

This also explained why there were no old people. If you were going to take a skin, I guessed that a more youthful skin was preferred.

This also explained why people were dressed so oddly. The wraiths could be of various ages just holding on to what fashion in their prime looked like.

We weren't geniuses. Why had no one done something about this problem? We'd seen so much in just a few days. Either killings were few and far between and had just happened to increase upon our arrival, or the people here were just too incompetent to handle the issue. Maybe it was both.

Felix glanced back at me. "Any other questions to ask?"

I looked up at the ceiling in thought before looking back down. "Do you have a den or a place where you all liv—Oh, shit, she's dead," I said, grimacing at her quickly deflating body.

Felix swore. "And we didn't even get to see what she really looked like."

Yusan cleared his throat. "What are we doing about the crying kid behind me?"

I got up. Between us, I probably looked the least scary. However, when I walked closer, the girl huddled even tighter to herself. "I won't hurt you, little girl," I said in as sweet a voice as I could muster.

"You're drenched in blood," Yusan cracked. "I don't think she believes you."

I looked down at myself. He did have a point. I waved a hand over my body and did a little Cinderella magic as I called it and cleaned myself up so that I was sparkling and new again. I then smiled at her and offered my hand. "Come on, honey. Let's find your family."

~

*U*nsurprisingly, the girl's parents had been slaughtered. Once we got her to her house, located in a small town not far from us, all that was left of her parents were their skinless dead bodies. I asked if the wraiths we killed earlier were wearing her parents, for lack of a better word, but thankfully they were not. The girl would have enough trauma for a lifetime, glad there was one less thing to add to it. Of course, now I had to figure out who was walking around wearing her parents. I grabbed a photo of the parents to take with me. If I saw anyone that looked like them walking around, I'd know they were wraiths.

We left the girl with a kind neighbor whom she seemed to trust and had no evil aura around them. Once we got back to the hotel, Felix went to fill in Azrael and Faith, and I went back to my room for a proper cleaning. My magic as a half-fae was diluted and only allowed me a show of looking brand spanking new. I was still funky under the façade.

I went to the bedroom and pulled out clothes from my suitcase, still refusing to unpack and get too comfortable. As I bent over my clothes, the hairs on the back of my neck stood to attention.

What now? Couldn't a girl get a proper wash before she started something new? If this was Yusan again, popping up unannounced, I was going to have Azrael exorcise him.

I sighed, turned and sucked in a breath.

Squiggly red lines floated in the air in front of me, taking shape to make what I could only assume were words.

Well, this was new.

I waited patiently as the lines quickly came together to form sentences.

*I request a meeting with you. Tonight, at midnight. A portal will appear at that time for you to enter. Only you will be able to pass. You will not be harmed.*
*King Herrod*

The words then started to melt, dripping like blood to the carpet but disappearing before they hit the floor.

One of the most powerful demon kings wanted to meet with me. And I had no idea why. Oh, shit.

# CHAPTER 15

"*I*'m going with you," Felix stated, his arms crossed in resolution as he sat back on our couch.

Azrael, who was currently pacing back and forth in the living area of our hotel room, paused. "You won't get through the portal. Herrod wants only her and if you try, you could get killed or maimed. Don't test him. My bigger question is why would he want to even meet with you?" Azrael gave me accusatory eyes. "Do you know him?"

I sat down at the dining room table and narrowed my eyes at the angel. "No. I think I would have told you if I was friends with another demon King. I hadn't even met him when I was with Alister. The first time I met the guy was in the soulmate battle."

Faith twisted her lips, looking slightly doubtful. "Right, when he just let you live for no reason."

I shrugged. I didn't care if she believed me. I knew the truth. "Yes, that's what happened. He knew my mother. Maybe nostalgia kept me alive. We couldn't really have a deep conversation at that time."

"So, he waits over two months to follow up?"

"Maybe he's busy. Look, why do any of you even care? I

don't have any secrets to give away. I want to go see what he wants. If you think I'll be tainted after seeing him, I won't come back to Silver Spring." I wrinkled my nose when I spoke. They already thought I was a bad influence so what did this matter? I was done trying to look good for them.

Felix uncrossed his arms and looked over at me with uncharacteristically stern eyes. "I don't want that."

Azrael shook their head, running a hand through their hair in agitation. "We spent all this time trying to keep you from your demon side, only for you to keep walking right into Hell."

I chuckled. "Okay, you spent all this time keeping Felix from his demon side. I've been there the whole time. I was engaged to a freaking demon King. And look, I made it out okay. I'm not eating kids and flaying people alive."

Azrael tilted their head from side to side with a deep frown. "Fair point. Fine go, report back."

Clearly, this angel thought they were my boss. "If there is anything to share with you, I will." I got up, done with the conversation. "I'm going to go take a nap before my meeting. You guys can go talk to the incompetent mayor about her wraith pack without me."

The others rose as well. Faith patted me on the shoulder before heading to the door. "Be careful."

I raised my brows in surprise. "Aww, you care about me?"

Faith scrunched her face. "Uh, no. I just know if something happens to you that big oaf on the couch will be destroyed and we can't have that."

I gave her a squinty eyed smile. "I'm still going to take that as you caring about me."

I tried to pretend I wasn't worried about seeing a demon King but I was. I never took demons for granted, especially the high-ranking ones. I had no idea what Herrod wanted from me but I was really hoping I wasn't walking into some kind of trap. I could have enemies I didn't even know about.

When you didn't remember your past, you kind of open yourself up to not knowing what was really dangerous out there.

~

*J*ust as the red message stated, a portal opened up in my bedroom exactly at midnight. A large circle giving way to smoky blackness faced the foot of my bed.

Felix coughed behind me and I turned to him. His arms were open wide and he waved his hands back. "I need a hug before you go."

I shook my head and walked to him. "I'm coming back," I said into his chest and he embraced me in a breath-stealing hug. I didn't mind it. Any hug from him was welcomed even if I didn't let him know that.

"I know, I'll be waiting here. If you aren't back in an hour, I might do something stupid like rip open a portal into Hell. I'm not sure; let's not find out."

I slowly pulled away from him. I really didn't want to, he felt so comforting. "Well, we don't want that. So, I'll make sure I'm back."

I turned to the portal and headed through, waving a hand behind me. As soon as I stepped through, the portal snapped closed behind me. The cold, empty darkness soon gave way to what appeared to be a study. I faced a wall of books, behind me was a door, to my left was a desk and chair, and to my right were lounge chairs, a couch and a coffee table facing wall length windows overlooking an expansive, lush green lawn. In one section of the lawn were several rows of purple flowers that looked almost like morning glories. I was sure this place had to be a mansion; the grounds seemed so expansive.

Many demon higher-ups lived in the underworld, others

lived on earth with a foothold in the underworld where one could easily pass through the realms without even noticing, like Nadia. I assumed this was the same, otherwise we'd be shrouded in the darkness of the underworld, not over-looking a bright sunny day.

I plopped down on the leather couch facing the windows and waited. Minutes later, the door opened behind me and I remained seated as Herrod appeared and took a seat in a matching leather chair.

He looked less grand than last time without his crown and armor. However, he was still impressively dressed in a blue suede suit and crisp white button down. I felt a little underdressed in my black jeans and white short sleeved shirt.

"So glad you decided to come," Herrod stated. He leaned forward and waved his hand over the coffee table. A bottle of brown liquid and two glasses appeared. "Are you a whiskey woman?"

I was an any type of liquor woman, but he didn't need to know that. I nodded, and he poured me a glass and passed it to me before pouring his own.

"This one is a good tasting whiskey. It goes down much easier than many others, with a tinge of sweetness." He took a sniff before sipping.

I'd have to take his word for it. I took a sniff as well, wanting to appear sophisticated.

Herrod sat back, crossing an ankle over his knee and resting his whiskey glass on his thigh. "So, I'm sure you are wondering why I asked you to meet with me. I wanted to talk to you some time ago, but life became busy."

I nodded slowly. "Well, torturing souls will take up your time."

He gave a slight chuckle, and then his eyes became dark as he looked over at his expansive lawn. "Do you know that I used to be a slave on this very land so many years ago?"

I raised my brows in surprise. I couldn't imagine him ever

being human, let alone a slave. He seemed so powerful. Of course, many demons, most demons in fact, began as humans. Through various reasons, punishment or trickery, like Yusan, they became demons. Only the ancient ones, closer to the time of arch angels, were originally demons.

Now this didn't mean that Herrod was not powerful. He was a King, after all. For angels and demons, age only played part of a role in power level. Herrod had grown strength in other ways. Possibly soul collecting or even consuming other demons. Rarely, demons could grow strength from belief and faithful followers. It's what helped Lucifer become all-powerful in the underworld. I didn't know much about Herrod or his rise in power, but I was very open to learn and maybe get some tips myself.

Herrod continued looking out of the window. "I worked these fields my whole adult life. Before that, I was royalty back in our motherland. I was beaten, maimed, had my family torn from me, and called everything but the name I was born with."

My mind was a buzz with questions. I was shocked yet excited at the same time. What he had lived through and endured made him much more complex than I imagined. "How did you become a demon?"

He gave me a slight wistful smile before taking a sip of his whiskey. "I made a deal with a devil. I'd collect souls in exchange for becoming immortal and protecting my people. And that's what I did. For hundreds of years. I started by stealing any soul I could but then I became more purposeful."

He snapped his fingers and soon the sunny field of green and purple flowers became a black skied nightmare. People hung from crosses or by the neck on trees, spanning the entire field. I squinted my eyes and saw some of the faces and bodies of the men and women on the crosses. They were badly beaten and bloodied. Some had their mouths sewn shut, others were eyeless. Still others were missing limbs. In between the victims were several hellhounds barking and gnawing at their bodies. Every so often, balls of fire would shoot down from the sky and land on a victim, burning them alive. I could hear the piercing screams from the people all the way from our location.

My body ran cold with fear.

Herrod's eyes were closed. He smiled and shook his head slightly as if listening to a masterful classic melody.

Well, he was a demon. I supposed screams of tortured souls was like music to him. It was all nightmares to me.

"Who are all those people?" I whispered, fear gripping my vocal cords.

He opened his eyes and they seemed almost pleasant. Which made him all the more scary. "That is but a fraction of the souls I have collected. But those are my favorites. The souls of those who have murdered and harmed the innocent. Slave traders, owners, and hunters. Klansmen and other racists who have killed, maimed, and raped our people. Not every soul out there was one I captured, but the evil will always come to the underworld. We then bargain, trade or bid on such souls. Most know to send those types of souls to me, and I will pay or trade well for them. I don't just relegate it to those from this country either. There is racial oppression and violence all over the world. And it has kept me plenty fed."

I gave a hard gulp. I had no doubt the world gave him enough power to thrive. As an Unseelie fae, I found his cause useful and noble. I only really knew the Unseelie fae and we were no fans of humans. Part of that was for the very reason Herrod hated many of them.

Still, a field full of evil people was less appealing than the flowers. This was probably why I really rejected the demon part of me. The Unseelie were often referred to as evil fae but we weren't. Okay, many of us were but many of us just didn't like humans. Some more so than others. Some for good reason, some for no reason. I tended to just keep my distance from them. This is what pissed me off so much about Felix's friends not understanding me. I struggled so hard against any evil in me. Meanwhile, Azrael feared Felix was letting it in but it was through no effort on my part. I was not the bad influence they believed. I never was.

I looked down at my whiskey, thinking of my next question. I wanted to keep Herrod talking. I felt a burning need to know and understand him. I wasn't sure I'd be able to tap into such power again, even if it was terrifying. "What you're doing seems like a necessary evil to me. Literally. Is that how you grew your strength?" I looked up at him and took a sip of the slightly sweet liquid.

Herrod tilted his head back, his dark eyes were filled with an intimidating intelligence that made me uncomfortable. I couldn't figure him out or understand his temperament. For all I knew he was reading my mind. Heck, he could be controlling my mind. The slight smile on his lips didn't help matters. "That was a good part of it. The other part was, my believers."

I scrunched my eyes in confusion. I'd never heard of a cult or group that worshipped Herrod.

Herrod looked back to his lawn and this time it was pleasant and bright again with no hanging bodies. "Do you know what those purple flowers are called?"

I shook my head. "Botany isn't my specialty, sorry."

"Ipomea purga. Part of the morning glory family. Many also call them High John the Conqueror. That is the name I often went by to my followers."

I gasped in spite of myself and then closed my mouth with an audible click. I'd heard that name before, I was sure of it. Of course, without my memories I couldn't place it exactly, but it felt important.

Herrod nodded as if understanding my predicament. "I am not a religion. I'm not a deity. I have no worshipers.

However, I am a folklore to many. My name has given strength to our people for years. I am a protector of our Black brothers and sisters in this country. There are stories and songs about me. It has kept me strong. And even as times changed and I became less known, I was still well known in the hoodoo community." He pointed slightly to the flowers. "Many in the magic community use the root of those flowers to make amulets and spells. Others use it to summon me. A good portion of my business is through the use of humans and the paranormal summoning me or using the flowers for magic."

"That's impressive," I replied, because it really was. He was able to bring a long-forgotten folklore into the present so that he could maintain his strength.

His eyes became gentle.

I still found that unnerving because he was anything but. Providing a false sense of comfort was the easiest way to catch your prey off guard.

"I'll give you a list of resources about me you might find entertaining to read," he offered.

"Thanks, I appreciate it." I'd let him believe I was falling for his kindness until I got some answers, but I was so tense I could snap any moment.

"You'd think with the world changing to one mostly of magic that my brand of punishment would no longer be needed but hatred continues even if it's less so because of race. Although that is still very much present."

"So, you take the souls of more than just people who have wronged Black people now?"

He nodded. "I'd like to think I am the weapon of the oppressed. I am the karma set upon those who have harmed the marginalized. My hands are fine dripping in blood." He grinned again, showing his pearly whites and once again I was reminded that folklore legend or not, he was still evil incarnate of a degree I truly couldn't comprehend. "Does what I say disturb you?"

I shook my head swiftly. "No."

"You lived with a demon so I suppose you wouldn't mind."

I leaned back slightly. Did he really know about me? "You knew that?"

"I know many things about you, Francesca."

I suppose I shouldn't be surprised now.

He gave me a knowing grin. "Francesca, do you know who you are? I heard you lost your memory."

I sighed. "No. The angels have tried to return my memories but haven't had any success."

He gave a snort and a short shake of the head. "Not surprising. Your memories were already tampered with to keep you from your kind."

"Wait, so you know about my past and my lineage?"

"I know everything about you, and I think it's time you did too."

# CHAPTER 16

*J* finished off the last of my whiskey and put the empty glass on the coffee table.

Herrod eyed the glass. "Need a refill?"

I shook my head. "No, thanks. I need to remain sober. Why do you even care if I know the truth about myself? That's like being nice and let's face it, that isn't a demon's specialty."

"Kindness is relative."

I scratched my head. "Is it though?"

"Relative? Yes. Especially when the relative is my daughter."

Was he? Was he saying what I think he was saying? I looked back down at my empty glass and reached for it with shaky hands. "I think I *will* need another drink."

Herrod reached over and poured me another glass. A slightly heavier amount this time. "You look just like her, you know. Your mother, Dalia. It's like she cloned herself. But still, you are definitely mine as well. You have the same temperament. Your mother was always so graceful and reserved. But you were a wildfire. Just like me." He furrowed his brows and looked away. "I wish that I would have been there for you. I'm afraid I've never had the chance to truly be the father that I wanted to be."

"You didn't raise me?" I asked before taking a shaky sip. Yes, I knew I had a parent for a demon. I didn't know that demon would be a King of the Underworld who was also an African American folklore hero. Couple that with a mother that was a fae Queen and I was starting to feel like a bit of a disappointment in my current homeless, jobless status.

Herrod shook his head. "Your mother and I were in love but we weren't married. In my role I couldn't, I can't be in love. It's a liability. And yet, she found a way to weaken my heart and I'm grateful for it."

"I was told I lived in the fae court. They allowed demons? She was a Queen."

Herrod sat back. "Yes, she was and no they did not allow demons. Our love affair was a secret. She even went on to marry a man who would take the throne as the King. Although she was the real power. All queens are in her court. But even then, we never stopped seeing each other in secret. And then one day our secret became a baby. You."

He gave me a smile that struck me as tender.

If he was lying, he was a darn good actor. Then again, most demons were. "I assume her family wasn't too happy about her being pregnant by another man."

His eyes cooled as he sat back. "They didn't know you weren't the King's…at first. You lived many years in the court and then one day an enemy of your mother's spread the truth. Even though her husband married into the royal family, no one was going to accept a fae Queen who'd allowed herself to get pregnant by a demon. The family tried to deny the rumors, but even the King began to believe them and then he and his cohorts began a campaign to get rid of you and your mother." A tightness grew in his eyes at the

175

memory and he gazed back out of the window. "You speak of demons being unkind, but the Unseelie fae, they are ruthless. No one protected your mother, not even her own kin. Eventually, she was forced to leave with you. That is when you entered the human world."

I thought about the family I could not recall. Had my own grandparents and aunts and uncles really run us off because they couldn't stand that I was half-demon? Had my mother given it all up to keep me? So Marcus had to have known me from before but not while I was in the human world. "Do you know a fae by the name of Marcus?"

He nodded. "Vaguely. He was from another royal family that was close to yours. You spoke of him often when we were together. I imagine you had a crush on him."

I twisted my lips. That wasn't surprising knowledge, but I did learn that he was not my brother. Perhaps he wasn't a threat to me. "When we came to the human realm did you join us?" I already knew the answer. If he had been around, he wouldn't be popping up only now to talk to me.

He looked over to me with pained eyes. "I'm sorry, my daughter. I could not. Our enemies were too powerful. It was safer for us to stay apart. Safer for you not to remember your past life or know who I was."

I let out a breath and rubbed my forehead, feeling suddenly tired. Perhaps it was the whiskey or maybe I didn't nap long enough, but my mind was still working just fine. "You bespelled me to make me forget that I was fae and your daughter?"

"Your mother did. She thought it would make things easier for you. You were twelve or thirteen going from living in a grand kingdom to a tiny two-bedroom apartment in the city. You would not have been happy at such a downgrade. But with a fresh slate, you were able to start anew. She was able to find love or something like it and he adopted you." He spat out the last sentence as if it tasted awful and I guessed it did. He couldn't be with the woman he loved and had to stand by while she married not once but twice.

"How did she die?"

Herrod rocked his glass slightly in a contemplative mode. "When the paranormal came back to the human world, so did our enemies. She was murdered. That was not long after the paranormal event."

I closed my eyes and rubbed my lids. I had suspected that my mother was gone but it still hurt to hear it be verified. Assuming, of course, that he could be trusted. "Why didn't you show up then, after she died?"

"My daughter, the danger was still there for you. I arranged things so that you could go back to the fae world. Just not to your family. They weren't safe."

That would explain how I came up working for Misandre. I wasn't sure he was much help in that department but I guess he could get a point for effort. "Am I still a danger now?"

At this, he smiled again, sitting back. "No, you are a warrior. You require no protection. Seeing you on that battlefield was quite impressive." I could already see his chest swell with pride.

"Why didn't you tell me then that I was your daughter?"

"At the time, I was not ready to admit to you the truth."

I twisted my lips in disbelief. That answer seemed lame to me. Only a couple months had passed and now he had an epiphany or something? Lies. "You thought I was going to die in battle and you didn't want to get attached."

Herrod chuckled. "There's my smart girl. The thought was fair, no? The odds weren't in your favor. At least not in the beginning."

I cocked a brow. Was he saying what I think he was saying? Did we have more allies than we thought? "Are you saying you helped us defeat the soulmates?"

"No, the defeat of the soulmates was all the work of those

177

children, Amina and Phillip. Such a waste we had to fight our own." He gave a displeased, wistful look as he stared back down at his whiskey.

He must have been thinking about what also ran through my mind. Both Amina and Phillip were Black, and so was one of the original soulmates we fought, Gedeyon. If I believed Herrod regarding his earlier goals, a battle between people of the African diaspora would not have been his preference. That only made it odder that he'd joined the battle in the first place.

"So, you helped just me out there on the battlefield?"

He gave a slight shrug which I took as a yes.

"Why'd you even join that fight to begin with?"

He sighed and tilted his head back, looking at the ceiling as he seemingly searched for the right words. "Gedeyon had many negatives going for him, but he also had some good ideas. He was very adamant about stopping continued injustices. It was appealing to me to see two people of color, an African and an Indian, essentially rule the world. It felt just."

I rolled my eyes. He was reaching if he thought Gedeyon and Rima had been going to heal the world of racial oppression. They had only been in it for themselves. "Well, sorry we took away your would-be civil rights icons," I said, dryly.

He snorted and a part of me was pleased that I made him laugh a little. It certainly made things less tense.

I couldn't forget that I was sitting in some mysterious location with a demon King. "So, *dad*, tell me the real reason why you struggled these past months with contacting me?"

His smiled relaxed and he took another sip of his drink before speaking. "I have lived most of my days since my mortal death as something different. I adopted a new name that signified my change. Being a father was too reminiscent of my old life. I no longer could afford that luxury."

"So then why tell me now?"

"Because I see you wasting your life. You are meant for greatness, only now I see you working for the angels like some sort of lackey." Darkness filled his eyes. "Never trust the angels."

"Says the demon." How the hell did he even know what I'd been doing? My mind went to Yusan. What if that little demon spirit was actually a spying flunky for Herrod?

He ignored my remark and continued. "I've been following you for a while now, especially since magic returned. You are bigger than what the angels would have you be."

"They are helping me get my memories."

"At a price."

"Isn't everything?" I shrugged. What was his deal? Right now, my plan for my future was all I had going. Did he want me to leave the others and rule in the underworld with him? "What do you want me to do? Stay here and have you make up for lost time?"

He gave a slight smile and sat back. "No."

I had to admit. That one word stung a bit. But, as I always did, I brushed aside any feelings. "Well, what do you want me to do? Marry Felix and be a housewife?"

His eyes darkened again. "I would hope not."

Well, that was an interesting reaction. As weird as the guy was, Felix was very likable. What the hell had Felix done to him? "Care to elaborate? Yes, he's half-angel, but he's also part demon. So, you should like him."

"Daughter, you must know that demons aren't all friends. In fact, the words don't go together. Your Felix has an interesting family history. One you probably want to keep clear of. Even if he may not know it himself." He took another sip of his whiskey.

Well, that was cryptic as hell.

"Francesca, I want you to take your rightful place with the

fae. I'm going to work on a way to return your memories. If you are to really be protected from our—well my, enemies, you will need an army behind you. Your mother's court can give you that."

"You think my big brother's going to give me the throne?"

"No, but I can help you with that. Stay here with me. We will come up with a plan. I'll work on getting your memories back."

Felix's face popped up in my mind. I could see him now pacing back and forth in our hotel room, waiting for me to return.

I had to admit, I wasn't okay with leaving him behind. Even when I'd stayed with Nadia, I'd still been comforted with the notion that I could go see him whenever I wanted. I knew that if I stayed with Herrod, he would probably make it very difficult for me to come and go as I pleased. Especially if it was to see Felix. And this was all assuming I even trusted this guy. I didn't know for certain that he was my father. Sure, there was a bit of resemblance but that didn't mean anything. For all I knew he was the enemy. I was in no mood to be manipulated by another demon.

Also, I kind of wanted to see this mission through. I was invested now. Being a hero wasn't my thing but something rubbed me the wrong way about monsters that liked to chomp on kids. Even I had a limit on how much I could ignore.

I was going back. If this guy really was my dad and he really cared about me, then what was a few more days for him to wait until I stopped those predators from hurting more kids. I stood up. "Sorry, Herrod. I've got to go do a good deed to balance my energy and all that. Sorry to disappoint you. We can meet again. You have a number I can call?"

Herrod stood up as well. He dug into his jacket pocket and pulled out what looked like a shiny, golden credit card. He passed it to me.

All that I saw was an old looking symbol. It looked close to Japanese lettering except I knew that it wasn't.

Herrod pointed to it. "Draw that symbol and you'll get my attention. I would give you a flower from the field but it takes much longer to get my attention with those. This is quickest."

I was slightly surprised he was being so understanding. I thought he would try to stop me but he seemed unbothered. "You're okay with me leaving?"

He gave a slight nod. "You'll be back."

"So confident."

"You are ambitious. And you will find that fighting for Misandre's unimpressive court is not worthy of your time. You'll need to get all the aid you can find. I have that to give. In the meantime, if you must mingle with the angels, be careful of that town."

"You know about those demons?"

He cocked a brow, giving me a look that said 'obviously.' "Wraiths are more than you think. Powerful ones will also manipulate your mind. Have you believing all is well while they are eating you alive."

"And here I thought that was what the paralytic was for."

"Yes, but if they want aid in getting more victims, they can manipulate a person to doing their bidding. Never let your guard down around them." He snapped his fingers, and a portal appeared behind me.

I headed to the portal, walking backwards. "Thanks for the chat. It was very informative. I'll be back for sure."

I turned to cross into the portal.

Herrod called my name. "You should know, that that town is well aware of their wraith problem. So, you should ask, why have they not dealt with it?"

I gave him a curt nod before crossing over. He had a good point. That floosy mayor had to have known what she was dealing with when we found the skin that first night and definitely the night Faith and I killed that skinwalker. Yet, she acted surprised and confused. What was with the act?

It seemed I learned more from this visit than I anticipated. I would definitely be back and I expected more answers.

# CHAPTER 17

*F*elix wrapped me in a bear hug so tight I almost passed out. I wiggled in his arms. "Can't breathe," I said into his shoulder.

He put me down, gently and looked me over with concerned eyes.

"I'm fine," I grumbled but a little pleased at the attention. Darn, this man made himself too likable.

"What'd he want?"

I yawned and flopped down on my bed. I gave him a quick recap, omitting the part where Herrod admitted he was my dad. Instead, I stated that he used to know my parents and made a promise to look out for me. I felt like crap lying to Felix but there was a nagging feeling in my gut that said telling my true identity was not a wise decision. At least not yet. Felix was a trustworthy guy but he was acting a little off and on lately and I didn't trust Azrael fully. They already hated me because I was half-demon. If they found out I was the child of a demon King, well, who knew what they would try to do. I wanted to be in a better place before I told them the truth.

I kicked my shoes off and unbuttoned my jeans, far from

concerned about flashing Felix because I already knew what he would do.

Except he didn't turn around.

I paused and raised my brows. "Turn around, you perv."

He chuckled, slowly turning and heading to his bed. "You can't blame me. When a woman gets undressed in front of me with no warning, what do you expect?"

"I expect you to turn like you always do." I kicked my jeans off and grabbed some sleeper shorts I'd left on the bed, quickly putting them on while giving Felix's back the stink eye. He really was changing.

"By the way, we're paying a visit to the mayor tomorrow," I said, laying my head on my pillow.

Felix turned slightly to me. "Why?"

"Because she knows more than she's letting on. She's got an infestation of wraith and she's not dealing with it. That puts her people in danger and all the foolish tourist who come to this town. The kid disclaimer isn't enough, especially when these things go after paranormals as well. I want to know what her deal is. No more games."

~

The following day we reconnected with Azrael and Faith over breakfast in their room. I gave them the abridged version of my meeting with Herrod, also leaving out the lineage part. Azrael gave me a look of pure suspicion but I ignored the angel. I really didn't owe Azrael or any of those tarnished halo wearing know-it-alls anything. They'd manipulated me and withheld my truth from me. I trusted the angels only as far as I could throw them. Which in reality was pretty far since I was a super strong faerie but that wasn't the point!

As I got up to head to the mayor, Azrael stood as well, still giving me distrustful eyes. "You will tell us everything you discussed later, right." The angel said this more than asked which only pissed me off.

I rolled my eyes and walked to the door. "I'll tell you to mind your own business."

Azrael growled and I heard them loudly say to the others. "We don't even know if we can trust her. He could have manipulated her mind while she was with him."

I paused at the door and glared back at them, ready to give Azrael a verbal beat down.

Felix raised a hand and headed my way. "I trust her. We don't need to keep talking about this." He gave me a wink and opened the door for me.

I stepped back, a little impressed—okay turned on, by his cocky assuredness. I don't know. Maybe I kind of liked this new, edgy Felix.

We decided to walk to the mayor's office since it wasn't that far and it was nice out. Azrael kept giving me the stink eye but Faith seemed unbothered, maybe she was starting to take a liking to me. Maybe she didn't care. It was probably the last option.

Fatih walked up to Felix's side and glanced at us with concerned eyes. "So, what's the plan? We tell her she's got a wraith problem and bounce? I mean, we're sticking around to help clear them out. Find the nest. We should come with a plan. Let her know her town police force is trash."

I nodded waving my hand dismissively. "All that sounds good. Let's do that."

Faith narrowed her eyes. "Okay, you are incredibly unhelpful. I'm asking, how do we sus out a wraith nest? We need to come looking like experts not some new and diverse Scooby-Doo and the gang."

I snorted. The image of the four of us creeping around trying to solve a supernatural mystery popped in my head. If only we had our Scooby. Well, no, we had Yusan. That made me cackle harder. "I'm fine with that."

Faith twisted her lips in annoyance. "Okay, woman, well I am not. We have a reputation to keep up. Felix and I are part of the Six. People expect big things from us and if we look all disorganized, then that could bring down the good that Lisa, Charles and Erik are doing. It could ruin Amina and Phillip's legacy."

Felix frowned and looked down at her with quizzical eyes. "Since when do you care what others think?" He looked over to Azrael. "This your doing?"

The angel gave a nonchalant shrug. "She isn't wrong."

This *was* their doing.

Faith stopped walking and placed a hand on her chest, her face fixed in shocked. "How about maybe I care about doing this right. I've grown over the past year. I'm not just a bartender. I'm a bartender with a passion for justice."

We all stopped walking as well and looked at her with disbelieving eyes. I was still getting to know Faith and although I wouldn't call her cold-hearted, she certainly wasn't a bleeding heart either. I always figured she was a do-gooder because of Felix. Maybe I was wrong. Could she really be some justice warrior inside and all her fighting with the Six had just uncovered it?

She relaxed her face upon seeing our expressions and began to walk again. "You guys are assholes."

I chuckled and began to walk again as she stormed past me.

Azrael caught up to her. "Perhaps we can tell them for now that we will help them find the nest. We certainly are better equipped to do so."

We definitely were better fighters. So far, I was under-whelmed by the weirdos in town.

My thoughts were disrupted as I slammed into Felix's back. He didn't seem to notice as he stood still, looking across the street.

I followed his gaze but nothing was there except for a row of shops on the street and a few people walking about.

"What is it?"

He kept looking, a frown etched on his face. "I thought I saw...myself."

I looked around. Crap, one doppelganger was bad enough but we really didn't need two to distract us. "Where?"

"He disappeared. He was there one moment waving at me with a dumb, dopey look on his face and then he faded away." He glanced back at me. "You think it's evil if it looks friendly?"

Before I could answer, Azrael spoke up. "Yes. And your definition of friendly needs to be examined. The doppelganger is only giving you what he thinks you are. It is a pale imitation. It doesn't know how to be its own being."

Felix pushed his hair back from his face. "So, I look that dumb?"

I smiled and patted him on the shoulder. "No. Seriously, why are these face stealers popping up now? And in this town? I bet you the fearful mayor knows." I poked Felix in the back to get him moving and he immediately started walking again.

When I glanced back there, I was smiling and waving back at me in the same spot Felix's doppelganger had supposedly been. I stumbled over a bump in the sidewalk and fell into Felix's back again.

He turned as I righted myself again and he lifted his upper lip as I assumed he caught my evil twin across the street. He moved towards the street to approach it.

"Ignore it for now!" Azrael called back as they continued to walk. "It's a waste of time to approach it now. It's trying to distract you."

How did the angel know? Azrael didn't seem to be an expert before, now we were being told to ignore evil beings out to kill us and take our places? Easy for the angel to say.

Once again, I was reminded that I couldn't trust the angels. Just like my dear, old, alleged dad said.

Either I was going to have to use some violence to get these angels to tell me the truth or chuck it all and go to Herrod. Assuming I could really trust anything he was saying, he seemed pretty open to telling me what I wanted to know. Mostly.

When we got to the mayor's office with no more incidents, we were told to wait in the lobby as she was in a meeting.

I slouched in my seat. "Like she has real work to do."

"Actually, I do. And now I'm free," came a tight, female voice from behind me.

I turned to find Mayor Yasmine coldly staring at me with an arched brow and hands on her full hips.

I shrugged. She wasn't going to scare me with her principal glare like I was kid getting caught talking about her.

She tilted her head to the door behind her. "Come into my office, all of you."

We gathered in her office, Faith and I sitting in two leather chairs in front of her desk as she perched on it, starring down at us. "How can I help you?"

Azrael spoke first, back turned to us as they studied books on Yasmine's bookcase near the left of the room. "Do you know you have a wraith problem?"

I sat forward. We needed to put it all out there. "And doppelgangers."

Yasmine looked at all of us with unperturbed eyes. "Yes, well not doppelgangers."

I shook my head quickly, annoyed with her seemingly unshocked response. "And you didn't want to tell us?"

She narrowed her eyes as she looked down at me. "And why would I?"

I grabbed my chin and looked up at the ceiling. What was this woman's angle? Earlier she seemed all innocent damsel in distress. Now she was a cold smart-aleck. "Uh, because we are guest here and it's dangerous."

She huffed with an amused look. "Everywhere is dangerous. Even before the world changed, does a city with high crime advertise that in their tourist promotions?" She spread her hands out in front of her body. "Come to our town, you just might get shot. No. No one does that. And when you encounter crime, we wouldn't tell you about the details of the crime problem here. You are right, you are a guest here. Not the police come to investigate. Although, maybe that is what you're here for and you just haven't told me, yet."

I studied her as she looked around at the four of us with expectant eyes. She had been playing us all along. She knew we were here to find out what was up with this town. The question then was, why did she hide it? What would she have to gain by not working with us to solve her supernatural crime problem?

Azrael turned around, hands behind their back as they stood erect. The angel's face remained neutral. "I take it you know the truth of why we're here? Why hide that?"

It was like he'd read my mind. Wait, could angels read minds?

Yasmine smiled. "Because we don't need your help. Things are just fine here."

Either she was crazy or she wanted her town full of wraiths.

"You're a wraith, aren't you?" Azrael demanded, taking a step forward.

Damn it, he kept taking the words out of my mouth. Although, at this point, it was pretty obvious.

I jumped up, not waiting for Yasmine to respond. There wasn't a need to, she was still smiling, which seemed like a very inappropriate reaction to Azrael's question. And if she was so calm about wraiths in her town, that got me to wondering if maybe the nest was actually the town. "You're all wraiths, aren't you? That's why you want tourist to come here? Easy prey."

Yasmine raised her shoulders and threw her hands out to the side. "Mystery solved. Aren't you so smart?"

"Why didn't you eat the other angels?"

"In due time. They're so happy to be here, though and they can bring us more to eat."

"Also your doing."

I heard Felix swear behind me. "Is that why you offered to let us stay longer? Wanted more time to get in our heads and make us pliable?"

She pointed at him, affirming his guess. "Well, you are tough nuts to crack. Although I wasn't going to eat *you*." She batted her eyelashes at him. "I know, I know, you must think us monsters, but what choice do we have to survive? We didn't ask to be this way. Without bodies, we can't live."

I chuckled before conjuring my sword. "Don't play the victim. No one just became a wraith when the event happened. You guys were demons and spirits who took advantage of magic returning and found a way to take skins and live again."

Yasmine glared at me crossed her arms. "You know everything, it seems."

I pointed my sword at her. "I know enough. This ends now."

Felix jumped in front of me before I could bring my sword down.

I looked up at him in shock. "Are you serious right now?"

He turned from me and eyed Yasmine who was looking up at him like he was her hero. "Is this really the nest? Everyone who lives here is a wraith?"

She grinned again, this time showing razor-sharp teeth. "Yes. Do you want to join us?"

"Fuck no. I just want to make sure that everyone we kill is actually a wraith."

She hissed and in one quick motion jumped in the air and landed behind her large oak desk. "If you think you're going to get out of here alive, you are mistaken. This town is now warded, you won't even be able to teleport out. I assumed after your most recent killing that you would be on to us. The town is on alert about you and behind that door is a lobby full of my people ready to kill you on my orders."

Faith, who had already stood up, banged her fists together, her tattoos glowing and powering her up. "We have no problem with fighting our way out of here. You wraiths aren't that hard to beat."

I mean, they were a little hard but now wasn't the time to argue. They clearly wanted to fight but we had no plan or backup. We needed to get the hell out of here.

Yasmine's smile grew, practically splitting her face in half in a horrific mask like the others. Her eyes went from brown to green, her pupils narrowing similar to a snake's. Now this was different. She pulled at her hair and it slid off. A wig. As she rolled her shoulders back, her skin faded and changed into a brick red. Cracks in her skin formed, turning scaly like a lizard.

Well, she was clearly no spirit. "You're a demon. And if I looked like you, I would probably skin people, too."

Her eyes flickered in that lizard-like way as a thin film covered her eyes then receded. "I am going to enjoy skinning you alive. I would eat you too, but I can smell the demon on you, so your body is worthless to me."

"That's the first time anyone's ever said that to me. How'd you know I was a demon?"

"You smell familiar."

"Why couldn't we smell that you were a demon?"

"She masked her scent," Azrael replied, heading to the door.

"Okay, got all my answers," I cried before leaping on the desk and bringing my sword down on Yasmine.

She quickly pushed out her arm and I found myself flying through the air but someone grabbed me before I hit a wall. I turned my neck slightly to see it was Felix.

Before I could give a thank you, the door to the office flung open and several wraiths stormed the room. Felix released me and I slid to my feet, already swinging my sword and connecting with the wraiths I hit. I caught several in the neck and shoulders as Faith did her power pummels, and Azrael and Felix brought out their magic weapons.

Azrael's weapon of choice being a giant silver sickle that was almost the size of the angel's body. Azrael decapitated several wraiths in one spin. To my right Felix pulled out his trusty machetes and began to slice away, flinging wraiths off of him as he stabbed.

I turned to find Yasmine standing on her desk and looking down at the fighting below her with a smug smile. I planned to make that smile wider by slicing her face in half. I ran toward her, ducking and slicing as I made my way back to her desk.

Suddenly my sword shook in my hands and I tightened my grip in confusion. What was going on? My sword pulled forward and yanked me with it. I pulled back and crouched down just in time to avoid being bitten by an attacking wraith. I tried to swing my sword forward at it but my sword was resistant, still pulling in the other direction like it was drawn to a magnet. I instead kicked my leg out and caught the wraith in the stomach, knocking it to the ground. That slight distraction caused my sword to gain ground and fly out of my hand.

I wanted to see where it went but the wraith was already back up and charging for me. I pushed out my faerie magic and zapped it with my electricity, its body convulsing before dropping to the ground. It wasn't strong enough to kill it without concerted energy that I just didn't have right now.

However, the creature was unconscious for the moment and I had bigger fish to fry.

Spinning around, I narrowly missed being cut in half and leaped to my right as Yasmine brought down my golden sword in the space I just vacated. What in the entire hell? How dare she put her lizard hands on my sword. And, how did my sword betray me like this? I pushed out my hand, willing my sword back to me but it refused to come back.

Yasmine made a fake shocked face. "Oops, did you lose your sword?" She waved it in the air. "Why don't you try to get it back?"

I pushed again, swearing, but my sword did not even look like it was moving at all. How had she gotten such control over my weapon and why was I so weak to get it back? What level demon was this bitch?

Screw it, no time to figure that out. I zapped her with my magic and Yasmine fell to the floor, still clutching my sword. Her body darkened and smoke blew off her body from my electrocution but she seemed unbothered as she stood up. She ran toward me, sword in the air and I quickly teleported to another part of the room. The fighting had now carried out into the hall and I could no longer see the others.

We were in trouble here. We had a whole town against just the four of us and I was assuming no backup would magically appear that quick. If she was as powerful a demon as I thought she was then her ward had probably prevented telepathic calls for help from getting out as well. For now, we were on our own and the odds weren't good. We had to get the hell out of here and we'd probably have to fight our way out.

# CHAPTER 18

*B*efore Yasmine could stab me, I teleported again. I hated running away from her but she was a tough one and I had to fight smart. I needed to cut her head off. That always worked. Unless she could get it back with her body. I dug into my pocket and flung my *shuriken* at her. It landed in her shoulder and quickly exploded, tearing her arm away from her body before she could pull it out. Unfortunately, I wasn't able to get the shoulder that had my sword. Still, one arm was better than nothing.

Yasmine screeched a room shaking sound that startled me for a moment. Just a moment. I teleported in front of her and grabbed the hand holding my sword. I yanked against her still tight grip but for someone squirting blood out of her body, she was still pretty damn strong. I grabbed another *shuriken* out of my pocket and began to bring it down on her hand when an agonizing heat hit my fingers, making me drop my weapons. I looked up and was shocked to find that Yasmine's eyes were now two orbs of laser beams which were now retracting back into her head.

I teleported out of the room and stumbled over the dead body of a wraith in the hallway. Laser eyes? What kind of demon was she? Felix appeared in front of me, battered, bruised, and bloodied. However, he didn't seem to be concerned about his own condition as his eyes narrowed to my right hand that had previously held my *shuriken*. "Shit, Fran." He bent forward and grabbed my hand.

I looked down and noticed for the first time the tips of several fingers were missing from my hand. She'd lasered part of my fingers off. The fighting adrenaline must still have been working in my favor because I could only feel cold numbness.

Felix hovered his hand over mine and a healing magic warmed my fingers. "Azrael can grow the tips back but I want to make sure it doesn't get infected or hurt."

I nodded, absentmindedly, still in shock as I looked at Faith and Azrael stand back-to-back as more wraiths approached. Was everyone a fighter in this town? They probably were and they were all in young, healthy bodies too. I dropped my shoulders. We had to call this fight or we would get hurt more.

Yasmine walked out of the room, still holding my sword with her hand pressed against her bloody stump of an arm. "Give up?" She looked to me, clearly thinking that I ran the show.

I looked back at the others. They all looked tired but they stared back at me with fighter's eyes. They wouldn't go down without a fight. It made me like them more. However, dying right now would get us nowhere. Yasmine wasn't planning to kill us right now, which meant we still had something she wanted for later. That meant we had time. Time to find a way out of here or to break the ward and get back up.

I looked back at the grotesque demon bitch. "Fine."

She gave me a face splitting demon grin. "Wonderful. Send them to their rooms for now. I need to reattach my arm. If they cause any trouble, kill them. I did want to wait until the full moon when their magic is at its most potent and delectable but they may not be worth the trouble."

We were our most powerful under a full moon? Hadn't read that on the internet. We made the walk back to our hotel surrounded by jittery wraith with all manner of weapons pointed at us.

I leaned toward Felix. "When's the full moon?"

"Tuesday night," Azrael answered for him, walking up to my left.

It was a Monday. We had one day to find a miracle.

The wraith minions shoved us all in my room instead of allowing us our two suites.

Azrael turned to the guard. "Is it too much to ask for to let us get our things from our room?"

The male wraith smirked. "For what? You aren't going to need them," he replied before slamming the door.

From his perspective he was right. We'd be dead tomorrow, who cared about a toothbrush?

Apparently, Azrael did because the angel disappeared and then quickly reappeared a minute later with their things as well as Faith's.

I collapsed on the couch, feeling incredibly exhausted. I wasn't used to losing. In my mind I felt like I was the greatest warrior there was but I'd just had my greatest weapon snatched from me with barely a struggle. Had being Alister's girlfriend all this time made me weak?

Azrael appeared in front of me and then sat on the coffee table. The angel took my injured hand and inspected it. "This was a clean cut. Very few demons have laser eyes. The dark prince being one of them."

I shrugged, not really caring about Yasmine's brand of demon. I just needed her gone. "Well, maybe she's his cousin."

Azrael caught my poor humor and kept a serious face as they covered both my hands with theirs. The angel then lowered their head and began to speak in a language I did not know. The angelic language? A bright silvery light shown from their eyes, flooding our hands with a tingling heat. Soon after an irritating itch began to trouble my fingertips. I could only assume that was the healing magic. I wanted to snatch my hand away and submerge it in a bucket of ice. Instead, I stayed still and gritted my teeth as pools of sweat began to spread under my arms and down my back from the healing pain.

Faith leaned toward me with amused eyes. "Need me to knock you out so you don't feel anything?"

I glared up at her, exposing my gritted teeth. She thought she was so funny. "You want to die before tomorrow?"

She straightened up and winked at me, clearly unbothered by the poor weakling that I had now become for the moment. Maybe Herrod and the angels were lying. How could I be the child of a powerful fae Queen and a demon King and get my ass kicked by a demon who wasn't even ruling an underworld?

Something didn't add up and I knew, assuming I could trust him, Herrod could give me answers and also help us from certain death. However, if I went and used his calling card now then that would only draw more suspicion from the others. Did I really want to keep this secret from them? The others already didn't trust me, if they thought I was getting close to a demon King and that he was my father, they'd never trust me.

But did I even care? I looked over to Felix who gazed down at Azrael still working on my hand like he was an instructor overseeing his student's work and realized that yes, maybe I did care what he thought of me. Sure, he was half-demon but not of royalty. Did that make it better or worse?

Less important than what they thought of me was the overwhelming fear of owing a demon. After Alister, I didn't really want to be at the mercy of any other demon ever again.

Nadia was different because she was my bestie. There was also the fact that I was unemployed and needed a place to stay.

There would be no telling what Herrod would really want if I called for help. And without a blood test, I really didn't know if he was my father. Wait, did demons have DNA?

On the other hand, if I died because I was so insistent on my independence, what the hell would it matter?

"Everything okay?" Azrael looked at me with suspicious eyes as the angel leaned back on the coffee table.

"Huh?"

"I asked you, how does your hand feel?"

I looked down at my hand and noticed it was now resting on my thigh as good as new. I'd been so deep in thought I had successfully blocked out the pain and the angel's voice. I looked up at Azrael and nodded. "It feels great. Thank you." I began to wiggle my fingers and press the tips to my thumb. Yup, felt normal.

Felix moved to sit down beside me. "I haven't been able to make contact with anyone telepathically. Just like Yasmine said."

Faith sat back in a dining room chair and balanced on the back two legs. "Me either. You think Amina being asleep really is disrupting our connection?"

He rubbed at his face before moving his hand back through his long hair. He looked exhausted but less battered than earlier. I could only assume he used some of his healing magic on himself. "Yeah, I haven't been able to reach Lisa telepathically when she goes to help Joo-won. We aren't as powerful without Amina."

Faith gave a displeased sigh. "So, we're just basic bitches now."

I wanted to laugh. Basic bitches didn't touch people and kill them or power-up through their tattoos. "Well, not everyone has to be part of the fabulous Six to be special.

You're not some elite group to us peons. You were just six people brought together by a spell to do public good. You're basically public servants. Thank you for your service."

Felix rubbed my shoulder but his face looked distracted. "We didn't mean it like that, Franny."

Azrael stood up and stretched. "Beyond all of that, I haven't been able to connect with Monica either. We knew this could happen. It's probably why she wasn't able to connect with the other angels."

Yeah, that was one way to take it. Or she could be ignoring us. For all we knew she was sending some fireball down on the whole town, looking at the place like a lost cause. I had a tough time believing she didn't know this town was full of wraiths. "Or she could be ignoring you."

Azrael gave me tired eyes before turning toward the balcony. "She has a lot on her plate."

I made a fart noise with my mouth. She knew we were in jeopardy here and she could have kept a close eye. Now she was all M.I.A. when we needed her.

"You have a right to your doubts but we won't know for certain why we can't reach her until we can confirm we are warded in. We can do that tonight when there are fewer people around. Assuming we aren't able to break the ward to this room that I'm sure we are under. How did Amina break the ward cutting off communication to Hagerstown those months ago?"

Felix leaned his head back on the couch and closed his eyes. "Witches worked together around the clock."

Of course, she had help. "Welp, guess we don't have that option. Even if we can break down the ward to this inn, we aren't strong enough to break a ward to a whole town."

Azrael let out an exasperated sigh. "So, without trying, what would you have us do?"

"I need to think." I got up and went to the bathroom, turning on the exhaust fan and sink for privacy. If we snuck out to test the ward we'd be killed on the spot if we couldn't get out. I needed to see if my link with Herrod could work and if it did, I'd have to find a way to get his help without the others knowing.

I took out a small knife hidden underneath my left breast. We'd gotten a very unthorough pat down from the wraiths, although they'd taken all my *shuriken*. No matter, I could easily make more with my magic.

I pricked my finger with the knife and drew Herrod's symbol with my blood on the sink. I stood still, having no idea where he would appear.

Minutes passed. If he didn't hurry up, they'd think I was doing something more in here. And although I shouldn't care what they thought, I really didn't want them to think I was stinking up the bathroom. I'd turned off the sink and decided to turn the shower on. It was better for them to think I was washing.

I sat on the bathtub ledge waiting, leaning my elbows on my thighs.

"Sorry for the delay, my daughter," came a quiet voice from inside the bathroom.

I jumped up and looked around, landing my eyes on the mirror above the sink where an image of my father appeared. It'd worked! That meant that dear old, alleged, dad was stronger than the magic here if we could connect even with the ward up. Good to know.

"I didn't expect to be hearing from you this quickly," he stated, a hovering half body in the mirror.

"I'm in trouble and I need your indirect help."

He raised a brow with a look of confusion. "Please define trouble."

"So remember when you said to be careful."

"Yes," he said in a cautious voice.

"Yeah, so I wasn't and we got in a big fight and are now trapped by the wraiths and warded in."

Herrod slapped his forehead, closing his eyes.

I gave him a wide smile knowing I'd messed up. "But wait, there's more. If we don't get out before tomorrow night, we're going to be eaten. We can't take on the whole town to even try to get to the ward and break it. We need back up."

"I'll send a horde."

I shook my head quickly. "No, please don't. I haven't told anyone about our connection and they might get suspicious if they know you saved me. Can you get in touch with my friend Nadia? I'm sure you know who she is. Tell her where I am and that I need help."

Herrod worked his jaw from left to right and then gave a nod. "Smart. The fewer people that know about our connection the safer you'll be."

I hadn't even thought of that point but it was a good one.

"I'll contact her." He put up an index finger. "One moment."

He closed his eyes and I waited patiently as he telepathically dialed up my BFF. He then opened his eyes. "Sorry, line's busy."

Was he kidding me? "What? That's not how it works."

"It actually is. I can't connect with her. She could be busy defending her territory. Rumor has it that there are some who still aren't happy with her being the leader."

That was true and very inconvenient for me now.

"Shall I come now?"

I raised a hand. "Nope. Keep dialing or whatever."

"And if I can't reach her?"

Didn't I have any other friends I could contact that I didn't mind knowing I had a friend in a demon King? I really didn't have a lot of people on my side. That was depressing. Then one name popped in my head. I threw my head back in frustration because it was not a person I wanted to rely on either. I would definitely have to owe him but he was one step better than Herrod.

"There's Marcus. We got back in touch recently."

Herrod gave a curt nod. "I am aware." He really had been keeping an eye on me. "You don't mind him knowing?"

"You think he'll use our connection against me?"

"Of course. But whatever he wants, you'll be able to give him."

Not if it was giving him my body. I wasn't a whore.

As if sensing my thoughts, Herrod raised a hand. "If it's undesirable, I will kill him. Not to worry. But it won't be."

I narrowed my eyes. He seemed awfully sure of himself. The others would be wondering if I collapsed in the shower, so I didn't have time for all the questions. "And you know this how?"

"I know more than you imagine. You will learn that I will not steer you wrong. Marcus won't betray you. However, I will continue contacting Nadia. One way or the other, you will be rescued before tomorrow night, even if I have to send my hordes. As a last resort."

"Thank you."

"And in the meantime, if you can, kill that demon Yasmine. Wraiths are made by demons and witches. She controls them all."

"So, if she goes, they all die?"

"Not that simple. But they will lose direction and their numbers won't grow. They can't procreate. The magic in them from her will weaken. They will be less formidable and thus easier to kill."

Someone pounded at the door. "Can you hurry up in there? Some of us have to use the bathroom," Faith called.

I kicked my shoes off. I needed to get undressed to pull my lie together. "Okay, be done in a minute."

I looked at Herrod. "Thank you."

He nodded before disappearing.

I quickly jumped in the shower and took an unnecessary

speedy wash, and then wrapped myself in a towel, grabbing my clothes in a pile in my arms.

Faith stood outside the door when I opened it, arms crossed. "Took you long enough," she grumbled, pushing past me.

I headed into the bedroom and sat down on my bed. My heart was racing and I had to acknowledge that I was a little scared of being caught talking to Herrod. Fear wasn't my usual go to button but the angels always made me nervous. Except for Carlos. Azrael still freaked me out.

Angels were mysterious and powerful. They were the first paranormals, according to everything I'd read. I didn't like being around them because I didn't understand their full power. The fact that we were trapped in here with a guardian angel, which was one step down from an archangel, confirmed to me that Yasmine was no low-level demon. She could make wraiths, shoot lasers out her eyes, and put up a ward that prevented us from contacting our friends and most likely from getting out.

"Everything all right?" Azrael asked.

I sucked in a breath and looked up at the angel, leaning against the door frame to the room. Did they know about Herrod? Did I have I'm-keeping-a-secret written all over my face?

"I'm fine, stop asking me that." I got up and grabbed some fresh clothes from my suitcase.

Azrael walked further in the room and sat at the foot of the other bed. "You seem distracted. This is a time to have your head in the game."

I rolled my eyes and put my fresh clothes on the bed and sat back down not planning to give the angel any type of show.

The angel continued talking. "I know you don't like me. I know you don't like angels and you think Monica is playing us. I suppose you have every reason to doubt us.

We didn't do you any favors and in retrospect, what we did was overkill but you have to admit that we'd have had a hard time getting Felix to the Six without him giving you up."

Why was the angel wanting to rehash old issues with me right now? While I was vulnerable in my damn towel with the air conditioner giving me goosebumps?

"What do you want to talk about, Azrael?"

The angel pursed their lips and scratched their neck as they gathered a response. "Angels aren't saints. The only saints are actual saints. We have our infighting. We have our own hopes and dreams. Monica is no exception. But you have to know whose side to be on. Your doubting of Monica might not work in your favor. She has a lot of pull. Trust that her goal is not to see your demise. That doesn't help her. Having a demon ally would actually be good for her. Help keep tabs on the underworld."

Did they think I was going to be some type of snitch? That was not my calling.

"She will get you the answers you're looking for. And the more good you do for her, the cleaner your aura. Don't go down that dark path to the demons. And don't pull Felix with you."

Ah, so this is what it was all about. Azrael was, as I thought the angel would be, concerned about my connection to Herrod. Keeping my alleged true identity was a good thing after all.

"Is this because of my meeting with Herod?"

Azrael leaned back, balancing on their arms. "And that minion, Yusan."

"I can't help that I'm a demon magnet."

Azrael cocked a brow as if they weren't buying what I was selling. "We can help with that."

He was going to proposition something and I probably wasn't going to like it. "How so?"

"Like I said, the better your aura, the lesser the demon part of you will thrive."

"Now how does that work?"

"Let me let you in on a little secret. Angel and demon blood? Not that different. It's easy for an angel to become a demon. We all know that. A little harder the other way around. Well, a lot harder. I've only heard one tale of a demon becoming an angel. In the few cases we can convert a demon, we are only able to neutralize their blood for them to become just a normal human. It takes more than good deeds but that's a start."

Suddenly everything made even more sense. They didn't care about saving our proverbial souls or removing us from evil. No, the angels, especially Monica, wanted two less power threats running around, especially one that was half-angel and part of the magical Six. "So that's the end game here. You want to remove us from our demon side and if you succeed, we would just be un-gifted humans. In a paranormal post-apocalyptic world." I twisted my lips so the angel could clearly see how undesirable I thought that alternative was.

Azrael gave a tight smile before sitting upright. "It's better than having your souls damned to hell because you are part-demon."

Felix appeared in the doorway with Faith peeking under his arm. "Why would we go to Hell? We're good people."

I cut my eyes at him. By the look on his face, it appeared that his guardian angel hadn't filled him in on the plan. "You know about this?"

"Not fully."

Faith ducked under his arm. "If Felix becomes a regular human, would we even be the Six anymore after Amina wakes up?"

Azrael turned slightly to her. "That I don't know."

She sat down on the bed near the angel, her face a mask

of concern. "Well, that's a pretty big risk then. We were brought together to do good because of our magic. We don't know that the original soulmates were the only mega threat in this world. Not to mention we're all more powerful individually because we bonded as the Six. So, we could all lose power in this."

"Would you want Felix going to Hell because you'd lose a little power?"

Faith scrunched her face up and gave Azrael a look that was a mix of annoyance and confusion. It was a dumb question but even dumber if one wasn't a believer. I wasn't sure where Faith's religious beliefs fell, but the look on her face said she wasn't one for regular Sunday worship.

I rubbed my arms. It was getting chilly in here, and I was starting to feel exposed with only a towel. I wasn't interested in this conversation or the angel agenda. Azrael thought I was a fool and they were playing us like we were some weak-minded followers.

Felix cleared his throat, still standing in the doorway. He looked down at Azrael with a stern gaze. "We all know Hell or the underworld is real but it's not a certainty if any of us go there just because of who our parents are. We are more than blood and bones. Now I'm fine with doing good deeds to help the world and if it makes my aura a little bit shiny, I'm all for it. But I like who I am and I believe in what brought the Six together. I don't know the demon side of me. Maybe I don't need to. I do know my mother raised me well and she was a good woman. That's the important part." He tilted his head over to me. "And maybe Fran's father was a good man, too."

I worked hard to keep my face neutral at that last sentence. I was certainly iffy on how much good he'd done versus evil. He had a slew of believers who he helped but I wasn't sure what evil he did to balance it out. Most importantly, I wasn't going to give up my powers to become a regular human. I couldn't even imagine what'd I do without magic. I was barely forming a path when I thought I was just a faerie. Who knew what my mind was like before magic? I didn't know if I was focused or not but I did know that of all the things I could have become with fae magic, I'd willingly chosen to become a hitman. And even when my mind was screwed over by the angels I still went to fighting.

I stood up with my clothes, heading back to the bathroom to change. Before leaving the room, I looked back at Azrael. "You keep working off the premise that angels are the greatest good. That we should follow you without question. Just because you're old and work for the man or woman upstairs doesn't mean you know everything. Maybe we're all equal. How scary would that be to you if you found out angels weren't the most powerful paranormals out there? I mean, didn't Amina and Phillip do your dirty work?"

Azrael turned quickly to me with blazing eyes and I gave the angel a saccharine smile. "I'm not going to stamp out my light to make you brighter."

# CHAPTER 19

*I* had just zipped up my jeans when Yusan appeared in the bathroom. I jumped, falling back on the toilet seat. "You're doing this on purpose!"

Yusan bowed his head. "Sorry, Francesca. I was in a rush."

"Well, I'm glad you're here. I need you to try to get out and send word to someone." It wasn't that I didn't fully trust that Herrod was working on it but- No, it was exactly that.

Yusan nodded quickly. "Yes, yes. I tried to get out as soon as I saw what happened to you at the mayor's office. No joy. The ward keeps even spirits out."

I sighed. Well at least he was smart enough to try.

"I can help sneak you out of the hotel if you want to check. I'm not very strong so my not getting through isn't that shocking. But we can do that later. I came here to tell you that Yasmine is on her way."

I jumped up. What the hell did she want now? I thought we had until tomorrow. "You could have led with that."

I raced out of the bathroom into my room where the other three still stood. "Yasmine's on her way here."

Felix, now sitting on his bed, looked over at me with surprised eyes. "How do you know?"

"Yusan told me."

I felt the demon's presence behind me and I moved to my side. "Maybe she's going to kill you now."

Azrael stood up calmly. "It would probably be me. As a full angel, she couldn't get any strength from eating me. We cancel each other out. But my skin is still valuable."

Faith shook her head, frustration in her eyes. "We have to hide you."

Azrael wasn't my favorite person but I knew that the others would be devastated if something were to happen to them. Plus, the angel was powerful, losing that strength would be to our detriment right now. "I could try my invisibility cloak. All fae can do it."

Azrael walked toward the door. "It would do no good. She could probably still sense my presence at her power level and it might put the rest of you in danger. The only other option I would have if we cannot defeat her is for me to leave to the heavens, without my body. I'm certain the ward can't contain an angel's essence. Very few things can."

Well, what was the hold-up? Why hadn't he done that in the beginning? "Okay, well then leave your body and go get some angel help."

Azrael continued to walk. "Yes, I can do that. Of course, once I leave my body, if I don't return in a certain amount of time, I won't be able to get back in it. And of course, there are many other beings itching to get into human skins, as we all know. Anytime one leaves their body they are risking permanent eviction the longer they are gone from it."

Like I cared. This wasn't the angel's body to start anyway. Yes, angels took on human bodies through consent, unlike demons, but the bodies still weren't their own. "Get a new body."

The angel turned slightly to me before heading to the hotel door, their eyes slightly saddened. "I like this one."

Faith raced past me to grab Azrael's hand. I suppose she

would be upset that her angel with benefits was possibly leaving their body permanently. "So do I."

They touched her cheek, giving her a nostalgic smile.

Suddenly, the front door swung open and I quickly made my way to the living area, with Felix on my heels, in time to see Yasmine, back in human form, walk casually in. Her minions stayed on the outside. Her arm was in a sling as it healed, I assumed. I took only a mild satisfaction since she was able to get her arm reattached.

Azrael blocked her path. "Why are you here?"

She patted their shoulder and moved around the angel. "I wanted to have more of a chat without fighting. Now that you know the truth, perhaps, we can have more of a sensible discussion. We've never been lucky enough to have any guest as powerful as you enter our town."

Had she lost her mind? We weren't going to sit here and have a chit-chat like old friends just to pass the time. No, her tune had changed from just an hour ago. Could it be that she didn't really want to kill us and if so, why?

Faith stood beside Azrael, hands formed in fists ready to fight. "I call bull-shit, why are you here?"

She continued to move into the room, sitting down at the dining room table. "Believe it or not, killing you, well some of you, was not in my plan when I first met you. As you have surmised, the wraith nest is in this town. If you know anything about wraiths, then you know they cannot travel far from the nest, which is wherever the creator, in this case myself, resides."

I silently moved into the living room, resting my back on a nearby wall. I wanted to ask a question but decided to keep quiet as I figured she'd quickly realize how much she'd given away. She'd basically said her people couldn't leave her side. So, what happened if she left them? Would they wither and die? Could she leave them for any period of time? What if she visited another realm? If we killed her, maybe they would all die? Even if we kidnapped her, they could possibly die. And, if we escaped, they couldn't come after us unless she was with them. The whole town would have to pick up and leave to find us. Not very efficient if they needed to focus on bringing in food sources. And now it made sense why they heavily advertised this place as a vacation town. They couldn't go out far and get their food. Only Yasmine could, and who knew how long she could be off without them dying when she was away from residence.

Yasmine tilted her head and looked up at me from the corner of her eyes. It was an unsettling look even in her human disguise. "I can feel your mind working overtime, Francesca. You won't be able to use your magic to kill me right now, even if you tried. You are strong but not strong enough. At least not yet."

How'd she know how strong I really was?

Azrael sat down at the table across from her. If the angel was nervous or scared, they never showed it. "Why are you really here? Aren't we supposed to be the tastiest of treats on a full moon?"

Yasmine nodded, tapping the table with her index finger. "Yes, you are. However, we could also use some scouters. Maybe some help bringing people to our town."

"To eat?" The angel's face distorted into an uncharacteristic look of disdain. "You want us to kidnap people and bring them here for you to kill? Have you lost your mind?"

"Not at all. See I know some things and have connections. I think we could make a good deal." She looked over to Felix. "You could run this town with me."

I sucked my teeth and rolled my eyes. Of course, she'd want him by her side. She'd been eyeing Felix from day one but he didn't want her.

"Azrael, you don't have to worry about doing anything since I know you could no longer be an angel if you did. I'd let you go if you keep the angels away. I'd even return your angels to you."

"How noble of you," the angel replied with deadpan eyes.

Yasmine looked to Faith, unfazed by Azrael's sarcasm. "You and Fran could work for me. Even send us evil people so your conscious could rest."

I made a pff noise at the same time as Faith and we glanced quickly at each other with somewhat renewed respect. There would be no way I'd work for another demon. I barely wanted to work for Nadia.

Yasmine raised her shoulders and widened her cold eyes. "This is the deal so you can live. You all sit here and judge me but you have no idea what life was like for many lost souls. They just want a chance to live a life they were prevented from earlier. I'm not saying everyone here is virtuous but many were just regular beings, killed before their prime."

I needed to stop her right there from making her sob story about everyone just being victims. "What is the benefit to you to even make wraiths?"

She lifted a shoulder. "I'll admit, I get more power from my wraith followers. What they eat, I get energized from that as well. We're all just trying to survive. We eat or die, what more can we do? Listen, this is a great deal."

Felix pushed away from the wall he was leaning against. "No dice. We aren't doing your dirty work."

Yasmine batted her eyes at him. "I can sweeten the pot." She clapped her hands.

Seconds later the door opened. I turned my head and saw a tall woman with light brown eyes and short, bob length black hair enter the room. She had smooth honey skin that made her look deceptively younger but I could tell by her eyes that she was perhaps in her early fifties. There was something very elegant about her as she walked with an almost graceful stride in black stilettos and a red fitted shift dress that hit just below her knees.

What was it about her that seemed so familiar?

"Felix!" she cried, walking swiftly towards him with arms open.

Felix's face crumbled in a jumble of emotions and he quickly cleared the gap between them, embracing her in a tight hug.

Huh, what was this now? A twinge of jealousy flared through me. I hadn't seen him hug anyone that tightly that wasn't me or his friends.

"Mom?" his voice cracked with emotion.

I dropped my mouth open. Mom?

# CHAPTER 20

*F*elix turned to us, his arm wrapped around the shoulders of the woman he called mom. "Everyone, this is my mother, Olivia." He was practically beaming, his chest puffed out with pride. He looked back down at her. "Where have you been? Do you want to sit? Have a seat."

He ushered her to the couch and sat down beside her.

Olivia looked around at us, quickly looking past me. "Pleasure meeting you all." She patted Felix's back. "I was imprisoned for years by another demon. It was a few years after the magic returned. I'd been trying to get in touch with you until that point but in the early days of this, it was hard," she explained as they sat down.

Felix balled his hands resting on his thighs. "What demon? I'll kill him."

"It's okay, there is time to get into that. Just know that if it wasn't for Yasmine here, I wouldn't have been able to escape."

Ah, of course she was behind this. Was it all a coincidence or had Yasmine known exactly who Felix was? His mother was supposed to be a high-ranking demon so it wouldn't be a surprise except she'd been living as human since Felix was a child. Would anyone have known they were related?

It certainly made sense why all she requested of Felix was for him to be by her side. I wondered if his mother had made some kind of arranged marriage deal. Well, if he liked old lizard face then good for him.

Felix moved his head in Yasmine's direction but didn't look at her. "Thank you for saving my mother. Should I assume that there's a condition?"

Yasmine looked all too pleased with herself as she lifted her hands and studied her well-manicured, pointed nails. "The deal I offered still stands and you can stay here with your mother."

Azrael leaned forward on the table, their eyes ablaze with anger. Guess they weren't too fond of demon mother's returned. Yet another demon around Felix that he didn't like. "And what if we refuse? Would you kill a fellow demon's child?"

"She wouldn't dare, angel," Olivia spat, her own eyes narrowing at Azrael. Didn't appear to have any love lost there.

Yasmine nodded. "She's right. Now everyone else is fair game."

Felix finally looked at the other demon, his eyes looking just like his mother's a moment ago. "If you lay a hand on my future wife or my friends, I will destroy you. That's a promise."

Olivia gave a slight gasp. "Future wife? Are you engaged?"

Felix looked over to me, his eyes softened. "Mom, that beautiful woman over there is named Francesca Ross and she doesn't know it yet, but she's going to be my wife."

I gave a wobbly grin not sure how to reply in front of his mother. "Hi, Mrs. Gonzalez."

Olivia gave me her narrow-eyed stare and I felt like melting into the wall behind me and disappearing. She lifted her chin, still glaring at me. "Francesca. Did you have a mother named Dalia?"

I nodded slowly. Did she know my mother? How did that happen? "Or so I've been told. I have a memory issue."

"You are an Unseelie fae, correct?"

"Yes."

"There was a scandal in your court years ago. A rumor that filtered amongst the underworld that she had a child by a demon. A prominent one at that."

Oh shit. Please don't know him. Please don't know him.

I didn't respond, just looked at her with large eyes.

Olivia nodded, tapping her chin. "Yes, yes. I recall. Although I'd been living in the human world, I still had an old tie who would tell me some of the gossip from the underworld from time to time. It drove your father mad, Felix." Her shoulders seemed to sag at the mention of his father. "But yes, when her court found out that her child was half-demon, she ran off to the human realm. I can understand having to do such things myself. My family was very displeased with my relationship choice. You're from a prominent family yourself, Felix."

He gave a lopsided grin. "So, I'm like a noble?"

"Actually, yes. And your father, was no ordinary angel. He was an archangel."

That was news. And a welcomed one because it meant we weren't talking about my family anymore.

Felix's mouth formed into an 'o' shape. "What?" He looked to Azrael. "Did you know that?"

Azrael bowed their head. "I was aware. It changes nothing and was not relevant to who you are."

Of course, the angels would still withhold things.

Faith, who had been sitting on the arm of the couch, uncrossed her arms and placed her hands on her thighs. "Not to change the subject Mrs. Gonzalez. Sorry, I'm Faith Thomas by the way, Felix's best friend."

Olivia smiled at her. "Hi, dear."

Faith got a smile and I got a glare. I was half-demon, she was a demon, why did she not like me? Oh, that's right some strange woman she didn't know was allegedly going to steal her son away and marry him. Was he a mama's boy? Was she the type of woman who didn't like her son's girlfriends? Ugh, I didn't need that drama.

Faith continued. "Hi, so, did you know Fran's father? That would be helpful to us since she lost her memory."

Was Faith actually trying to be nice and look out for me? Aww...just when I *didn't* need it.

Olivia turned back to me, her face hardened again. What the hell? "I think I do. The word on the underworld street was that your father was none other than King Herrod. Although it was never proven. He has so many enemies that wouldn't be ideal for people to know."

Yasmine sat forward. "I had no idea. But when I found Olivia, through a mutual friend I had help me look on Felix's behalf, she told me."

How did she know Felix was looking? Who was spilling all our beans? Could he have said something? I looked over to him and he seemed unsurprised. Had he actually told Yasmine he was looking for his mother?

He nodded. "I've been putting out feelers to find her. Before I knew what Yasmine was, I mentioned I was looking for my mother. The paranormal world is large and small at the same time."

I twisted my lips. Of course, he'd be spreading his business all over town. Didn't he know that secrets were power?

Yasmine went on. "So, if it is true that you are his daughter, we wouldn't want to harm you. He is one foe we wouldn't want to have. Even if he's not well liked."

Well, that would be another reason why she was offering a deal to us instead of death. She now really had no power over me. If I shot down her offer, she still couldn't hurt me.

Olivia, still glaring at me, adjusted in her seat. "Herrod is the worst of demons. Our kingdoms have a history of disputes with his. He is a relatively young demon King but dangerous all the same. Ruthless and untrustworthy. He's killed many a friend and family members of mine. I'm sure he was behind my... detainment."

Oh, well that would explain the hate. I wondered if her family had done anything to Herrod's people? The thought then crossed my mind if she had anything to do with my mother's death. Herrod's M.O. seemed to be revenge. However, since there was obviously history and Olivia knew of me, he might have kept her locked up to protect me. Assuming I even believed her.

Azrael's neutral voice broke my thoughts. "Did you not know, Francesca? When you visited him, he said nothing?"

I looked around at all the faces in the room. I was an amazing liar and I could keep my knowledge hidden. After all, I wasn't in a room of friendly people. If Olivia really was an enemy to my father, then admitting my identity would put me in the very danger he claimed to want to protect me from.

"He knew my mother. He knew of me. He was a family friend checking in on me. He told me some things about my past that I didn't know."

In a way this was true. He'd never been a father to me.

Olivia gave a chuckle. "Is that what he said? And you think he'd take such special interest in you simply because he was friends with your family. Felix, I'd hoped you'd pick a smart woman to be your wife."

I clenched my jaw in annoyance. If she was trying to goad me into telling the truth well it was working. I needed to breathe in deep and let it go. I did not want her as a mother-in-law though.

Yasmine gave an exaggerated yawn and stood up. "How about we let the two of you play catch up? I can set you both up in another room. Of course, for now you'll have to understand that you cannot leave the town."

Olivia rose as well. "Of course." She patted Felix on the shoulder. "Come on, sweetheart."

Was she really okay with being confined again? You'd think as a royal demon she would be all types of pissed that Yasmine wouldn't let her leave. Why was she being so understanding? What kind of deal had been made?

Felix slowly got up and walked behind his mother. He avoided my eyes and said nothing as he left. That was not like him. He didn't believe me.

When the door slammed shut, I raised my shoulders, almost wincing. It felt painful to have Felix not acknowledge me.

I went to sit on the couch, avoiding the stairs of Faith and Azrael.

Faith plopped down beside me, stretching her legs out. "My grandmother had a saying. Tell the truth and shame the devil."

I side-eyed her. Clearly, she didn't believe my story either. Maybe I wasn't as good a liar as I thought.

Azrael thrummed their fingers on the table, their lids lowered but eyes fully on me. If they had a tail they'd be swinging it back and forth like a cat ready to pounce. I was not safe. "Now that the demons aren't here, you can tell us the truth. Is Herrod actually your father?"

I turned to the angel and gave him a hard stare. "No."

Azrael squinted their eye in disbelief. "Why lie? What do you think will happen? This news won't make us want to hurt you. We already know you're half-demon."

He thought I was an idiot. This would be clear ammunition. I gave him a tight smile. "If I was Herrod's daughter, and an ambitious someone like Monica found out, she would use me as bait to get Herrod to submit."

"What's wrong with that?"

"One, why do I want him to submit? Two, we don't know if she'd kill me after he did submit. She doesn't seem like the type to allow loose ends. I'm assuming I'm still around because she finds me useful. I'll do her bidding while she takes ridiculously slow baby steps to find a way to return my memories and feed me bits and pieces of my past."

Faith turned fully to me, one leg up on the sofa. She gave me a skeptical smile and scratched her head. "You expect us to believe that Herrod demanded a meeting with you after seeing you two months ago, just to play catch up? You can keep feeding us the bullshit but it's going to cost you a good man. Felix never just leaves quietly. Up until just now he was still calling you his wife to be. Then he leaves without even so much as a glance at you. He's not buying it and neither are we." She threw a hand out to the side. "So what if we know? Felix will still like you and we will still be okay with you."

I looked away although she did have a point. And how long did I think I could keep this secret? If Herrod and Olivia were really enemies—and based on Herrod's warning to me about Felix this seemed believable—then he wouldn't be happy I was friends with Felix either. It would get messy anyway. If the cat was out of the bag I might as well feed it some milk. I probably took that analogy too far.

I placed my feet on the coffee table and gave my best unbothered look. Might as well play it down with a cool face. "Fine, he told me I was his daughter. But I don't even know if I believe it. I need a DNA test or something."

Azrael shifted in their chair a deceivingly pleasant smile on their lips but eyes still eerily dead. Yup, the cat was about to pounce. "No need. I'll be able to confirm it if you both can be together. Angel ability. Why did you hide this from us earlier? We could have tried to protect you from Olivia's accusations if you wanted it secret."

I eyed the angel carefully. Why would they want to

220

protect me? "I didn't say anything because I didn't want to bring any unnecessary danger."

Faith huffed. "You don't trust us."

I tilted my head toward her to catch a confused frown on her face. Was she really surprised? "Look, I sort of trust you and Felix but I don't trust the angels." I looked back towards Azrael. "I don't believe you would cover up my true identity. What would be your reason for protecting me? As far as I'm concerned this works well for you. With Olivia not liking me for supposedly being Herrod's daughter, that can give you good footing to keep me away from Felix, which is what you wanted."

Azrael threw their head back and slouched low in the chair. "I wanted you away from him because you were part-demon and I didn't want that to heighten the demon half of him. But with him finally finding his mother, it doesn't matter anymore. Game over. He's never going to be separated from her. She's the loving woman who raised him, for all intents and purposes, well. He only knows her as human because that's how she presented herself all this time. At this moment, I can't think of a single thing that would make him step away from her, even you. Before his memories were tampered with, he'd been looking for her for years. And just a few words from her about you and he doesn't even argue. I thought his love for you was going to be the hardest thing to beat. I was wrong."

I wasn't sure if Azrael was truly frustrated or just trying to egg me on. For some reason I felt a queasy unsettled feeling in my gut. Everything they'd said was right. Perhaps I took for granted the sort of power I had over Felix. I liked the unfaltering devotion he seemed to have towards me. I'd never had anything like that, even with Alister.

Okay, I know I'd been pushing him away but still, I guess I kind of liked him around and maybe deep down thought he might be around for a while. Maybe I thought, that one day he and I could be a real thing. However, with his mother just ushering him out like that with barely a but from him, I wasn't so sure about that anymore. I'd seen Felix angry before. What would it look like when he was angry with me?

I needed to not care. I shook my head of the thought and caught Azrael's intense gaze on me.

"Is this why you've been so distracted?" the angel asked.

Nope, I wasn't going to have a heart to heart with Azrael. "What's the game plan? Olivia doesn't have the power here. She might have been a noble at one time but she's not anymore. She struck a deal with Yasmine and we know Felix will be protected. The rest of us are fair game. We still have to get out of here." I needed to check in with Herrod at some point. Now that everyone knew, perhaps having him rescue us wouldn't be a problem anymore.

"Herrod wouldn't let his daughter get killed and I'm not sure Yasmine looked up to fighting him. I'm assuming you called for help when you were in the bathroom for an excessively long time. Can Herrod break in?"

"He's willing to try. I asked him to contact Nadia or a fae friend of my mine. I was hesitant about owing him a favor. Still not sure he actually is my dad."

"Maybe Felix will help get us out of here?" Faith suggested. "Since his mom is friends with Yasmine."

That raised another point I wanted to highlight. "You can say all you want about me being a bad influence but listen here. I helped get rid of an original soulmate ally. Herrod protected me on the battlefield."

Faith tilted her head down, eyes wide. "He did?"

Had I left that part out? "Uh, yeah."

"But he's not your dad," she said, dryly.

I waved a hand at her in a dismissive fashion. "The point is, the demons around me are helpful. Like Yusan and Nadia. Olivia is aligning herself with a child eating skin stealer."

Azrael sighed. "Have you heard the tales of what Herrod has done? Let's not point fingers here."

"I wasn't. I'm just saying, what kind of person is Olivia for siding with Yasmine?"

Faith shrugged. "She freed her. Maybe Olivia doesn't have a choice."

Were they being difficult on purpose? "Fine, stay here and wait for Olivia to help you get out. I'm going to just have Herrod get me out."

"Now, hold up. No need to go so far. We get out anyway we can and come back with help to shut this place down."

I kept my mouth shut. If I got out of here, I wasn't coming back. Turns out this was more than I bargained for. It was time I took the easy road for a change. No need to stay where I wasn't wanted.

# CHAPTER 21

*B*y the next morning, I still hadn't heard from my father. Were Marcus and Nadia really that busy? I still had time, but something told me if Olivia laid eyes on me again, she might shorten that time.

My father wasn't the only one M.I.A. Felix hadn't returned that night or that morning. It was now noon. I had to admit. I was getting antsy. I lay on the bed looking at the ceiling and formulating how I planned to fight my own way out. Things felt so unclear. Now that I knew I had a family, perhaps I needed to refocus my energy on reconnecting with them. Then again, if they were willing to kick out a 12 year old, I wasn't so sure they'd be too happy to see me. Yet, if I came back as a fae Queen maybe they'd be more receptive. But did I care what they thought? They sounded like jerks.

I rubbed my face, feeling frustrated and overwhelmed. I now knew who I was but I still wasn't sure of my purpose. With my father's cause, perhaps ruling in the underworld wasn't such a horrible thing. I could now see how I could make a greater difference with that power. The fae side didn't want me but there were those on my demon side who did.

Yet, that nagging feeling of being let go by my fae family wouldn't go away. My mother died with them having turned their backs on her and me. I was a child and they didn't care if I left. Probably never checked in on me. That part made me sick. It also made me angry. No, I wanted to return to the fae realm and let them know that despite them throwing us out, I was still someone worthy and powerful.

I felt a chill in the room.

I looked down at the foot of the bed to find Yusan sitting cross legged. The demon still creeped me out. I had to remember that the shadow figure with glowing eyes and razor teeth was actually an ancient teenager.

"Why are you here?"

"Honestly, Francesca, what else do I have going on? Most people who can see me won't even talk to me. Some try to exorcise me. You treat me like I'm almost human. It's lonely for me. I need a friend."

I sat up. Well, that was sad. I guess it would suck to be in his position. Rarely being seen and when you are seen, you scare people. And I couldn't imagine other demons were especially kind to a low-level demon like him. Something pulled at me and I decided, when I got a chance, I'd help him get out of that demon form and set him free. He'd help me without getting anything in return so far. Why not?

"Well, since you're here and you're an old demon. Do you really think Herrod is my father?"

Yusan snickered. "Of course. It's like the worst kept secret around. If Herrod wanted to keep quiet that he had a kid, he shouldn't have hooked up with a fae Queen. Of course, we didn't know who you were exactly, especially when you were in the fae realm. And even when you were said to have come to this human realm, while magic was gone, there was no way to tell who you were and your mother went into really good hiding. I figure she glamoured herself and you too before she left her realm and that maybe it held. But now that magic is back, we can smell his scent on you."

"Why didn't you say anything earlier?"

Yusan shrugged. "Didn't think it needed saying."

I wondered if Alister and Nadia knew. I'd told Nadia about meeting Herrod on the battlefield, that would have been a good time for her to tell me who I was. Maybe she didn't know his scent. However, Alister, as a King, had to know. He probably kept it from me for the same reason he didn't let me know I'd broken up with him before my memories were stolen. It was his happy convenience that I'd gone right back to him, not realizing that I'd broken things off. He'd made Nadia keep it secret. Not telling me I was Herrod's daughter to keep me from leaving him seemed like an Alister thing to do. It made me want to kill him all over again.

If Yusan knew my father's scent, he must have been around him. "Wait, did my father send you to keep watch over me?"

Yusan gave me what I assumed was a sheepish look and hung his head. "He's had people watching over you since you were little."

"Even when I was with Alister? What about when the angels wiped my memories?"

"He's been trying to get those back. He didn't want any of us to step in unless absolutely necessary. He wanted you to be strong, and you are."

It sounded like he was the kind of dad who watched his kid get beat up by the school bully to teach her about strength.

How dangerous *was* my father? "He didn't think I needed help to get away from Alister?"

Yusan shrugged. "Guess not. I'm not in his inner circle, Francesca. I only recently got assigned to watch you when you came here."

I suppose I wasn't surprised. Alister was a bastard but he never actually hurt me. Of course, now I knew my father had dubious taste in who he would approve as a son-in-law. "Can I trust him? Will he really come and help?"

"The only reason he isn't here now is because you didn't want him, but he is ready and able if push comes to shove."

I felt like we were at the shoving stage.

Yusan leaned forward, patting my knee with a cold hand. I pressed my lips tightly together and held in a gasp so as not to hurt his feelings. "Don't worry. My dad was like that. He sent me into the desert to fend for myself for almost a week to gain strength. I almost died."

Yikes. And Yusan's father wasn't even a demon. "Hey, what's the deal with him and Olivia? Did he really keep her captive? Does he know she's free and here and Felix's mom?"

Yusan nodded. "Yes, there is some history there but I don't know it. He knows she's out."

"Can he come get her?"

Yusan laughed. I was only half-joking. "I can't explain how King Herrod works. He could have let her go for all we know."

"Why would he do that?"

"Your father is very wise. Also, very scary. So, the less I know the better for me. He promised he would help free me of this demon curse if I watched over you so I didn't ask anymore questions after that."

Was that possible? Seemed to me if he could do that, he could get my memories back. "Can he really do that?"

Yusan shrugged again. "He said he'd have his people work on it. Better to have that than just me finding a way."

Well, that made sense. "I'll help too."

Yusan bared his teeth in a smile before looking to the door and widening his eyes. I followed his gaze and saw Felix standing there glaring at the both of us.

"That's my cue." The demon snapped his fingers and faded away.

Felix walked further in the room and sat down on his bed, leaning his forearms on his thighs as he continued to stare at me with less than friendly eyes. "You knew."

Where there was possible doubt before, he was now looking at me with certainty. He knew I withheld the truth. Either the others had told him what I admitted or he was just going off the word of his mother.

I nodded my head but kept silent. I didn't think adding any other words would help the situation. Honestly, a dark part of me wanted to see angry Felix. Not just when he was fighting either.

The heat in his eyes dissipated but he still didn't look happy. "Why don't you trust me?"

Damn, this was worse than when your mom said 'I'm so disappointed in you'. "I do trust you. It's just the others I have an issue with."

He leaned back, looking away. "You're exhausting."

I wanted to say something smart but I wasn't in the mood to argue. I was in the mood to figure a way out of here if help didn't come in time. "Can your mother get us out?"

He snorted and shook his head. "Yasmine won't budge, but I won't let anything happen to you or the others. Did you tell us everything your father said?"

Was now really the time to focus on that? Was he sniffing for information to give dear old mom? "I told you everything except that he was my father. Sorry I don't have more information for your mother."

He got up and walked over to me, crouching down in front of me. He searched my eyes with such intensity that it made me nervous and I looked away. He gently touched my chin and turned my head back to him. "Just because our parents hate each other doesn't mean we have to. My mother's a good woman. She's understandably upset about what your father did. You shouldn't trust him so easily."

I pulled away from him. "I'm not gullible. My father is a King of hell and it sounds like your mother was a Queen so maybe we can't fully trust either of them."

He raised a brow. "Your dad wasn't the one locked up."

"Maybe he locked her up for good reason?"

"What good reason would a demon King have? My mother became good. She fell in love with an angel and raised me to be a good man."

I bit my lip in annoyance. Did he really want to act like his mother was a saint while implying my father was no good? Granted I didn't really know Herrod and I did have feelings for Felix but it didn't mean I agreed with his reasoning. Plus, something about his mother rubbed me the wrong way. "Well, slow clap for her for raising her child. My father didn't have that luxury. He stayed away to protect me. And he uses his power as a demon King to seek revenge on humans who commit injustices." I wasn't so sure I was sold on my father as a good guy either but I was not going to let others talk badly about him.

Felix gathered my hands, which were now in tight fists, and kissed them before placing them back on my lap. "Yeah, Yasmine and my mother mentioned that. Maybe he used to do that but he doesn't anymore." He stood up. "Your father isn't a good guy now. They told me stories."

I chuckled, shaking my head. "They could be lies."

Felix squinted his eyes. "My mother doesn't lie."

A strong wind lifted the hair on my shoulders and I jumped up as a tornado of sparkling onyx appeared in front of the window. Soon after Marcus stood with a fanged grin painted across his face. "The calvary has arrived." He opened his arms and gave me a wink with his dazzling blue eyes. "Now we don't have much time so pack your things and let's go. Or just leave them here. I'm sure you can get new stuff."

In retrospect of all the people to pick me up right now, he was probably the worst one. Felix frowned at him and then looked to me, pointing his thumb in Marcus' direction. "Who is this guy?"

Marcus walked up to him and offered a hand, which Felix inspected before shaking. "I'm Marcus. Royal Unseelie faerie. Childhood best friend of Francesca. I was sent by a-" he turned to me with questioning eyes. "What should I call him?"

I grabbed my suitcase which was already packed. "My father. My father sent him to get us out of here. We can finish this conversation later. Azrael and Faith, we are out!" I shouted towards the bedroom door. "Get here now or I'm leaving you behind." I looked to Marcus. "How'd you get in?"

He crossed his arms with a self-satisfied smile. "I have people. The court I'm from has many specialties. One of which is breaking wards."

I could imagine how useful that would be for an Unseelie. I was sure his court used that skill to conquer quite a few foes.

"I have a troop outside the town ready to attack but I'd rather not waste the energy so let's just get out of here while the ward is still down."

I looked to Felix who hadn't made a move. "Get your stuff."

He lowered his large shoulders and let out a breath. "I'm staying."

"Like hell you are," Faith cried, appearing at the door with her tote and Azrael standing behind her.

"I can't leave my mother."

"Well, then bring her with you."

"She won't leave. She's better protected from Herrod here. Yasmine's people will support her. And help her get justice."

He said that last sentence while looking at me. So, Olivia

was going to seek revenge on my father from imprisoning her. And maybe Felix would be helping. That would make things challenging.

I looked to Marcus. "Fine, let's go."

Marcus gave a curt nod and snapped his fingers. "Your ride awaits."

I clapped my hands. "With the ward down, I can teleport on my own. See ya."

I didn't wait to try to convince Felix to change his mind. I'd leave that for Azrael and Faith. I was done. I'd always known we weren't right for each other. Maybe it was finally time for us to go our separate ways.

# CHAPTER 22

*I* reappeared a mile out of town having no idea where I was going to go. Technically, I was homeless.

Marcus appeared beside me. "Lost, little lamb?"

I elbowed him in the ribs with all my force and he keeled forward. "Call me little lamb again and you'll be missing a testicle."

He covered his privates and backed away. "I don't feel that is an equivalent reaction."

I looked around the empty road and dark houses of the deserted neighborhood, trying to decide my next move. "No, but it'll make sure you won't say it again."

"Need a place to lay your head?" He asked, standing upright.

I actually did. Without Felix, I didn't think it right for me to go back to his town. Although it felt weird not telling the others. "I should go check in on Nadia."

"Can I join you?"

I eyed him with doubt. "Why do you want to go to a demon realm?"

"Because you're half-demon, which I find very intriguing.

I want to know more about that half of you. And let me say, thank you for considering me when you asked your father to find help. Imagine my surprise when I was contacted by a demon, a King no less."

"Why'd you help me?"

He looked around. "Can we have this conversation when we aren't so out in the open? Perhaps away from the wrath of Yasmine?"

Good point. I grabbed his hand and teleported us to Nadia's. When we arrived at her door, she answered with a look of shock on her face. "I thought you'd be gone longer," she stated, opening the door wider to let us in.

I never understood why she didn't have help in her mansion beyond a cook and housekeeper who showed up occasionally. She really shouldn't be answering her own door, she was a Queen. I expected her to look battle-worn but she appeared fine. "I heard you were in a fight?"

She made a pfft noise. "Eh, it wasn't anything I couldn't handle."

"My father tried to reach you."

She paused walking and we stopped in the foyer. She looked Marcus up and down and then glanced at me. "So many questions on that statement but first, who did I just let in my house?" She pointed a finger at him.

Marcus thrust out a hand and Nadia shook it with raised brows as he kissed her knuckles. "I'm Marcus, childhood friend of Francesca from the fae realm."

"He knows about your memory?"

I shook my head. At this point, there was no need to keep secrets. "My memory was wiped," I said, glancing over at Marcus.

He frowned. "So, do you remember me?"

"Nope. I don't remember anything from before five years ago. I just learned Herrod was my father."

"There was a rumor that your father was a demon and that's why you left. I thought it was a lie until today."

Nadia led us to her living room and called her cook to make us some food as I took a moment to figure out my next moves. I still had questions for Marcus. "Will you tell me now why you helped get us out of there?"

Marcus sat back on the couch, resting an ankle on this knee. "We were supposed to be partners, I couldn't let you get killed. I'd have gotten there sooner but rallying up troops to fight a demon for a fae not of their court took some bribing. I pulled a few favors."

I wasn't buying it. There was another reason he was so accommodating. "What do you really want from me?"

Nadia nudged my shoulder. "Maybe he just likes you."

Nadia was now a Queen of the Underworld. She hadn't been Alister's second because she was a dummy.

Before I even said a word, she raised her hands in surrender. "I know, I know, it's probably more. It's just that he's so cute." She gave Marcus a wink.

He gave her a wide grin. "Thank you, love."

"Give her the answers she wants, pretty boy or I'll boot your ass out of here so fast you won't have time to blink. You're cute but not that cute." She gave a wiggle of fingers at us. "Keep talking. I have work to do. And I'm sorry about being unreachable. I knew being a ruler would keep me busy but I'm not sure it's worth the pay."

"Have fun." I waved goodbye after her and then turned to Marcus. I didn't speak, just gave him a tightlipped stare to let him know I meant business. He was going to tell me the truth.

Marcus snapped his fingers and onyx glitter swirled above his fingers forming zig zag patterns in the air. Soon the swirl of glitter moved into the shape of a small dragon. The glittery dragon breathed out a tiny ring of smoke.

I looked at it in gleeful awe, like a little child at bubbles. It was actually impressively beautiful.

"When you were little, you used to like when I made these sparkling animals."

"I'm not a kid." Really, it did look cool.

"No, you aren't." He eyed me like he wanted to eat me for dinner and that made me do an uncomfortable shift in my seat. "Now that I know you don't have your memory, I guess you wouldn't remember that we were promised to each other when we were little. It was a deal your step-father made with mine."

I chuckled. Of course, leave it to a man to manipulate how a woman lives her life. "I thought my mother was the head of our court?"

Marcus blew on the magic dragon and the glitter dispersed into nothing to my sadness. "She was. I was a kid so I don't know much, but apparently she wasn't happy about it. However, it was supposed to grow our courts. The bigger the court, the more powerful the court. Your mother understood that and we got along so it wasn't a horrible match. Then the scandal happened and you left. My family still wanted me to marry you. Your mother's bloodline is strong even if you were half-demon. We looked for you for a long time. It was hard to do with hardly any magic in the human realm. Then when magic came back, I found you."

I scrunched my eyes not sure I believed him. Was my blood that potent that he'd search for me for over a decade? I guess they didn't know I couldn't have kids. "How'd you find me?"

"It wasn't that hard. Your mother didn't strengthen her magic when the world changed so it got easier to find you. When I went to you, you remembered me. I told you about our arranged marriage and you would have none of that even if it might get you back in your family's good graces."

Now *that* I believed. "So, what did I do?"

"You sent me on my merry little way only to end up a few years later engaged to a demon. Perhaps that's your preference, just as it was your mother?"

"The way you say it sounds like an insult."

"It's no offense. Perhaps I'm a bit jealous."

I pondered his words. I knew the annoying side of my brain wanted that family acceptance by the fae and this would be an easy path but the more independent side of my brain also hated for men to dictate my future and an arranged marriage was just that. "I never wanted to be told what to do or be a kept woman. I'm sure at some point I fell in love with Alister. He was my choice. I wasn't forced. Except when my memory was snatched. In that case, I was fooled to stay with him. So, it wasn't that I didn't like you. It was more that I didn't want to be told what to do. I guess I have a good idea what you want now."

Marcus smiled and scooted to the edge of his seat, closer to me. "Just hear me out. We were already thinking about supporting each other in our bid for the throne. Instead, why don't we go for the throne together? As a married couple. You want power. Your brother is already on the throne for your family's court, this is a good way to still get you to rule. We'd be equal partners. Something you rarely see. But I know I couldn't make you submit no matter how hard I tried."

He had that right. Still, marriage. I wasn't exactly jumping up and down for that idea. "You saved me not knowing if I would say yes. I owe you a favor but it doesn't have to be that and if you try to send me back to that town I won't go without a fight."

Marcus leaned back with a look of disdain. "I would not do that. First, it's cruel and I consider you a friend. Second, your father would murder me rather painfully."

"Did you tell my father what you want to do?"

"He was the one who suggested it. He knew of our prior arrangement. Apparently, daddy approves."

As if I would ever go to Herrod for approval for any of my decisions. "Like that matters."

He tilted his head from side to side. "No, but it does give me a little hope. Who was the bloke in the hotel room?"

"A friend."

Marcus gave me a lopsided grin, exposing one fang. "From the way that he looked at you and then glared at me, I'd say he was more than a friend. My proposal doesn't have to get in the way of whatever you have going on."

Okay, now I was confused. "You think Felix is going to want to be with me if I get married to you?"

"Do you want to be with him?"

I didn't know what I wanted. I knew I didn't like how we left things. I didn't like that he was still in that town and that he seemed so disappointed in me.

Marcus lowered his head and his eyes became mischievous. The way he kept looking at me was starting to make me uncomfortable. "I don't mind sharing."

Crap, that hadn't entered my mind. I wasn't sure I was that enlightened. "Maybe I don't want to be shared." I'd actually never thought about entertaining an open relationship before. Nadia was in one. It'd be any day now that she'd officially tie the knot with her boyfriend and girlfriend. Some would call her a lucky girl. I just thought it was too much of a headache. More importantly I didn't want someone else. Felix had occupied pretty much all the romantic residency in my mind and I didn't have room for any more.

"Think on it. You're not going to get a fae throne if you're with a Nephilim."

"Who told you about him?"

"Your dad."

He must really dislike Felix.

Marcus balled his fist and put it in front of his mouth. "Ooh, you really like him."

I lifted my upper lip and looked away. Were my complex internal feelings about this guy that obvious? I wanted to wince again just seeing the look on his face when I left. He looked, emotionless.

The cook came in carrying a large tray of goodies with utensils and placed them on the wide coffee table before leaving.

I took in a deep breath and grabbed half of a sandwich off the tray. "Maybe I don't need to marry. I can run a throne alone." I took a bite but it felt dry in my throat. I felt queasy and unsettled. Was it all because of Felix? Maybe I was upset because we hadn't taken Yasmine out and stopped her wraiths.

Marcus sat back and chuckled. "No, no, no. You like him. I can see it all over that pretty face of yours." He pointed at me and made a circle with his index finger. "Looks like I came too late. Another man has stolen your heart."

"Don't say that," I growled, taking another large bite of my sandwich in spite of my stomach issues. "I have no heart."

Marcus moved closer to me and tapped under my chin with a finger. "Sure, you do, love. Problem is, he's not the best pick for a royal."

"He's not my pick."

Marcus chuckled and picked up a sandwich. "Stubborn as always. Listen, you do need to be married to continue the line."

I couldn't continue a bloodline because I couldn't have kids but I could adopt a powerful kid and that's all that was needed. Power.

Marcus continued. "Only you can't do it with Felix. What I'm offering you is a business deal. You marry me and carry on your affair of the heart with Felix behind the scenes. Having your cake and eating it too and all that."

I didn't want a marriage out of strategy. It was what my mother clearly had and she'd ended up giving up everything and then eventually dying because of it. I wasn't interested in repeating that life.

I looked at Marcus as he finished eating his sandwich, seemingly oblivious to my gaze. I didn't really know him but he behaved like we were old pals. It felt nice but also unsettling. Without my memories I couldn't confirm anything. Everyone was a threat. It was an exhausting way to live. Part of me believed that I'd stuck it out with Alister so long because it was scary living on my own without anyone I could trust, including myself. Felix was lucky to have Faith and Azrael had always stuck with him. Carlos was my guardian but I'd abandoned him like an idiot.

Things weren't the same now. I did have those I could trust. Nadia was free to be the full friend she'd wanted to be without fear from Alister. Felix, at least until now, had seemed devoted to me and by extension his friends seemed to support me. Maybe I was in a position to live differently than my mother. Change the rules. Didn't Marcus want better, too? "Don't you want love?"

Marcus slouched back down on the couch, another sandwich in his hand. He looked ahead at Nadia's outside patio through her glass doors. "I want power. Love is over-rated. I thought you were just like me. Perhaps I was mistaken."

"I *am* just like you." Or so I thought at first. Now, things were fuzzier. He didn't need to know that yet while I sorted things out.

He tilted his head towards me with a side grin. "No, you aren't. And that's quite all right. In theory. You aren't going to win this battle for the throne running after that man and doing the bidding of the angels. You want your memories back, you have your dad and me. Forget the others. Forget that town."

I frowned. He was right. I knew that but another part of

me still hated the idea of leaving those monsters alive to harm more children. It would also make me look more formidable as a fae leader if I had a reputation of eradicating threats which the wraiths were. They'd eat fae all the same. "It's a town full of wraiths that eat children."

"What business is it of ours? We're Unseelie. You've been too long in the human realm."

"Through no fault of my own. They also eat paranormals. They'd eat you and wear your skin. They are a danger to everyone."

He waved a hand at me. "Let your boyfriend and his mates deal with it." He sat up, running his tongue over his bottom lip and removing any crumbs from his mouth. The look had a very sexual effect and I wasn't sure that wasn't his duel purpose. "You need to focus on the campaign. You have that weasel Sylvester on the loose bad-mouthing you whenever he can. And he's been trying to dig up dirt on who you are. It won't be long before he finds what he's looking for. You won't be seen as one of us as a half-demon who grew up in the human world without the right spin. You'll need support to convince voters. And I need your royal lineage combined with mine to make us a formidable pair. Others may doubt your strength but those who remember your mother and those in her ancestry know full well what you are capable of. If you reconnect with your family, it will aid our cause. Let's help each other."

Everything he said made sense. He could get me to where I needed to go. Unfortunately, my currently adolescent mind was stuck on one thing. Talking to Felix.

I shook my head at him. I had to start thinking with my brain. Marcus made perfect sense and without my memories, I really was at a disadvantage. "Fine. Let's do the fake marriage thing. No love."

Marcus stood up. "Glad to hear it. That makes me very

happy. I'll get started on our joint campaign. You realize it's less than a month until decision day."

My eyes grew wide. Did I know that? It seemed like just yesterday I was learning the campaign rules. I slapped my forehead, realizing that time was different and I'd allowed myself to get confused again with fae human time. Even demon realm time ran at the same speed as human time. "Shit, I got confused about the time."

"See this is why you need me. I'll let you rest up. I'll be back later to take you back where you belong." He kissed the top of my head before disappearing.

I let out a breath. I'd made the right decision. I was sure of it. But it didn't feel good.

# CHAPTER 23

*S*ince sleep hadn't come easy while I was at St. Michaels, I'd fallen asleep in Nadia's guest room quickly. The next morning Nadia's housekeeper, a short, stout woman with green skin and red eyes, told me I had a visitor. I figured it was Marcus coming to whisk me away to the world of the fae.

I finished getting ready for the day and strolled in the living room, surprised to see Felix standing there. He had his broad back to me, arms crossed as he stared out at the pool in the backyard. I felt a giddy excitement at seeing him, inwardly pleased that he seemed to still, well, want me. I wanted to kick myself for that thought.

I sat down on the couch. "Didn't expect to see you so soon. Don't still want to hang out with mommy dearest?"

Felix turned slightly to me, golden-brown eyes dead. Something cold wormed its way inside of me. There was no love in his eyes like I was used to seeing. Had my omission of the truth really broken this man? Or maybe his mother had?

He opened his arms. "Come here, I need a hug," he said with very little enthusiasm.

I remained where I sat. I wasn't a woman who jumped at any man's beck and call. "Your feet work fine to come to me."

He twisted his lips, eyes still emotionless. "You lied to me, can't you give me one win?"

I grumbled and stood up. I suppose if this would smooth the waters, I could be accommodating this one time. I walked over to him and he wrapped me tightly in his embrace. I rested my cheek on his chest and closed my eyes as he stroked my back lightly. It was a distinctly Felix thing to do and for a moment, I was content in his attention.

"You disappointed me, Francesca."

"I did explain to you why I did what I did."

He moved me slightly from him and stared into my eyes as if searching for more truth. What else did he really think I was lying about? I'd told him everything. "I know. And I'm having a hard time staying away from you," he replied simply before taking my face between his large hands and leaning his head towards me.

His lips found mine, tongue tickling my own, replacing the coldness in me with heat. He pressed me to him tighter and I dug my hands into his arms. I didn't want to let him go.

However, he had other ideas as he slowly pulled away from me. "I'm sorry, Francesca."

Why was he calling me by my full name? He never did that. "What are you sorry for?"

"Because I think it's time we go our separate ways."

Something stabbed at my heart that I wasn't expecting. Was he dumping me?

He gave me a sad smile and brushed the back of my cheek with his knuckle. "Look, you fully don't trust me and maybe I don't fully trust you. Not to mention our families have some sort of Hatfield-McCoy hate for each other. And you've wanted to get rid of me from day one."

"Not true." Okay, it was very much true. But I was an idiot who didn't know what she really wanted. I was headstrong and sure about most things but when it came to him, I couldn't make a decision and stick to it.

Felix patted me on my head and I felt my eyes burn with anger. Did he really have to seal the deal with an insulting head pat? I fought the urge to kick him in the kneecaps. "You pat me on the head again and I will break you."

Felix threw his head back with a laugh. "Why are you so mad? It's what you want."

"I said it wasn't."

He looked down at me with a frown, his eyes were still a bit lifeless but at least I could feel some type of emotion from him. Was he even sad about this? How had I gone from wifey to some chick he wanted to break up with? "If it's not, renounce your father and come back with me. My mother won't hurt you if you stay under me."

I jutted my chin out, perplexed. Something about what he said hit me wrong. It sounded almost like submission. And let's not even get to the whole giving up my father bit. I may not know the demon, but he had access to getting my memories back. "When you say stay under you, what do you mean?"

"Oh, Francesca, I think you know what I mean." His began to stroke my cheek again but this time I found it agitating.

I shook him off of me. "I submit to no one."

"Well, that's not true. You submitted to Alister. I'm ten times better than him."

"You know that was different. Why are you being a dick?"

He lifted a shoulder, biting his lip as he looked at me with bedroom eyes. I didn't like it. I didn't like this Felix. Was this the dark side of him that Azrael had warned me about?

"Why don't you just come back with me and let me make it up to you?" He reached out and began to rub my arm. "If you really do like me, maybe you can prove it to me."

Something about the way he said it made it very clear

what he meant by proving it to him. This wasn't my Felix. I wanted to be angry but a deep sadness began to take root. How did I fix this? How did I get my old Felix back? Was it too late? Was being next to his demon mother the final nail in the coffin?

Tears stung the back of my eyes against my will. I backed away from him, fighting against showing him any emotion. He couldn't know how sad I was. I puffed out my chest. "You can go. I'm fine with not seeing you again." I turned my back to him holding onto a small hope that he would snap out of whatever he was in and apologize, leaving St. Michaels behind.

"Good," he said simply.

I turned to have the last word but he was gone.

~

It took all the energy I had to focus on campaigning in the fae realm later. We sat in a grand conference room as stuffy looking fae on our campaign team discussed what amounted to the fae version of polling numbers, strategies and debates. The news of Marcus and my engagement seemed to bring a boost to our chances. It seemed even Unseelie fae liked a good love story and as far as I could tell no one knew my background. We'd decided to play it close to the chest for now but the truth would find its way out once we became more popular and the other courts took notice. Of course, I was older but I didn't look unrecognizable from my 12-year-old self.

However, the fae court wasn't front and center on my mind. I still kept thinking about Felix and his cold eyes and overall creepiness toward me. It made my insides feel queasy. I didn't like where we left things. I found myself downright distraught that Felix had turned so frigid towards me. He was the one person I had foolishly believed was unconditional. There was just something about him that gave me comfort. I'd taken for granted that he would always be there. Even when I knew our relationship couldn't last I secretly thought we'd stay connected in some form. Of course, playing it out in your head wasn't the same as feeling the real loss. I wasn't prepared for this kind of pain. Our last encounter replayed in my mind and I couldn't shake it away. Had I really lost him for good? Why was I so stupid to think it wouldn't hurt me? Was I really so foolish to think he would never get tired of me? That I would be the one always in control? I felt like lying on a bed and never getting up.

I also thought of St. Michaels and the wraith. Were more people being lured to their death as I sat in this boring campaign meeting? Had the angels got off their asses and invaded?

A hand snapped in front of my face and I sucked in a breath, sitting upright. I looked over to Marcus who eyed me with slight amusement in his eyes. "If you're going to be a leader, beautiful, you're going to have to pay attention to even the boring bits."

I gave him a tight smile. "Maybe that can be your thing since we're joined."

He raised a brow. "Why should I get stuck with all the boring work? What's on your mind?"

I looked away, staring out at the indigo sky through the tall arched windows of the massive conference room. "Nothing."

"Lies." He leaned into me, looking me over. "Did you break up with the giant?"

I sucked my teeth and turned my back to him.

"Did you tell him about our arrangement and it sent him flying into a jealous rage?"

I looked at his smiling face. Why did he look so damn happy at what he thought was my heartbreak? "No, he left me for his mother."

His smile dropped. "That sounds very inappropriate."

I shrugged as I glared at Sylvester shimmy his way into the palace conference room. "Why is he here?"

Marcus closed his eyes and rubbed the bridge of his nose. "I suppose you really did hear nothing. All the candidates are now to cover the most pressing issues to the fae realm for court discussion."

I scrunched my face in thought. Who knew faes were this organized? Honestly, I'd thought Misandre had gotten the throne by killing someone or from inheriting it. Had that wench really been civil enough to go through a campaign? Well, she did know how to rock a pants suit. Maybe she had. Then when she won, she just did whatever the hell she wanted. I knew for sure that she did not go about working on the needs of the Unseelie fae realm to help her people. She was all about self. That's why everyone hated her. Except no one verbally objected to her under their court because she was powerful and would kill them. She also had dirt on just about every royal in the Unseelie realm, even beyond her court. So, she didn't have to worry about any uprisings.

It was quite impressive in retrospect. She spouted the most hateful, useless rhetoric yet people defended her at every angle they could in public. The only reason I knew that there were many who thought she was self-serving trash was because I was nosey and had some ties in the gossip world.

As I watched Sylvester take a seat across from me, with his smug, pig-nosed face, I wondered if he would be the same kind of leader if he won. Did he know the dirt that Misandre knew to blackmail her supporters? If that was the case, would I even have a chance at winning the throne?

"So," Sylvester began before waving his fingers in our direction. "I heard the two of you are getting married. Congratulations. What nonsense is this?"

Marcus tilted his head back slightly, he flicked a tongue over a fang and lowered his lids.

The whole action gave him an undeniable sexy appeal and I wasn't the only one who noticed. Sylvester dropped his mouth open then caught himself, wiggling in his seat and straightening up.

Marcus gave a cocky smile. Oh, he knew what he was doing. "It's the truth, Sylvie. It was love at first sight for me." He looked over to me with adoring eyes.

All right, this dude was laying it on thick.

Sylvester lifted his chin in obvious disdain. "I can hardly believe that."

This asshole. I bared my teeth. "Of course, you wouldn't, you little rodent. That's because you don't even know what love is. Jealous no one is crazy enough to even like you a little?"

"I'll have you know, you dusty wench, that I have plenty of suitors."

I put a hand to my forehead as if searching off in the distance for something. "Where?"

Marcus placed a hand over mine and leaned in close to me. "Play nice, won't you. If you keep rising to his bait, people won't think you're emotionally strong. A good leader rises above pettiness," he whispered in my ear before giving me a quick peck on the cheek.

I pressed my lips together against my teeth. Misandre was the definition of petty. Guess we were just going to ignore her shoddy leadership and take the higher road. I gave Sylvester a tiny smile. "Sorry, Sylvester for implying no one loved you." Even if it was true.

Sylvester gave me a 'humph' and looked away. I wanted to step on him.

However, for the rest of the meeting I played nice. Actually, it was interesting learning about the challenges to fae kind, both Seelie and Unseelie. Everyone was still worried about the paranormal illness, which had made its way into our realms despite our best efforts to keep it out. There was renewed discussion about building a truce with some of the Seelie fae courts. Something Misandre had actually done for a short time.

My interest also peaked when they talked of the rise of demon interactions ever since the return of the original soulmates, especially in connection with the Unseelie. Misandre teaming up with demons and ghouls hadn't done the reputation of Unseelie fae any good. Some suggested exploring relations with them since there was a mutual disdain for humans. Others opposed it since they felt demons were beneath them and although Unseelie cared little for humans, not all actively went out of their way to destroy them as demons did.

I wasn't opposed to alliances with certain demons, like my father. It also would make news of me being half more palatable to the fae. However, we had to be very careful about who we decided to join. I was still human enough to know that I didn't want to be allies with a child-eating demon like Yasmine. At the thought of her, Felix's face popped in my mind. I couldn't shake him. I wanted to know how he was doing. Being in the fae realm for a few days would mean almost two weeks had passed in the human world. What had happened during that time?

A dramatic sigh interrupted my thoughts. "You really refuse to pay attention, don't you?" Marcus stated, standing up.

I gave him wide, innocent eyes. "I was paying attention. I swear. I was deep in thought about our strategy and the important issues of our world."

He narrowed his eyes and bit his lower lip, studying in me. "Go back to the humans. It's clearly going to be a distraction to us if you don't resolve things with your giant, check on that demonic town, and talk to your father. Do all that, then come back with your pretty head clear. If we are going to have a successful fake marriage you've got to play the part better."

It dawned on me then that Marcus was much more than a pretty face. He was quite perceptive. I understood why my family thought he'd make a good match for me. Good looks, intelligence, and wealth. However, none of that mattered. A formerly jolly half-angel, half-demon kept occupying my heart.

Marcus was putting way more effort into our campaign than me and I was starting to understand it was because my heart wasn't as entirely behind it. However, until I figured out what path I really wanted to take, I had an image to uphold. If I acted or even looked like the weaker half of this arrangement then it would be even harder to make sure people respected us as equals and if I did decide that this was my certain path, I couldn't risk losing my ground. We could campaign as husband and wife all we wanted, but many fae still looked to a man as the leader. As a married couple, if Marcus took any lead, I'd forever be relegated to second status. I'd be no better than a vice-president to him.

I cleared my throat and looked around the now empty room. "I'm not going back for a guy. But I have to go back to talk to my father and get all the answers I can before the truth of what I am comes out."

Marcus gave a twisted smile that successfully displayed how little he believed my words. "I'll make you a portal and send you home." He pulled what appeared to be a small purple box out of his pocket. He took my hand and placed the box there. "Open it."

I did as he requested and raised my brows as I stared down at a large diamond-shaped, sapphire ring. "Engagement ring?"

Marcus moved his head from side to side. "And a communication ring. Since you're only half-fae, I know you can't easily teleport here or communicate across realms. This will let you do that. So, you have a two for one. Lucky you."

I took the ring out of the box and put it on my right ring finger.

Marcus made a noise of disapproval. "Please do me the favor of not embarrassing me by putting your engagement ring on your right hand. I know it is a human tradition to put it on the left finger, but it is one we've taken quite a liking to."

I shook my head, feeling like an idiot. What was going on with me? "Right." I switched the ring and gave him a cheesy smile. I guess I could be happy that I had a ring that could easily come off this time. I grimaced at the thought of the tracking ring that I'd gotten from Alister.

I looked up at Marcus and gave a salute. "Okay, send me back to the human realm."

# CHAPTER 24

$\mathcal{T}$he first person I went to see was Faith. I had to know the outcome of the St. Michaels situation, which I assumed was resolved by now. I figured that would be the quickest matter to get over. Then I'd call dear old dad and get some more answers before returning to the fae.

When Faith answered her door back in Silver Spring, she looked less than thrilled to see me. "Where the fuck have you been?" she grumbled before opening her door wider for me to enter.

"And hello to you, too," I said as I walked into her apartment. "I've been in the fae realm."

She paused in front of her door after closing it, not inviting me further in. "You ditched us."

"What else was there for me to do? I owed a friend a favor for breaking the ward and getting us out. And Felix made it very clear he didn't care about me. We solved the mystery. We're good, right?"

Faith scoffed and crossed her arms. "Hell, no we aren't good. St. Michaels is still operating. Monica is still M.I.A. Then when we finally went to the town, the wards were back up and we can't break it. We think Olivia helped amplify it."

"Felix can't convince his allegedly awesome mother to help us take out an evil demon and her wraiths? I'm beginning to doubt she was such a good woman or that Felix is such a good guy. I mean he's still in that rotten town, after all."

Faith squinted her eyes. "No, he's not. He's back. He left to try to figure out a way to get rid of Yasmine and her people. He's off visiting that old witch, Charlie, now to find a spell or something."

Well that wasn't what I expected to hear after my last meeting with Felix. "No, he wouldn't leave his mother. He told me that."

"Yeah, well his conscience got to him and his mother is refusing to leave. She's able to hold her own so I guess he felt okay leaving even though he risked not getting back in the town."

"People are still leaving the town to get victims, right?"

Faith shook her head. "No. The ward is so strong because it won't let anyone in or out. We're hoping as a last resort we can just starve them out. We have folks posted out there 24/7. The only issue is there are still victims trapped in there."

I scratched my head, thoroughly confused. "How did Felix get out then?"

"He left before that particular ward went up. We should have had your friends fight while the first ward was down."

I closed my eyes, frustrated. Something wasn't right about her story. "Marcus wasn't going to use his resources to start a fight with demons without a benefit to him. But Felix said he was staying in the town. He told me when I was at Nadia's after I left with Marcus."

Faith lifted a brow. "Not possible. Unless he just lied to you and why would he do that?"

"I'm not going crazy. I had a whole conversation with him."

I heard footsteps from further in the apartment and Azrael soon appeared. Had that angel been eavesdropping the whole time? The jerk. "You weren't talking to Felix," they announced, walking closer to us.

"Come again?"

"You were most likely talking to his doppelganger. We've been with Felix up until now."

Faith shivered. "That's creepy as fuck. What was the point?"

Faith wasn't wrong. I'd been totally fooled and, even worse, vulnerable to being attacked. Why hadn't he harmed me?

The angel shrugged. "What did he say?"

"That he felt we weren't right for each other. It felt like a breakup." Just saying it out loud made me feel nauseous. If I didn't know how I felt about Felix before, my body was telling me now. I deeply cared about him and I did not want to let him go. Not for anything. Shit.

Azrael scratched their chin, squinting their eyes as they pondered my response. "Well, that would keep you from coming back to town if you thought Felix wouldn't want you."

"So, we think the demons really are behind these doppel-gangers?" It certainly made sense being that we hadn't encountered them until we got to the town. It just freaked me out that now they were on the move and this thing had come to visit me in the demon realm with no problems. "He could have killed me. I suspected nothing."

Azrael gave a slow nod. "Yes, he could have."

I didn't have time for this. "Okay, let's get rid of that town. If his mother doesn't want to come out then she has to go too." Of course, that would do nothing to repair any rela-tionship I was even thinking about with Felix.

Faith snorted. "Or maybe we can get some help clearing out the demons before we go destroying a whole town with innocent people in it. We've been trying to reach you because we wanted to see if you could get your dad to come and break the ward but you left."

That certainly sounded like a less destructive option and I did need to talk to the man. Of course, getting my father to help us might not be realistic. "My father is a demon King. I'm not saying he's horrible but I need to give him a reason to go break that ward."

Azrael tapped the back of their head against the wall. "Your father and Olivia are enemies. Wouldn't he want to break the ward to get her back?"

I chewed on the inside of my cheek as I thought. Assuming my father had actually captured Olivia, then it would stand to reason that he would want her back. However, it felt wrong to set up a situation where Felix could lose his mother. "If he breaks the ward, he'll want to take Felix's mother."

"We won't allow that."

I snorted. "Like you'll have a choice. My father is not weak. If Olivia could help put up a ward that you guys can't break, how easy do you think it will be to get my father to back off when he was strong enough to trap her?"

Faith grumbled something intelligible. "You're his daughter. Can't you just ask him not to hurt the mother of your kind of boyfriend?"

I lifted my upper lip in a silent snarl. Did she want me to lie? Believe it or not, that wasn't my specialty. "Felix can't stand me right now. I don't think that's going to fly."

Azrael pushed themselves from the wall and lightly tapped the top of my head with their fist. "How many times do I have to say that the Felix you spoke to was a doppelganger?"

I winced and plucked the angel in the forehead. Was Azrael being playful with me? Were they, dare I say, liking me now? "Well, even before then, he didn't want to leave. But fine, whatever, I'll try. And what's the backup plan if my father refuses or decides to come for Olivia?"

Azrael ruffled my hair and I swatted the angel's hand away. "We'll work it out."

"Would you stop touching my head? What is wrong with you?"

"We thought all along that you were the problem. But you aren't, are you?" The angel looked almost shocked at this statement. "You're in love with him."

I leaned back. "I'm not. Shut up. What?" I rolled my eyes and looked away. Was it love that I was feeling? Maybe, but I definitely didn't want to discuss my feelings with the two of them.

Faith waved her hands in the air. "Girl, you aren't in middle school, it's okay to love. Felix is lovable."

I cut my eyes at her. "Says the girl who can't commit to anyone."

She shot me the middle finger. "It's not about me. Go to Hell."

I glared at her. Maybe we weren't friends just yet.

Faith smirked. "I was talking literally. Go to the underworld and talk to your dad. We're wasting time."

～

The next time I crossed the portal to the underworld after summoning my father, I did not end up in his nice spacious mansion in the south. Nope, this looked clearly like Hell. I stood in what appeared to be a large cavern. Orb lights hung in the air along with sconces holding fire. The air felt stifling and immobile and I opened my mouth just a crack in order to breathe. Sweat started to pull at my hairline and neck and I wiped at it absent-mindedly.

Black and red etchings of languages I didn't know

covered the cave walls. The place smelled like mildew and something very burnt and foul. Far off, in a direction I couldn't determine, I heard faint screams and deep laughter.

Out of the depths of the cavern a dark figure approached. The shape did not match my father's. Soon a man dressed all in black with a buzz cut appeared. He looked no older than his mid-twenties and his eyes were entirely black, no whites.

One of Herrod's minions. He had many of these humanoid beings to do his dirty work. Outside of the eyes they looked unassuming but they were very powerful.

"Where's my father?"

"Indisposed. He told me to have you wait in his study." He snapped his fingers and instantly the surrounding cavern morphed away, replaced by the same room I was in when I first visited Herrod.

I spun around, a little freaked out by the sudden change. When I turned to look back to buzzcut, he was now standing with a tray holding a short glass full of brown liquid. He didn't say anything to me, just looked at me with those same creepy dead eyes. I took the glass and lifted it slightly in an unspoken thanks. The buzzcut bowed and then stepped back, standing against the nearest wall in the shadows of the room.

I sat down on the couch near the window. "You gonna stay there?"

"Yes, I am your minion."

"Say what now?"

"I am your minion."

I didn't have minions. What the hell was he talking about? "I didn't ask for a minion."

"Your father assigned me to you. I am to serve at your call."

"What's your name?"

"Lucas."

I nodded slowly. My father had given me a minion. What

the hell was I supposed to do with him? "You stay here, right?"

"I am to go where you go."

"Like a bodyguard?"

Lucas nodded. I rolled my eyes and shook my head. How the hell was I going to explain that to the fae? I couldn't just walk around with a black-eyed demon like it was no biggie. I took a sip of my drink as I pondered my predicament. I really needed my own place to live. Maybe I could hide him out there.

Before I could think further into possible living arrangements, my father appeared in the leather chair beside me. Since I was used to how demons and fae just liked to materialized, I wasn't surprised.

Herrod gave me a gentle smile. "I'm glad you returned so quickly. I was just about to contact you."

I squinted my eyes at him and leaned forward. There was a speck of red on his crisp white button down. "You got a little blood on you," I stated, pointing at his collar.

Herrod looked down and then snapped his fingers, magically erasing the blood. "I do hate when they make a mess."

I nodded slowly. "Yeah, me too. Anyway, I'm actually here to get your help on the town. And to stop some doppelgangers."

He propped his elbow on the arm of his chair and rested his cheek against his fist. He gave me a look of boredom. Something told me he wasn't going to be jumping up and down to help us out. "Beware of doppelgangers. They are harbingers of death."

"One that looked like Felix fooled me. I couldn't even tell it really wasn't him."

Herrod sat up at that. "That would make it a strong doppelganger. It is a possibility that your Felix may die then."

My heart dropped. "What? Don't say that."

Herrod raised his brows but no sympathy showed on his

face. "I'm sorry, my daughter but that is usually the way that it is. You must get rid of it if you wish to avoid the fates."

"How do I do that?"

"By ridding yourself of whoever conjured it."

If that was Yasmine, I'd have no problem with that. "It might be the demon lady from St. Michaels. Problem is, we can't break into the town to get to her. That's where I was hoping you'd come in to help."

Herrod chuckled. "I know you like the boy but perhaps things are better this way. Getting into a whole messy affair with another demon is a waste of my resources."

"Olivia is there."

He gave me a confused look.

So, he wanted to play dumb, huh? "Sir, Olivia. The demon you held captive. Felix's mother. Which I think you knew. Why are you holding women in cells?"

He narrowed his eyes. "You have no idea who Olivia is. She played human very well around that son of hers but she is far from it. It is a long story and we have more important matters to discuss. Just know she is not your friend and she means nothing good for you. Stay far from her."

I frowned. "Uh, I'd like to hear more about that. She's a demon, they aren't known for meaning good for anyone. What did she do that made you want to lock her up even though she'd left that world and was being a mother?"

Herrod rubbed his head as if I'd asked something ridiculous. "Oh, daughter there is so much to teach you. I will say this, Olivia is a higher echelon demon. I tried to weaken her and she's probably a bit rusty from being in hiding before that but with this freedom she has, she'll get back to her old glory in no time."

That sounded foreboding. What kind of woman was Felix's mother? That she was siding with Yasmine definitely made her morally questionable. However, I had worked for Misandre and Alister so I couldn't throw stones too hard.

The major point was if my father didn't like her and saw her as a threat then he should have been agreeable to helping us. "So, you will join us in taking down the ward?"

"My dear, that is still more trouble than I'm willing to direct right now. If push comes to shove, then I suppose I can help as a favor to you. However, I think you'll be able to do away with that Yasmine just fine. If I go, I'm only going for one thing: Olivia. Are you ready for the consequences of me killing that boy's mother?"

I sighed and put my drink down on the coffee table. Why did it have to go so far and right now? Couldn't he hold his anger for another day? What had this woman done to him? If I allowed my father to help us, knowing he would kill Felix's mother, Felix would never forgive me. I could be conflicted about my feelings towards him all I wanted but I knew that him hating me was not what I wanted. No, if I made the decision to get Herrod's help, I'd have to tell Felix everything and prepare him for that possibility. Maybe that might get Olivia to get off her ass and disappear from the town, and take her wards with her?

I glared at my father. "You are being difficult."

He waved a hand at me. "Fine, fine. I suppose I can gift you this for all our time apart. I can break the ward for you. But the rest is up to you. If you call me to do more just know what I will do."

I clapped my hands and shook them. "Thank you."

"Wouldn't you rather hear why I was going to contact you?"

Oops, I'd forgotten that part. Of course, I did. I figured if he'd wanted to reach out to me, it was to give me more information I needed to know. "Sure."

He smiled slowly. "I can return your memories. All of them."

I blinked several times, my heart speeding up. "Uh, could you have led with that?"

He raised a shoulder. "I tried."

"Not hard enough. How?"

"I've been working on it. I thought I said? I finally have a potion that I believe will work. I was told it might take a while for all of your memories to come. Apparently having them all come crashing back to you at once might be overwhelming for your body."

I looked around the room as if it would hold the secret to regaining my memories. "Well, let's get this show on the road. Where is the potion?"

Herrod glanced down at my drink. "You drink too slow."

I pointed to the brown liquid. I had just taken a couple of sips. It tasted like scotch. "This? Did you poison me?"

Herrod gave me an incredulous look, adjusting in his seat. "Do you still not believe that you are my daughter? Why would I do such a monstrous thing?"

"Is there anyone else who I can trust who can verify your story?"

He let out a breath. "No, because we were keeping you secret. If you'd just drink that potion, you'd remember it all."

I sucked my teeth not sure I believed him. I couldn't quite figure out his angle for lying but it didn't mean there wasn't one. "What if that's a potion that manipulates my mind?"

"It's possible."

He didn't elaborate and I glared at him. He blinked but kept quiet and we engaged in a short starring match until finally I swore and growled. Curiosity and maybe desperation had won out.

"Fine. But if I die or turn into some mindless robot, there is a rather large half-angel/half-demon that will come here and ruin your world." Did I know if Felix could really kill Herrod? No, but he'd defeated Alister so it wasn't a reach. I picked up the drink and gulped it down quickly without waiting for any confirmation from Herrod.

I put the glass down and paused, waiting for some type of feeling to overcome me. Nothing. "I didn't taste anything."

Herrod stood up. "You wouldn't." He offered me his hand. "You're going to be very sleepy so let's get you to a bed."

I still felt fine but I stood up anyway. "No, I don't want to sleep here. I need to be ho-" A sudden dizziness racked my brain and I stumbled slightly. Herrod gripped my hand and he led me through the dark halls of his mansion to a guest room. The walls were a pale pink and the bedspread was white with white and pink pillows over it. There was a dollhouse off to the left near a tall bay window.

"Was a little girl living here?" I asked, sitting down on the bed. My vision was starting to blur and I fell back on the pillows. I hated sleeping in strange places but some part of me felt this place wasn't so foreign. I felt way too vulnerable. The only good thing is that others knew I was coming here, including Nadia.

"Yes, there was for a short time," Herrod answered, taking my shoes off and putting them near the bed. "You." He kissed my forehead and my eyes closed.

That was oddly tender of him. Was it possible he really was my father? Could I really trust him? It was too late to second guess myself now. My mind clouded over before I could think of any other questions to ask.

# CHAPTER 25

*I* was in a dream or a memory, I couldn't tell.

*I was sitting on a couch, a beer in one hand and fries in another. I was laughing, staring at the TV. An elbow lightly nudged my arm and I looked to my right.*

*Felix pointed at the screen. "This is funny."*

*"You do realize I am watching this with you," I muttered, shaking my head. "You always point out the funny parts like I can't see that it's funny."*

*He gave me a toothy smile, nodding. "I know. I like annoying you," he replied before taking a swig of his beer and looking back at the screen.*

*I studied the profile of his face. He was, at this time, clean-shaven. His hair wasn't as long as I knew it now but it was long enough to push behind his ears. I smiled. I loved his face. His body was amazing but it was his face. Those kind smiling eyes and strong jaw, which I could now see without the beard, and those full lips. I'd always thought he was handsome but I tried not to look at him too often. If Alister ever caught me even glancing too long at Felix he would kill him. That was one of many reasons why I had to break up with the demon.*

*Felix didn't know I was going to do so. I wasn't sure I wanted to* tell him. He'd think it was because of him. Maybe he was a reason. I'd realized for a while that my feelings were shifting for him. My stupid heart would beat faster around him at the most random of moments. Even then as I watched him, I could feel butterflies forming.

I shook my head quickly and stuffed several fries in my mouth, staring back at the TV.

"You've been looking at me a lot. Why is that?" Felix asked.

I nearly choked on my fries and covered my mouth, coughing. Felix reached over and patted my back. I took a swig of my beer and swallowed before answering. "I think it's all in your head."

I glanced over at him and he wasn't smiling now. He looked contemplative as he studied me.

"What?" I asked, leaning back.

"Break up with him."

I knew he meant Alister. I definitely couldn't tell him my plan now. Even when I broke up with Alister I couldn't go to Felix. The demon would kill him, assuming he was the reason, no matter what I said. And with everything in my being, I wanted to protect this man. Because I–

~

*I* woke up to a dark room but as my eyes adjusted, I could see it was the same child's room I'd passed out in. Memories crashed into my mind like a jackhammer and I closed my eyes tightly. I rubbed my forehead with the heel of my hand to push away the pain but it was fruitless.

Images continued to flash before my mind's eye. Me running around in a garden. Hiding behind bushes and yelling, happily, when a little boy popped out in front of me. Marcus. We were playing tag.

More images. Me sitting at a long table in what appeared to be a fancy dining room. A grim-looking but handsome older man with a well-trimmed white beard sat at the head of the table cutting his food as he spoke. Closest to him was a beautiful woman with eyes like mine. My mother. She nodded her head, talking back. Across from me sat a boy a few years older than me with shining dark blue eyes and light brown skin. He stuck his tongue out and flicked food at me. I wiped my face and tossed a biscuit at him.

Another image of a man that looked an awful lot like Herrod picking me up and swinging me in the air. He had a squinty eyed smile and I was giggling. I couldn't have been more than five.

More images. My father and mother in an embrace as the three of us sat outside staring at the field of purple flowers.

Another one. My mother crying, walking down a palace hall. I followed closely behind, picking up a chair and tossing it against a wall.

Then us living in a small two-bedroom apartment. Me screaming at seeing a cockroach. Me bullied by a tall girl. Me having my first kiss at 15 with a drummer in the school band. Me starting college and pulling all-nighters with my roommate.

I saw my mother in a hospital bed. Her grave. I remembered the Event and magic flooding my body. Me hiding in buildings, scared.

I remembered Nadia and I gossiping in our shared apartment. Meeting Alister, then his profession of love. Felix. I remembered Felix. My core flooded with feelings. Love, lust, happiness, sadness, anger, fear.

I remembered it all.

Tears flooded my eyes as my headache persisted. I bent my body forward in a tight ball, grinding my teeth as the memories continued. How long would this go on?

"Go back to sleep, daughter." Herrod's voice cut through the darkness of my pain.

A soothing warmth spread through me and darkness entered my mind.

*I* wasn't sure how much time had passed when I woke back up. It was brighter in the room so I assumed it was daytime. I yawned and sat up, rubbing my eyes. My headache was gone but my memories and the emotions were still there. I had memories now that I'd forgotten well before the angels wiped my mind. My father was right, my mother had erased my mind of my prior life. I was twelve then, how had I not questioned that? She must have implanted other memories but those did not come with me this time.

The door to the room opened and Herrod walked in holding a tray of food. He placed it on my bedside table before sitting down at the foot of the bed, eyes not showing emotion as he looked at me.

"You're my dad."

He nodded. "You remember me."

I smiled. I remembered loving my father. I loved the man who adopted me but I'd loved Herrod too before we came to the human world. Shame crashed over me for being so cruel to him earlier but hell, I hadn't known know him then.

My eyes watered again against my will. I had so much emotion for him. I hadn't seen my father in over fifteen years. I wasn't an emotional person but something pushed me to crawl over and give him the tightest hug I could. "Dad." I couldn't say anything else. I was feeling too much. All the memories coming back to me at once were now attacking me with emotion and throwing me out of whack.

Herrod hugged me just as tightly. "Baby girl."

We remained in an embrace for a long while before I slowly pulled away. I had so many questions running through my mind even with my memories. "I remember everything. Living in the fae realm with my mother, the man I called father and my brother. I remember hanging out with

Marcus. I had a memory of me being at the hospital. I was maybe thirteen or fourteen. I think I had my tonsils taken out?"

Herrod just nodded his head. "Do you remember how you got your golden sword?"

I frowned and searched my now healing mind. I raised my brows, spotting the memory. "It was a birthday gift I received. Alister threw me a party and I had a table full of gifts. The sword came from an unknown recipient. Alister was pissed because I loved that gift more than any other." Wait, why did my father ask me that? I looked over to Herrod with wide eyes. "Did you get me that sword?"

He smiled. "Yes. I've gotten you many gifts throughout the years. When I'd lost track of you, it was devastating. I was thankful to have found you again. Although you were dating that demon, which wasn't the most ideal, at least I knew you were safe. Alister was an ally of sorts."

"Did he know I was your daughter?"

"He had suspicions but I never confirmed. For all his faults, Alister seemed to really love you."

I felt a pang of regret. "Should I have not killed him?"

Herrod chuckled. "No, you did what you had to do. Just because he loved you didn't mean he could do as he pleased. He was too possessive. You aren't a thing to lock up and keep behind glass. As much as I'd like to do that. No, you are a warrior. Plus, he was a prick. Just because he was an ally didn't mean I liked him."

I slumped my shoulders in relief. Seems dear old dad was a bit protective himself. He didn't like Alister. He didn't like Felix. "Seems you don't like my taste in men."

Herrod stroked his chin. "I don't know. I think I like that Marcus fellow."

I rolled my eyes. Of course, he would. "You'll have to get over that. You brought my memories back, dad. And I now remember something I didn't before."

"What's that?'

I swung my legs to the side of the bed. "I'm in love."

Herrod stared at me for a beat then ran a hand down his face in exasperation. "Have better taste in men, my daughter."

I jumped up and put my shoes on. "Too late. Okay, I have to run off. I'll contact you when we are ready for the ward to come down. You'll come through, right?" I gave him an expectant look. Now that I knew he was my father, I did have expectations that he wouldn't let me down. He wasn't exactly a dead-beat dad. He had solid reasons for keeping his distance and then there was me going off the grid. Still, I wasn't too good to make him feel guilty.

Herrod sighed. "I will clear my schedule."

I smiled and leaned down to give him another tight hug. I couldn't explain how knowing my past and being with my own flesh and blood had just renewed me. I was still jobless and homeless but I wasn't alone. Okay, my father was a demon King from Hell who had once sided with evil soul-mates out to rule the world and had kidnapped and locked up my love interest's mother but we couldn't pick our family, could we?

## CHAPTER 26

When I arrived back at Faith's place, she wasn't alone. Azrael was still there and this time Felix had returned. As soon as I saw him my heartbeat hammered in my ears. I wanted to run to him and have him wrap me in his bear hug and never let go. However, my pride wouldn't let me. I pressed my lips together and strolled into her living room with as much nonchalant energy as I could muster.

Felix immediately jumped up from the couch but he didn't move, just stared at me with wide sorrowful eyes. What was that about? "They told me about the doppelganger."

Ah. "I know it wasn't you now. But it's still a problem. My father said doppelgangers can be a foreshadowing of death." I didn't think to ask him if that death would be the person the doppelganger visited or the person they were mimicking. I'd have to follow up on that.

Felix gave a curt nod. "I'm sorry about how we left things."

I shrugged as I sat down at Faith's dining room table. I hadn't realized the last time I visited, but Faith's place was a pig stye. She had shoes thrown about the place and books scattered across her coffee table. Past the dining room I could see dishes piling up in the sink and dirty pots on the stove. I looked back down at the table and saw it had food crumbs and stains on the wood. How did she not have a roach problem? Maybe she did.

I backed my chair away from the table, ignoring her sloppy digs for now. I had news to share. "So, I spoke to my father and he agreed to help us take down the ward at St. Michaels."

Azrael tilted their head, raising their brows in surprise. "Really? That easy?"

I shrugged. "I'm his daughter. He did say he couldn't help us actually fight but we don't need him for that."

"You sure he won't help us fight? Yasmine's a powerful demon."

"True, but maybe she isn't that strong when Olivia isn't there." I avoided Felix's eyes at that. I really didn't want to talk about how my father planned to harm his mother if he did help us fight. "Anyway, we can pool a group together from here and get the angels. That should be enough to fight Yasmine's wraiths and rescue her victims. We aren't some low-level group. I'm the daughter of a demon king and fae queen, I've got power. Felix is stupid powerful, Azrael you're a high-ranking angel and Faith's a superpowered member of the Six. We can do this."

Azrael gave me a wink. "I like your confidence."

I pointed at him, acknowledging their compliment. "And, no big deal, but I got my memories back."

The three of them looked at me with shocked eyes.

Faith leaned toward me from the couch. "Say what now?"

I then began to replay my visit with Herrod. I shared some of my memories. Felix confirmed some of the ones he knew from our experiences together or things I'd shared before I lost my memories.

Faith placed her hands on her face, squishing her cheeks. "How do we know he didn't insert himself into your memories?"

Azrael walked over to me and leaned forward, staring at my face as if searching for something. I looked back at them with questioning eyes. "Problem?"

The angel stood up straight and nodded. "I don't sense that you're bespelled. That doesn't mean you aren't, though. We'll keep an eye on you. If Herrod has a plan to use you, we won't let it happen."

It was unusual that Azrael was so caring. Naturally, I was suspicious. I didn't need my memories to know how untrustworthy angels were. What I did recall was that they were dangerous. Yet, Azrael had never made me feel threatened like my past encounters with angels. Maybe they weren't all bad.

I looked over to Felix who stared back at me with intense eyes. He looked like he was struggling with what to do. His hands were balled into tight fists and I could actually see the strain in his body. He was holding himself back from me, probably waiting until I gave him a sign that it was okay for him to come to me.

I gave him a soft smile. "Felix, do you have time to talk back at your place?"

"Absolutely," he replied in a low voice. The baritone of the sound shook me slightly.

Azrael rapped the table with their knuckles. "All right you crazy kids, go reconnect or whatever you call it. We'll go rally the troops. I'll get in touch with Carlos and tell him you've recovered. He'd be happy to hear that. Meet back here tomorrow morning. 6 am sharp."

I got up and glared at the angel. "Really, that early?"

Azrael nodded with amused eyes. "I'd make it today but-" the angel glanced over to Felix who was walking over to me like a man possessed. "We do need to strategize. And I think he might explode if we don't give you two some alone time."

And before I could reply with embarrassment, Felix grabbed my hand and whisked us out of there.

～

We reappeared in Felix's apartment and I looked around his clean space, noticing the drastic difference between Faith's and his place. I'd always known he was neat but after coming from Faith's, his place looked even more spotless. "How did I not know your place was so clean?"

Felix squeezed my hand. "Francesca."

I looked up at him and saw that his eyes were almost fearful. Did he think I was lying? Perhaps he still thought I wouldn't remember him. Why the hell wasn't he speaking?

I bit my lip, racking my brain on how to break the silence. I was the one who asked to speak to him separately after all. Why was I waiting on him? Then it hit me. I chuckled before talking, a memory coming to the front of my brain. "We would have the most mundane conversations when we were on stakeouts. The last one was about you wishing we could eat hot wings again. Then that went into a conversation about your favorite type of wings. I acted so annoyed but I wasn't. I never was." I avoided his eyes, nervous about the confession I was making. "I liked our talks. They always calmed me. You always calmed me. I'd never met a man who seemed so damn content with life. No matter what was going on. When we'd fight Alister's enemies you did it smiling. I mean, that was a little psychotic but you were just always so happy. You were mostly why I broke it off with Alister. You were mostly why I wanted to retire from being an enforcer. It was you. It was always you."

I kept my head low, still too coward to look up at him.

The longer his silence stretched the more embarrassed I felt about it all. Maybe he really wasn't into me anymore.

Felix let go of my hand and moved his own to my face, brushing my jaw with his thumb. His eyes had softened now, almost glistening. "Francesca. I've been waiting for you." He dropped his shoulders as if letting go of a great weight. He must have been exhausted all this time waiting for me to remember him.

I touched his hand. "I'm here."

He tapped his forehead to mine. "Can I kiss you?"

"Please."

The right corner of his mouth turned up again and he leaned forward, pressing his lips to mine. The kiss was soft and slow, as if we had all the time in the world. But it wasn't enough for me. "More," I whispered into his mouth and raised a hand to rest on his chest.

A short chuckle released from him that I felt vibrate into my fingers. He pressed a free hand to my lower back and brought me closer to him as our lips parted and tongues began an impassioned dance together. Each touch of his tongue awakened my core. I moved my hands, wrapping them around his neck so that I could press even closer to him, my breast mashing against his chest.

He gently grazed my lower lip and I returned it with a nip of his upper lip. I could kiss, lick and bite his lips for eternity but right now I wanted something else. "More," I whispered.

"Yes, ma'am," he growled back before moving his tongue to my neck, tracing an invisible pattern on my skin and sending me on the edge of control.

A sudden gust of wind surrounded us, lifting my hair slightly and sending me out of sorts. Suddenly we were in his bedroom. Had he just teleported us there without warning? Show off. I liked it.

He nibbled on the other side of my neck as if to remind me that he was there. Not that I needed it. My neck was a key zone for me so I was practically a puddle at that point and yet I wanted – "More."

"Can I take control?" he whispered, his mouth now near my collarbone. This too had me weak. At this point maybe my whole body was an erogenous zone with him.

"Hell, yeah."

"Lift up your leg."

I did as he told me and wrapped a leg as near to his waist as I could lift it. My boot slipped off my foot but his hands were still on me. I raised a brow and looked down at my bare foot, puzzled. Now how had that happened?

"Other leg," Felix ordered. A hand was now under my shirt, thumb rubbing over my rib cage ever so lightly. Again, it sent tingles through me.

I raised my other leg and did as I was told and my boot and socks also shot off all on their own. When I lowered my leg back down, I felt my jeans unbuckle, the zipper sliding down. I was sure Felix was doing this and it was damn impressive and sexy as hell.

His large hand moved up to one of my bra covered breast and I threw my head back at the sudden sensation as my jeans and now soaked panties moved down my legs to my ankles.

He brought his mouth to my right ear. "Jump on me," he breathed out and I could have exploded right then and there.

However, I did not. I wanted to see where this was going. I jumped up and wrapped my legs around his waist. He kicked jeans and panties from his path and walked us to his bed. We leaned forward until my back was on his bed. He pointed his index and middle finger in an upwards motion and my shirt rose up and over my head. My bra unclasped and moved down my shoulders before floating away with the rest of my discarded clothes.

Was he doing this with his angel magic or his demon magic? Did I care? "Neat trick," I cracked.

He gave me a devilish grin before taking his own shirt off the old fashioned away, kicking his shoes off at the same time. Once again, I was reminded of how damn fine he was. Broad, cut shoulders. Toned arms. He didn't have a six-pack but that didn't matter. It was close and I wanted to lick my way down his center but I stayed where I was. He was running this show and this was one time I didn't mind falling back.

He leaned over me again, licking the tips of my breast teasingly before placing his hands on my knees and spreading my legs apart. The air hit my center and I arched up and closed my eyes, tickled.

"I'm going to taste you now."

My eyes popped open and I looked down. Felix was already on his knees in between my legs and then I felt his lips on mine. When his tongue licked me, I sighed. I actually sighed. His mouth felt like silk. I melted for him more, spreading my legs wider as he continued to bring me to climax.

The feeling was more than I could have expected. My body felt weightless as I buzzed with ecstasy. I grasped at his covers, wrapping a leg around his back as I moved with the pace of his tongue. Soon the buildup met its end and I crashed, screaming as I was taken beyond my control.

"Baby girl, you're floating," I heard Felix say.

I opened my eyes to see him looking up at me, licking his lips. Just the sight of him doing that melted me again but something was off. The angle was wrong. I shouldn't have been looking down at him. I looked around and sure enough I was floating. I was only a few inches above his bed but it was still something. I'd floated before, being fae and all that. However, I didn't recall every doing so with sex.

I allowed my body to float as I coasted in the afterglow. I wanted to say something but I was too speechless. Felix

275

could be a silly, lovable oaf many occasions but he knew how to step up when the time was right.

I glanced at him as he stood up. "More." I smiled.

He bit his lip as he undid his pants and stepped out of them. I turned my body so that I was in a kneeling position, still hovering over the bed. He seemed to understand what I wanted and he laid on the bed under me. I looked down at the length of him and let in a breath. I had to admit, I was slightly intimidated but I knew we were made for each other. We would fit.

I floated down to him and let out a gasp as I felt him enter me. He breathed a soft curse as his hands found my hips. I started a slow grind, closing my eyes as I let my body take over. His hands moved to my breast. Massaging, tweaking. I felt a lick on my nipple and I scrunched my face, lost in pleasure.

He brought his hands back down to my hips and took control, moving upwards to counter my moves as he set the pace. I let him, still happy to give up control. He quickened his movements then slowed down. I leaned forward and balanced my hands back on his chest. His skin was slick with sweat under my fingers but I knew I was glistening just as much. I grinned, catching his eyes as he looked up at me. He looked completely mesmerized. By me? My heart clenched and I moved forward, kissing him.

Soon weightlessness returned and I felt him mumble something through my mouth. I pulled away slightly, glancing over his shoulder to see we were higher off the bed than I was earlier. Felix looked sideways to catch his bearings and I increased my pace to draw his attention back to me. He tilted his head back, swearing again and that was all the encouragement I needed. I quickened even more, giving my thighs a workout and soon felt his fingers on my center, bringing me along with him. I crashed again, trembling over him, but I kept moving until seconds later he joined me in an explosion of pleasure. He bucked up, rapidly, before gradually slowing down, cursing all the way. Funny, I hadn't known Felix to curse much. I guess I now know what did it for him.

I chuckled, falling into him as we continued to float and relax from our mutual high.

He stroked my hair and kissed the top of my head. "Why are you laughing? Did I make a stupid face?"

I laughed again. "No. I'm just happy."

He gave me a gentle squeeze before continuing to stroke my hair. I felt like a cat being petted but I loved it. "I'm happy too. I can't believe this is real. Do you know how long I've loved you?"

I closed my eyes, the squeeze on my heart returning. To hear him say those words. They were the words I was hoping to hear one day when I was finally free of Alister. They felt amazing. I knew I'd been bespelled with no memory but I still felt foolish for not having known how much I cared about this man from before. It made me hate the angels even more. It also made me a little annoyed at my father for not stepping in sooner to help me get away from Alister. However, I was no damsel. I supposed this journey had to happen like this.

Felix kicked a leg down and it hung loosely in the air. "This is crazy but kind of cool. I'm not sure but I think floating made things more intense if you know what I mean."

I plucked at his chest. "Yes, it can do that. But you're the one with the trickery."

His chest moved me up and down with a chuckle. "I did warn you months ago what I would do."

Yes, I remembered. When I had tried to make the moves on him, he had shot me down until my memory returned. He'd promised me it would be well worth the wait. And it sure as hell was.

"I've got more secrets up my sleeve."

"Well, damn. Don't tease me."

"Marry me."

I stiffened. I'd just gotten my memory back. I couldn't wrap my mind around that concept. Marriage? After Alister, I didn't think it would ever be for me. However, Felix was nothing like that asshole but, still, I needed time. Everything was still so fresh for me. Now that my mind was complete I needed to learn myself again and—Oh crap.

I squeezed my eyes shut, cursing inside my brain. I'd told Marcus I'd agree to marry him. Even if it was just a business arrangement, it wouldn't fly with Felix and me. I had to tell him. Maybe I could just go to Marcus and call the whole thing off. Things were different now that I had my memories and I knew the Felix I spoke to at Nadia's wasn't the real him. What would Marcus do if I fell back from that promise? Did I really care? What if we became enemies? The truth was, there was no way I would win that throne if Marcus was against me. What if I just gave it up and focused on the throne I deserved by lineage? That would be a fight with a brother I hadn't seen in almost two decades.

Sensing what he probably thought was my hesitation Felix spoke again. "Look at me."

I moved my head to see him better.

He brushed my cheek with his thumb. "Take your time on giving me an answer but I am serious. We'll work out everything with our parents. Don't worry about that. And even if you become a fae Queen, we can navigate our way there too. I just want to be with you. That's all that matters to me."

He was so sincere, so beautiful in every way. I couldn't hurt him. I had to get out of this marriage arrangement. There was no need in telling him about something that wasn't going to happen.

# CHAPTER 27

The morning came faster than I wanted it to which was never surprising. I looked at the ceiling as I psyched myself up for the impending fight at St. Michaels. I never took a battle for granted. It was always possible that some or all of us wouldn't make it out alive. I didn't want to die with regrets but also didn't want to die with any misunderstandings. If I told Felix the truth now without having it resolved with Marcus before our fight then our short-term love affair would end on a sour note if one of us died in battle. No, it was better to keep this hidden for now after such an amazing night.

But my mind wandered all night as I took in old memories and fretted about what to do with Marcus and what exactly I wanted to do with my life. I sat up, staring at Felix's carpeted floor knowing I needed to get moving. I felt Felix move beside me and soon a light kiss on my shoulder.

"Think we have time this morning?" He wiggled his brows with a devilish grin.

I knew exactly what he was implying. We'd been up half the night doing what he was implying. As much as I wanted to, Azrael had us meeting them at stupid-early o'clock. I leaned forward and gave him a quick kiss. "I don't think we have time. We better not have time."

Felix snorted. "You're right, I like to take my time with you." He grazed my shoulder with his teeth before getting up.

An instant heat flushed my core remembering the night's events and the selfish part of me wanted to rethink the whole being on time things when we heard a knock at the door.

"That's probably Azrael coming to light a fire under us," Felix started slipping on his briefs and pants before heading to the door.

I got dressed as well, soon hearing an exclamation from Felix that sounded like a happy surprise. He called my name a second later. I walked out to the front, fully dressed but wanting a shower and a toothbrush. This might be a fae magic cleaning kind of day.

I paused at the entrance to the living room. Felix stood beside Carlos dressed in all white armor except for silver etchings that seemingly glowed. I always considered him a handsome older man and today he looked almost regal. It was a shame that he was going to have to get blood on it.

"Carlos! You look fancy," I exclaimed, opening my arms.

Carlos quickly embraced me in a tight hug. "I heard you got your memories back. I'm so happy for you. And you met your father."

I nodded cautiously. The way he said it, the look in his eyes. Something made me suspicious. "Did you know Herrod was my father? Did all the angels know?"

Felix cleared his throat. "I'm going to wash up quickly and let you guys talk." He then walked down the hall to his bedroom and bath. I looked back at Carlos, expectedly.

He shrugged, sitting down on the couch. "Some of us did. I did. Azrael did not. I only came into that knowledge recently."

"Why not tell me?"

Carlos tilted his head and gave me a patient smile. "He's a

demon lord of Hell. Despite what you are, you've been slowly working your way to a path of light. Reconnecting you two was not ideal. However, if I'd known he'd have the power to return your memories, I would have rethought things."

"Thanks," I said dryly. I was pissed but I had to remind myself he was an elite angel, he wouldn't do me any favors if it involved connecting to a demon.

Carlos leaned forward, resting his forearms on his thighs. "I'm sorry. And I'm sorry I haven't been around lately."

I rolled my eyes. "I'm not a child. I don't need to be up under you."

He pursed his lips together. "And now that you have your father, you don't need me anymore."

I huffed out a breath. He did look sad. Had he really thought of me like a daughter? Despite his role in my memory loss, I'd forgiven him and I mostly trusted him since I understood how his angel mind worked. "Of course, I need you. I got a demon dad and an angel guardian. I feel balanced."

He patted me lightly on the cheek. "I must have done something right; you're still going to help those in need even though you have what you wanted."

That thought wasn't lost on me. Honestly, I wasn't a monster. I'd been so self-absorbed the past few months but maybe seeing that little girl in the kitchen and even dealing with Yusan got me thinking about helping those in need for nothing more than it was the right thing to do. Heck, even hearing about how my father went after evildoers was a somewhat noble cause. I couldn't make my life perfect right now but I wasn't going to waste my gifts while I was finding my way, either.

"Listen, I also came over to tell you that the other angels might be a little late in today's fight," Carlos continued.

I blinked rapidly, confused. This was Monica's deal, how

was she not fighting? "Excuse me? Two of the people we are trying to rescues are her angels."

"I know, I know. The thing about Monica is, she believes that angels are of the highest order. So, they should be used sparingly. In this case, the good people of this town are willing to go in and fight."

I was surprised we'd gotten anyone to fight with us at all. St. Michaels really wasn't their problem. However, Silver Spring had recently earned the reputation as a place that helped those in need. Especially other paranormals. Right now, we had two angels and several other stuck tourists-paranormal and human- that needed our help. The fact that there were child killers was enough to get the town's attention on its own.

"Just because these people are willing to risk their lives to help those in need doesn't mean the angels are off the hook. I think it's pretty messed up that she roped us into this and then backed away for us to do the dirty work. That is not what I would think an angel should do. They're supposed to protect us, right?"

Carlos looked up at the ceiling, as if searching for a response. "Angels protect humans and each other. She is allowing Azrael and myself and a couple of other angels to assist."

I squinted my eyes, hearing what he wasn't saying. "Angels don't protect paranormals. She is supplying just enough to get her angels out of there and any of the few humans. The rest are on their own. Right?"

He nodded.

"Your boss is a bitch." I looked away, not wanting to spend any more energy on the discussion. The more I learned about angels, the less I liked them. "Felix put a move on it. We have some lives to save!"

Felix appeared a minute later. "All right, I'm read-" He suddenly keeled over, grabbing his stomach.

I took a cautious step toward him. "You okay? Stomach ache?"

He looked up at me, still bent over, eyes watering but he didn't speak.

I saw Carlos get up and walk over from the corner of my eye. "Let me heal you."

Before he could get closer, Felix's body cracked and broke apart. I couldn't quite describe what I was seeing. It was like he was turning into a puzzle of himself. Soon those pieces separated and scattered to the floor, dispersing into dust before disappearing.

My mind froze. Unable to process what I was seeing, I dropped to my knees in shock. "What the fuck just happened? Is he dead? Did he just explode?"

Carlos placed his hands on my arms and guided me back to my feet. "No. He was teleported away."

"I've never seen any teleportation like that." I fought between relief and disbelief. I'd seen teleportation go wrong before, with only part of a person's body crossing over or the body combining with something else like furniture. This was just as horrifying.

"Looked evil. Teleportation shouldn't do that to someone."

"You think Yasmine or Olivia did that?" I refused to believe it was my father. However, I thought Yasmine allowed Felix to leave willingly? What had I missed? "I'm getting him back, now."

"That was the plan, let's go get the others."

I shook my head quickly. "You tell them what happened. I'll meet you there," I replied before teleporting myself away.

Before going to St. Michaels, I went to Nadia's house where I put on my fighting gear and grabbed some weapons. I was still angry I didn't have my sword. If Yasmine had gotten rid of it, I was going to enjoy killing her even more.

Nadia offered to help me fight but I told her to just go on

283

standby. We both needed to be conscious of the fights she entered. If her people thought they were doing battle without any direct benefit to them, they would lose faith in her and demons weren't above being disloyal. It was always a precarious thing to be a demon leader unless you had an insane amount of power. Nadia was strong but she wasn't at Herrod's level or possibly even Yasmine's.

When I left Nadia's, I arrived at the warded entrance of St. Michaels, part of the main street near a shopping center, where my father was already working on the ward after I had contacted him while at Nadia's.

He stood, arms wide and eyes closed. I'd expected him to recite a spell or something but he seemed just to stand there, perhaps expelling energy to force the ward down.

"How long is this going to take?" I asked, pacing back and forth behind him.

"As long as it takes," he replied in a neutral tone, eyes still closed. "I know you are antsy to save your boyfriend but your nervous energy is distracting."

I took a step back. "Sorry. I'm just pissed. It was probably Olivia who summoned him back to get him away from me. What kind of mother is she to bring back her son in such a cruel way?"

Herrod really looked unbothered. Of course, he wouldn't care. "I don't know why I'm talking to you. You're probably glad he's gone."

"Not true. However, you should be certain of who you give credit to in these things. It would help you to prepare."

Why did my father talk in riddles? What was he talking about? I looked around, straining my neck to see if the others were going to show up down the road. I had expected them to be here by now.

"Daughter, do you care about what I was trying to say?"

"No."

He tsked. "I was implying that Yasmine was the possible

source behind Felix's disappearance. Do not underestimate her. She is quite formidable."

"Do you think I can fight her?"

"I think you can do anything you put your mind to." He snapped his fingers. "And take this."

A golden sword materialized in front of me, hovering horizontally. "My sword!" I grabbed it and began to swing, testing my arm.

He kept his eyes closed, continuing to focus on the ward. "It is a new one. To replace the one I gifted you before. No need to go in unprepared."

"Thank you," I exclaimed, still practicing with my shiny new toy.

"This one can't magically be taken away from you."

I glanced over at him but he was still focused on the ward. Nostalgia flashed through me at a vision of him surprising me with a birthday present when I was maybe eight. At the time, a toy had materialized out of thin air and danced across the air. "Can you teach me how to break a high-level ward?"

"Of course." He stiffened. "Wraith are on the way."

"Crap, no one's here and the ward's not down. What if they restrengthen it?"

Carlos materialized by my side. Azrael, also in angel armor, and Faith soon appeared after him. Other Silver Spring people, including some of the Six, appeared as well, soon I was surrounded by a tiny, but hopefully tough, group of maybe one hundred people. St Michaels probably held two times that many people but I was still going to think positive. I'd gone in as an enforcer to groups where I was outnumbered and won before.

Herrod stood back and opened his eyes. "Ward is down." He moved over to me as if he was going to give me a hug or kiss on the head. "Do well in your battle. Remember, the sword is nice but you don't need it. You have magic."

"I know. I have fae magic."

He placed a hand on my shoulder and stared down at me with dark eyes. "There are pulse points on some demons, not me of course, that if jabbed or stabbed can kill them."

I widened my eyes in surprise and annoyance. "Now you tell me?"

He looked over to the others. "It's not something we want others to know about."

"Can you make an exception for me? At least give me one point to know."

He smiled. "Give your father a hug for good luck."

My eyes widened and I stepped back. Guess he wasn't going to tell me "No, dad. Not in front of my friends," I cracked, although I did have a bit of the warm and fuzzies at his request. I guess a girl never got tired of having a parent's love. Especially one you hadn't seen in almost twenty years. I leaned back in for a hug.

He wrapped his arms around me. "Spine," he whispered before surrounding me in a cloud of dark smoke as he disappeared.

I mouthed the word 'thanks' to the air. I then turned and caught Azrael looking at me with something like amusement, which I ignored. "Let's go save our guy."

I then turned around and led us through the ward just as Sheriff Asshole appeared with several wraiths behind him. I gripped my sword, ready to swing.

Dante gave a light snort, seemingly unimpressed at my shiny new toy. "We were expecting you." He looked around at the large group, all in fighting stance, weapons aimed. "Tell your people to fall back if you want Felix to live."

"You wouldn't kill Felix, not with Olivia all BFF with your mayor."

He chuckled and a few of his wraiths joined him. Really, what was so damn funny today? I'd have to change that. "We aren't concerned about someone who's dead."

My heart stopped cold. "What are you talking about?"

Dante leaned forward. "We ate Olivia. Can't have such a powerful demon possibly challenging our leader, can we people?" The wraiths around him gave cries in affirmation. "Plus she has really nice skin."

My mind was having challenges registering what he was saying. Yasmine had gone through the trouble to rescue Olivia and then used her as an enticement to keep Felix by her side. Not to mention we were sure Olivia had helped her to keep the wards strong. Unless Olivia used a symbol, which could outlast her life to form a ward, then the wards would have been weakened by her death. It took a while for my father to break it, but maybe not long enough?

Faith walked up to my side. "I thought Olivia was a friend to you all."

A female wraith sneered at us. "Demons don't have friends. They just use each other until the other serves no purpose."

Dante glared back at the woman, I guess not agreeing with her observation, before turning fully to us again. "Felix chose to leave his mother here."

"He was coming back, you animals!" Faith shouted. I could practically feel her magic simmering like a pot ready to boil over.

"Felix made a deal with us. He could leave for a short period of time. Say his goodbyes and then he would come back to serve by Mayor Yasmine's side. He was due by midnight. He did not return."

I let out a breath. He didn't return because he was with me. He couldn't have forgotten he had to go back just because of the news of my returned memory. Sure, that had been exciting but not exciting enough to risk getting your mother killed. Why hadn't he said he was on borrowed time?

I leaned toward Faith. "Did you know about this?" I asked through gritted teeth.

287

"No," she said back in an angry snarl, still glaring at the wraiths.

Something wasn't right. I hadn't even caught a moment of distraction from Felix last night. He had seemed totally focused on me. Even this morning, he had seemed to not be in any sort of rush. "Did he know his mother would be killed if he didn't return?"

Dante gave an overly dramatic stroke of his chin, squinting his eyes up at the sky. "You know, we might have forgotten to mention that to him."

I thought of how Felix had just reconnected with his mother after all of these years. As much as I didn't care for, I knew that he loved her. If he had known that his mother's life was at stake, he would never have missed his time let alone even left. He had only left in the first place to help the poor tourist left behind. He'd done nothing for himself. Then they had brought him back just to, what, show him that his mother was dead? Disrespectfully treated as food for the masses? Anger entwined itself around me and I shot out my hand without thinking, electrocuting Dante's lower half.

The sheriff lifted his knees high, stomping up and down as if to put out the fire now erupting from his legs. He then stopped and wiped his hands over his body and the fire went away.

Now that was not a wraith power. I rolled my eyes in realization. "You're a demon, too. You guys really know how to hide what you are."

Dante took a step towards me and I lifted a chin defiantly, I was ready for him to try something. "You are lucky it is not your time to die yet."

Faith snarled. "What the fuck does that mean?"

"You want a chance to save your friend?"

"We want to save all the innocent people in this death trap, you piece of shit."

Dante bared his teeth which were now fully sharp. "We

288

have a match that we put on from time to time to decide who gets the best skins. Sometimes it can end in death. This time, with you and your two friends joining, it will most certainly end in death. If one of you dies in the matches, you all lose and no one is saved and you all will be worn by our fiercest fighters."

Now that didn't sound like a fair deal. "We are in the town now. We can just kill you all."

"And we will immediately kill Felix and the others before you take another step. You don't have the upper hand here. We are offering you the chance to save people."

Faith made a pfft sound. "Like we would believe you."

"Fine, don't take our deal. I'll let our Mayor know. Is there a message you'd like me to give to Felix before he dies?"

I raised a hand to stop him. They didn't have us fully over a barrel. If they turned on their word or added some unknown stipulation that none of us knew about, we still had our supporters who could come in and fight. Both Azrael and I could teleport and Azrael would telepathically communicate with Carlos who could lead the others.

"Can we at least see him first?"

Dante chuckled again. I was really tired of his laughter. I was going to have to punch his teeth out when the time came. "Like we would trust you. No, you'll see him after you accept our offer and come to the field to fight. Everyone but those in the tournament stays out here."

Azrael nodded. "Fine, we accept."

I wanted to be annoyed with the angel for accepting the offer without discussing it with us but the truth was, we all were going to accept. I wasn't going to let my guy die.

# CHAPTER 28

*O*ur fight, whatever it was called, was held in a grassy field near the water. Bleachers were set up around the outside of the field filled with wraiths, the fighters stood in different sections of the field, and a platform stood between bleachers facing the water where Yasmine sat in the center.

However, it wasn't Yasmine that I was looking at. To her side, Felix lay on the ground bound and muzzled like some wild animal. His feet and hands were tied behind his back. He lay sideways on the floor of the platform and he didn't move but he was awake, his eyes a shocking red. I'd never seen his eyes like that before. It had to be the demon side of him. Even from a distance, I could see the tears in his eyes. It broke my heart.

Azrael touched my shoulder. "I know you want to go over there and free him and burn this place down with damn near everyone in it. I want to, as well. However, we can't risk it right now. Your father said Yasmine is powerful and she has to be in order to turn beings into wraiths and free Olivia from his cage. We can't take for granted that she could kill

Felix on the spot if we approach. You won't let that happen, right?"

I shook my head, blinking rapidly at the tears forming in my own eyes. Was I crying because it hurt to see him so broken? Was I that in love with him? Yes, yes I was.

Yasmine stood up and hushed the crowd with a raised hand. "Today's tournament is going to be extra special. We are fortunate to have an angel, a member of the infamous Six and a fae in our midst. They are entering as a team together and the stakes are higher than before. Our fighters will be fighting to the death. You know the deal. We will have several teams compete in brackets, resulting in three levels of fighting until we are down to the final two teams standing, who will battle to the death."

Faith turned to us looking all too excited. "That's just three rounds of fighting. We can do it. We've already fought some wraiths."

I was less excited seeing as our past fights with the wraiths were not easy ones. "Uh-huh, just keep that same energy on the field. We don't know who we are fighting. We could have just encountered the easy marks. There could be demons on the field as well. I don't see the Sheriff up there. I see him over there." I pointed to Dante standing with two other people to make up what appeared to be a team. "Not that I'm intimidated. I just know demons are a very different breed to fight. They play dirty."

Azrael nodded. "Yes, they do." The angel patted my shoulder. "But we can do this."

I raised my brows, still surprised that Azrael was starting to be kinder to me. Was it because they were seeing I wasn't such a horrible person to be around? I hoped so because I was going to be relying on them to have my back out there. I looked over to Faith but she was too busy looking on at the crowd of wraiths in disgust.

She curled her upper lip up. "I can't believe we are going

to be battling gladiator-style over skin like some *Silence of the Lambs* shit."

I wasn't as surprised. Demons loved their battle royals, especially tournaments. Alister used to hold many of them. They were popular betting events. I didn't want to keep thinking about it. I just wanted to get this over with so I could get to Felix. "Can I count on you out there?"

She turned to me, eyes incredulous. "Do you think I won't have your back? Listen, we may not have started off so well but I see the love you have for my friend. I'm not going to let anything happen to you out there. Felix would never get over it." She gave me the slightest of smiles.

"So we're best friends now." I looked on at the field of fighters, feeling only a tinge better.

"That is not what I said."

"That's what I heard."

"Me too," Azrael added, much to my amusement.

Faith grumbled but didn't say anything as I surveyed our situation.

There were eight teams in total, counting ours. Each match had to be no longer than fifteen minutes. I assumed this was because they didn't want to drag out the fighting because watching people kill each other could get so boring. I lowered my head and rolled my eyes. If neither team finished their kills in the allotted time, they both died. I had a hard time believing she would kill her own people. After all, they were what made her powerful. No, I was sure that rule only applied to us three.

That made for one hour of fighting for the first round. The second round with the four remaining teams consisting of two fights allowed for twenty minutes each and the final battle with the last two teams was thirty minutes. So, I just had to survive less than two hours worth of fighting. I could do that.

I had hopes we wouldn't have to go first so we could see

how the tournament was played. So far, the only rules I could gather was that we couldn't leave the field. That would result in automatic death for the whole team. However, our team was called up first. I figured Yasmine knew this was disadvantageous. Of course, if we won, it allowed for the most rest time. I guess she didn't have that much faith in us.

Since we were up first, maybe we would go up against Dante's team. It wasn't because I thought we could beat him easily. I just figured that if we did beat him, it would all be down hill from there since I assumed he was our strongest opponent. But, yet again, Yasmine didn't do us any favors and we were up against a group of seemingly all wraiths. It looked like she wasn't going to take for granted that we would lose and wanted to save her right hand for later when we would most likely be too tired. If we made it past the second round and so did Dante, I was very sure Yasmine would not have us fight first again and ensure Dante's group fought first and us second so that if we won, we'd be tired as hell by the time we got to round three. Of course, we might also be hopped up on adrenaline. Who knew what Azrael's angel reserves allowed for them and Faith had the bond of her Six to help power her, although Amina being sleep might affect their energy boosting abilities.

At the thought of the Six, I looked back over to Felix who stared out onto the field with still angry red eyes. If he was coherent, why hadn't he gotten someone from the Six to come help him? Had Yasmine locked his mind so that he couldn't telepathically communicate? I'd heard of that happening before. Felix had mentioned something similar occurring with Amina when she was banished to Ireland several months ago.

Faith patted me on the back. "Head in the game, Fran."

She was right, of course, but it was going to be a challenge to ignore Felix lying there without wanting to run right to him. I looked to our opponents. There was nothing physically concerning about them. They were all men, very youthful in appearance. However, a wraith's strength came through their magic. They would be deceptively strong and they had the ability to rip your throat out with just one bite. They also were holding various weapons. Swords, axes and what appeared to be a sledgehammer.

Faith tapped her fist together as if recharging her already glowing tattoos. Azrael took out their gigantic sickle from thin air, and I grounded myself, lifting my sword to swing.

A loud horn blared and the clock began. We only had fifteen minutes to kill these guys and we hadn't talked strategy.

"Let them come to us," Azrael said in a low voice. "Conserve your energy."

I gave a curt nod in understanding.

The trio raced at us, growling like animals. I caught the eye of one of the men, holding the sword, I guess he wanted to spar. He looked like a man on a mission as he raced towards me, eyes laser focused. When he was only several feet away, he veered off course and swung at Faith, who jumped back, narrowly missing his sword, which sliced into just the thread of her light jacket. Clever fellow.

However, I didn't have time to get pissed about my miscalculation. My skin tingled as the air buzzed behind me. I dropped and rolled forward, just missing the massive sledgehammer holding wraith. He raced towards me in a blur and I flipped backwards into a stance, swinging my sword before my feet touched the ground. My weapon clanged against his, leaving a very unpleasant vibration that rocked my body.

The man swung again and I teleported away, appearing behind him and striking forward, stabbing into the man's back. He howled and spun around before I could pull the sword out, flinging me to the side. I ran towards him and teleported in mid-run, grabbing my sword back from his body just as he sped away. Damn, these wraiths were fast.

"Behind you!" I heard Azrael's voice.

I lowered to the ground but that wasn't the right move because I caught an axe right in my left shoulder. I screamed as agonizing pain rocked my body, burring my vision. I teleported several feet away and struggled to my feet. I had no time to wait for my fae/demon magic to heal my arm. My arm burned with shocking pain, and nausea hit my stomach. Believe it or not, I'd been cut in the shoulder with an axe before. Life of a hitwoman. However, this pain felt ten times worse. I had been out of the pain game for a while.

I couldn't focus on the pain. Sledgehammer dude was missing from my vision. Which meant one thing. I lowered into a crouching spin and swiped my sword out, cutting into the wraith appearing behind me. My sword bit into his leg, severing the leg with one slice.

Damn, Dad. What was this sword made of?

The wraith toppled forward, off balance and I tumbled to the side to avoid being crushed. I jumped up as the now one-legged wraith moved to their back, hand still holding the sledgehammer. I swung my sword above my head but caught him glance behind me. Instead of hitting him, I spun around and met my sword with the other sword welding wraith. Why were they all taking turns on me? I was sure Yasmine had given them their focus.

He swung at me again and I struggled to match his speed with my impaired arm.

"Five minutes!" Cried an announcer from the podium.

Damn, we had to end this. Had we killed anyone?

Sword guy swung again and I blocked him with my sword, then quickly kicked him in the privates with all my force. I have never heard a scream that high pitched before. I wondered if it was because I had my special retractable blade boots on. I guessed it hurt getting stabbed in the privates.

The wraith hunched forward, knees pressed together and one hand covering his now bloody privates. I didn't waste a second and swung my sword up, quickly beheading him. I spun around to finish off the one-legged wraith but Azrael had already taken care of him, kicking the wraith's head from his body like a football. Their sickle bloodied. I turned to my left and saw that Faith had taken care of the axe wraith, its body quickly deflating to an empty skin suit.

The horn blared again and the announcer called out our victory.

The crowd booed. Assholes.

We left the field and sat on the perimeter, looking at the four other battles and studying our opponents. Some were stronger, bigger and faster than the wraiths we just beat. Others were much weaker.

At the end of the first round, there was a brief intermission where the audience was given time to grab more food and drink. It was sickening that they were watching us kill each other while chomping on hotdogs like they were at a freaking baseball game.

I looked back over to Felix who was still immobile. His eyes were closed now but I knew he wasn't asleep. "What if while we are fighting, one of us just teleports to him and gets him out?"

Faith tilted her head from side to side. "We did something like that a while ago when he was unjustly found guilty of murder. Some of us battled the pack police back in Silver Spring while Lisa teleported him out of there. That was before he knew he could teleport himself. You know, come to think of it, Felix keeps getting captured for something or another. For a guy that big we constantly have to save his ass."

She had a point there. He was the biggest damsel in distress I'd ever seen.

Azrael shook their head. "As sadly accurate as that is, that plan wouldn't work. There are too many variables. We don't know what kind of spell is keeping him bound. We don't know how to prevent her from teleporting him back again. I'm not willing to risk his life without knowing for certain."

I didn't tell them that I doubted we would get Felix back by playing by the rules anyway. We'd win this whole thing and they could easily change their mind about letting him go. They were demons, after all. If that happened, I'd have to call dad to break him out quickly.

Round two soon began and we found out who we'd be battling next. I got tired just looking at them but I'd have to pull from my reserves. My left shoulder wasn't fully healed but I could move it with less pain attached.

Faith cursed beside me. "Why do they all look like they used to play for the NFL? Including that woman. Damn, they're large."

I ran my tongue over my front teeth as I studied them. They were huge. All three looked like they were over six foot. One of them, the male, looked vaguely familiar. I kept staring until recognition took hold. He was the father of the little girl we'd saved. I took a picture of her parents so that I would remember to kill them. It was just unfortunate that the wraith in the mother's skin wasn't out there. No matter, I would find her.

In the meantime, I had to keep my head in the game and in this game, our opponents were well-armed. One had a bow and arrow, another a sledgehammer, and the final one, the dad skinsuit, had what appeared to be a large razor-sharp boomerang. Where the hell did they get some of these weapons? I was being dense. Of course, I knew. From their powerful demon Queen. She had all sorts of access to demonic and underworldly weapons to let them use. And it made total sense why it hurt more to get cut with those weapons. The wounds would be healing slower as well. Just great.

Like I thought, we didn't go first and I spent the time watching Dante's team annihilate their opponents in under twenty minutes. It was slightly intimidating. I was mildly surprised that they were actually killing each other. This wasn't their usual norm and perhaps they were playing a tiny bit fair by having everyone's life up for grabs, not just ours.

When they were finished, the horn blared for our time to start. Like the first round, we didn't run for them. However, they didn't run for us either.

We weren't surprised. They'd done the same thing during their first-round battle. However, I had a plan that I'd shared as soon as I saw that. I looked over to Azrael and the angel nodded at me. We then teleported and reappeared in front of and behind one of the male wraiths holding the sledgehammer. I immediately stuck my sword in his back and Azrael thrust their fist in the man's chest, ripping out his heart. We had agreed earlier to both double up on the first wraith on the right which happened to be sledgehammer wraith.

The two remaining wraiths charged at Faith who leapt high in the air before lowering down and kicking the bow and arrow holding female wraith clear out of the field. Her power was impressive. We had no idea how far she'd sent the woman. The wraiths were fast, but we hoped it would buy us enough time to take out the remaining boomerang wraith.

As Azrael beheaded the sledgehammer wraith for good measure, Faith and I went after the boomerang wraith. He zoomed out of the way and flung the boomerang towards us. We separated, missing the weapon. However, instead of it returning to him, it changed course and zoomed towards me.

I ran like my life depended on it because it did. However, I could hear the sound of the boomerang cutting the air way too close behind me. I dove to the ground, looking up to see the boomerang sail past me before flipping and coming back my way except at a lower angle. Way too low for me to remain on the ground. It would slice the top of my head off even if I smashed my face into the grass. When all this was said and done, I really needed to invest in one of those weapons. But for now, I got up and played a game of teleport around the field as the boomerang continued to chase me. I had to either disable it or kill the wraith.

I reappeared just as the boomerang was inches away from me and batted it back with my sword, sending it spinning. I could see my sword had cut into it. Perhaps if I kept slicing away at it, that would do the trick. Or leave two halves of a boomerang to come at me.

I readied my sword as the boomerang spun back my way but suddenly, it dropped to the ground several feet away from me. I looked up and found Faith bashing in the head of the wraith owner until it didn't really look like the wraith had a face anymore. It was safe to say the creature was dead, although I could see it had taken a sizable chunk out of Faith's forearm. No wonder she was pounding it into oblivion. I was a little disgruntled that Faith got to be the one to kill the parent killing wraith but I'd get over it.

The hairs on the back of my neck rose and I dropped low, spinning around in time to see Azrael in front of me, stumbling backwards. A steel arrow the size of my sword protruded through the angel's chest. They had jumped in front of me to save me. I wouldn't let this moment go to waste.

I got up and raced to the angel.

Azrael dropped to their knees, clearly not okay. "Don't mind me," the angel said through gritted teeth as they grabbed the arrow. "Finish this."

I gave them a curt nod and looked forward as the female wraith let loose another arrow, this time in Faith's direction. Faith jumped to the side, falling to the ground but the arrow changed course and zoomed back towards her at a downward diagonal.

I took out one of my *shuriken* and flung it at the wraith

who was now aiming her arrow at me. Just as she pulled the bow, the *shuriken* caught in her throat. I swiped my index finger in the air to my right and the *shuriken* dug further into the wraith's skin, slicing deeply across her throat. The wraith's eyes bulged and she dropped her weapon, grabbing at the star making good work of decapitating her. She yanked it out, her neck gushing blood, the severing only halfway complete. Faith rushed to her side and landed a forceful punch to the wraith's head, tearing it away from the rest of her neck.

"Teamwork makes the dream work," she said with a menacing grin, her face splattered with blood. I think she was actually enjoying this fight.

I looked back at the platform. We were done with a couple of minutes to spare.

"Call that shit!" Faith shouted at the announcer who glared at us before sounding the horn.

I looked over to Dante who gave me a wide sharped tooth grin. He was holding a blow torch. Really? And I though the boomerang was bad. He rolled his shoulders back. "This will be fun."

"There will be no interim. We will go into the final round at the sound of the horn," the announcer called. "But first, we must make a substitution."

I frowned and looked as one of the wraiths on Dante's team left the field. "Wait a fucking minute. I thought no one could leave the field!"

The announcer sneered at me. "We made a rule change. Sue us."

Faith kicked the grass, cursing as she headed over to Azrael. "This asshole. I knew they would pull some last-minute shit."

I wasn't surprised either. It's what I'd feared.

She helped the angel to their feet. The arrow was now

gone but it would heal slow if it was demonic. "Then we can break the rules too."

"Except this set-up isn't in our favor," Azrael huffed, face scrunched in pain.

We watched as a figure approached the field and I cursed upon seeing one of Monica's angels, Dean, appear. He looked dead-eyed and unbothered about his situation. I looked to Azrael and the angel's eyes were wide with furry. We'd come here to help rescue Dean, we couldn't fight him. However, if we didn't kill him, we couldn't rescue Felix. There was no question who was more important to me but for Azrael I wasn't so sure. This made me hate Monica even more. Here we were having to fight her people and she was nowhere in sight. She should be here fighting with us. If I had to kill this angel, I didn't want any repercussions from it.

"I can't kill him," Azrael whispered, shoulders sagging.

I don't think I'd ever seen the angel look so defeated before. "You won't have to. Maybe this is the moment that we risk getting Felix out of here. They clearly aren't going to play fair. Even if we win, they would have gotten us to kill an angel."

Faith shook her head, her lips a thin line of anger. "Assuming they hold on to the deal. Do we want to risk it?"

I looked over to Felix who now had open eyes but they were emotionless. That was disturbing, especially since they were still red.

We didn't have time to further decide what to do because the horn blared at that moment.

"If Dean comes for us, we will have to subdue him," I began. "I'll do the best I can to just make him unconscious but I won't make any promises."

Azrael didn't respond. Instead, they spread their wings and held open their hand, the giant sickle appearing. The angel looked slightly paler and with them badly wounded and my shoulder still a mess, I didn't know how great we were going to be. Faith still looked in perfect shape, her bite wound was already healing from her succubus magic. I could only assume her powerful Six magic had avoided the effects of becoming paralyzed. Must be nice to have a battery of energy on standby.

Dean also expanded his wings and a standard issued silver angel sword appeared in his right hand. It was the typical weapon of choice for angels, especially lower-level ones. His eyes went full silver. Guess he meant business now.

The other wraith had no weapon. I guess she was pretty confident. She raced towards us in a blur of motion. I spun, expecting her to appear behind me because, didn't they all? Only instead of showing up in front of me, she appeared next to Faith, ramming her to the ground and windmilling her claws at her.

I swung my sword almost hitting the wraith when a spray of fire met my sword, sending a fiery heat to my hands. I dropped the sword and stumbled back, my hands now painfully red and already blistering.

Dante walked toward me in a slow pace, still grinning. He was loving this. I pushed my magic to teleport away and buy some time since I wouldn't be getting any help right then. Azrael was fighting Dean and they seemed to be losing. I wasn't sure if it was because of Azrael's injury or if they were being half-hearted because they were fighting a fellow angel.

More importantly, was why had I not moved? I shut my eyes and tried to teleport again. Nothing.

Dante gave me a pitying pout. "Having problems running away? Did you know that demonic weapons can curb your powers if you are injured by them? You and your angel friend were both hit by our weapons. Sorry for you." He then let loose another blast of fire, and I dove to the ground, tumbling away. I'd had my powers earlier when I out tele-ported from the boomerang. I guess it took a while for the demon wound to zap me of my gifts.

How the hell did I outrun a magic blow torch? I needed to get the weapon from him. Maybe I could find a way to cut Dante's hands off? He had to use both hands to work the machine so even one hand down would give me a leg up. Of course, having my sword which I had dropped to the ground would help. Not that my damaged hands would do well swinging a sword now. Well, that and getting close enough to him to even swing the sword before me getting fried was another thing.

Of course, I had other magic. I was a faerie and demon, after all. It was time to stop fighting like a blind soldier and time to get creative. Herrod told me to stab or jab the spine. Was it any part of the spine? Was just a finger enough? I had to make sure I knew what I was doing because as soon as I tried it, Dante would know what was happening. If I hit the wrong spot then he would be on notice and would ensure he wasn't so exposed. However, first I had to get rid of the torch to even get close enough.

I jumped up and shot out my hands, sending an electrical current of magic around Dante, shaking his body. However, he held tightly to the blow torch as if it were a part of him. I ran to my sword and cried in pain as my burned hands picked up the weapon, which still looked undamaged but no longer hot. I swore through the pain, shaking at the throbbing burning.

I raced toward Dante, sword in my right hand and left hand up, still emitting my electrocuting magic. My damaged shoulder screamed at the continued strain but I was strong. I could do this. I was part demon, a wound by a demonic weapon shouldn't keep me down for long.

Dante stopped shaking and turned his torch back to me. Fire shot out and I swiped my left arm, sending him flying backwards but not before my arm was wrapped in fire. Tears of pain tore through me, and I let out a guttural scream. I gritted my teeth so hard I thought I would shatter them but I kept focus. I looked to the blow torch and lifted it in the air with my magic. I then began to bend it tightly as if it was made of just paper until it became nothing but a steel ball. Sweat poured down my forehead, burning my eyes but I stayed focus. I felt like I was on my last reserve. Using my magic, demonic or fae, was not an endless supply. Between my injuries and fighting fatigue, I was running close to empty.

And Dante could sense it as he ran toward me, disappearing mid-run. He reappeared in front of me and lifted his hand, using his magic to send me in the air swinging like a rag doll. Azrael raced to his side, swinging their sickle. Dante, spotting the motion from his peripheral vision, teleported away, dropping me hard to the ground. But he was too late, I saw the sickle biting into his side.

I got to my feet, slightly off-balance, as my damaged left arm hung limply. These bastards really liked to come for the arms. How smart of them. I spun around, looking for Dante. I could only see him teleport here and there at different parts of the field. He was trying to confuse me. If he kept moving, we wouldn't be able to get him. I could already see Faith providing a killing blow to the other wraith but Azrael was still having trouble with Dean. I wanted to help but I had to keep my guard out for Dante. Was he running the clock? Did he think he could finish me off if he just kept me tired? No, I needed to get him out and end this before I actually passed out. I was about to make my move. If there was any part of the spine that could be the most damaging, it had to be the top, right? I was part demon, maybe my demon intuition would guide me correctly. It was a long shot but I needed this win.

"You scared to fight me, Dante!" I shouted. "You just keep running." I sheathed my sword. "See, I'm putting away my weapon. So, we're even. Still scared?"

Dante appeared in front of me, swinging his fist and

connecting with my jaw. I did a very fake but dramatic fall to the ground. That wasn't to say it didn't hurt like hell because it very much did, however, I needed him to position himself in a manner to allow me easy access. Dante jumped on top of me as I expected. He wrapped his hands around my neck and a burning heat choked me. I widened my eyes as more pain from his fire hands tore the life out of me. I had to remain conscious. Not struggling against his grasp, I moved my hands around his back. I began to touch the top of his spine but at the last minute, something compelled me to move lower, in between his shoulder blades.

I jabbed all my fingers into that space at once with all my force.

Dante let out a thunderous howl, loosening his hold on my throat and throwing his head back. He looked down at me with murderous eyes. "You bi-" He didn't finish his sentence as his body broke apart, crumbling to ash all over me.

It worked! I had no clue which finger was the magic touch but I would think about that later. Right now, I felt like I was going to suffocate.

I let out a hacking cough, rubbing my burning throat and wincing at the pain of the tender skin. I wouldn't need a mirror to know my neck was probably burned as badly as my hands and arm.

I heard shouting to my right and turned my head to see Azrael slice their sickle across Dean's body just as he was about to impale Faith with his sword. The angel's body slid apart in the midsection, toppling to the ground in different directions. Even from my distance, I could see tears pouring from Azrael's silver eyes.

I continued my coughing, closing my eyes in frustration. I could barely move. I felt like shit. We were supposed to help him avoid killing another angel. However, I couldn't get to them in time. I clenched my teeth again from pain and anger.

When I got my second wind, I was going to destroy Yasmine. I just had to get up. In my mind I was doing it but my body refused to match my thoughts.

The horn blared and I sucked in a breath, grunting as I sat upright. I looked to the platform and saw Yasmine standing next to the announcer. Her face a mask of fury. I knew right then and there that she wasn't going to honor what she promised.

Azrael and Faith joined me. Azrael had an arm over her shoulder as she kept the angel upright. Azrael looked ready to crumble. I'd never seen the angel so weak and I could still see their chest wound unhealed. If we didn't get a healer on them soon, the angel might not make it.

Yasmine grabbed the microphone from the announcer. "Whoever kills them gets their skins!" Yasmine shouted, pointing to us. I looked to the crowd and the wraiths looked down at us with hungry eyes.

Did our skins even look worth it now? We were all battered and bruised. Then again, maybe our skin could still heal when worn by a wraith. And our bodies were still good food for them.

I struggled to my feet. What little energy I had left wasn't going to get me through fighting all these wraiths. My throat felt raw and burned from Dante's fiery choking. Through the commotion of the wraiths charging towards us, we could see our allies bursting past the podium and bleachers. I was so thankful I could have fainted. We were still heavily outnumbered but it was better than being just the three of us fighting.

I looked over to Yasmine and pulled out my sword, feeling a second wind. Okay, maybe it was more of a light breeze but it was enough to get me to fight again. I pointed my sword at her. "I'm coming for you, bitch."

# CHAPTER 29

asmine had the audacity to laugh as I charged at her. "Haven't you learned enough from our last fight?" she called. "Shall I take your sword again? It should be easy now. You can barely hold it upright."

She was right but I wasn't going to let her know that. She threw her hand out and I felt a slight pull of my sword but it stayed with me. This sword was loyal. Also, dad magic.

I gave Yasmine a triumphant smile as she frowned at me. "Not as weak as you thought." With my magic, I flung her into the bleachers. I wished I could teleport. Stupid demon injury. I charged toward her again but she teleported away.

She reappeared in front of me and I swung my sword at her. She bent backwards, missing my blade by mere inches. I thrust my sword at her again and she moved to the side with ease. She didn't look the least bit hurt by any of my actions. I pushed off the ground and leaped into the air, bringing my sword down onto her in a last attempt to stab her.

Yasmine looked up and snapped her fingers. Instantly I felt the bones in my right wrist break. I fell to the ground, dropping my sword. I was in so much pain now that I wasn't sure what hurt more. Nausea threatened to force the contents of my stomach to the surface but I held it back, steadying my breath.

Yasmine smirked down at me. "I'm kind of disappointed that killing you will be this easy. You're the daughter of a high-level demon. Of course, I'm sure it was Herrod who told you about the death jab. That bastard."

I saw Azrael appear behind her but she must have felt the presence of the angel because she lifted her hand in a fist and Azrael fell to the ground. The angel didn't move but their eyes were wide open and I could see them struggle against an invisible hold as their body slowly sunk into the ground. She was burying them. I had to kill her before she killed them.

Both my hands were pretty much useless right now but I didn't need them to protect myself. If she snapped her fingers again, I didn't want her breaking anything else on me. I lowered my head and pushed out my magic to send an electric current her way. Her body froze, shaking at a speed too fast to catch with the naked, non-paranormal eye. I lifted my chin and her body rose in the air. Maintaining control, I raised my sword and flung it through her, impaling her in the throat. She gurgled, grabbing at the sword sinking into her skin. I could decapitate her like this.

"Francesca, watch out!" called a voice. It sounded like Azrael.

I looked over my shoulder, too late to see two wraiths ram into me and knock me to the ground. They clamped their teeth into my arms and I shouted in pain as I looked up at Yasmine who was fighting my control. She ripped out the sword and tossed it to the ground. She then grabbed her neck, gagging with the effort as she covered the gushing wound. I knew she would heal but it wouldn't be fast. If I could shake free of these wraiths, I could actually finish the job.

She floated towards me, one hand outstretched. Her face changed to the bald, bloody mess from before, her teeth growing sharp and nails black and long. I struggled against the wraiths and they soon tore away from me, ripping my skin as they moved. I saw Azrael lift a hand in the air and I knew the angel had helped remove the wraiths from me even from their stuck position in the dirt. I would have preferred they do it in a way that didn't involve tearing of my skin but I'd move on from that.

I felt a sharp pain in my gut, as if my intestines were being moved around. I looked up and Yasmine hovered above me with a sneer of a smile on her face, blood leaking from her lips from the damage I'd caused her. However, this had not stopped her from trying to kill me. She was literally trying to gut me. It felt like snakes were inside me, struggling to escape. I was close to passing out from the feeling.

I was on borrowed time now before I became paralyzed from the wraith bites so time was running out. I tried to push my power back at her and she dropped to the ground but that would not be enough. I was starting to feel the effects of my blood loss and burns. My fighting energy burned away like a candle. Between that and the agonizing pain in my stomach, I hardly had any juice left in me. However, I would not give up. I was the daughter of a warrior fae Queen and a King of the Underworld. I was made of the strongest stuff. I could take down this no-name demon. I would fight. I would sometimes lose. But I would never give up. It wasn't in my D.N.A.

I lifted my burnt hand in the air. I would electrocute her with whatever energy I had left. Even if I died, I was taking her with me. I poured everything I had through me and magically lifted the *Shuriken* and every weapon I had at my disposal, sending it all in her. Since she was now electrified again, she couldn't dodge my weapons and they all landed in her body like some kind of horrific push pin doll. She keeled forward from the attack, her eyes bulging in shock. She cried out and more blood spurted from her mouth but she did not stop her magical attack on me. I knew she was hurt, it was all over her face. Her body continued to shake like a rag doll from my attack. Why was she not at least retreating? That was okay. It only meant I had to kill her right now.

I closed my eyes and continued my magic, feeling like I was on my last bit of strength and not wanting to waste anymore by even looking at her. I really needed her to die already. At this point we were both inflicting the maximum harm on each other and I needed her gone before she gutted me.

A woman shrieked. The sound shook the ground and pierced the air louder than the horn. It was like a banshee, banging against my ear drums. I opened my eyes and saw Felix floating in the air, awash in blood. Yasmine's body was torn, for lack of a better word, in two from the torso. His eyes were still fully red and now I noticed his nails were sharp and black like Yasmine's.

Felix held her two halves by the leg and arm like they were some human-shaped trash bags. Yasmine, still alive, cursed and shook in Felix's hands. He flung her lower body across the field and I didn't bother to look where it landed. I was too horrified by this demonic Felix. With both hands, he clutched Yasmine's upper body whose head was aimed towards the ground. He then shot down, bashing Yasmine's skull into the hard dirt.

And it splattered. As if that wasn't enough, he then slapped her back and a blinding white light spread across her body until it was nothing. Had he just exorcised her as well?

I remained where I lay, too stunned and paralyzed with pain to move. Several wraiths descended upon Felix in anger. Seemingly fearless, he grabbed wraiths by the collar like they were nothing and bashed the creature's heads together. The wraith's heads exploded against each other like they were humanoid pumpkins. More gore splashed across Felix but he

310

seemed unfazed as he went through wraith upon wraith. Crumbling them like paper waste.

Some wraith were finally getting the picture that he was not to be messed with and started running away only to get put down by our allies. However, Felix was relentless. He charged after the wraiths, tearing them apart with what seemed like ease until his fighting and our allies left no wraith standing.

Carlos appeared in front of me, crouching down. "Looks like you need some healing," he observed.

I groaned. "Thanks, captain obvious. Do you know how Felix got out? He came just in time."

Carlos hovered his hand over my burned neck. I had so many injuries I didn't know how he chose which one to heal first. "No idea."

"Well, he doesn't look good."

Commotion stole my attention as I saw Felix fling several of our allies out of the way. He was now charging towards me with blazingly, angry eyes. Something cold spread in my chest. He looked horrifying. Like he would kill me. What the hell had I done to him? I was here to save him.

Carlos paused and turned slightly, eyes narrowing towards the bulldozing maniac. "I knew he was falling into his demonic side but I had hoped he could control it."

"Did you not see him tear bodies apart like paper?"

Azrael stood in front of Felix, shoving him backwards in the chest. "Friend. Find your peace. We won," the angel commanded, stumbling slightly. They were covered in dirt and still wounded, but I was glad they were no longer being buried alive.

Felix looked down at the angel's hand on his chest and then back up at Azrael. To my shock and horror, he picked up the angel and tossed them to the side. Faith wasted no time and punched him in the side of his face. Felix replied by back-slapping her to the ground besides Azrael.

Others ran up to hold him down. Felix was taller and bigger than anyone around. Add his magic and he was very intimidating. He elbowed and punched his way through his friends and allies who were all surprised at his destruction. Felix definitely was not in his right mind. I was only thankful that he hadn't killed anyone on our side. Yet. Had Olivia's death sent him over the edge? His dark side had clearly taken over and he seemed to want to focus his rage on one person. Me. Was he angry that I had kept him from returning to town, leaving his mother to die?

I scooted backwards in the dirt, suddenly very afraid. There would be no fighting Felix. If I used my magic, it would be to kill him. There would be no middle ground. This guy was a beast that you would have to put down to defeat. At least, that's all my magic knew how to do. And I didn't want to. "We need to get out of here."

"Felix!" shouted a familiar woman's voice.

Felix paused his rampage and turned.

Several feet behind him stood Olivia, besides a member of the Six, his name was Charles I recalled. "Son, I'm not dead. They lied to you. They locked me up but this gentleman here got me out. I'm sorry I couldn't get free sooner."

Was it odd in that moment that all I could think was like mother like son? They both seemed to have a knack for getting captured.

Olivia clasped her hands together walking slowly towards him "You did good, Felix. You're so strong. But you don't have to keep going. You're done now. I know that the type of demon you are loves a fight. You get that from me, but there just isn't anyone left to battle. Let that side of you rest for now. Until we can control it better. And leave that young woman alone. I know seeing her hurt is upsetting you. But she has an angel there to heal her. It's best if you stay back."

Was that what he was coming to do? Heal me? Not kill

me? He needed to have a different face then because his healing face was not a comfort.

Felix remained looking at her, his shoulders rising and falling with each rapid breath. I wondered if he was calming down or thinking of his next move. I searched his eyes for the man I knew but could not find him. He actually glared at me. But then he turned and walked away, exiting the park, away from the crowd.

Where the hell was he going? Panic took hold of me. If he left, we wouldn't know where he went. I didn't think he was clear-headed enough to go home. He could go to the demon realm and we'd lose him. If he shut out his connection to the Six, they wouldn't be able to communicate with him. If he was a battle demon like Olivia stated, then he would want to look for a fight. Or to start one. That's what those types of demons thrived on. The fact that he hadn't tried to fight us more let me know that his angel half was not too far from the surface but I didn't know how long that would last.

I struggled to my feet, Carlos helping me up. If we let him go, we could lose him. He would hurt an innocent person and we would never get him back then. We'd just reunited, at least in my memories. I had to reach him even though I felt like garbage. I was still in so much pain from my injuries but Carlos' healing was already taking effect. My throat was soothing over and my broken wrist and wraith bites were healing but everything else was still a wreak. However, I didn't have time for Carlos to help me anymore. I had to get Felix's attention before he teleported away.

"You can't leave us," I yelled. "Felix, stop!"

He kept walking.

Faith got up. "Hey, asshole!" Faith shouted, walking towards him with a slight limp.

Felix paused but then kept walking.

Hmm, seemed he didn't like being called names. That could get him to stay.

"Do you think name calling is the right way to go?" Carlos asked from behind me.

Faith looked over to us and shrugged.

Was it the right way? Who knows, but it did get him to stop.

"Hey, you big dummy, we're talking to you!"

He stopped again and turned his head to glare at me this time. His brows furrowed together in a scowl. I'd never seen him look that way before.

So much for being nice. I guess there was a reason why foul-mouthed Faith was his best friend.

Felix didn't speak, but his attention was back on me, like he wondering if he should squash me like an ant or flick me like a fly. Either way, I was registering a look of annoyance from him. But heck, it could have been love. Demon Felix was kind of hard to read.

I moved my hands near my hips then a shot of pain flared through me and I hung my hands back at my sides. *Okay, Fran, be mean to the man you love. It's not a reach for you.* "You are a big jerk. Hitting your friends like that makes you a trash ass person." I looked to Faith after using her words for Monica and she gave me a thumbs up. "Do you really want to be *that* guy? How'd you even get out, anyway?"

He turned fully to me, squinting his eyes, still pondering my existence probably. I knew this was the part where, instead of throwing insults, I was supposed to tell him how much I loved him and tell him to come back to us. However, this seemed to be holding him so I would go with what worked. Felix hadn't lost his mind. He wasn't feral, or loupe like a were or blood lust like a vampire. He had just given in to his darker bases.

"I'd been working on my bonds and I finally broke them" he said in a base heavy voice that, admittedly, shook me a little. I was so used to Felix being so jolly all the time that I forgot that he could be quite intimidating if he wanted to be.

"You couldn't break them earlier when we were fighting all those damn wraiths in that battle royal?"

"Do you want to fight me?"

Against my wiser instincts, I took a step forward. "No, because as I am right now, you would kick my ass. I mean, it's really unfair that you get to showboat at the last minute. I've been in, like, four fights in the past couple of hours. I'm beat all to hell. I want a break. We all do. You'll have plenty of fights in the future. Plus, we are supposed to be a couple or something. And I, your woman, as you referred to me before, am hurting." I waved a hand vertically in front of me to showcase my injuries. I instantly regretted it as I shut my eyes and pressed my lips together in pain. "You should be helping me heal. Surely, a lame-ass half battle demon can do that." Battle demons were far from lame. They were actually a pretty powerful brand of demon, comparable in power to hate and chaos demons.

Felix took a step towards me and I held my breath, standing my ground. He kept moving, his eyes not betraying his intentions. I really couldn't tell if he would hit me or hug me. My words certainly hadn't made him feel the love but they had gotten him to stay. I could feel Carlos growing restless behind me with several mutterings hitting the air. I really hoped he didn't make a move. I had a feeling that would just make things worse.

I remained motionless until Felix reached me, bending my head back to stare up at him. He gave me stern eyes back before eventually switching to a lopsided grin, wrapping me in his arms. I winced at the pain his squeezing me caused my injuries but I didn't care. I'd take it over him disappearing.

"You got a lot of balls, baby girl," he whispered.

I chuckled. "That whole sentence sounded inaccurate."

He rested his chin lightly on the top of my head and I pressed my cheek against his chest, not wanting to move. Then I felt a radiating warmth spread throughout my body.

A burning itch from Felix's magic surrounded me in healing. I let out a comforting breath and maybe collapsed a little in his arms. I was exhausted and for once didn't mind having someone take care of me.

I felt Felix kiss the top of my head. "Thank you."

I wanted to say for what but I knew. Maybe he had needed to be brought back and we had done that for him. No, it wasn't with words of love but he knew I cared. And I would be there for him. Always.

EPILOGUE

$\mathcal{T}$he next evening, I found myself rotating between rolling my eyes and glaring at Monica as Azrael, Carlos, Faith, Felix, and I gathered in a private room of some fancy restaurant near the DC Wharf. The area was a newer community run by humans and witches, although it was not part of the federation.

I sat back in my chair, arms crossed, as our waitress came in to deliver our drink orders. The restaurant was an Afro-Caribbean fusion and the menu looked mouth-watering, but I needed Monica to be gone to enjoy it. Of course, she was paying for it all.

Azrael continued to talk about the events from the prior day and Monica gave us wide eyes, nodding her head as if she was impressed at all the right parts. When the angel was done talking, they picked up their cocktail and eyed the archangel expectantly. I knew Azrael respected Monica but some part of me thought that maybe their view of her was no longer as high.

Monica cleared her throat, clasping her fingers together on the table. "Well, I am so very impressed. I knew you all could do it. Of course, I apologize that I could not make it

317

myself. You'd be surprised how much work goes into being an angel leader. But I'm happy I was able to send support."

She paused as if expecting accolades for doing absolutely nothing.

Azrael looked down at their cocktail. "Thank you for helping us." Their voice sounded a bit stiff. I wasn't buying that gratitude.

Monica nodded again, a slight smile on her lips, her brows wrinkled in sympathy. "Of course, I would never leave my people to suffer."

Faith snorted. "Bitch, please."

Carlos swore and Felix rubbed his temples.

Azrael dropped their head to their chest.

I let out a snorting laugh. I was so glad Faith was who she was. She really knew how to say what we were all thinking.

She glared around at us, unashamed. "I'm sorry but some-body had to let the truth out. You did nothing. And you certainly didn't care about those angels stuck in that town or the few tourists there. The man or woman upstairs probably gave you that assignment and you pawned it off on us for something more high level. It's because of you one of your angels is dead."

Monica bristled at that and her eyes flashed silver. "I did not kill Dean."

Faith's eyes blazed like fire to match Monica's; she was really not intimidated by the angel. "Yes, Azrael had to do it. But he wouldn't have if you had come into the town to get your angels. You're supposed to be powerful. You could have beat that demon bitch. Or at least teleported the victims out of there. You were supposed to be on this mission. Not us. Thank you for letting some angels help us. Round of applause for you." She patted Azrael's thigh in concern. "Azrael could have died. I could have died. And an angel did die."

I was ready to tap in now. Encouraged by her outburst

and thankful I wasn't the only one who wanted to tell Monica off for once. "You sent us on that fool's errand, dangling little bits of knowledge about my past and then you disappeared. You didn't care about helping me undo the mess you made by wiping my mind. And a real leader knows how to get down in the field with her people, not just point her finger from afar."

Monica tightened her fingers together. "You have no idea what I have on my plate, little girl."

I gave her a squinty eyed frown, lips pursed together in doubt. "Don't call me little girl. There's nothing little about me. I'm a grown-ass woman who was handling *your* business."

Faith scrunched her face and clapped her hands in approval.

"Jesus," I heard Carlos whisper, wiping a hand over his face. I think he was sweating.

I was on a role. I couldn't stop myself. "You are not the president. You are one of God's minions. Okay? And you have two jobs to do. Keep people safe and lead your angels. You didn't do either of those things. We did. Can we be archangels? I want some cool wings."

Felix reached over and rubbed my back. It was most likely less an attempt to soothe me and more of an attempt to get me to fall back before Monica burnt me to a crisp with angel laser eyes. Maybe I had taken things a bit too far but I was pissed. Getting burned and bitten and chopped hurt more when I saw her stroll in the restaurant in an impeccably tailored ox-blood colored suit and her hair laid to perfection like she was about to run shit.

Monica cleared her throat again and lifted her chin as she looked around the room. "It's clear you all misunderstand my role here. I assign my angels things to do and they do them. I intervene only when needed. I can't and will not do everyone's job." She lowered her chin and looked at me, eyes wide and cold.

Maybe she really was going to laser beam me. Perhaps I needed to think more before I spoke. It was Faith's thing to go off at the handle but I really couldn't do that. Right? You know, maybe it was time to change the script of what I could and couldn't do.

Monica continued. "Do not mistake you and me as equals. Just because your father is a high-level demon does not make you invincible. You should know your place if you want to survive. You have time, little girl, to get where I am. Until then, sit back and learn and don't presume to know all that is going on. You have no clue of this world and the threats that await you. Any of you. You want me as your friend, not your enemy."

Oh, I had a good idea of the threats that were out there. She was one of them. If she thought I was going to bow to her anymore, she was out of her mind. She no longer had anything I needed and I could find my own way to use my powers for good.

Monica sighed as if suddenly bored with our conversation and looked at the others before getting up. "I'll let you enjoy this dinner together. I will cover the bill. I am really impressed with you all." She glanced at me, a slight smile on her lips. "Try the jerk chicken. It's to die for."

She then turned and walked away, vanishing into a white cloud of smoke.

I let out a breath I didn't know I was holding.

Azrael laid their head on the table.

Faith knocked back her drink. "Can we get another?" she called out with a playful glint in her still fire rimmed eyes.

"I thought she was going to kill you both," Carlos murmured, patting his forehead with a napkin.

Felix chuckled. "I think Faith has rubbed off on you."

Faith smirked. "Could be worse."

I frowned, deeply annoyed. "What did she mean by 'try the jerk chicken, it's to die for'?" I asked in a lousy imitation of Monica. "Was she calling me a jerk? Was she threatening me?"

The group looked at me with a mixture of stunned and amused eyes before they all burst out laughing.

~

*I* flopped down on the bed of my new apartment back in Silver Spring. Yes, I decided to move into Felix's town for just the time being to be closer to him. It had been a couple days since the big fight and I was just taking a moment to regroup and enjoy Felix fully with both our memories intact. I had deferred any contact from Marcus about the campaign but I would have to get back to him. I needed to tell him that there was no way we could get married now and I still had no intention of telling Felix about the arrangement. I was still trying to keep his emotions in a good place.

Carlos had made it clear that as Felix had finally let loose his demon side, he was more prone to having it be released again. I wanted to remove any unnecessary anger and need to fight. I knew enough about battle demons to know they could be ticking time bombs. This was not Felix and he was only half but there was no reason to poke the bear.

Felix turned to his side and lifted up on his elbow, gazing down at me. "How long do I have you?" He trailed a finger over my collarbone as he waited for my answer.

I blew out a breath. "I should probably stick my head into the fae realm sometime tomorrow and then I've got to run to the underworld to do something with a minion my dad gifted me." That was still weird to me. I really didn't need a demon servant. However, he had popped up to help us during the battle so I suppose he was useful.

He leaned in and kissed my shoulder. "I'd ask to come with you but I know that wouldn't help your cause. I still don't know how it'll work between us when you're made Queen."

I had no clue either but then again being Queen was no longer my only viable option. I could live in the human realm and just use my fae and demon magic to help others and stay as a council member to pay the bills. I could go to the underworld and rule with my father while still making a difference for the good. Or I could seek my proper place in my fae family.

Even if being a fae Queen or royalty was still my only goal, I could change things. Live the way my mother was never allowed to live. Of course, if I were made Queen, I'd have to live in the fae realm. I wasn't sure if Felix was willing to come with me. Especially now that he had his mother back. I doubted she'd be welcomed in my realm or honestly even want to go. I decided I'd cross that bridge when I got to it.

He continued to sprinkle kisses over my shoulder and I began to want to get past this conversation and move to something more fun. "What does your dad say?"

I turned to face him and flipped a leg over his. "I have to go see him. He hasn't reached out but he helped us so I really want to thank him. I also need to find Yusan and work on a way to set him free."

Felix brushed the hair from my face. "Ah, I forgot about him. Where is he?"

"Back with my father."

"Speaking of parents, do you think we're going to have a tough time on our hands with them?"

I snorted. "Uh, yeah." When I had calmed Felix down on the field, I'd caught Olivia giving me the stink eye when Felix released me from his embrace. You'd think she'd be grateful that I had helped her son from disappearing. And since that day she'd practically been following him like a shadow. I was surprised she hadn't come over here with him. She practically lived with him now.

I needed to understand this feud my father had with Olivia. It must have been deep-rooted for both parents to not only hate each other but for them to hate Felix and I as well. We seemed to be innocent victims in a Hatfield-McCoy type battle and I wanted to get to the root of it.

I also had a family in the fae realm that I wanted to reconnect with. My brother was on the throne by default because my mother and I were forced out. Would he want to reconnect with me or be annoyed by my return? Would the rest of my relatives who let me go, care? I remembered my grandmother on my mother's side. She had loved me. We had good times together. How had she just let us leave? I needed answers.

Felix kissed my cheek. "I don't know what's running through your mind right now, but let it rest for at least tonight. Just allow yourself to be happy."

"I'm not sure I know how."

"When I was going berserk on that field, do you know what brought me back?"

"My kind, loving words?" I cracked.

"In a way, yes. No matter what happens to me; I'm going to know you. I'm going to love you. That will always ground me. Even battle demons and warrior faeries can love."

I looked up at him and snuggled closer. He really knew how to say the kindest things.

He began to slowly rub my back and I allowed myself to melt into his touch. "So, whatever comes our way, we can handle it. And we will save talk of the new mission Azrael just told me Monica sent us for tomorrow."

New mission? The hell? I shot up, ready to fight the air. Did that wench really think we were going to work for her again?

Upon seeing my rage-filled face, Felix grinned and rolled me on top of him. "Tomorrow." He kissed me again, this time on the lips, instantly simmering my boiling anger.

Yep, he was right, save telling off an archangel for another day. Tonight, I would enjoy my bit of happiness. I didn't know when I would have it again.

*If you enjoyed this story, please consider leaving a review on Amazon and Goodreads.*

## ABOUT THE AUTHOR

C.C. is originally from Baltimore, Maryland, and has actively written fiction since the age of eleven. She's an avid "chick lit" reader and urban fantasy fan. During her days, she works in Civil Rights for the federal government. In her free time, she sings karaoke, travels the globe, and watches too much TV...when she's not writing, of course.

To keep updated on future books and C.C.'s travel and life-style website, go to:

**www.ccsolomon.com**

CC Solomon: Nerdy Travelista Newsletter

Cat's Corner: New Adult Urban Fantasy and Paranormal Romance Reader Group

You can also reach C.C. at the following social media sites:

OTHER BOOKS BY CC SOLOMON

**Paranormal World Series**

Mystic Bonds

Mystic Journeys

Mystic Awakenings

Mystic Souls

**Paranormal Rising Series**

Deathly Touch

**Paranormal Times Series**

Mystic Memories/Dark Memories: A Novella

Dark Hauntings

**Paranormal Realms Standalone Series**

Mystic Realms/Lightning and Realms: A Novella

*Lightning and Curses: Coming Fall 2021*

**Standalones**

Girls of Might and Magic Anthology

www.ingramcontent.com/pod-product-compliance
Lightning Source LLC
Chambersburg PA
CBHW031617100726
47898CB00006B/1828